JODI TAYLOR

HARD
TIME

Headline

First published in Great Britain in 2020 by
HEADLINE PUBLISHING GROUP

First published in Great Britain in paperback in 2021 by
HEADLINE PUBLISHING GROUP

2

Cataloguing in Publication Data is available from the British Library

ISBN 978 1 4722 7318 5

Typeset in Times New Roman by CC Book Production

Printed and bound in Great Britain by Clays Ltd, Elcograf S.p.A.

Headline's policy is to use papers that are natural, renewable and recyclable
products and made from wood grown in well-managed forests and other
controlled sources. The logging and manufacturing processes are expected
to conform to the environmental regulations of the country of origin.

HEADLINE PUBLISHING GROUP
An Hachette UK Company
Carmelite House
50 Victoria Embankment
London EC4Y 0DZ

www.headline.co.uk
www.hachette.co.uk

For Isabella

Jodi Taylor is the internationally bestselling author of the Chronicles of St Mary's series, the story of a bunch of disaster-prone individuals who investigate major historical events in contemporary time. Do NOT call it time travel! She is also the author of the Time Police series – a St Mary's spinoff and gateway into the world of an all-powerful, international organisation who are NOTHING like St Mary's. Except, when they are.

Alongside these, Jodi is known for her gripping supernatural thrillers featuring Elizabeth Cage, together with the enchanting Frogmorton Farm series – a fairy story for adults.

Born in Bristol and now living in Gloucester (facts both cities vigorously deny), she spent many years with her head somewhere else, much to the dismay of family, teachers and employers, before finally deciding to put all that daydreaming to good use and write a novel. Over twenty books later, she still has no idea what she wants to do when she grows up.

By Jodi Taylor and available from Headline

TIME POLICE SERIES

DOING TIME   HARD TIME
SAVING TIME

THE CHRONICLES OF ST MARY'S SERIES

JUST ONE DAMNED THING AFTER ANOTHER
A SYMPHONY OF ECHOES
A SECOND CHANCE
A TRAIL THROUGH TIME
NO TIME LIKE THE PAST
WHAT COULD POSSIBLY GO WRONG?
LIES, DAMNED LIES, AND HISTORY
AND THE REST IS HISTORY
AN ARGUMENTATION OF HISTORIANS
HOPE FOR THE BEST
PLAN FOR THE WORST
ANOTHER TIME, ANOTHER PLACE

SHORT-STORY COLLECTIONS

THE LONG AND SHORT OF IT   LONG STORY SHORT

THE CHRONICLES OF ST MARY'S DIGITAL SHORTS

WHEN A CHILD IS BORN
ROMAN HOLIDAY
CHRISTMAS PRESENT
SHIPS AND STINGS AND WEDDING RINGS
THE VERY FIRST DAMNED THING
THE GREAT ST MARY'S DAY OUT
MY NAME IS MARKHAM
A PERFECT STORM
CHRISTMAS PAST
BATTERSEA BARRICADES
THE STEAM-PUMP JUMP
AND NOW FOR SOMETHING COMPLETELY DIFFERENT
WHEN DID YOU LAST SEE YOUR FATHER?
WHY IS NOTHING EVER SIMPLE?
THE ORDEAL OF THE HAUNTED ROOM

ELIZABETH CAGE NOVELS

WHITE SILENCE
DARK LIGHT
LONG SHADOWS

FROGMORTON FARM SERIES

THE NOTHING GIRL   LITTLE DONKEY (digital short)
THE SOMETHING GIRL   JOY TO THE WORLD (digital short)

A BACHELOR ESTABLISHMENT

Time is an arrow.
Isaac Newton

Time is a river.
Albert Einstein

Time is fluid and not linear in any way.
The Time Police

*Time is a chunk and most of it is missing. I must have been
off my face last night. Jesus, my head is killing me.*
Luke Parrish

Roll Call

TIME POLICE PERSONNEL

Commander Hay	Beginning to realise Team 236 has its disadvantages as well as its advantages.
Captain Farenden	Keeping his boss on track. Mostly.
Major Callen	Now Head of the Hunter Division.
Officer North	Newly recruited Hunter.
Major Ellis	Surprisingly gunshot-free in this story.
Lt Grint	Is Hay now regretting giving him a second chance?
The Map Master	Possibly like Gollum, she's forgotten her real name. Even her mum calls her Map Master.
Officer Connor	Quite normal.
The doctor	Surprisingly compassionate in the face of an officer's personal disaster.
Officer Varma	Member of security team.
Other Time Police officers	Who come and go but rarely hang around long enough to say anything.

TEAM 236 – TEAM WEIRD

| Trainee Farrell | Still not got his hair cut. Wounded again but this time by accident so that's all right then. |

Trainee Farrell — Still not got his hair cut. Wounded again but this time by accident so that's all right then.

Trainee Lockland — Still blushing at her own shadow. Now developing signs of schizophrenia as well. It never rains . . .

Trainee Parrish — Completely unchanged. You'd think recent experiences would have rendered him thoughtful, considerate and hard-working . . . but no.

TEAM 235
Just for once, they're the screw-ups.

Trainee Hansen

Trainee Kohl

Trainee Rossi

ST MARY'S PERSONNEL

A bunch of feckless pod jockeys, none of whom
you'd want to meet on a dark night. Or even on a
sunny afternoon at a charming riverside pub. Which
might or might not be suffering from a nasty case
of St Mary's-related E. coli. Or possibly salmonella.
Whichever is the most serious, anyway.

Dr Maxwell	Matthew's mum.
Chief Technical Officer Farrell	Matthew's dad.
Dr Peterson	One of Matthew's many uncles.
Miss Lingoss	One of Matthew's many aunts.
Mikey	Matthew's special girl.
Professor Rapson and Dr Dowson	What those two can do with half a lime and two beer mats has been banned across seven continents.
Mr Markham	Head of Security. Another of Matthew's uncles.
Mr Evans	Yes, yet another, etc. Member of the Security Section and unofficial doorstop.

Previously on the Time Police . . .

A long time ago in the future, the secret of time travel was discovered and, people being what they are, the world nearly ended.

Just for once, however, and to the surprise of all, the world pulled itself together in time to avert disaster. Nation cooperated with nation and the Time Police were formed. Their purpose was to eradicate illegal time travel and restore the timeline – or as much of it as could be restored. Sometimes it was nothing better than a cut-and-shut job, but if that was what it took then that was what was done.

Ruthless, efficient and with their famous *couldn't give a rat's arse* attitude, the Time Police paid a high price – at one point there were only thirteen officers still standing – but they succeeded. Time travel was, more or less, eradicated.

Of course, once the situation was under control, the governments that had been so enthusiastic now began to regard the Time Police as pretty much having outlived their usefulness. No government is ever happy with an organisation better equipped, better funded and more efficient than they are. Especially one not answerable to that bunch of mindless, ungrateful, demanding, awkward-question-asking bunch of

1

troublemakers usually referred to in public as the electorate. Behind the scenes, the diplomatic wheels began to turn.

The Time Police themselves were not unaware that, ironically, times were changing. The more astute among them prepared to adapt themselves to the hazards of peacetime. A new commander was appointed to guide Time Police boots down gentler paths.

But, although Time moves on, old threats can reappear in a new guise. Temporal Tourism, for instance, is illegal but extremely lucrative for those prepared to take the risks. And Big Business, often more powerful and frequently more intelligent than any government, is prepared to take that risk. As Commander Hay repeatedly reminds her unit, new threats require new methods of attack. Bursting in, shooting everyone within a five-mile radius and torching anything left standing – while having its merits – is not conducive to intel gathering. And intel is now a large part of the game. Under her direction, the Hunter Division has been strengthened and, under Major Callen, given virtual autonomy.

Grumbling and dragging their feet, the Time Police are preparing to meet new threats.

Enter Team Weird.

2

Luke

I can't believe I'm still in the Time Police. And this time it's all my own fault. I can't say I wasn't given every opportunity to blow them off for good. All I had to do was what my dad wanted – which is probably where it all went wrong because I've never been that brilliant at doing as dear old Dad wants.

Let's be clear – at this very moment, I could be sprawled in a luxurious, rent-free Hong Kong hideaway, with an Asian lovely in one hand and something long and cold in the other. A statement open to misinterpretation but I'm too frozen to care. My point is that I could be out there enjoying the excitement, the exhilaration, the buzz of cosmopolitan life and the wonderful, life-giving, incredibly hot sunshine.

I'd have my own office – *offices*, even. My own staff, every one of them absolutely drop-dead gorgeous, all leaping to do my bidding whenever I bidded. My every need would be catered for, and trust me, my needs are many and imaginative.

Instead of which I'm trapped here in the Time Police as a trainee, the lowest of the low. I've been shot at and scared shitless on an Egyptian hillside. I've been menaced by a rabbit – and before you laugh, you should have seen the size of the bloody thing. And it was pregnant. If you think pregnant women are cranky, you should meet an artificially engineered, lab-produced super-rabbit. We had to chase it nearly the length and breadth of Australia – a country which, I might add, has been very slow to show the sort of monetary gratitude that might have made it all worthwhile. I've been attacked by barely sentient denizens of the 20th century and their feral children. And don't even get me started on Sarah Smith. The list goes on and on and I'm not even a fully qualified officer yet.

Nor ever likely to be if someone doesn't find us soon. I think Jane's already slipped away. I can't wake her. I should let her go. I can't save her. I'd be doing her a kindness. I'll just close my eyes for a minute.

Perhaps I should have listened to dear old Dad after all . . .

Jane

It's so cold. I'm so cold I can hardly think. I just want to sleep. Luke is doing his best to keep us both alive, but he's as far gone as me. He thinks he's talking to me but he's just spewing words to keep me conscious. Every now and then he'll stop and I wonder if he's gone and then he jerks himself awake and starts again and all the time his voice is getting further and further away and I don't know if he's losing me or I'm losing him . . .

Matthew

Where are they?
What went wrong?
What can I do?

1

Marietta Hay, commander of the Time Police, settled herself at her desk, fired up her scratchpad and gazed at her adjutant.

'Good morning, Charlie – what do you have for me today?'

'Well, ma'am, as you must be aware – an important part of my duties is, as far as I can, to mitigate the bad news with little snippets of good news. To lighten your working day, so to speak.'

She sighed. 'This does not bode well. All right, Charlie – hit me with a snippet.'

'Alas, ma'am. There are no snippets.'

'What? No good news at all?'

'Regrettably, ma'am . . .'

'Not even anything decent for lunch today?'

'Not even that, ma'am.'

'Well – I can regroup. Hit me with the least of the bad news.'

'Trainee Farrell's hair is still not benefitting from the adoption of a regulation hairstyle.'

'I thought he'd been specifically instructed . . .'

'He was, ma'am, and he did. Last Thursday.'

'Are you sure? I saw him this morning and couldn't see any difference. Did the barber actually have the nerve to charge him for that?'

'I doubt it, ma'am. He has it done at St Mary's.'

'That accounts for a lot. Who does it?'

'A Miss Lingoss.'

'Isn't she the weird one?'

'We are discussing St Mary's, ma'am. You will have to be more specific.'

She sighed. 'Tell him to put it up.'

'Er . . . put it up what, ma'am?'

'All female officers with long hair must wear it either up or back. Offer him a choice. Pigtail or ponytail. Tell him his benevolent leader recognises the importance of employee autonomy and therefore it is his choice. Up or back. Just make it very clear there is no third way and ribbons are not an option.'

'Yes, ma'am. If you have no objections, I will relay your instructions to Major Ellis for onward transmission to Trainee Farrell. As team leader, the appearance of his crew is his responsibility.'

'As you wish, Charlie. Just let me know which option he chooses, will you?'

'Happily, ma'am.'

'There – that wasn't so bad, was it? Next.'

'The reorganisation is not proceeding without problems, ma'am.'

'*Challenges*, Charlie, challenges. The Time Police do not have problems. We have challenges. To meet and overcome. Please can you draft an all-staff memo to the effect that if a great deal more meeting and overcoming doesn't start taking place PDQ then I will be forced to leave the safety and security of my office and *mingle*.'

He grinned. 'Steady on, ma'am.'

'Exactly, Charlie. I suspect the prospect of rounding a corner and finding themselves face to face with me will induce levels of challenge-meeting-and-overcoming my people did not know they possessed.'

'As you wish, ma'am.'

She moved a file across her desk. 'Well – so far so not too bad. What's next? What's the big one you've kept for the end?'

'Raymond Parrish has withdrawn his opposition to the parliamentary bill, ma'am. The one curtailing Time Police powers and responsibilities. Apparently, since his son has chosen to go his own way, Mr Parrish has no further interest in the future of the Time Police. We are, it would seem, on our own.'

She shrugged. 'I suspect the price of his support would have increased exponentially over the years. Looking on the bright side – we have escaped that partnership unscathed.'

'Not quite unscathed, ma'am. We are still the proud owners of his son. Luke Parrish, despite all forecasts to the contrary, is not only still with us but is actually on the verge of completing his gruntwork.'

'Yes, interesting, isn't it? Between you and me, Charlie, I'm rather hoping that bad business with Officer Smith has taught him a far more effective lesson than anything we could have done. Short of shooting him, that is.'

'It may yet come to that.'

'You see, Charlie – it's not all bad – something for us to look forward to. I shall implement a new strategy. Every Friday morning, I shall select someone at random and shoot them. To encourage the others. You know, I could really see that working.'

'I'm not sure shooting random staff would send quite the right message, ma'am.'

'All right. I'm not unreasonable. Forget the random bit – I'll shoot a specifically selected member of staff instead. A much better idea. It will make them feel valued to know they've been specially chosen. And with the additional bonus of encouraging the survivors to think more positively about our upcoming reorganisation. Genius, Charlie.'

'I'm happy to think my poor abilities have contributed to your unique solution to our difficulties, ma'am.'

'Yes, sometimes I don't know what I'd do without you. Anything else?'

'Actually, yes. The Rt Hon Patricia Farnborough has requested a private meeting.'

'The cabinet minister?'

'At 1400 hours this afternoon.'

'I feel sure I'm busy at that time.'

'I feel equally sure that you are not, ma'am.'

She sighed. 'You always manage to get your own way, don't you?'

'Only sometimes, ma'am.' He stood up. 'I shall go and look out the best crockery.'

The Rt Hon Patricia Farnborough was punctual almost to the second.

Captain Farenden collected her from the downstairs atrium and personally escorted her to Commander Hay's office.

Patricia Farnborough was the long-serving MP for South Rushfordshire. She was popular with neither her fellow members nor the public. So far, she had consistently refused to participate in any of the political activities so beloved of her colleagues. She had, for instance, refused to live in a jungle, or become embroiled in a sex scandal on a popular ballroom-dancing programme. Nor had she ever been compelled to apologise, photogenically tearful, for not having completely understood the really very complex rules pertaining to the claiming of what were almost perfectly legitimate expenses. Nor had she, for any reason, been obliged to welcome the opportunity to spend more time with her family.

'Much to her family's relief,' as one of the whips had once remarked.

She was, however, respected and known to be a safe, if unimaginative, pair of hands and a strong upholder of trad-itional values. Not *family* values, as she always made very clear – those frequently being a kind of shorthand for bigotry, intolerance and prejudice – but the traditional values of honesty, hard work and loyalty.

'Definitely in the wrong job,' the same whip had remarked to the same confidant.

Patricia Farnborough halted on the threshold of Commander Hay's office and turned to Captain Farenden. 'Thank you, Cap-tain, but I think I can find my way from here.'

Captain Farenden raised an eyebrow at Commander Hay, who nodded and said, 'Thank you, Charlie.'

'And I shan't require any refreshments, either. What I do require is an uninterrupted thirty minutes with your com-mander.'

'In that case, ma'am ...' said Captain Farenden, with well-concealed relief, and closed the door behind him.

The two took stock of each other. Commander Hay was a small, slight woman. It's not unusual to describe someone as being of indeterminate age but in this case, it was an accurate description. As a young officer, Marietta Hay had fought in the Time Wars and there had been an accident. Her pod had sustained serious damage and the door had blown off in mid-jump. The results had not been for the squeamish. One side of her face was now considerably older than the other. The rescue party had managed to get her out of the wreckage, but she had been the only survivor.

Patricia Farnborough was a large woman who strode the corridors of power with a firm tread. She wore her hair short, favoured dark suits, and her voice had been designed to be heard above the clamour of battle. The adversarial atmosphere of the House of Commons suited her perfectly.

'Like one of those Valkyrie women coming at you,' yet another colleague had said, recovering in the bar after a shattering three-minute interview.

The precise whereabouts of *Mr* Patricia Farnborough were currently unknown. And had been for some time. Unkind rumours postulated the theory that he had, at some point, been consumed during the mating process. Which, given the size of the Right Honourable lady, was entirely possible.

Mrs Farnborough seated herself and both women looked at each other in silence. Eventually, Commander Hay enquired politely how she might be of service.

'I will not insult you by swearing you to secrecy.'

If Commander Hay thought she just had, she said nothing.

'And before you ask, this is a private matter. Nothing to do with the government or politics. I should also make it clear I am not seeking any special treatment for my daughter. She has been foolish and must bear the consequences of her actions.'

'I think,' said Commander Hay, 'I understand you. However,

12

I must make things clear. This is the Time Police and I am their commander. Should I become aware of any unlawful actions . . . I am legally bound to proceed accordingly. Do you wish to reconsider?'

'No. I understand.'

'You understand also that anything said now cannot later be unsaid?'

'I do. Thank you for the warning but it is unnecessary. I am here because I do wish you to proceed accordingly.'

'Very well. Now that we have established the parameters, would you like to begin?'

Mrs Farnborough smoothed her skirt, clasped her hands on her lap and began.

'I have a daughter. Imogen. She's not . . . she's not a bad girl. She's just the typical product of her age and class. And she has been foolish.'

'What has she done? Let me rephrase that: what has she done that involves my organisation?'

'She and a friend were offered an opportunity and they took it.'

'Could you be more specific?'

'They were approached and offered the opportunity to travel.'

'In Time, I am assuming. Please be clear, Mrs Farnborough. You are telling me your daughter and her friend have committed a crime. A serious crime.'

'It's worse than that.'

Commander Hay waited. As always, her face gave nothing away and she never hesitated to use that to her advantage.

'She . . . what is the expression?'

'Jumped?'

'Yes – she jumped back in time . . .' Mrs Farnborough stopped again.

'Yes, it really is difficult to describe this sort of thing without sounding like a bad science fiction novel, isn't it, but your expression is perfectly correct.'

Rather in the manner of one wanting to get the unpleasant part over with as quickly as possible, Mrs Farnborough said in a rush, 'She has gone off somewhere . . . jumped . . . and she did not return. I would like to take shameless advantage of your organisation, Commander, and ask if you could find her and bring her back.'

Commander Hay pulled out her scratchpad, set it to record, and laid it on the desk between them. Mrs Farnborough stared out of the window and watched the Paris airship descending through the clouds.

Commander Hay gestured towards her scratchpad. 'You understand, Mrs Farnborough, that from this moment on . . .'

'I do, Commander. Please proceed.'

'I have several questions.'

'Please.'

'How do you know that your daughter has engaged in illegal temporal activity?'

'The friend – who has taken steps to ensure they cannot be identified – although I'm sure you would have no trouble tracking them down should you wish – has sent me the information. I suspect out of a spirit of revenge.'

'I see. We'll get to that in a minute. Firstly, do you know to where and when they jumped?'

'I do.'

'It would be enormously helpful if you had the actual co-ordinates?'

'I do.' Mrs Farnborough took out a sheet of paper, folded very small, and laid it on the desk at a point midway between them.

Commander Hay did not so much as glance at it. 'And the location is . . . ?'

'I have been led to believe . . . 17th-century England.'

'Was this her own choice?'

'The trip – planned by her friend – was to be a gift.' She gripped her hands in her lap. 'It was – the trip was supposed to incorporate – a proposal.'

'Of marriage.'

'Yes. The plan was to whisk Imogen away to somewhere exotic and, during the excitement of the . . .'

'The jump . . .'

'Yes, the jump . . . to propose marriage.'

'The plan being that Imogen would be so thrilled and excited that she would fall into her friend's arms and say yes.'

Mrs Farnborough nodded, remembered the recorder and said, 'Yes.'

'And what did actually happen?'

'I don't know all the details. The friend seemed disinclined to give them, but it would appear that events did not progress quite as planned.' Mrs Farnborough swallowed. 'This is the friend's version of events, of course, but it would appear that no sooner had they finished their proposal than Imogen . . .'

She stopped.

'Declined the honour?'

Mrs Farnborough closed her eyes briefly. 'She said she'd

15

rather die in a ditch than be married to anyone, and when the friend pointed out the honour they were doing her and how much the trip . . . jump had cost, she announced she couldn't be bought and disappeared off into the crowds.'

There was a stunned silence.

'Pardon me,' said Commander Hay, recovering the power of speech. 'I wish to be perfectly sure I understand you. Miss Farnborough and a . . . close friend . . . embarked upon an illegal enterprise for romantic purposes . . .'

'I'm not sure Imogen can have been aware of the true purpose of the jump. Not initially. From things she has let drop recently, I don't think she regarded this person as anything other than a friend who was offering an exciting opportunity to do something new and different. Imogen does not deal well with long periods of boredom.' She considered for a moment before adding, 'Or short ones, either.'

'So, your daughter had no idea a marriage proposal was in the offing?'

'As far as I am aware – no.'

'And the young man . . . I am assuming it was a young man?'

Somewhat stiffly, Mrs Farnborough agreed that yes, the party in question was a young man.

'Only in these days . . .'

'I can confirm the person in question was definitely a young man.'

'This young man goes down on one knee – so to speak – and Imogen not only rejects the proposal, but the young man as well.'

'That would appear to be the case, yes.'

'Forgive me, but where exactly did this take place? Were

there other people present? Did no one try to prevent her from leaving? Was the young man in question quite happy to just return to the present and leave your daughter there?'

'To take your questions in order, I believe Imogen and her friend had stepped outside to savour their surroundings, and when he returned to the pod to tell his tale, the people . . . the crew . . . simply packed up and brought him home.'

'Packed up?'

'From what I can gather, the . . . company . . . offers a number of what they call "packages", including the "Special Occasion" experience. It's extremely expensive – something Imogen's friend mentioned several times – and consists of an exclusive, specifically tailored excursion including costumes, catering, champagne and such, all of which had been brought with them and set up, but was, of course, not needed.'

'And they just packed up and left her there? Did the young man offer any sort of protest?'

'I do not believe that at that point he was inclined to consider Imogen's future welfare to be one of his priorities.'

'I can imagine.'

'The consensus seemed to be Imogen had made her bed and must lie on it. The company offers no sort of guarantee or accepts liability of any kind. It is clearly understood that everything is at the customer's own risk.'

'And having returned to this Time, this unfortunate young man came straight to you.'

Mrs Farnborough gritted her teeth. 'Actually, no. His feelings were, apparently, somewhat bruised, and his initial reaction was that she could bloody well stay in the 17th century and good riddance.'

Commander Hay, who had been in charge of the Time Police for some years now, found herself temporarily with nothing to say.

'However,' Mrs Farnborough continued, 'after several days elapsed, he appeared to relent and passed me a message detailing Imogen's recent . . . exploits.'

'And where is this young man now?'

Mrs Farnborough's expression was professionally blank. 'I am not aware of his current location.'

Commander Hay filed away that particular line of enquiry for future action. 'And Miss Farnborough is still, to the best of your knowledge, in 17th-century England.'

'Yes. London, to be precise. And has been for some days now.'

'Well, to put your mind at rest – that is not necessarily the case. We can jump back to these coordinates . . .' Hay gestured to the piece of paper still lying between them, 'and it is very possible we will be on the scene only an hour or so behind Imogen. Which might easily be long enough for her to have decided the 17th century is not a particularly safe place in which to reside. With luck, she won't have been there long enough to have incurred any serious injury. I suspect that with no training, no background knowledge and very little prep-aration for surviving in this period, she will almost certainly welcome the opportunity to be taken home. From our point of view, setting aside – temporarily – her illegal actions, she should certainly be removed as quickly as possible before any permanent damage occurs. Either to her or, more importantly, to the timeline. Which, I must inform you, Mrs Farnborough, will be our first priority.'

Mrs Farnborough lifted her head. 'I know I am in no position to ask a favour . . .'

'But you are about to nevertheless.'

'I ask – no, I plead – for leniency. There have been faults in Imogen's upbringing which should not be laid at her door.'

'That will be a matter for discussion on Imogen's return,' said Commander Hay, drily. 'And I must inform you I am unable to influence the courts. Those powers are denied me. Any recommendations I make will be taken into account, but the ultimate decision is not mine.'

'I understand. But I wondered . . .'

'Yes?'

'Imogen will be willing to provide you with valuable information in exchange for a light sentence.'

'Does Imogen know she will be willing to provide me with this valuable info?'

For one very brief moment, Mrs Farnborough's face showed the expression that had once, famously, caused a back-bencher to wet himself. 'Not at the moment, but you may rest assured she will.'

Commander Hay did not doubt it for one moment. 'I want us both to be clear about this. You wish us to locate your daughter and bring her home.'

'Yes.'

Commander Hay paused. 'Whatever it takes?'

'Imogen does not always act in her own best interests. This is one of those occasions.'

'If what you say is true, then Imogen has broken the law. I should tell you we make no exceptions. We cannot afford to. Each and every offence is prosecuted and we always push for the strongest possible sentence. Sometimes even . . .' She left the rest of the sentence unspoken.

Mrs Farnborough said quietly, 'I believe we might be able to come to some arrangement.'

Commander Hay tilted her head to one side and said sardonically, 'Do you now?'

'I would be willing to use my influence – my not inconsiderable influence – on your behalf.'

Commander Hay smiled and leaned back in her chair. 'I have learned to be wary of such offers.' She picked up her paper knife, turning it over in her fingers, an action that, had he been present, would have filled Captain Farenden with the gravest misgivings. 'However, as you say, it is very possible Imogen might have something we need.'

'You're speaking of my offer of intel. Information. Names. Places. Details of how they were approached and by whom.'

'Yes. Such information could be very valuable to us. However, you must understand – I don't want to be accused of misleading you – no matter how helpful Miss Farnborough is – or isn't – there *will* be a prosecution. There *will* be a prison sentence. I'm sorry, but we cannot be seen to display favouritism. Especially to a high-ranking member of the government. If such a thing ever came out it would cost me my job, you would lose yours as well and there would be a prison sentence for both of us. And Imogen. So, I will ask you now – is this a deal-breaker for you?'

'Not at all. Imogen out of circulation for a while might not be a bad thing. A short, sharp shock will do her no harm. She must learn to accept the consequences of her actions.'

Commander Hay chose not to mention that Imogen's shock

20

might be less short and more sharp than her mother envisaged. 'I can despatch a team . . .'

'When?'

'Tomorrow.'

'But why the delay? You have the coordinates. You could go now.'

'This is a time-travelling organisation. It doesn't matter when we leave – it's when we arrive that's important. We could leave next year and still arrive at exactly the right Time and place.'

'Oh. I see. Foolish of me.'

'Not at all. It takes some time to get one's head around it. Do you have any details at all of the organisation that took her there?'

She said with some difficulty, 'No. Imogen and I do not converse daily.'

'No notes left behind? Any irregularities with her bank statement?'

'Imogen's bank statement is full of irregularities, but I know what you mean and no.'

'Did you have any idea? Any idea at all?'

'No, of course not.'

'Then neither you nor Imogen put up any part of the not inconsiderable sum of money required?'

'No. And you're right – it wasn't cheap. Imogen couldn't possibly have afforded it on her allowance, generous though it is.'

Commander Hay regarded the folded piece of paper still on her desk. 'And you want us to bring her back?'

'Of course I do.'

There was a long silence. Eventually, Mrs Farnborough said, 'So what will happen now?'

'I'll send a team. As I said.'

'No, I mean, how will they get her back? What will they do?'

Commander Hay smiled. 'Whatever it takes.'

Returning to Commander Hay's office, Captain Farenden reported he had escorted Mrs Farnborough off the premises.

'Did she say anything?'

'Nothing, ma'am. Apart from goodbye.'

'Charlie, ask Major Ellis if he can spare me a moment, will you?'

Ten minutes later Major Ellis was standing in front of her. 'Good afternoon, ma'am.'

'Good afternoon, Major. Something a little different for your team today.'

Catching a glimpse of Captain Farenden's grin, Major Ellis said neutrally, 'Oh?'

'Yes. A task requiring tact and diplomacy and when that fails – as I'm sure it will – brute force and ignorance.'

Bristling slightly at this unflattering description of his team's abilities, Major Ellis enquired whether, whatever the mission was, might not a clean-up team be more appropriate?

'Yes, if I wanted an almighty temporal and political scandal. Clean-up crews are not noted for their tact and diplomacy.'

Major Ellis listened with growing disquiet as she outlined the situation and concluded by handing him a piece of paper. 'You should find the appropriate coordinates on this, Major. Other than that, there's nothing more I can tell you. The situation will be fluid in the extreme. There are two possible scenarios:

either the young woman has fared badly during her time there and cooperates fully in her rescue, or . . .'

'Or she fights us every inch of the way.'

'I hesitate to contradict you, Major, but your use of the word "us" is inappropriate. You are still on light duties. Your team must manage without you.'

'Ma'am . . .'

'No, Major.' She gestured at his arm, still strapped up.

'Then perhaps, ma'am, my original suggestion of a clean-up team . . .'

'The young woman involved is the daughter of a high-ranking government minister.'

If Major Ellis groaned, he had the sense not to do so aloud.

'Even more importantly, it's the 17th century and not that long since the Restoration. Charles II is still not secure on his throne and there's enormous anti-Catholic feeling throughout the country. The last thing we need is some entitled little baggage destabilising the situation and plunging the country into such chaos that, when the Dutch attempt to invade, the only force the English will be able to muster will be two old women with a skillet and a pack of geese.'

'Gaggle, ma'am.'

'I'm sorry?'

'Gaggle. A pack of geese is a gaggle.'

There was an un-encouraging silence.

'Or,' said Major Ellis, avoiding Captain Farenden's innocent gaze and swiftly recovering lost ground, 'I believe, pack is a perfectly acceptable alternative.'

Commander Hay nodded. 'And while I have no time for politicians, having them on our side is marginally safer than having them against us. Which we will if anything happens to Imogen Farnborough. Personally, I always feel we'd probably be better off with the geese in charge but someone has to round up the country's idiots and put them somewhere they can't do any harm and so we invented Parliament.'

'But my team, ma'am? A man down, not yet qualified, and I'm unable to accompany them.'

'They've always been a man down – I don't count Smith's short and ineffective stint. And your team do things differently.'

'But . . .'

'And you're still here, Major.'

Major Ellis took the hint. 'Not any longer, ma'am.'

2

'Good morning,' said Jane, seating herself alongside Matthew and opposite Luke. 'Pass the marmalade, please.'

Luke slid it across the table. 'Guess what? We've only four weeks to go on our gruntwork. Our six months are nearly up. I worked it out last night.'

Tremendous enthusiasm was conspicuous by its absence.

Luke persevered. 'No, come on – we're nearly full Time Police officers. Have you decided yet which jobs you'll put in for?'

Matthew shrugged. 'The Time Map, I suppose.'

Luke looked at him. 'You don't sound very keen. I thought that was what you wanted. It's definitely what Commander Hay wants.'

'Mm,' said Matthew and no more.

'And you'll soon be off to Records, Jane. No more dark places or concussing yourself on garden implements or being pursued by feral children. A nice quiet life for you.'

'Mm.' She smothered marmalade on her toast. 'What about you, Luke? Didn't you rather burn your bridges telling your dad you wanted to stay in the Time Police? Can I have some more coffee, please?'

He poured. 'Dunno. I mean, I don't know what job to put in for. You two both know what you want but I never thought I'd be here long enough to qualify so I haven't given it a lot of consideration.'

'Well, Grint'll be looking for a new team when Rossi and the others graduate. You could apply to join him.'

'Oh yeah – I can just see Grint welcoming me with open arms.'

A cloud of gloom descended over the breakfast table.

'Well,' said Matthew, rousing himself. 'Never mind. With a bit of luck, you'll be dead before then and it won't matter.'

'You really sound like your mother sometimes, you know that? How is she, by the way?'

'Last time I saw her she was alternately pissed off at missing the assassination of Julius Caesar and laughing herself sick at Time Police stupidity.'

The room went temporarily dark as an enormous officer stopped at their table. 'Team Two-Three-Six?'

Luke leaned back in his seat, the better to take him all in. 'Who wants to know?'

'I do, Gobby. You want to make me ask again?'

'No,' said Jane, quickly, unwilling to encounter hostility this early in the day. 'And yes.'

The officer peered at her suspiciously. 'You pissing me about?'

'No,' said Matthew, even more quickly.

'And yes,' said Luke, who could never help himself.

The officer abandoned his questioning. 'Hay wants to see you.'

Luke blinked. 'What? Why?'

He shrugged. 'The smart money's on you all being handed your papers and told to piss off before you make us look any more ridiculous.'

Luke shook his head. 'Don't think us pissing off would help that much, mate. You looked ridiculous long before we turned up.'

The officer swelled and it was perhaps very fortunate that Officer North, carrying an elegant breakfast of coffee and a croissant, was passing by.

'Why are you three still here? Commander Hay wants you.'

'Now?'

'Ten minutes ago. Move.'

She passed on.

'See,' said Luke. 'That's how a proper officer does it.'

Jane pushed him out of the door in the interests of his own safety. 'I really don't get paid enough for doing this. Seriously, how do you manage to get through the day unscathed?'

'He doesn't,' said Matthew. 'He frequently needs rescuing from the consequences of not being able to keep his mouth shut.'

'But not by Jane,' said Luke hastily. 'I don't think Mr Todger could survive another of her rescue attempts.'

'Well,' said Jane, 'other than your blonde in Logistics, I'm not sure anyone would care.'

Luke assumed a melancholy air. 'Actually, I've rather gone off women.'

Matthew raised his eyebrows. 'Even more than they've gone off you?'

Luke sighed. 'I preferred both of you when you never spoke.'

'What a coincidence,' said Jane, summoning the lift.

*　　*　　*

Captain Farenden was waiting for them in the outer office. 'Please come with me.'

In silence, he led them to Briefing Room 3. 'Wait outside, please.'

'Do we know why we're here?' asked Luke.

'Well, I do,' Farenden said and left it at that, limping into the briefing room to announce their arrival and closing the door behind him.

They waited nervously and in silence. Team 236. Or Team Weird, as they were frequently known. Jane Lockland, the mouse. Matthew Farrell, the weirdo. And Luke Parrish, voted most likely to get his arse kicked. In fact, it was rumoured a queue was forming.

After two or three minutes, the door opened and Captain Farenden motioned them to enter.

Commander Hay was seated at the briefing table. Standing behind her, Major Ellis, their team leader, surveyed his crew.

'Good morning,' said Luke, brightly.

Commander Hay ignored him, saying, 'If you would, please, Charlie.'

Captain Farenden brought up an image on the screen. 'This . . . is Ms Jones.'

The screen showed a formally posed photograph of a young woman in her mid-twenties, dark-haired and with the expression of one just waiting to see what sort of trouble she could get into next.

'No, it isn't,' said Luke, still, despite the best efforts of Major Ellis, Officer North and the entire training section, apparently unaware of the correct method of addressing senior officers.

'I beg your pardon?'

'Parrish – shut up,' said Ellis.

'Well, I'm sorry, but I have to point out you're working from duff intel here. That's not Ms Jones – whoever *she* is. That's Imogen Farnborough. Her mother's something in the government. Terrifying woman. Built like the red-brick Victorian privy she so closely resembles. Estates in Gloucestershire. Advocate of hunting foxes but would prefer peasants. Speaks to people in Latin. Wants the poorhouses reinstated. Gets paint flung at her twice a month. Very big on traditional values.' He paused to reflect. 'Although now I come to think of it, some of our traditional values are pretty dire and . . .'

'Parrish . . .'

'Anyway, I went out with Imogen a couple of times and I can tell you that's definitely her. Didn't come to anything because I met her mother. You know what they say – always check out the mother if you want to see how the daughter will turn out. Got a birthmark on her . . . Imogen, I mean, not her mother. Shit-hot skier. Tried out for the Olympics once and . . .'

'Parrish – shut up.'

'I think my info's a bit more up to date than yours, that's all. I was just trying to help.'

'Make a start by not saying a word for the next twenty minutes.'

A slightly gritty silence fell.

Commander Hay twisted in her chair to look up at Ellis. 'Does this change anything?'

'I don't think so, ma'am. It might even prove useful if . . . Ms Jones . . . is already familiar with one of the people involved.'

'Good thought. Proceed, please, Charlie.'

'Anyway,' said Captain Farenden, and waited until all eyes

were on him again. 'This is the young woman ...' he fixed Trainee Parrish with a look, 'known, for our purposes, as Ms Jones.'

He paused but Parrish was staring vaguely out of the window and showing no signs of paying attention.

'It would appear Ms Jones is in need of our assistance.'

Silence fell again. Jane, unsure whether questions were allowed, said nothing. Matthew pursued his usual policy of silence and Luke was apparently enjoying the novel experience of doing as he was told.

Captain Farenden continued. 'This briefing is for your ears only. You will not discuss this matter outside this room. You will receive your instructions, clarify any points necessary with Major Ellis and then depart.'

He paused but again, Team 236 uttered not a word.

'We have received a request for assistance. From, shall we say, a member of Ms Jones's immediate family.'

'From her mother,' were the words definitely not uttered by Luke Parrish.

'It would appear our Ms Jones has managed to get herself into a little difficulty.'

Luke Parrish shifted his weight, managing to convey, surprisingly clearly, that in his opinion, Ms Jones had always been a little bit of a minx and it had been bound to happen one day.

Captain Farenden persevered. 'It would seem that Temporal Tourism is raising its head again. According to information received, at least one small and discreet organisation has sprung up, offering various opportunities for the historically interested and/or extremely rich.'

Luke sighed, thus communicating his opinion of the historically interested and/or extremely rich.

'Presumably dazzled by the opportunity to observe, at first hand, some exciting historical event, Ms Jones, together with a male companion, has allowed herself to be tempted.'

A slight sound from Mr Parrish indicated that he was able, from personal experience, to understand just how easily Ms Jones could allow herself to become tempted.

'Ms Jones has departed for 17th-century London, from which location she has failed to return. We're not sure of the reason why. We don't know if it's a reluctance to return here or an attraction to remain there. Ms Jones's mother is naturally most concerned for her safety and has requested speedy, discreet and above all, effective action from us.'

More silence. Team 236 eyed each other sideways. Ellis sighed. 'Parrish, you may speak.'

'Well, I was just going to say that if no one else has been able to persuade her to return home, I'm pretty sure there's nothing we could do that—'

Ellis interrupted him. 'Your instructions are to locate Ms Jones and bring her home. By any means.'

'What if she doesn't want to come?'

'You weren't listening, Parrish, were you?'

'Eh? Oh. You mean kidnap her?'

'Whatever it takes. Whatever her feelings on the matter, Ms Jones is to be returned to her proper Time and place. With all speed.'

'Um . . .' said Luke. 'I have a difficult question. Difficult for you, I mean. As far as I'm concerned, difficult questions are fun.'

'Yes, Parrish?'

'What is Ms Jones's status?'

'I beg your pardon?'

'Well, if it was anyone other than a cabinet minister's daughter, you'd have sent in a couple of clean-up teams, and if she'd survived that, then she'd be under arrest and due a long spell in prison, wouldn't she? You know – the wrath of the Time Police and all that. But, I'm assuming, with the double standards so prevalent among politicians, that that will not happen. I quite agree that our Imogen is a little bit of a baggage, but even so . . .'

Ellis sighed. 'Firstly, and we have had this conversation before, what happens to those brought in on legally issued warrants is not your concern. Secondly, however, it is hoped that in response for clemency, Ms Jones can be induced to provide some much-needed intel on illegal Temporal Tourism.'

Luke stared. 'You've never actually met Imogen, have you?'

'No, Trainee Parrish, but we have met you.'

'Oh. OK then.'

'A pod is being prepped for you at this moment. Lockland, you do the research. Farrell, you can assist. Get yourselves as much background info as you can and flash it to the AI.'

'When would . . .'

'Now, Trainee Parrish.'

'Right. Gotcha.'

3

'I've been doing some digging,' said Jane, half an hour later, 'and these coordinates are very specific. London, Covent Garden, 7th May 1663. It would seem that Imogen's friend had planned to take her to the theatre. And not just any theatre. Apparently, it's the opening night of the recently restored Theatre Royal in Brydges Street.'

'Never heard of it,' said Luke.

Jane sighed. 'Yes, you have. Drury Lane.'

'Really? I *have* been there. In fact, I think I went with Imogen.'

'You don't remember?'

He grinned down at her. 'Well, you know how it is, Jane. After a while they all just merge into one another.'

'No,' she said tartly. 'I do not know how it is. No one does except you.'

'Don't be crabby, Jane.'

Ellis nodded to Jane. 'Well done, Lockland. Good, solid groundwork.'

Jane felt her face burn with her usual self-consciousness.

'Still not stopped doing that, then?' said Bolshy Jane, from her permanent position inside Jane's head.

33

Ellis continued. 'I think that's the place you should begin your search. We're not sure what Miss Farnborough . . . Jones . . . all right, Farnborough might get up to, but it's the only specific information we have. She was to attend a performance with her young man and she might still try to gain entry to the theatre.'

'That may not end well,' said Matthew, frowning heavily. 'Unaccompanied woman and all that. She won't even have a maid with her.'

'I doubt she'll understand or be interested in the accepted forms of behaviour for women in the 17th century,' said Luke. 'I think we should be prepared for fireworks. And not the celebratory kind.'

'Well, if it's such a big night, then the place will be packed. Surely she won't want to draw attention to herself?' said Jane, without much optimism.

Luke, reading the data over her shoulder, shook his head. '*Au contraire*, Jane.' He pointed at the screen. 'Samuel Pepys was definitely there so probably the king was, as well. And if he's there, then most of his court will be, too. And if that's where all the attention and excitement is, then, trust me, that's where Imogen will be. Simple.'

'Why? Why was this night so important?' She drew a breath to interrogate the AI.

'For God's sake, don't do that,' said Luke quickly. 'You know what it's like. Anyway, I know this one. During Cromwell's reign and as part of Parliament's ongoing attempts to render people's lives as miserable as possible – nothing ever changes, does it? – in addition to banning happiness, Christmas, good food and extra-marital hugs – they also shut down the theatres. On his reinstatement, one of Charles' first actions was

34

to issue Letters Patent reopening them again. This is opening night.'

'That's right,' said Jane, copying details from the screen into her trusty notebook. 'The play is, apparently, *The Humorous Lieutenant*. Oh look – Nell Gwyn performed there.'

'Who?'

'You know – the Protestant whore.'

Luke blinked. 'Jane – I'm astonished at you.'

'No,' said Jane, patiently. 'Charles had many mistresses – often simultaneously – but at one point the leading contenders were Nell Gwyn and a French woman. Louise de Something. She was very unpopular – you know – Catholic – and the mob besieged what they thought was her coach. Only they got the wrong coach and Nell stuck her head out of the window shouting, "Fear not, good people, 'tis only the Protestant whore," and they laughed and left her alone.'

Matthew and Luke exchanged glances. 'You're not turning into Officer North, are you, Jane?'

Officer North had joined the Time Police from St Mary's, a small outfit just outside Rushford, where they would explain, until your ears began to bleed, that they didn't do time travel – they investigated major historical events in contemporary time. How or why St Mary's was allowed to continue was a constant mystery to the Time Police and it was the aim of nearly every officer to eradicate this pestilential organisation from the face of the earth. With extreme prejudice. While everyone agreed Officer North appeared relatively uncontaminated by St Mary's, there were still deep suspicions over what was sometimes seen as her overattention to historical detail.

Jane ignored them. 'Wouldn't it be amazing to see Nell Gwyn?'

'Possibly,' said Ellis, attempting to return his team to the task in hand. 'But mostly, I'd like you all to concentrate on identifying and retrieving Imogen Farnborough.'

Jane blushed again.

'Can we go fully armed?' asked Luke.

'Are you yet fully qualified?'

'Very nearly.'

'Then you can very nearly go armed. Go and get yourselves kitted out. I'll meet you in ten.'

By the time they'd kitted themselves out, the mechs had their pod ready and waiting for them in the Pod Bay.

For safety's sake, this enormous structure had been built underground. A good part of it was actually under the River Thames itself. *To minimise the risk of radiation in the event of pod failure* was the cheerful explanation they'd been given during their basic training. Which, Luke reflected, seemed a very long time ago.

'Aren't you coming with us?' he enquired of Major Ellis as he slapped a sonic on his sticky patch and hung his liquid string and baton off his utility belt. Only fully qualified officers went properly armed with proper weapons. The sort of stuff that could level a building and everything in it.

'I'm not yet completely fit but I am here to ensure you understand the importance of returning with Ms Jones. Intact. Whatever she knows – we need to know too.'

'Yes, yes, we know. Return with Ms Jones or don't return at all. Like the Spartans and their shields.'

Major Ellis heaved a long-suffering sigh. 'What are you talking about, Parrish?'

Luke assumed a muscular pose and deepened his voice. '"Spartan – come home with your shield or on it." That sort of thing.'

'Should I find, Trainee Parrish, that you have, at any point in this assignment, made any attempt to return *on* Ms Jones instead of with her, I shall lock you in a small room with her mother and abandon you there.'

Luke blinked. 'I'm sure you're not allowed to threaten junior ranks with . . .'

'Just get in the bloody pod, Parrish.'

Inside the pod, Jane was at the console, laying in the coordinates, and Matthew was checking them over. None of the Time Police pods are discreet and anonymous. Their stated purpose is to spread shock and awe on the widest possible scale so that for anyone teetering on the verge of something temporally dubious, the sudden appearance of a small, featureless, black hut with no apparent doors or windows was never going to be good news. As a concession to the delicacy of this mission, however, this pod was smaller and slightly less shocking and aweing than usual.

Official procedure decreed that, on landing, officers would noisily emerge and give the buggers point five of a nanosecond to stop what they were doing, lay down their weapons and surrender themselves to the might and majesty of the Time Police. And there was always the unspoken implication that anyone taking the opportunity to shoot themselves dead, thus saving hard-working officers the strain and struggle of all that paperwork, would be greatly appreciated.

Those not achieving this point five of a nanosecond deadline would find themselves either crushed as Time Police boots thundered down the heavy-duty ramp, or zapped into pants-wetting unconsciousness prior to being removed for some quality time at TPHQ. Or just plain shot if those officers were in a particular hurry to be somewhere else. Like the bar, for instance.

Inside this particular pod, the console stood to the left of the door with lockers on the far side and with a row of seats bolted between them. The interior was clean, functional and smelled pleasantly of Apple Orchard.

Luke sniffed unappreciatively. 'I've always felt that Bloody Aftermath or Pants-Filling Terror would be a more appropriate fragrance, don't you?'

'Do we have a team leader for this one?' said Jane, vaguely, all her attention focused on the information being displayed on the console.

Luke sighed. 'Well, it'll be me, won't it? It's always me. No one else ever volunteers.'

'No one else ever gets a word in,' said Matthew. 'Besides, she's your girlfriend.'

'Ex-girlfriend,' said Luke quickly, looking around. The pod door was still open and mechs were criss-crossing the bay.

'Worried your blonde in Logistics might hear?' asked Matthew, innocently.

Jane looked up. 'I thought he'd taken up with that brunette in IT.'

'Is that the one with the guide dog?'

'Very funny,' said Luke, drawing himself up. 'Your team leader instructs you to get a move on.'

'Before the blonde finds out about the brunette and they both find out about Ms Jones?'

'Just get on with it, will you.'

'Ready when you are.'

'OK – everyone got everything? Sonics? Liquid string? Then let's go. Matthew, get the door shut. Jane, commence jump procedures.'

The pod responded. 'Jump procedures commenced.'

The world flickered.

4

London. May, 1663.

'Oh my God,' said Jane, staring at the screen. 'Is this a riot? Are we in the wrong place? What is going on?'

Matthew surveyed the milling, shouting crowds. So many people jam-packed into such narrow spaces. 'Don't think a drone is going to be much use here.'

'Right,' said Luke, leaning over the screen to look more closely. 'Let's have a recap. What do we know about this Time and place? Wait – don't ask the . . .'

Too late.

'Pod,' said Jane, not without a sideways glance at Matthew, who was grinning. 'Please provide details of this location.'

The AI responded in its pleasant female voice.

'London, 1663, during the reign of Charles II. This period is known as the Restoration and is characterised by . . .'

'Never mind all that,' said Luke, impatiently. 'Where is . . . ?'

The AI ignored him. Not for the first time.

'After the restrictions of the . . .'

'We don't need all that.'

'This area predates the Great Fire of 1666 when . . .'

'Nor that.'

'The buildings are constructed mainly of . . .'

'We don't need that, either.'

'. . . wood, thatch, wattle and daub. The invention of the chimney means that smoke from internal fires . . .'

Luke ground his teeth. 'I don't care about the fire-trucking smoke. Is there any evidence of a pod signature in this area?'

'The most recent signature appeared precisely three point three minutes ago and . . .'

'That's *us*, you moron. Anything earlier than that?'

'Yes.'

There was a long pause. Jane busied herself checking the read-outs and power levels and shutting things down while Matthew appeared to be in some sort of light trance. Neither caught each other's eye.

'Yes, what? Jesus, it's like pulling teeth.'

'Yes, there is evidence of recent pod activity unrelated to this one.'

'Where? When?'

'Initial scans indicate a pod departed this vicinity approximately three hours ago.'

'That's good news. We're not too far behind,' muttered Matthew.

'Not long enough for Imogen to have got herself into any serious trouble, surely?' said Jane, packing her notebook away.

'You don't know Imogen,' muttered Luke.

The AI continued. 'I have the signature recorded. A return to HQ will enable comparisons to be made with similar . . .'

'Forget that. It's not the pod we're after this time. Do your scans indicate the presence of any contemporaries?'

'Please indicate the area to be scanned.'

His voice rose to a shout. 'Here. In this place. Where we are now. London. We are looking for an illegal. How much easier would you like me to make it for you, because it's quicker just to switch you off, open the door and take a look ourselves!'

Jane judged it time to intervene. 'Pod, is it possible to locate the illegal in this vicinity, please?'

'You don't have to say please,' shouted Luke. 'It's a fire-trucking machine.'

Until she joined the Time Police, Jane's life had been a sheltered one. She had had little experience of the casual swearing now occurring all around her on a continual basis. After a few months, however, her horizons had broadened. She still wasn't quite ready for the f word – nor could she ever imagine she would be – but life with Luke Parrish had taught her a lot and use of the word fire truck as an acceptable alternative to the word beginning with f and ending in uck was one of them. She was aware its use was being picked up by other officers, although whether this was a compliment or mockery was unclear.

As unstoppable as Time itself, the AI swept on. 'I am unable to detect any anomalous readings but this may possibly be due to the large number of people in this area.'

'Thank you,' said Jane.

'You're welcome,' said the AI, pleasantly.

'Piece of fire-trucking crap,' said Luke.

Team Weird wrapped themselves in the Time Police long black cloaks and exited the pod.

'The AI was right,' Luke said, as they stood outside getting their bearings.

'Who'd have thought?' murmured Matthew and was ignored.

Luke consulted his scratchpad again. 'There's definitely been something here. I can pick up the signature but it's very faint. I doubt we'd be able to track it even if we wanted to.'

'I can't believe they would leave without her,' said Jane, still struggling with how she imagined Imogen must have felt on learning she'd been abandoned.

'Well, it's Imogen, so you never know. She can get on your nerves a bit. She certainly got on mine.'

'Or vice versa,' muttered Matthew.

Luke persevered. 'She's carved an entire career out of never doing what people expect. Or want.'

'With luck,' said Jane, optimistically, 'she will have been horrified to find they'd pushed off without her and will be very happy to go back with us.'

'Or,' continued Luke, 'she's an ungrateful little madam, puts up a fight when we eventually locate her, and we find ourselves in the middle of a riot.'

'Or,' persisted Jane, 'she's been here alone for a couple of hours now and she's frightened out of her wits and is actually pleased to see us.'

'Yes,' said Matthew. 'This job could be a piece of doddle.'

'Although, if she wouldn't leave with her boyfriend, then she's hardly likely to want to leave with us,' said Jane, suddenly abandoning her uncharacteristically optimistic outlook. 'Even if one of us is you, Luke.'

'That's a point,' said Matthew. He peered at his team leader from under his non-regulation haircut. 'And we probably should have asked this earlier, but will she be pleased to see you or is she likely to reach for the nearest weapon?'

'Ah . . .' said Luke, carefully.

Matthew looked at his team leader and rolled his eyes. 'You couldn't have mentioned this before? Jane, if we find her, *you* do the talking.'

Jane looked down at herself. Unlike those pod jockeys at the Institute of Historical Research at St Mary's Priory, where historians go to enormous lengths to achieve historical precision with their attire, the sole Time Police concession to temporal accuracy were their black cloaks, beneath which they wore their normal day-to-day uniform. Body armour, black T-shirt, black combats, boots. Since they weren't expecting any trouble, and to avoid panic and possibly over-hasty actions on the part of any contemporaries, Team 236 had left their helmets back in the pod.

'We're not going to blend in at all,' she said, anxiously.

Luke sighed. 'Jane, I keep telling you. We're the Time Police. We don't have to blend in. We're utter bastards and we want people to know it. Besides, you know what the English are like – they'll just think we're foreigners and pity us.'

'So, what's the plan?' said Matthew, carefully checking the pod door was closed behind them. 'Do we just march up to Imogen, grab her and throw her into the pod, clean-up-crew style?'

'I strongly advise against anything physical,' said Luke. 'Even without her anti-kidnap training, I know she captained the hockey team at Cheltenham Ladies' College. I believe doubts were raised at the time on the advisability of weaponising her but it was too late by then. No, I think our best plan will be to locate her with all speed and then adapt ourselves to whatever circumstances are prevailing at the time, devising and executing a simple but effective plan to achieve our primary goal.'

Matthew eyed him suspiciously. 'You mean make it all up as we go.'

'Pretty much, yeah.'

Jane surreptitiously consulted her by now very dog-eared notebook and pointed. 'This way,' she said, and with some misgivings, the three of them stepped out into the seething mass of humanity. It was impossible to put one foot in front of another without colliding with someone else. The streets were packed and noisy.

'Bloody hell,' shouted Luke, battling to stay on his feet. 'What's that smell? I swear it's making my nose hair curl.'

Matthew tried to squint up Luke's nostrils. 'You have nose hair?'

'Probably not any longer.'

They were buffeted on all sides by citizens going about their normal day-to-day business. Horses shied at all the noises and sights around them. Shopkeepers bawled their wares. Shrieking women, their aprons covered in blood and guts, held up reeking fish. Beggars pleaded for alms. Seeming lunatics – or possibly street preachers – wandered past, shouting randomly. Armed men, grim-faced, marched purposefully. Well-dressed nobles forced their way through the crowds. Dogs trotted determinedly to the next butcher's shop. Pickpockets did what it said on the tin. Indescribably filthy children smelling worse than the fishwives dodged between people's legs. Rats scuttled. Pedlars peddled. And every single one of them, as Luke put it, suffering every personal hygiene issue known to man and a few more besides.

The streets seethed with life and vitality. There were eleven years of Puritan rigour to overcome and it would appear that everyone had already made a great start. The pubs were open. The theatres were open. Christmas was back. Riot, drunkenness and bawdy behaviour were the norm.

'I'm sure no one ever buffets real Time Police officers,' said Luke crossly, rebounding off a sooty wall. 'For God's sake, Jane, stay between me and Matthew, otherwise you'll be swept away to a life of sin and debauchery. Not that you would probably notice.'

'Hey,' she said indignantly, but such was the racket around her that no one heard.

'I could do debauchery,' she muttered to herself.

'Don't think they heard you, sweetie,' said Bolshy Jane, making her unwelcome presence felt again. 'And no, you couldn't.'

Jane wondered if anyone else had voices inside their head or whether, as she suspected, it was just her.

The Theatre Royal was approached by a narrow, dark alleyway running between two rows of barely upright tall wooden buildings whose upper storeys very nearly met over their heads.

Luke halted, looking up. 'Why do they do that?'

'What?' said Jane.

'Build them like that. No – don't ask the . . .'

Too late. The AI spoke in his ear. 'Rent was calculated according to the size of the ground area. In an effort to avoid taxes, the ground floor was designed to be as small as possible while no restraints were placed on the size of the upper floors. When traversing the streets, it is advisable . . .'

'Shut that thing up,' muttered Luke.

'It is important to note . . .'

'Be quiet.'

'I am endeavouring to . . .'

'*Shut up.*'

'Yes,' said Matthew, thoughtfully. 'Shouting at a machine. That's always a sign of intelligence.'

'You have only to say thank you,' said Jane.

'I am not saying thank you to a bloody machine.'

'Not surprised,' said Matthew. 'You barely say thank you to us humans.'

'Can we get on, please?'

At the far end of the alleyway they could just make out a three-storey-high wooden structure. The Theatre Royal.

'Excellent,' said Matthew, drawing back against a wall. 'We'll wait here. Easy to monitor. Ideal for our purposes.'

'Actually,' said Luke, peering down the alleyway. 'No.'

Matthew frowned. 'Why not?'

'Well, a dark, narrow alleyway leading to a theatre – a place of sin and iniquity according to the religious – also makes it an ideal place for commercial transactions.'

Jane was puzzled. 'You mean selling oranges? Nell Gwyn sold oranges.'

'Yes,' said Matthew firmly before Luke could speak. 'They're selling oranges.'

'You can see the Great Fire hasn't happened yet,' said Jane, looking around. 'Everything's made of wood and thatch and it's all crammed together and there are open fires everywhere.'

'Yep,' said Luke. 'I reckon even St Mary's would call this a bit of a death trap.'

Remembering Luke's frequent comments on his taciturnity, Matthew made an effort at conversation. 'My mum was at the Great Fire.'

'Oh my God,' said Luke. 'She didn't start it, did she?'

'No, of course not. But she did get lost and Uncle Markham nearly had to shoot her.'

They stared at him. 'Was it something she said?' said Luke. 'Because I can definitely see *someone* shooting her one day.'

'She outstayed her welcome. A second Maxwell was about to appear in Mauritius.'

Jane shivered. There had been one infamous instance of a person being in the same Time twice and the subsequent consequences were required learning for all trainees before they were even allowed to think about getting in a pod. 'Imagine trying to get two hands in the same glove,' their instructor had said. 'Simultaneously.'

They peered again down the narrow alleyway, which was lined with women ranging from the well-dressed to the barely dressed at all.

'Wow,' said Luke, blinking. 'Don't look, Jane. You'll only have questions Matthew and I can't answer.'

But they'd been spotted. A woman – probably much younger than she looked – was approaching them. Her greasy red hair was piled bird's-nest-like on top of her head and hung in tangled snarls either side of her face. Her gown had once been a dark red but the years had faded it to an indeterminate rusty colour. Dark patches stained under her arms and down the front of her bodice. Her skin was terrible, pitted and scarred, cruelly emphasised by her artificially red cheeks and lips. Jane felt desperately sorry for her and resolved never to complain about her lot again.

Adjusting the bodice of her dress for maximum impact, she parked herself squarely in front of Matthew, smiled gappily at him, inserted a shoulder between him and Jane and expertly separated him from the herd.

Matthew froze. Rabbit in car headlights, was Jane's first thought.

What the hell? was Luke's first thought.

He, Luke Parrish, had never regarded himself as overly conceited. Blessed with a sense of humour, he was well aware of his many and varied faults – and if he wasn't, then his team informed him of them quickly enough – but given that he was tall, handsome, charming, and most importantly, rich, the idea that someone – anyone – could be more desirable than he himself was as surprising as it was unthinkable. That that someone could be Matthew Farrell – short, scrawny, shaggy and with weird eyes . . . What the hell was the matter with this woman? Was she blind? At the very least her professional genes should have homed in on him – Luke Parrish – everyone's first choice. Instead of which . . .

This was a first on a number of levels for Team 236. Luke struggling to comprehend a world where he wasn't automatically someone's first pick. Jane meeting her first prostitute. Matthew suddenly face to face with his first sexual encounter. He and Jane were both incandescent with embarrassment.

'Just say no,' said Luke, amused.

Matthew shook his head. Whereas Luke never had any problem with words, speech was never his first choice when dealing with new situations. His childhood had been bloody, violent, and over with very quickly. Conversation had been a luxury for other people. Those days were gone but old habits die hard.

'You've never done this before, have you?' said Luke.

Matthew shook his head again.

'OK – just smile politely – no point in upsetting anyone in case her pimp's not far away – it's all right, Jane, I'll explain about pimps later . . .'

'I know what a pimp is,' said Jane, indignantly and incorrectly.

The young woman, possibly considering she hadn't made her intentions quite clear, moved closer still, running her fingers down Matthew's arm.

Matthew tried to step back and collided heavily with the wall behind.

Having manoeuvred him into the optimum position, the young woman uttered a few words in an accent so strong he had no chance of understanding her.

He panicked. 'What did she say? I didn't catch what she said.'

Luke grinned. 'I think she's agreeing the price. Would you like me to negotiate on your behalf? I could probably get you quite a good deal.'

'No. Just tell her I'm not interested.'

'Easily done, Matthew. Shake your head and move away.'

'She's got my arm,' whispered Matthew. 'What do I do?'

Luke pretended to consult his watch. 'Well, we do have a few minutes in hand if you fancy having a man made of you behind the wall.'

A faint sound from Matthew indicated he had every objection to having a man made of him behind the wall.

'Oh, for heaven's sake,' said Jane.

'No, hang on,' said Bolshy Jane. 'This is funny.'

'He's spoken for,' said Jane, as firmly as she could, placing herself between the young woman and her potential customer.

She was ignored.

'You two really don't have a clue, do you?' said Luke. He addressed the young woman and shrugged. 'No money. Sorry.'

The young woman stared at Matthew for a moment. He wondered what would happen to her if she failed to earn her quota for the evening. Nothing good, that was for sure.

Bowing to her, he said, 'I'm so sorry – I don't have enough money for someone as special as you, but it was nice to meet you today.'

For a moment she stared, then, getting the message if not the individual words, she smiled at Matthew, curled her lip at Luke, ignored Jane completely, identified a more promising customer on the other side of the street and sauntered away.

Jane and Matthew heaved huge sighs of relief. Jane's blush began to fade.

Luke sighed and regarded them both. 'Am I going to have to have The Talk with you two?'

Both Jane and Matthew stared at their feet.

'Really?' said Luke. 'You're both . . . ?'

'Members of the Time Police,' said Jane, quickly. 'And can we concentrate, please.'

'Fine with me,' said Luke, grinning.

They drew back behind a small cart loaded with empty barrels and waited in silence, broken only by the occasional snigger from Luke.

'So, what's our next step?' asked Matthew, attempting to distract him.

Luke surveyed the jostling crowds. 'We wait here. If she's here for the play, then Imogen must pass this way sooner or later. She probably thinks her boyfriend will meet her here. She doesn't know she's been missing for days. We just have to be patient.'

'Do we know what she's wearing?' enquired Jane.

'Actually, yes,' said Matthew helpfully and hardly in the spirit of revenge at all. 'I believe the AI has full . . .'

Luke groaned.

'. . . details. Pod, provide a description of Imogen Farnborough's clothing.'

The AI responded. 'A long blue dress.'

They waited. After a while it dawned on them that no more information would be forthcoming.

Luke rolled his eyes. 'Is that it?'

'I do possess supplementary information.'

'And what is that?'

'Supplementary information is information that is supplementary.'

'I *meant* – of what does this supplementary information consist?'

'A big skirt.'

'What?'

'A big skirt.'

'*What's* a big skirt?'

'A skirt is commonly regarded as a garment, usually but not always worn by a female, that descends downwards from the waist, while big is another word for large and usually relates to size, height, weight or amount.'

Matthew clutched at his scratchpad before Luke could send it flying across the street.

Robbed of revenge, Luke took refuge in sarcasm. 'Is that the best you can come up with? Brain the size of a . . .' He paused, seeking inspiration.

'Planet,' supplied the AI.

'What? What are you talking about now?'

'The accepted expression is "Brain the size of a—"'

'*Shut up.*'

There was silence. Jane suspected even the AI could see it had pushed Luke too far.

Luke inhaled deeply. 'And that's all we've got to go on?'

Jane nodded. 'Yes.'

He gestured dramatically. 'Every third woman out there is wearing – or mostly wearing – a long blue dress with a big skirt.'

Neither Jane nor Matthew could find anything constructive to say.

Luke shook his head. 'Well, if it helps in any way, it'll be the poshest and most expensive outfit on the street. Trust me, that girl is not cheap.'

Jane peered around the wagon and surveyed the jam-packed street again.

Even though they were in the middle of the city, there was a strong smell of pigs. Dogs and chickens appeared to roam as they pleased. Steam arose from the midden carefully situated adjacent to the back door of an inn – for the comfort and convenience of their valued customers, she assumed. Just for once, she found herself in complete agreement with Luke, who always regarded picturesque as just another word for primitive. And smelly. And uncomfortable. And a massive health hazard.

The only good thing happening was that no one else appeared to be taking the slightest notice of them. As Matthew said, so much for projecting the traditional Time Police aura of shock and awe.

'Suppose Imogen slips past us?' whispered Jane. Although why she whispered was a bit of a mystery in this racket. 'What if we miss her?'

'Oh,' said Luke reassuringly, 'I wouldn't despair. Imogen has a habit of making her presence felt.'

'If we don't locate her before it gets dark, we may have to walk the streets looking for her,' said Jane.

'We have to find her before then,' muttered Luke. 'Something tells me this is not a good place to be after dark.'

'And we can't possibly leave her here,' said Jane, shivering despite the hot, airless street.

Matthew nodded. 'My mum says living outside your own Time is not easy.'

'Can I ask –' enquired Jane, 'is she likely to come quietly?'

'Imogen? Probably not. Depends how she's spent the last couple of hours. She might be desperate to return to a cleaner time, or, being Imogen, she might already have found some other poor sap with a fortune for her to plunder. Could go either way.'

'Oh my God, Luke, are we actually going to have to kidnap her?'

'No, no,' said Luke hastily. 'It's not kidnapping when *we* do it – it's person-retrieval. We'll find somewhere quiet and talk to her, putting forwards our strong and well-reasoned arguments for her returning home . . .' He paused.

'And then we'll have to sonic her.'

'Very probably, yes.'

'She might have become someone's property by now,' said Matthew. 'You know, those predators who look for inexperienced young people to exploit – and if that's happened, then they're bound to make a fight of it. I can't see this going at all well.'

'Nothing ever goes well for us,' said Luke, 'but somehow, we get there in the end. That's why they've sent us and not Grint and his gang of thugs.'

'Anyway,' said Matthew. 'Even if we do locate her, we still have the problem of persuading this fearsome young woman who doesn't like you to return with us . . .'

'Without incurring any personal injuries ourselves . . .' said Jane.

They both looked at Luke.

'As team leader,' he said, with dignity, 'it is my duty to remain positive. An opportunity is bound to present itself. I mean, without being indelicate, sooner or later she's going to have to slip away somewhere private to do the biz. We follow her and at the strategic moment – we pounce.'

'*What?*' said Jane, who could see so many things wrong with this plan it was hard to know where to begin.

'Before, during or after?' enquired Matthew, curiously.

'What?' said Luke, temporarily confused.

'Before, during or after Imogen doing the biz?'

'At the first opportunity, obviously.'

Matthew wouldn't let it go. 'Only if we try our luck *before*, then she'll be too busy trying to hold it in to listen to us. And if we approach her *during*, then she'll scream her head off. And if we try *afterwards*, then she'll accuse us of being a bunch of perverts and hit you over the head with the nearest handcart.'

'Why will she hit *me*?'

'Because Jane and I will be half a mile away by then.'

'I think,' said Luke, 'we should employ the same tactics we used in Australia to capture the rampant rabbit.'

Matthew blinked. 'What – Jane hits herself over the head with a rake and you nearly get us arrested for child molesting? Those tactics?'

'No. Obviously. I mean we simply bide our time and await an opportunity. Seize the moment, so to speak.'

Matthew innocently enquired which they should seize first. Imogen or the moment.

Luke declined to respond and they went back to watching the crowds again.

'It's nearly three,' said Jane, anxiously. She consulted her scratchpad. 'The play will start at three. Even allowing for fashionable lateness . . .'

'Who *are* all these people?' said Luke in exasperation, staring about him at the people still flocking towards the theatre. 'Why aren't they all as culturally deficient as the people in our time? Why aren't theatre prices beyond the reach of the hoi polloi as they are in better-ordered societies? Why don't they all have jobs they should be doing, thus enabling us to walk off with Imogen before anyone – including the half-witted, pain in the arse herself – realises what's going on?'

'That's a little unkind, Luke,' said Jane.

'She's an upper-class Englishwoman,' said Luke, impatiently.

'She's been bred to look good on a horse and that's about the limit of her accomplishments. And even then, the horse is doing most of the work.'

'I heard that,' said a voice behind them.

Jane's first thought was, what could possibly have attracted Imogen Farnborough to Luke Parrish? Yes, she was a spoiled little rich girl – lines of discontent were already carving themselves at the corners of her mouth, and her default expression appeared to be that of a thwarted kitten – but her eyes, a deep brown beneath fashionably thick brows, were quick and intelligent. Brains were not usually high on Luke's list of requirements for the ideal woman.

Imogen's dark hair was done up in a knot on top of her head with corkscrew curls falling around her face and Jane could see the AI had nailed the sartorial details – she was indeed dressed in a long blue dress with a big skirt, its hem already dark with dirt and wet.

To be fair, Luke did his best to be conciliatory. 'Hey, Imogen. Looking good.'

'What the hell are you doing here, Parrish? I'm almost certain the words *I never want to see you again* were uttered during our final conversation. By me,' she added, just in case anyone was in any doubt. 'Many times.'

'We've come to rescue you, Immy.'

She put her hands on her hips. 'Don't call me that. Unless

you want me to resume calling you Loo and tell everyone why.'

It began to dawn on both Matthew and Jane that Luke might not have been the ideal choice for this mission after all. Stepping forwards, Jane said, 'Hello. I'm Jane. We've been sent to ...' she paused, changed what she had been about to say and amended it to, 'look for you.'

Imogen stared them up and down. 'You're the Time Police. Bloody hell, Parrish – you're Time Police now? Jesus – whatever did they do to deserve that?'

'Yes, we are Time Police,' said Jane, 'and ...'

'I can't believe it,' Imogen continued, circling Luke. 'Although I've got to say the uniform suits you. Was that why you chose it?'

'Not the entire reason,' said Luke, stiffly. 'Anyway, we're here to ...'

He broke off as someone pushed past him, causing him to stagger.

Imogen took advantage. 'I'm not going anywhere with you.'

Luke regained his balance. 'You don't have a choice, Imogen. By the powers vested in ...'

He was buffeted by a woman carrying a basket of fish well past their sell-by date. The smell, sadly, was at peak performance.

Imogen laughed. 'Do you know how ridiculous you sound?' She looked at Matthew and Jane. 'Not you two. I'm sure you're lovely people. No offence.'

'None taken,' said Matthew. 'And we are. Is there any chance of hearing more about why you broke up with Luke?'

'Absolutely none,' snapped Luke, attempting to regain lost authority. 'Immy ... ogen, we've been sent by ...'

'We're here to make sure you're here by your own choice,' said Jane quickly, realising that disclosing parental involvement might not play well just at this moment. 'Some of these . . . um . . . time travel organisations . . . can be a little bit . . . well . . . casual. I'm sure you understand that it's our duty to make sure you haven't been callously abandoned. Marooned here against your will. By someone who just took the money and ran, perhaps.' She paused hopefully for Imogen to avail herself of this opening.

'Oh no,' said Imogen, airily. 'Nothing like that. They were very good.'

'Well, that's a relief,' said Jane. 'Perhaps you could give us some details, just to put our minds at rest, and then we can be on our way.'

A gaggle of women, all talking nineteen to the dozen, elbowed their way through their group. 'Sure,' said Imogen, retreating back into a convenient doorway and leaving the other three to be battered to death by eager 17th-century theatre-goers. 'I met someone – he was much nicer than you, Luke – and after we'd been together for a while, he said did I want to do something exciting and I said yes and here I am.'

'Oh?' said Jane. 'So, these people approached you and your friend?'

'Well, we were given a time and a place to meet – by someone who knew someone. You know how these things work . . .'

Jane nodded, hoping very much she was giving the impression of someone who knew exactly how these things worked.

'And here I am,' finished Imogen triumphantly, effortlessly omitting all the important details of her story.

Luke rejoined the conversation. 'So, this other bloke . . . ?'

'Eric.'

'Eric?' said Luke incredulously. 'You're in a relationship with someone called *Eric*?'

'Eric Portman. Son of *the* Portman of Portman and Webber Technical. Yes, he's a bit wet but quite nice. He's almost certainly never stood up his girlfriend to go gambling. Or refused to take her to Monaco. Or two-timed her with that horse-faced . . .'

'*Eric Portman?* That . . .'

'Handsome, well-connected, very rich, powerful man with excellent taste in women? Yes, that Eric . . .'

'That's the same wonderful Eric who left you here?'

'Well, you left me at Grimaud's. All night, if I remember. If John . . . whatshisname hadn't come along . . .'

'I turned my back for five minutes and you pushed off with that . . .' Luke groped for adequate words.

Imogen smirked. Which might not have been wise.

Luke loomed over her. 'Well, the boot's on the other foot now, Immy, because now the wonderful Eric has abandoned you here . . .'

She laughed. 'No, he hasn't.'

'Yes, he has.'

Jane and Matthew could only watch in wonder.

'He pushed off and left you, you petulant . . .'

'No, he hasn't.'

It dawned on Jane that Imogen must think Eric was still somewhere in Restoration London, frantically searching the streets for her, and was waiting for him to appear at any moment, full of contrition and expensive presents.

Luke looked around him in an exaggerated fashion. 'Oh. Is Eric here and we can't see him? Let me see – is he over there? Oh – no, he isn't. Is he over there? Well, what a surprise – again, no.'

'He can't have abandoned me, stupid. Look, we had a bit of a disagreement, that's all, and . . .'

'That's not all, Immy.'

'. . . and he'll turn up any moment now. We're going to the theatre.'

She gestured. In the wrong direction.

'He's not coming back,' said Luke, flatly.

'Yes, he is.'

'No, he's not.'

Jane intervened in an effort to propel the conversation in a more constructive direction.

'I'm afraid he's not, Imogen. Not coming, I mean.'

For the first time, Imogen appeared uncertain. 'You mean . . .'

'I'm afraid so.'

'Oh,' she said, in relief. 'Got it. He's sent you instead.'

'We're not some bloody nursemaid service for airheads with more money than brains,' exploded Luke. 'We're here to arrest you and take you in.'

'You can't arrest me.'

Luke loomed again. 'Try me.'

'What for?'

He was thrown. 'What?'

'What are you arresting me for?'

Another group of eager theatre-goers swarmed past them. Luke fended them off as best he could, raising his voice in response over the eager chatter. 'Illegal time travel, Immy.

Surely even someone as self-absorbed as you will have noticed it's against the law.'

She laughed. 'No, it's not.'

Luke pointed at his colleagues. 'Time Police.' He pointed at her. 'Time criminal.'

A sudden silence fell around their little group. Jane would not have believed it possible, but somehow, the universe arranged it.

Luke took advantage. 'This isn't a game, you know. Did you think that if you ran away then Eric would rescue you like some sort of knight in shining armour? Dear God. Imogen, how manipulative are you? Your mother's worried sick.'

'Eric adores me, Luke.'

'Not when he discovers you've involved him with the Time Police, he won't.'

That hit home. Again, Imogen looked uncertain.

'Think about it, Immy. Eric tipped off your mother, but he kept his identity secret. As did your mother. *You're* the one who let his name slip just now. I'm betting he won't be quite so adoring when he discovers you've grassed him up. And he hasn't sent anyone to save you. It was your mother who initiated this rescue. Eric's probably off somewhere having a stiff drink with his mates and congratulating himself on his lucky escape.'

Imogen stepped back. 'Eric *loves* me.' She lifted her chin defiantly. 'And I love him.'

'Oh, come on, Imogen. You don't love anyone. You don't have it in you and I'm bloody certain this prat Eric doesn't either.'

She flushed with rage. 'Just because you . . .'

63

'Yes, as you've already pointed out – many times actually – I'm selfish and self-centred and care only for myself. You're just pissed off because I'm even more selfish and self-centred than *you*.'

'I think we should marry them off,' whispered Matthew to Jane. 'Take them both out of circulation. Think of the favour we'd be doing the world.'

At this point, Jane still carried a faint hope that they could persuade Imogen to return peacefully to their pod. Sadly, this was shattered by Luke's next words.

'Imogen, you imbecile, it's not *love*. Men like him don't marry girls like you. His parents will see to that. He's the heir to Portman and Thingummy. Minor royalty is the very least they'll be aiming for, not some here-today-gone-tomorrow politician's daughter. You really do have to rid yourself of this idea you're the centre of the universe. In fact, I wouldn't mind betting that your tantrums have pushed your Eric so far that when you so spitefully rejected him and flounced off, he seized the opportunity to reject you as well. And who could blame him? I suspect he was dazzled by you – as so many are,' Luke added bitterly, 'and because you're too stupid to keep your petty nature to yourself, the scales fell from his eyes and today was the final straw. He went to a lot of trouble bringing you here and you've publicly humiliated him.

'And,' he continued, well into his stride by now, picking up speed and seemingly oblivious to Jane's attempts to rein him in, 'don't make the mistake of thinking you'll fall on your feet here. Trust me – you won't last ten minutes. You haven't the faintest idea of the position of women in this society, and by the time you do, it'll be far too late.' He gestured to her blue silk dress. 'Someone might think you're rich and well-connected . . .'

Imogen tossed her curls. 'I *am* rich and well-connected.'

'Not in this Time, you're not.'

'And I've already met some very nice young men. They were very helpful and sympathetic and one's going to take me to meet his sister and . . .'

'Oh, for God's sake, use your brains, Immy. They're not *nice young men*. They're the 17th-century equivalent of the pervies who hang around the cheap airship stations looking for naïve young women who've just arrived in town to seek their fortune – but the only fortune involved is the one you'll make for them. Their leader will have a quick shag or two – just to let you know what's required of you from now on – and once he's had them, he'll pass you around until everyone's had you and you're living with the pigs as the town bike and even your long-suffering mother won't have you back.'

There was a moment's disbelieving silence and then Imogen planted her feet, bunched her fist and landed Luke one squarely on the nose. He reeled backwards, caught his foot on an uneven cobble and toppled over.

Imogen picked up her skirts and prepared to flee.

'Dode led her ged away,' shouted Luke, sprawled in a greasy puddle.

The Time Police have procedures for this sort of thing. Matthew and Jane grabbed an arm each.

Imogen struggled violently. And then she screamed. Ear-splittingly.

'Bloody hell,' said Matthew, wincing. 'I bet they can hear her all the way to Oxford.'

'By dode,' said Luke, tenderly fingering his throbbing nose. 'We deed to go.'

And indeed, they were attracting far more attention than Jane was happy with. Two or three men – she wouldn't mind betting they were some of the very nice young men Imogen had met – were pushing their way towards them, shouting angrily. They didn't look at all thrilled at the prospect of Luke muscling in on their naïve country girl, and the future earnings she was sure to bring them.

'Shid,' said Luke. He heaved himself to his feet and wiped the blood off his nose with his sleeve. 'Back to the pod.'

Imogen was struggling like a maniac against Jane and Matthew's grip. Luke glanced at the advancing men, cursed, surveyed his puny teammates and found them wanting. In one quick movement, he threw Imogen over his shoulder and did his best to run.

She did not go quietly. She wriggled frantically, twisted her hands in his hair and pulled hard, trying to kick him. Jane and Matthew moved into position behind him. They staggered down the street. People moved aside – some were laughing, but the shouts behind them were drawing closer. Imogen was wriggling and kicking. And, Jane realised, they were running *away* from the pod.

A stone whizzed past and bounced off the wall to their right.

'You two get in front of me,' shouted Luke. 'I'll protect you.'

'What about you?'

'Not a problem. They'll hit Immy before they hit me.'

Imogen's shriek of rage could, indeed, probably be heard in Oxford.

'Down here,' shouted Matthew, veering off to the right. 'There's another alleyway. Run like stink.'

'We always run like stink,' panted Jane, skidding into the alley. 'We don't know any other way.'

Luke was slowing as Imogen alternately pummelled at his back or attempted to give him some kind of wedgie.

'For the love of God, Immy!' Her struggles had caused her skirts to wrap around his face and he was nearly blind. Desperately he tried to claw them away with one hand and retain his grip on the squirming Imogen with the other. 'I'm trying to save you.'

She lifted her head and shrieked, 'Help, help! I'm over here. Help!'

'Is there no way of shutting her up?' panted Matthew. 'We'll never lose them with her shouting her head off all the time and it looks as if we're the bad guys. We'll have the mob after us in no time.'

Skidding around a corner, they found themselves entangled in that popular 17th-century street entertainment – a cock fight. Around ten or twelve people – men and women – stood in a rough circle as two bedraggled cocks closed with each other in a flurry of gore and feathers. The runnels ran red with blood. Even over the jeers from the crowd they could hear the chink as coins were thrown into the ring. And the faces turning towards them were not friendly.

'Left,' shouted Matthew and suddenly they were in a maze of narrow, foetid and almost identical streets. All the doors, though ramshackle, were firmly closed. There was nowhere to go. There was shouting behind them. There was shouting ahead of them too. They appeared to be surrounded.

Luke unloaded Imogen like a sack of coals.

'Well,' he said, unslinging his baton. 'We always knew this

would happen one day. Back to back, people. Remember the drill.'

'All for one,' said Jane.

'And one for all,' said Matthew.

'This is it,' said Bolshy Jane, presumably in case Jane hadn't noticed what was going on.

Either say something useful or fire truck off, thought Jane, turning to face the two men coming up on her left, liquid string in one hand, baton in the other, in the approved Time Police manner. She gritted her teeth.

'Please don't let this hurt too much,' whimpered Wimpy Jane.

'Sonics as last resort,' instructed Luke. 'Only if batons won't hold them.'

He was right, thought Jane. Batons for close combat – sonics for covering their retreat.

There were at least five of them that she could see. Four men wore greasy leather doublets and the one Jane assumed to be the leader sported a long, scruffy and much-stained coat. Jane couldn't help feeling they looked rather too down at heel for Imogen. She wasn't the type to be attracted to the rougher element. And this lot looked very rough indeed. A thought struck her. Perhaps they were servants – sent by Imogen's nice young men with instructions to retrieve Imogen. Or could they be casual cut-throats availing themselves of an unexpected opportunity?

'Never mind who they are,' shouted Bolshy Jane. 'Just get stuck in.'

The one with a coat had a sword, already drawn and brandished in a manner that showed he knew how to use it. The

68

others were armed with nasty-looking cudgels, one or two of which were dark with sinister stains.

Jane could hear Imogen shouting behind her. Whether she was still haranguing Luke, or encouraging the men, or just having a whinge in general, Jane was unable to say. And she had more important things to worry about.

In holos, this sort of thing is always carefully choreographed and everyone knows exactly what to do, to whom, and where to do it. People fight neatly and cleanly and then the villains run away. Narrative imperative. Villains are always worthless cowards who run away when faced with anything more threatening than an angry chicken.

Needless to say, this lot clearly hadn't read the *Handbook for Villains*. They were quick and professional. They fanned out and charged simultaneously.

Fire truck, thought Jane, momentarily paralysed.

'Baton, you thicko,' shouted Bolshy Jane, jolting her back to the moment.

Jane flicked open her baton – its range was greater than that of the advancing man's cudgel – and prepared for her first street fight.

The Time Police have a procedure for this sort of thing. The first stage is to draw batons. The second is to flourish them in a menacing manner, making sure all their prospective assailants get a good view of the shit coming their way any moment now. Having done that, the third is to raise the baton and begin the advance.

'Remember,' said Luke. 'Five paces. One . . . two . . .'

Jane picked her target – a small rat-like man on her left who had made the mistake of thinking she would be the weak link.

At five paces, they broke into a run, batons at head height. Jane opened her mouth and yelled. Partly to frighten the opposition and partly to give herself courage. Rat man filled her vision. She swung her baton, aiming for his upper arm. She struck hard, not letting the knowledge this was her first live target to overcome her instinct to survive.

He yelled in pain. She whipped it back again across his thigh. He screamed this time.

'Stay together,' shouted Luke. 'Watch your backs. Stay defensive. Don't let them split us up.'

Trusting Matthew to have her other side, Jane swung again, cracking rat man's shin. That was him out of the fight.

'Remember your training,' said Bolshy Jane, who could, on occasions, be useful. 'Concentrate on what's around you but be aware of your flanks and rear.'

Her left side was brick wall. Her rear was more brick wall. Matthew was on her right. She could do this.

Rat man was on the ground. She gave him a quick stringing to keep him there and turned her attention to her right. Matthew had engaged two of them. Where Luke was and what he was up to was anyone's guess.

Jane moved away from the protection of the wall to get behind Matthew's assailants and fetched one a stinging blow across the kidneys – a painful and disabling move straight from the pages of the unofficial Time Police training manual – a considerably more useful handbook than the official version.

Sadly, his leather doublet protected him to a great extent and he whirled around to deal with this new threat. That she was female certainly surprised him. Jane fumbled with her string, aiming for his arms. It was more important to disarm the weapon than the man. Although if he wanted to run away, she would have no problem with that.

The man looked down at the rapidly hardening yellow festoons with surprise and she seized the opportunity to whack him one across his thigh. Down he went.

Oh my God, that's two, thought Jane. I'm a proper utter bastard now.

Someone crashed into her, knocking her to the ground. Time Police procedures are very clear about lying on the ground in the middle of a street fight. Don't.

She rolled to get clear and collided with rat man, still struggling to break free of his string. His free hand grabbed for her and quite instinctively she stringed his face.

He yelled. Opening his mouth was not a wise move. She filled it with liquid string. Rolling again, she left him to it. Matthew was struggling – his baton lay on the ground. Down the street, two of them had pushed Luke against the wall. Even as she looked, he brought up his knee and gouged at one assailant's eyes. It occurred to Jane that Imogen probably wasn't the only one who'd had anti-kidnap training.

Matthew still needed her. Adrenalin fizzing, with a yell, she waded in, baton swinging. To the left. To the right. To the left again. And squirt the string. The bloody stuff didn't harden quickly enough, that was the problem. The small part of her mind not concentrating on staying alive made a note to mention this in her report.

One of Luke's assailants whirled about and ran straight into her. She fell to the ground again, hitting her head. There was the sound of footsteps running away and then Matthew's face appeared.

'All right?' He pulled her to her feet.

She looked down at herself. Dishevelled and muddy but everything seemed to be in the right place and more or less functioning normally.

'Yes,' she said in disbelief. And then, more strongly, 'Yes. You?'

'Fine. Where's our fearless leader?'

'Here,' said Luke, pushing himself off the wall. He looked at the two on the ground. 'Did we win?'

'We did but they'll be back. With friends.'

'Who were they?' said Matthew, looking around.

Luke shrugged. 'Street thieves, perhaps, who thought we'd be an easy target.'

'They got that wrong,' said Matthew in some satisfaction.

Jane wiped the sweat from her face. 'I thought they might be connected to Imogen's nice young men.'

'If so,' said Luke, stowing his baton, 'she's really got herself in with the wrong crowd and we should get out of here as quickly as possible. Everyone back to the pod. Mission accomplished.'

They turned.

No, it wasn't. Imogen Farnborough had disappeared.

6

Team 236 stared about them in dismay. At some point in the proceedings, she'd buggered off. Jane's first reaction was that Luke had done the right thing when he'd ditched Imogen Farnborough. That girl really was more trouble than she was worth.

Luke was looking up and down the deserted street. 'Did someone grab her while we were busy?'

'No one got past me,' said Jane stoutly.

Matthew shook his head in agreement.

'She ran away again,' said Luke in disgust. 'We saved her from that bunch of thugs and she just pushed off.'

'Now what?' said Jane, stowing her baton and checking her aerosol. 'Because I'm nearly out of string.'

Matthew nodded.

'Back to the pod,' said Luke. 'We don't have a lot of choice. They might be back with reinforcements. We'll clean ourselves up, recharge our weapons – and ourselves – and formulate our next plan of action. God knows where the silly bint is by now. This way.'

Jane stood still, frowning.

'Jane? What is it? Are you hurt?'

'She thought we were sent by Eric to save her but what she

actually got was not so much a knight in shining armour as a pair of tatty wimps and an ex-boyfriend.'

'So?'

'Look, she made a big mistake when she ran away from Eric – I mean running off into the 17th century, not turning down his proposal – but she'll never admit it. What we have to do now is make things easy for her. Luke, you have to plead with her . . .'

'What?'

'And then she can do you a favour and agree to come back with us.'

'I'm not doing that.'

'You have to. Our mission is to get her back – whatever it takes – and you might be the best person to do that.'

'In which case,' said Matthew slowly, 'she might even be waiting for us at the pod.'

Jane shook her head. 'No – that would be too easy. I think she'll give us time to get back and then stroll up immaculate and unconcerned . . .' She looked down at her muddy self. 'Then she'll probably saunter into the pod and demand to be taken home because we're just a bloody taxi service.'

There was a silence while they all thought about this.

'I am not, in general, an advocate of violence against women,' said Luke, gently touching his still tender nose. 'Trust me – the boot is usually on the other foot – but the second I clap eyes on Imogen Farnborough I'm going to throttle her. Until that happy moment, however . . . back to the pod.'

They set off at a swift trot, covering themselves at all times. 'Just like real officers,' said Luke, chattily. 'How happy Ellis would be to see us now.'

'What – after being involved in a back-alley brawl and losing our prisoner?' said Matthew. 'I don't think *happy* is the word you're looking for.'

'The word *unsurprised* would probably be more accurate,' said Jane, gloomily.

'I'll tell you something,' said Luke. 'We are *not* going back without her. If it takes the rest of our lives, we will track that girl down and make sure she gets what's coming to her.'

They ran on. Past twisted wooden buildings whose wooden supports had warped over the years. Past piles of filth. A dog shot out of a doorway and snapped at their ankles. The over-hanging buildings rendered the day dark. Air barely moved in these tight spaces. Jane tried very hard not to imagine millions and millions of plague rats watching her pass, just waiting for the opportunity . . . There were another couple of years before the Great Plague of 1665 would rip through London, closely followed by the Great Fire a year later. This was definitely not a good time to be a Londoner.

The meandering lanes were mean, narrow and unpaved. The street level was considerably higher than the narrow houses on either side. In London, the streets were not paved with gold. They were paved with household refuse. Some of it was very squidgy underfoot. People just opened the door or the shutter and chucked it all out. Which must have been a complete waste of time since whenever it rained, surely it all got washed straight back in again.

'Makes the 20th century look good, doesn't it?' said Matthew cheerfully to their leader, who ignored him.

Luke was in front, Jane in the middle. Matthew brought up the rear. He stopped suddenly. 'Listen.'

They pulled up, turned and listened.

Somewhere, not too far away, they could hear sounds of an altercation. A woman screamed. The voice was familiar.

'Fire-trucking hell,' shouted Luke. 'This way. Sound and fury, people.'

He ripped out his baton and shouted. Jane and Matthew followed suit. Roaring Time Police defiance, they pounded down the alley and rounded a corner. Imogen was on the ground surrounded by five or six women. One had a nasty-looking knife. The others were kicking and stamping and she'd rolled into a ball in an attempt to save herself. There was blood on the stones.

Luke waded in, baton swinging. Jane and Matthew were only slightly behind him. Since Imogen had already proved herself to be a bit of a flight risk, Jane left her teammates to deal with whatever was happening around them and knelt alongside her.

'Quick,' she said, pulling out her sonic to cover them. 'Can you stand? You must get up.'

Imogen groaned.

'Use my shoulder,' said Jane. 'Pull yourself up.'

Somehow, Imogen heaved herself to her feet. Jane stood in front of her, her sonic raised, her mouth set in a grim line. Anyone not Imogen Farnborough or Time Police were about to find themselves with enormous – if temporary – bladder control problems. She was just in the mood.

'Attagirl,' said Bolshy Jane.

The women were proving far more formidable than the men had been. Two of them were prising up loose cobbles and hurling them at Luke's helmetless team. Luke and Matthew were falling back.

76

Luke turned to Imogen. 'Sorry, Immy, you're going to have to run like the rest of us. I need my hands free.'

Imogen, however, had no intention of running. 'Give me that.' She snatched Luke's baton from him, flicked it open with an ease he found more than disconcerting and advanced on their attackers. The addition of Imogen to their little party evened the odds. Even more so when it became apparent she had recent scores to settle. Whoever had paid for Imogen's anti-kidnap training had certainly got their money's worth. Luke's world suddenly became a maelstrom of shrieking, flailing, kicking women.

'We've got to get away,' shouted Jane. 'There's too many of them.'

Somewhere above them, a shutter was forced open. There was a shout – whether a warning, a curse or an order to take the fight somewhere else, they never knew. For some reason everyone drew back – except for Luke – and then someone hurled a bucket of what Jane optimistically hoped was pigswill out of the window. And then followed it up with the bucket.

Luke stood dripping. Imogen was wielding the baton like an expert, showing no sort of regard for either the official or unofficial Time Police handbook. People scattered before her. Matthew, possibly wisely, was standing back. Jane pushed Luke back against the wall under the upper storey where he should be safe from any further household-waste-related assaults and turned back to watch the fight.

One wild minute later, it was all over and Team 236 and their prisoner were alone. Imogen stood, chest heaving, baton raised, looking, had she known it, very like her mother single-handedly demolishing a back-bench rebellion. The only sound was her heavy panting. Matthew gently removed Luke's baton from her suddenly slackened grasp and handed it back to his leader.

'Nice,' he said to Imogen.

She smoothed back her tangled hair. 'Thank you. I just imagined each and every one of them was Luke Parrish and the rest was easy.'

Luke picked something purple and wobbly off his shoulder. 'Oh, dear God, what is that?' and dropped it on the ground. Four heads bent over it.

'No idea,' said Matthew. 'Do you want us to bag it and take it back?'

'No.' He retracted his baton and hung it off his belt. 'Back to the pod, I think.'

Imogen folded her arms. 'What sort of a moron are you, Parrish? I keep telling you – I'm not going back with you. *Eric will rescue me.*'

No one could say Luke Parrish wasn't a fast learner. In a flash Imogen was on the ground, hands zipped in front of her and in an even more furious temper than before. If such a thing were possible.

'Parrish, I swear . . .'

'Shut up, Imogen. Do you even understand why those women were beating you up?'

'How the hell should I know? I rescued myself from your attempt to kidnap me and ran. I stopped for breath and to get my bearings and a woman shouted at me. Then another. Then their friends turned up and the next moment I was on the ground.'

'Thought so,' said Luke.

'What do you mean – thought so?'

'Amateur prostitution, Imogen.'

'What?'

'They don't like it.'

'Who don't like what?'

Matthew glanced at Jane and raised an eyebrow. She shook her head, mystified.

Luke pulled Imogen to her feet. 'They thought you were muscling in on their patch.'

'What?'

He sighed. 'Prostitutes have their own particular areas.' He added hastily, 'Or so I'm told. Usually it's all negotiated by their pimps. They tell me. Everyone takes a very dim view of an amateur turning up and claiming another prostitute's patch for herself. Justice is swift and painful.'

Imogen was incensed. 'They thought I was . . .'

'They did. They would have killed you.' He drew a deep breath. 'You just haven't got a bloody clue about the real world, have you, Imogen?'

'How could they . . . ?'

'Well, look at yourself.'

Imogen looked down at her stained dress. Her once carefully styled ringlets hung in snarls around her face.

'You're looking a bit rough, Immy, and you've only been here a couple of hours. Imagine the state of you this time tomorrow. If you lived that long, of course.'

'I didn't look like this until you turned up, Luke Parrish.'

'Immy . . .'

'Dear God, how many times must I tell you not to call me that.' She raised her voice. 'Help! Help!'

Luke pushed her against the wall and covered her mouth with his hand. They waited apprehensively, but fortunately

17th-century London was a lawless place and something as trivial as a woman shouting for help in a sinister side street could safely be ignored.

Very, very slowly, Luke removed his hand.

'Let me go, you bastards.' She took a deep breath to scream and Luke hastily replaced his hand.

'Do you think she means us?' said Jane to Matthew, neither of them showing any inclination to go to their leader's aid.

'Oh no,' said Matthew. 'We're lovely people, remember?'

Imogen was pounding on Luke's chest.

'Immy, for God's sake, use your loaf. I'm armoured. All you're doing is hurting yourself. Calm down.'

She held his gaze furiously for one moment, then nodded.

Very, very slowly, Luke removed his hand.

'You arrogant bastard,' she screamed. 'Who the fu—'

'Now, now, Immy. We don't use that sort of language here. We prefer the term fire truck. You know – starts with f and ends in uck. Perfect for use in mixed company.'

Imogen absorbed this seamlessly. 'Who the fire truck do you think you are?'

'We are the Time Police,' said Luke, slightly puzzled. 'Hadn't you noticed? You know – long black cloaks, sinister expressions and . . .'

'And sweet Fanny Adams for brains.'

'That's rather offensive, Immy.'

'*Don't call me that.*'

'Immy . . . ogen . . . look . . .'

'I don't want to worry anyone,' said Jane, who had walked to the end of the street, 'but I think reinforcements might be on their way.'

'Good,' stormed Imogen.

'We need to get back to our pod,' said Luke. 'And I should warn you, Imogen, that damage to Time Police personnel will be taken into account when determining the length of your sentence.'

'I won't go to prison,' said Imogen smugly. 'Mummy will never allow it. Now get off me, you great lump.'

'You really have no idea how much trouble you're in, do you?' said Luke, pushing her along in front of him. 'I'm sorry, but this is official now and even your mother won't be able to get you out of this.'

There was a moment's shocked silence. Imogen stopped and turned to face him.

'I don't believe you,' she said uncertainly.

Luke shrugged. 'Don't care whether you do or not. The fact is, you dozy bint, you're going to prison. And for a very long time.'

'I can't go to prison,' she said, half-laughing in disbelief. 'I've got things to do.'

'Well, I'm sure they'll take the damage to your social life into account when passing sentence.'

'You bastard, Parrish. This is your revenge, isn't it? Because I dumped you.'

'I think you'll find, Immy, if you consult your one brain cell, that I dumped you. In the middle of the Ingrams' party. Remember?'

'I remember chucking a glass of champagne at you and telling you I never wanted to see you again. Ever. And yet, here you are. Again. Ballsing everything up as usual.'

'You know,' said Matthew, quietly to Jane, 'I'm beginning to see why the relationship didn't prosper.'

'I am not the criminal here, Imogen.'

'I'm not a criminal! You can shout and stamp your little foot and swirl your girlie cloak, Parrish, but I'm not going anywhere. You, on the other hand, are going to find yourself looking down the wrong end of Mummy's solicitors.'

'Immy – get it through your thick skull. We're the Time Police. We're utter bastards. Nothing frightens us – least of all some dim floozy with more money than sense who thinks she's immune because of Mummy. You've gone too far this time, Immy. Literally. Mummy sent us to bring you back and back you're going, and, for the first time ever in your sad and empty life, you'll face the consequences of your actions.'

'Parrish, I swear I'll have your balls for this.'

'Will you stop and take a look at yourself. What good have you ever done in this world? What good have you ever achieved?'

'Well, for a start, no one's ever died because of me. How's Orduroy Tannhauser these days? Shall we ask him? Oh, no, wait – we can't, can we?'

Everything went very quiet and then Luke said, 'Imogen, for two pins I'd give you the good hiding you so richly deserve.'

'Yeah? You tried that once before, remember? How did that work out for you?'

'I tripped,' he said with dignity.

'Yeah – over my left hook. Face it, Parrish – you're the useless one here. You live off someone else's money just like me. What are *you* good for? Absolutely nothing and . . .'

Luke clamped his hand across her face again, counted to ten and then took it away.

'. . . arrogant, conceited, self-important . . .'

'Shut *up*, Immy.'

She ignored him. She doesn't even pause for breath, thought Jane in admiration, stowing away the colourful phrase *colossal arsehat* for future use.

'Wow,' said Matthew to Luke. 'You really do have a way with women, don't you? I can't believe Ellis thought having you along would actually help our case.'

'Narcissistic, shallow, self-absorbed . . .'

'Immy . . .'

'Shit-for-brains pretty boy.'

Jane judged it time to intervene. Inserting herself between them, she said, 'For God's sake, both of you, keep your voices down.'

'I am not going anywhere with Luke Parrish,' said Imogen furiously. 'Why are you people so stupid? I'm staying here. It's my choice. It's my life and my . . .'

Jane checked her sonic was on minimum and fired.

Imogen sagged against a shaky-looking building, which did it no good at all, and then fell to the ground.

A relieved silence fell.

'I'm sorry,' said Jane, making her sonic safe and stowing it away, 'but she really was beginning to get on my nerves.'

Luke scowled. 'You're a nicer person than me, Jane. I was all ready to brain her with the nearest rock.'

'How long were the two of you together?' enquired Matthew.

'Nearly two months.'

'I'm surprised central London is still standing.'

'To be fair,' said Luke. 'There were compensations.'

'There must have been,' said Jane. 'And no, we don't want to know what they were.'

They stood around Imogen, who was lying on the ground and effortlessly soaking up the puddle of dirty water in which she was lying.

Luke looked down at her. 'There's going to be hell on when she wakes up. Can we get her delivered to security first? Let them bear the brunt.' He stirred her with his foot.

Jane touched his arm. 'Luke . . . don't do that. She has a tough time ahead of her.'

Luke laughed mirthlessly. 'Jane, your faith in the system is inspiring but misplaced. Imogen's absolutely right. She won't go to prison. Trust me. Her mother, Hay and a couple of others will do a deal and she'll get off scot-free. People like her – people like us,' he said with a sudden flash of insight, 'always do.'

'Can we at least get her back to the pod and try to clean her up a bit?'

Matthew glanced at his leader. 'Clean us all up a bit.'

Luke sighed. 'Jane, you lead the way. Matthew, you watch our backs. And once again, I'll carry madam.'

7

Ducking, dodging and diving, they made their way through the labyrinth of dark foetid lanes surrounding the Theatre Royal. Around them, the streets of London teemed with life. As did some of the citizens of London. Jane dreaded to think what particular forms of life were making the evolutionary leap from 17th-century citizen to modern Time Police officer.

Filth covered every surface. Soot, grime, grease, human and animal excrement. Jane could not, for one moment, imagine why Imogen would want to live here.

They passed a butcher's shop where dark meat with an ominous green sheen offered a home to every fly in London.

A metalworker hammered away at an old kettle, sparks flying perilously close to a heap of old straw currently being used partly as packing material by a potter's apprentice and partly as lunch by an aged horse.

A dog cocked his leg against a basket of vegetables set down for a moment by a gossiping woman. Apparently unnoticing, she picked it up and sauntered away. Given the lack of clean water, Jane wondered whether washing them would prove more or less risky.

Someone collided with her and passed on without even

noticing. There were people everywhere. Continually fighting her way through a solid mass of humanity was exhausting. Between the crush, the smell and Jane's own fatigue, she couldn't wait to get back to the pod. Looking down at her stained uniform, she realised a large part of the stink probably emanated from herself.

Imogen stirred several times, making faint mewing signs of protest.

Luke told her to keep quiet. 'We're taking you to safety, but I warn you now – give me any more grief and I'll drop you where we stand and go home and tell everyone we couldn't find you.'

'You wouldn't dare.'

'Scream and let's find out.'

'Can we pick up the pace,' said Matthew. 'There are people following us.'

Luke felt Imogen stiffen.

'I think it's those men again,' whispered Jane. 'We should try and lose them before we get back to the pod.'

'In here,' said Luke, drawing back into a recessed doorway. As Jane and Matthew crowded in after him, the door behind them gave way and swung inwards and with a shout of surprise, Luke and Imogen disappeared from view.

Jane and Matthew could hear the clatter of two people falling down a flight of wooden steps together with the language appropriate to two people falling down the same flight of wooden steps.

Matthew winced. 'Ouch. That had to hurt. He's really not having a good day, is he?'

Imogen's voice drifted up from the gloom. 'For fire truck's sake, Parrish – are you trying to kill me?'

'No trying about it, Immy. I am so bloody sick of today. Someone remind me again why I'm here.'

Matthew was struggling to push the door to. Jane was groping her way down the steps by torchlight. 'Hay thought we were the best people for the job.'

'Jesus,' said Imogen. 'What the hell were the others like?'

Eventually, Matthew got the door closed and now they were all in the dark.

A grunt and a muffled curse informed Jane she'd trodden on her team leader and a moment later, a squeak and a very unmuffled curse informed Matthew he'd trodden on their prisoner.

'Anyone else got a torch?' enquired Jane.

'Not sure if mine will still be working,' said Luke, but it was. He flashed it around.

A sinister-looking narrow stone passage stretched ahead of them.

'And the day just keeps getting better,' snarled Imogen.

Luke nudged her. 'Shush.'

Jane felt Imogen draw breath to expostulate – if not actually kill him – and then, above them, voices sounded on the other side of the door. The muttering seemed to go on for a very long time. Luke held up his hand and they all stood motionless, waiting for the moment the door was thrown open, exposing them in this narrow space.

It never happened. No one tried the door, but for how much longer would their luck last?

'Quick,' whispered Luke. 'This way.'

The passage was cold but dry. Cobwebs hung everywhere, through which they could see another wooden door at the end.

'Don't think anyone's been down here for ages,' whispered Jane.

'Then why was that door unlocked?'

'It wasn't,' said Luke. 'I think it was old and our combined weight was just too much for it. Lucky for us, although we shouldn't hang around here.'

They shuffled down the corridor in single file. Luke first, then Imogen, then Jane. Matthew brought up the rear.

They halted at the end. Luke put his ear to the door and listened. 'Can't hear anything.' He lifted the latch and pushed. Nothing happened. 'Damn.'

'Try pulling,' advised Imogen.

'Don't be so bloody . . .'

Awkwardly, she reached past him and pulled. The door opened easily.

'Moron,' said Imogen, pushing past him.

Jane could tell by the change of air they were in a large space. A cool breeze blew something light and feathery across her face but she didn't scream because Time Police officers don't scream, as had been drilled into them during their training. They were a cause of screaming in others.

Matthew shone his torch around. They were in a vaulted room. Jane was never afterwards able to describe it because, abruptly, she'd lost all interest in where they might be. Her only thought now was to escape this nightmare with all speed. She swallowed hard. Even Imogen was silent.

Dark recesses were set at intervals around the walls and each recess was shelved and each shelf was stacked with skulls. Scores and scores of neatly arranged skulls. Sightless eye sockets stared down at the four of them. Some were brown, some yellow, and a very few were gleaming white.

They've been put here recently, thought Jane, fighting down panic. But not the way we came. Which means there's another way out.

Imogen's breathing was fast and shallow. 'For God's sake, Parrish, where have you brought me now?'

'It's just some kind of ossuary,' said Jane, trying to convince herself. 'A place for storing bones. Look, there's long bones over there and . . . more bones over there . . . and . . .'

Luke was baffled. 'Why would anyone want to . . . ?'

Imogen clutched at him. 'Oh my God – that skull – that one on the end. It moved. It's alive.'

'No, it's not,' said Luke, reassuringly. 'It's just the rats.'

'*What?*'

'There's a rat inside the skull making it move. Look – you can see the tail hanging out of the eye socket. It's just having a bit of a play. You know – like a hamster in one of those ball things.'

Three pairs of eyes regarded him.

'What?' he said, hurt. 'Just trying to point out – only a normal rat in a normal skull. Nothing spooky at all.'

'This way,' said Matthew, who had been exploring. He flashed his torch on a side wall. 'There's a door over there.'

Luke led the way. 'Hope this one's unlocked as well or we could have a problem.'

Imogen stared at him. 'Don't you have those fire things? What do they call them? Blasters?'

Very patiently, Luke said, 'Not on us, no.'

'Why the fire truck not?'

'Imogen, your language has really deteriorated since we parted.'

'Really? That's a surprise because everything else perked up no end once you were out of my life.'

Jane was flashing her torch around. Something winked in the light. 'What's that?'

They inched their way closer.

'Ornaments?' said Matthew.

'Offerings,' said Jane. And indeed, when they looked along the shelves, they could see rosaries, tiny boxes, small ornaments – gifts left for the dead.

Why do we do this? thought Jane. Every culture does it – leaves gifts for the dead. Is it to ease them into the next world? To salve our consciences? To leave them a keepsake or a reminder? They hardly need it, so why do we do it?

Her musings were cut short as she was jostled by Imogen, presumably eager to leave this place of the dead. And, Jane reflected – who could blame her?

This door wasn't locked, either.

'It's a crypt,' said Jane, looking up. 'I think we're in a church. The steps are over there.'

They made their way up the stone stairs emerging very cautiously through a tiny wooden door into the nave and daylight.

'It's empty,' said Luke.

'It's abandoned,' said Jane, and it was. Dim light was making a bad job of streaming through dirty windows. The cavernous space before them was empty. No altar, no font, just a large, stone space. The floor was covered in a mixture of dust, bird droppings and broken twigs. Something flapped in the rafters overhead. Jane tried very hard not to think of every vampire story she had ever read.

'Yes,' said Bolshy Jane mockingly. 'Because vampires always hang out in churches in broad daylight. Famed for it.'

'There have been animals in here,' said Luke, stirring a small bone with his foot. 'There must be a way in.'

'Or, in our case, out,' said Matthew.

But the big wooden doors at the back of the building were locked.

'Oh my God, we're trapped,' cried Imogen.

Luke could not resist. 'Looks like it. Can the last one to die carry our bones downstairs, please.'

Imogen slumped to the floor, leaned against a pillar and closed her eyes.

Matthew and Jane began to work their way around the walls, looking for a way out.

'Stay together,' warned Luke. 'And watch where you put your feet.'

He propped himself against the pillar opposite Imogen, who ignored him.

'There's bound to be a door somewhere,' whispered Matthew. 'All these animal bones. Something's getting in and out. We just have to find where.'

The shadows were darker at the other end of the church. Both Jane and Matthew slowed.

Something moved.

An evil yellow eye glowed in the torchlight.

They didn't clutch at each other for mutual reassurance, but only because Time Police officers don't do that sort of thing.

The shadows hissed. They stood, rigid and unmoving.

'A snake?' said Matthew.

'An owl?' said Jane.

She became aware of Matthew's gaze. 'Owls hiss,' she said, defensively. 'Owls live in churches. Could be an owl.'

'More likely a hideous monster from the depths of hell preying on the soul of the unwary,' said Bolshy Jane, contributing nothing to Jane's peace of mind.

'A one-eyed cat,' said Matthew, shining his torch.

'With kittens,' said Jane, shining her torch. A soft bundle stirred and mewed. The cat's hiss changed to a growl of unmistakeable menace.

'We'll go the other way,' said Matthew, although whether he was speaking to Jane or the cat was unclear.

'No need to mention that to Luke,' said Jane as they edged away.

'No, he's got a lot on his plate at the moment with Imogen. Kinder not to bother him with it.'

It was Matthew who found the broken door halfway down the nave on the west side. Squeezing through, they found themselves in a very small churchyard, overgrown and dark. Tree branches met overhead and everything, gravestones included, was smothered in ivy.

'It's like every horror story you've ever read, isn't it?' said Luke cheerfully, looking around.

'Can we go?' said Imogen. 'I have what I can only hope are cobwebs in my hair.'

Jane was consulting her scratchpad. 'We're not far from the pod.'

'Good,' said Luke and took hold of Imogen's arm.

She stepped back. 'I'm not going over your shoulder again. You nearly killed me last time.'

'Fine – you were doing my back in anyway.'

She tried to pull free.

'Not a chance, Immy. Let's go, everyone.'

They made their way back to what passed for the main street. Where the excitement wasn't over.

'Something's happening,' said Jane and indeed, something was happening.

There was rising excitement in the crowd, who had ceased to mill aimlessly and were now craning their necks to see down the road, jostling and pushing for a better place. They could hear cheering in the distance. Uniformed guards pushed through the crowd, clearing a path.

'Someone's coming,' said Jane, in excitement. 'Do you think it could be the king?'

Imogen tried to wriggle from Luke's grasp. 'Where? Let me see.'

The sounds of shouting grew ever closer. King or not, something was approaching.

Imogen was galvanised. 'Let me go.'

'Out of the question,' said Luke.

'No, please. I want to see the king.'

'Tough.'

The cheering was upon them. 'Oh my God, that's him,' said Jane in excitement. 'That's his coach. There he is.'

Accustomed as she was to pictures of the monarch's state coach on the newscasts, this one was a little bit of a disappointment. Made of wood, it looked like a clumsy teacup slung between two sets of enormous wheels. The gold and black decorations were chipped in places. The streets are so narrow, thought Jane.

The door was emblazoned with the royal arms. The lion and the unicorn supported a shield which was, in turn, surmounted by a lion standing on a crown. She could even see the royal motto – *Dieu et mon droit*.

A coachman sat high above a pair of horses. They were struggling a little with the weight of the coach behind them. Jane guessed there should be four of them but the streets just weren't wide enough. Two footmen clung to the back of the coach. Both were armed. The king's close protection, Jane assumed. The coach rattled and bumped its way along the barely wide enough street.

The crowd, as they say, went wild. Women flung shrivelled flowers and waved wildly. Men took off their hats.

The leather curtains had been looped back so onlookers could see the occupant. Jane's first thought was that he was the ugliest man she had ever seen. Her second thought, following hard on the heels of the first, was – wow!

Charles II, recently restored to his kingdom after the mistake that had been Oliver Cromwell, was a very dark, swarthy man. Long nose-to-mouth lines were deeply impressed into his thin face. His eyebrows were thick and heavy over dark, heavily lidded eyes. His hair was improbably long, black and glossy – almost certainly a wig. He leaned forwards in his seat, apparently thoroughly enjoying all the attention, waving his handkerchief and smilingly acknowledging the crowd that pressed around the coach.

The horses, already sweating heavily, their bits covered in foam, skittered nervously. Two men went to their heads while more tried to shove the crowd out of the way. The crowd refused to be shoved, cheering with great enthusiasm.

It is said that Charles II was most famous for his mistresses – of whom there were many. Nell Gwyn, Barbara Palmer, Louise de Kérouaille, possibly the incredibly dim but incredibly beautiful Frances Stuart, Moll Davis . . . The list was, literally, almost endless. What was generally less well recognised was the diplomatic tightrope Charles walked with such skill. A precarious hold on his throne, Parliament to placate, perpetually short of funds and always the problem with the succession. For someone who reputedly only had to look at a woman to get her pregnant, Charles had no legitimate children. Jane had always thought of him as a bit of a serial shagger but there was kindness in his face and she remembered his constant refusal to divorce his queen, Catherine of Braganza, to whom he appeared to be quite devoted. Not devoted enough to stop rogering every woman in sight, of course, but he always refused to cast her aside. Not that the need had yet arisen. These were the early days of his marriage. All that grief was yet to come.

'He's very popular,' observed Jane.

'He's very ugly,' observed Luke.

'No, he's not,' trilled Bolshy Jane.

'You – behave,' said Jane.

'What?' said Luke.

'Nothing.'

The crowd forced the horses to a slow walk but even so, they caught only the very briefest glimpse of the king. A wave, a smile, a flutter of the royal handkerchief and then he was past them.

Jane turned to Luke, her eyes sparkling. 'We saw the king.'

'And the king saw us,' said Luke, smiling down at her.

'I didn't see him,' said Imogen, sourly.

'That's because you're not important,' said Luke. 'Get used to it. You'll be even less important where you're going.'

She tried to kick him. 'You are so dead, Parrish.'

'Just get in the fire-trucking pod, Imogen, before you do any more damage.'

Imogen stormed past him into the pod. A difficult task with her hands still zipped but Jane had to admit she managed it magnificently.

Unfortunately, with the better light, the full extent of her injuries became apparent.

Her fine blue dress had been ripped from the shoulder nearly to her waist. She was barely decent. Her skirts were torn around the hem and stained a dubious yellowish brown around her knees. She was soaking wet and there was more than a faint smell of the midden about her. On top of everything, she had a cut lip and a bloody nose.

'Same as she gave you,' said Matthew to Luke.

Luke cut her free. Imogen folded her arms tightly around herself and sniffed.

Matthew stirred, whispering, 'Jane, I think this might be one for you.'

'No,' said Luke, quietly. 'I think this one's for me.' He took off his cloak and carefully wrapped it around Imogen.

'Um, we'll wait outside if you like,' said Jane, and she and Matthew shuffled out. The door closed quietly behind them and Luke and Imogen were alone. With this barrier between her and the outside world, Imogen seemed to relax slightly.

'Would you like some coffee, Immy?'

'Oh, yes. Please.'

She hunched over the hot drink, warming her hands. Luke frowned at the black and blue contusions on her arms and face and busied himself with the medkit, laying out wipes and sterile dressings, seemingly paying her no attention as she sipped at her drink.

'Now then,' he said when it was ready. 'I'm not sure how best to do this. Can you manage for yourself and I wait outside, whistling, or do you need a bit of a hand?'

Her face quivered. 'It hurts, Luke.'

'Yes, I expect it does.'

Silence.

'What can I do?' she said suddenly, the words tumbling over each other. 'I can't go back. Not like this. And Eric . . . what will he say? And Mummy will probably put me in a nunnery.'

He crouched beside her. 'Convent.'

'What?'

'I think it's a convent – not a nunnery.'

'Shut up, Parrish.'

'Shutting up now.'

She sniffed again. 'What's going to happen to me, Luke? My life is over. Everything's ruined.'

'Well – and I hardly know how to break this to you, Immy – but you're not the centre of the universe and not everything is ruined. Now, I can see that's come as a shock to you, so I'll just give you a moment, shall I?'

'Idiot.'

'Ah. Good. Back to normal. There's a small fire axe by the door should you feel the need to reinforce the point.'

She managed a weak smile. 'I can hardly even stand up by myself.'

He tried again. 'If you don't want me to patch you up then I can call Jane back again.'

Silence.

'Immy, if you won't talk to me then I'll just have to call you Immy again.'

She shook her head, her hair obscuring her face.

He shifted his weight to ease his legs. 'Immy, you and I fight like cat and dog. This makes us old friends. Let me help you.'

She made a slight sound and clutched herself even more tightly.

'Look, I probably shouldn't say this – in fact I know I shouldn't say it – but perhaps you don't have to go to prison. When we get back to HQ, tell them everything. Every single little scrap of info you can remember. If you do that – and given who your mother is – you may not go to prison. But you mustn't hold anything back. Cooperate – do everything you can to assist with our enquiries and perhaps . . . well, perhaps you might just get away with it.'

Tears ran down her cheeks. 'Do you really think so?'

'I do,' said Luke, unthinkingly. 'Just tell them everything they want to know. Oh – and don't hit anyone. Otherwise, you should be fine.'

Imogen nodded. 'I will. I don't want to go to prison, Luke.'

'You won't. Now, are you sure you wouldn't prefer Jane to help you? It's all right if you do. I can get her back here in a minute.'

A bloodstained hand gripped his arm. 'No. Don't leave me.'

'OK, then – not Jane – although between you and me she's

not that scary.' He appeared to stop and think. 'Actually, now I come to think of it, she's got a powerful right knee and doesn't hesitate to use it. It was hours before I could walk properly again. You'd have loved it.'

Encouraged by Imogen's silence, he continued. 'And she emptied a fire extinguisher over half a dozen officers once. *And*, now I come to think of it, she was once arrested for murder, so you may be right – you're probably better off with me. Who'd have thought, eh?'

Still no reaction.

'It's a good five minutes now since you've told me I'm an idiot or tried to hit me and I'm becoming concerned about you.'

'Luke . . .' A tear rolled down her dirty face and she turned her head away again. 'I'm sorry. I can't even look at you.'

He sighed. 'I get that a lot from my ex-girlfriends. I'll go and get Jane. Don't be fooled by her mild-mannered exterior – she's the Tasmanian she-devil of the Time Police but you'll be fine as long as you don't make eye contact. Finish your coffee – I'll be back in a minute.'

He opened the door. Imogen could hear him talking quietly just outside. He'd left the door open and sounds and smells of London wafted into the pod. She huddled under Luke's cloak and closed her eyes – all the better to keep the world at bay.

She heard the door close and then Jane was beside her.

'Oh, good. Luke's got everything ready. I know you're probably most worried about your face, but I think I need to check you for broken bones first, then we'll . . .'

Imogen grabbed at her hand. 'Jane, you must help me. Let me go. I'll give you money. I can't go back. Everyone will know . . . all my friends . . . what happened.'

'Well, at the moment, even we don't know what happened, so I'm certain no one else will.'

She said bitterly, 'I think I'd rather stay in this shithole than have everyone think . . .'

Jane did not have the heart to tell her that the chances of her seeing *anyone* she knew – let alone the people important to her – were almost nil. And for a long time. Imogen was going to prison.

Imogen stared at the floor, asking in a tiny voice, 'What will they do to me?'

Jane busied herself examining and cleaning Imogen's cuts and bruises. 'Well, you'll be invited to give a statement.'

'I like your use of the word "invited".'

'And then there'll be a hearing. To ascertain exactly what happened.'

'And then?'

'And then,' said Jane, putting off the moment, 'they'll decide what to do with you.'

'Which will be?'

Jane started on the other arm. 'Well, probably a custodial sentence.'

'Luke said not if I cooperated. He said if I told them everything they'd let me off.'

Jane bent over her task, hoping Imogen couldn't see her face.

Imogen groaned. 'Oh God. How did this go so wrong? It was just supposed to be a bit of fun.'

'Imogen, prison is not the worst thing that could happen to you.' She swallowed. 'At least we're under instructions to bring you back. Sometimes . . .' She stopped.

'Yes?'

100

Jane busied herself bagging up the soiled wipes. 'Sometimes we don't bother bringing people back at all. Sometimes we just leave them. To send a message to anyone else who thinks it's fun to try this sort of thing.'

Imogen had gone very white. Her bruises showed stark and blue. 'Mummy won't let me go to prison.'

Jane was glad she was busy anointing Imogen's bruises with cream and could keep her face hidden.

Imogen was rocking, her bruised arms wrapped tightly around her body. 'It wasn't supposed to be like this.'

'Time travel is against the law.'

'But they said it would be all right. That it was a victimless crime. That no one would be hurt. That everyone was doing it.'

Jane looked down at the battered and bloody Imogen, huddled in the sad remains of her pretty blue gown, and wondered if she had any idea, bad though this was, how much worse things were about to get.

8

Ten minutes later, everyone had tidied themselves up, readjusted their clothes and, in Luke's case, were borderline fragrant again.

'Shouldn't we be going?' said Imogen nervously, looking at the screen. Matthew had muted the sound but crowds of people were still streaming past.

'It's all right – no one can get into this pod,' said Jane, reassuringly.

She and Matthew busied themselves at the console, doing nothing very conscientiously. Luke went to sit beside Imogen.

Imogen made a gallant effort. 'Look, we have matching black eyes.'

He took her hand. 'Immy – I've been thinking.'

'Is that something they taught you to do in the Time Police?'

'Believe it or not – yes.' He looked at her and said quietly, 'You're going to need something to tell people. An alibi.'

She blinked. 'What for?'

'Your absence.'

'But the Time Police know everything anyway . . .'

'No, not an alibi for us – one for your friends and so on.

And to save your mother professional embarrassment. This could finish her, you know.'

She swallowed hard, looking down at her hands. 'And what, according to you, is my alibi?'

'You've been with me for the past few days. At a discreet place in the country somewhere.'

'Oh yes? Doing what, exactly?'

'We've been researching 17th-century England. Always tell the truth where possible,' he said virtuously. 'Saves wear and tear on the memory.'

'And what was your role in this research?' said Jane, disbelievingly, not looking up from verifying the return coordinates.

'I needed the money now my dad's cut me off. Imogen hired me to give her the low-down on the Restoration.'

'Why?'

'She's thinking of going back to uni.'

'Am I?'

'Yes,' he said firmly.

'But you don't know the first thing about the . . .'

'Oh, I don't know,' said Matthew, turning around. 'Just from looking at what we pulled off Luke, we could tell you what they ate. How they cooked it. What they threw away. How they disposed of it. How it smelled. Their bowel movements. He's a whole chapter in himself.'

Imogen looked at Luke. 'You'd do that for me?'

He shrugged, not meeting her eye. 'Why not?'

'Why are you being so nice?'

He sighed. 'It's my fault this happened to you. I'm the team leader and I handled this mission badly. Frankly, Imogen – and you won't like this – I shouldn't have let you get away. I should have sonicked you on sight and dragged you back to the pod. I'd probably have two black eyes, but you would have been spared being beaten up by those women. It's my fault.'

'Well, half of me is quite glad you didn't and half of me wishes you had.'

'Immy, I urge you – when we get back – tell them everything they want to know. Don't hold anything back, no matter how unimportant it seems. The more you help us, the more we'll help you. Trust me.'

She nodded. 'I do trust you.'

He sighed. 'I'm sorry – we used to be friends once and I let you down.'

There was a long pause and then she said shakily, 'It's a good job you don't know how sexy you are when you're nice.'

'Actually, I know how sexy I am all the time. I just have to remember to tone it down a bit out of consideration for the weaker sex.'

Imogen slapped his arm.

Matthew turned around once more. 'Are you being beaten up again? Can we watch, because that's always fun.'

'Why are we still here, Farrell?'

He grinned. 'Waiting for our team leader to give the word.'

'You may consider the word given.'

Matthew turned back to the console. 'Commence jump procedures.'

The AI responded pleasantly, 'Unable to comply.'

'What?' said Luke, sitting bolt upright.

'I don't want to worry anyone,' said Jane, peering at the screen, 'but there are a lot of people heading towards us right now and they don't look very happy at all.'

Imogen pulled Luke's cloak around her and groaned.

'It's all right,' Jane said again. 'They can't get in.'

'No,' said Matthew, 'but they could pile a ton of wood around the pod and try to make a bonfire of us.'

Imogen's voice was shrill. 'Then let's go!'

'We can't,' said Jane. 'The AI's not happy.'

'It's never bloody happy,' said Luke. He stood up and assumed an authoritative stance. 'Pod – why did the jump fail?'

Imogen clutched him. 'Are we stuck here forever?'

'No. Pod – respond.'

'I am detecting an anomalous object.'

'What?'

'I am detecting the presence of an anomalous object.'

'Have we picked something up?' said Matthew, looking around.

'Everyone – check,' ordered Luke. 'Pockets, sticky patches, everything.'

'Why?' said Imogen.

'Because, somehow, we've picked something up. We're not allowed to remove things from their own Time. The pod won't jump. Everyone have a look around.'

Matthew checked under the seats. Jane was searching under the console. 'Nothing here.'

'There must be,' said Luke. 'The AI's detected something. Check nothing's on the bottom of your boots, check your cloaks, check everything.'

Matthew pulled off his cloak and shook it. Nothing fell out.

'Jane?'

'No.'

'Then what?' said Luke. 'I've wiped off most of the pigswill so it can't be that. Check your pockets.'

They did so. Again – nothing.

Someone thumped on the door and Imogen jumped a mile.

'Where is it?' cried Jane. 'We've checked each other – we've checked the pod – what's left?'

The truth hit them all simultaneously. As one, they all turned to look at Imogen. Who backed away from them, her face a mixture of guilt and defiance.

Luke said quietly, 'Imogen, what have you done?'

Someone pounded on the door again. It sounded as if they were trying to kick their way in.

'Nothing,' she said, unconvincingly. 'I haven't done anything.'

'OK. You have three choices. Jane searches you – probably quite gently – or I search you – not so gently – or you voluntarily hand over whatever it is you've stolen, right now. You choose.'

The pod reverberated to a dull booming noise. 'They're trying to force their way in, Immy. We need to get out of here.'

Imogen drew herself up. 'I haven't done anything. I don't know why you're assuming . . .'

'Matthew, stand by the door controls. Imogen, you have three seconds before we open the door and throw you out to face your fate. Three.'

'Luke, I'm telling . . .'

'Two.'

Imogen threw a glance at the screens, filled with images of angry men. Jane recognised rat man and one or two others from their earlier encounter and was struck by sudden inspiration.

106

'Luke, they're not thieves or thugs – they're the police – or whatever the 17th-century equivalent is. They're thief-takers. They think Imogen's a thief.' She turned to Imogen. 'They hang thieves here.'

'One,' said Luke, grabbing Imogen's arm.

Matthew raised his hand to the door control.

'No. Wait.' Imogen slipped her hand into some sort of pocket hidden in her wide skirts, pulled out a small wooden box and passed it over to Luke, who opened it.

'Spoons?' he said in astonishment. 'You risked your life – our lives – for spoons?'

'I think they're Apostle spoons,' said Jane, taking the box off him. 'My grandmother had a set.'

They looked down at the six silver spoons, each one with an image on the handle. 'Look,' Jane said. 'I don't recognise them all – and it's not a full set anyway – but this one is probably Judas because he's usually represented by a bag of money.' She looked at Imogen. 'How appropriate.'

Luke snapped the box shut. 'For God's sake, Immy, what were you even going to do with these?'

'Sell them, of course.'

'You idiot. They're brand new. If somehow you had managed to smuggle them back – which you can't – they'd have been rejected as forgeries. Yes, they have a 17th-century hallmark but they're obviously freshly minted. You'd have been rumbled in five minutes. Why would you take such a risk?'

She said quietly, 'I have a very generous allowance. If I ask for it. I can have almost everything I want. If I ask for it. It's her way of controlling me.' She paused. 'How did you know I'd taken them?'

'I did something very similar once. We're quite alike, you and me, Immy.'

She flared. 'I am nothing like you, Parrish.'

There was a long silence in the pod – apart from the angry mob outside trying to break in.

'So, what do we do?' said Jane to Luke, who was staring at Imogen.

'We need to get rid of them,' said Matthew. 'Luke?'

He didn't reply.

'Luke?'

He pulled himself together. 'Sorry – yes. We need to get rid of . . .' He tailed away.

'What?' cried Imogen. 'What do you need to get rid of?'

Luke looked pointedly at Imogen. She began to cry. Jane stepped forwards and put her hand on his arm. 'Luke . . .'

He shook her off. 'She's a waste of space, Jane.'

'Possibly, but I don't think it's really her you're angry with . . .' She took a step closer.

He was breathing heavily.

'Luke . . .'

'*All right.*' He continued more calmly. 'All right, Jane.' He drew in a breath and pulled out his sonic. 'Right. We can't jump with these bloody spoons on board. Jane, you open the door – Matthew, you throw them out – I'll cover you. I'll keep it wide beam and low setting. Imogen, stay back out of harm's way, for God's sake. OK, team – when I say go. Go.'

As soon as the door was open, Matthew flung out the box, which turned out to be an excellent diversionary tactic. A good part of the crowd scrabbled for it and a substantial number of those remaining fell over them. The thief-takers, however, were not so easily distracted. Two pikes were thrust into the pod, stabbing wildly. A cunningly wielded bucket wedged the door open.

'Oh, for heaven's sake.' Imogen seized the fire axe off the wall and began to hack at the bucket. Luke fired his sonic. One of the pitchforks was withdrawn but the other fell into the pod and clattered to the floor, narrowly missing Imogen.

'Get rid of it!' shouted Matthew.

Jane tried to kick it back out of the door, missed and kicked Matthew instead. He staggered sideways. Imogen was hacking at the bucket with frenzied blows, shrieking curses with every stroke.

Jane stood by ready to get the door closed. The bucket split and Imogen hurled it back outside. Seizing the axe off her, Luke began to swing wildly at the pitchfork, nearly taking his own leg off in the process. Matthew and Jane scrabbled to fling the bits out of the door.

'For fire truck's sake,' roared Luke, kicking at the remains. Matthew knelt quickly and discharged his own sonic. Suddenly, the pod was clear. Jane got the door closed and they all stood, panting slightly.

'Not our finest hour,' said Jane, sadly.

'Have we ever had a finest hour?' enquired Matthew, activating the screen. The citizens appeared to have given up, retreating as best they could and dragging the still slightly stunned with them.

Luke mopped his brow. 'Pod – for God's sake, can we go now?'

'There are now no constraints to making the jump.'

Nothing happened.

Luke gritted his teeth. 'Pod – why are we still here?'

'I am awaiting the correct command.'

'I gave you the correct command.'

'You might want to get comfortable,' whispered Matthew to Imogen. 'This can go on for some time.'

'That command was rendered invalid by the presence of an anomalous object.'

'Which has since been removed. Which, unfortunately, cannot be said of you.'

Silence.

'Why aren't we moving?'

'There are many theories, many of which postulate that the pod does not in fact, ever move. That the universe readjusts itself to accommodate . . .'

'Shift your arse or I swear I'll rip you out by your peripheries.'

The silence took on a sulky quality.

Imogen nudged Matthew. 'Does this happen a lot?'

'Every time. We'll get there eventually. When the AI stops enjoying itself.'

Imogen shook her head at Luke. 'He's really not that bright, is he?'

Jane, wiping the sweat from her forehead, said sunnily, 'You've noticed that, too.'

Matthew finally intervened. 'Pod – commence jump procedures, please.'

Luke scowled. 'Matthew, I keep telling you, you don't have to say please. It's a . . .'

'Commencing jump procedures.'

Matthew smiled. 'Thank you.'

110

'You're welcome.'

The world flickered.

'Well,' said Luke, throwing himself back in his seat. 'Anyone else think we made rather heavy weather of that one?'

9

'They're waiting for us,' said Jane, checking the screen.

They all clustered around the display. The Time Police Pod Bay was a large, echoing space running under the River Thames. It was rumoured that an exploding pod could take out half London, though which half was never specified. Jane was of the opinion it wouldn't do the Thames a lot of good either and the surviving part of London might one day wake up and find itself on the shores of a very large and very surprised lake.

Pods of varying sizes were ranged in neat lines. Gaps denoted pods currently in use. Two big hospital pods, white coloured and decorated with every medical symbol known to man, were parked next to the entrance to MedCen which, for operational reasons, was as close to the Pod Bay as it could possibly get. Double doors led through to Supplies and Logistics, source of equipment, tools, weapons and Luke Parrish's legendary blonde. Another set of doors led to security. Where Imogen would soon be lodged.

Imogen looked up in alarm. 'Mummy's not there, is she?'

'No, no,' said Luke reassuringly. 'Just a couple of heavily armed officers waiting for an excuse to blast you into oblivion.'

'That's a relief.'

Colour was coming back into her cheeks. Jane couldn't help but admire her. Whatever was coming her way, Imogen was meeting it on her terms.

They filed slowly out of the pod, with Luke grasping Imogen in a manner that could be construed as either custodial or supportive depending on your point of view.

Ellis stepped forwards to greet them. 'Well done, team.'

'Oh, they were marvellous,' gushed Imogen, causing Luke to nearly drop her in shock. 'They were so brave. I'm terribly, terribly grateful.'

By now, Ellis had caught a glimpse of Luke's black eye and generally battered appearance. 'Everything all right there, Parrish.'

'Yes, I'm fine, thank you.'

Behind him, Matthew and Jane nodded their reassurances.

'I shall never be able to thank you enough,' cooed Imogen, looking up at Luke with the huge pansy eyes that got her into – and out of – so much trouble. 'I shall certainly tell Mummy how wonderful the Time Police are.'

Those officers present, more accustomed to being shot, fled from, stabbed, kicked, blasted, knocked down or spat upon, were certainly unfamiliar with adulation and how to deal with it. Luke said afterwards he could actually see the years being shaved off her sentence.

'Well, Miss Farnborough,' said Ellis, equally unaccustomed to his team being regarded with enthusiasm, 'you'll need to be checked over in MedCen before . . . anything else. You too, Parrish.'

'Oh yes,' trilled Imogen, no stranger to over-egging the pudding. 'After they were so brave . . .'

113

She was led away but only after a brief scuffle among the officers over whose arm would support her on the way.

'She does know that as soon as we turn in our reports, they'll directly contradict everything she's just said, doesn't she?' said Jane, anxiously.

'Doesn't matter really, does it?' said Luke. 'She's not going to prison. You mark my words.'

'Do you think she'll ever change her ways?'

'Imogen? God, no. She'll be trouble until the end of her days, that one. My sort of person.'

Jane, whose turbulent teenage rebellion had consisted of wearing a red hair ribbon in direct contravention of her grandmother's instructions – although not until safely out of sight around the corner – tried to imagine what that would be like. Crashing through life doing what she wanted, when she wanted, to whom she wanted. And then accepting the consequences with a careless shrug and a witty comment.

She focused to find Luke watching her. 'Whatever are you thinking about now, Jane?'

'Doing what I wanted. You know – being assertive.'

'Jane, you've been arrested for murder. You severely impacted – good choice of word there – my chances of reproduction. You faced down Commander Hay and the entire Time Police to reveal a traitor. Trust me – lack of assertion is not a problem for you.'

He strode off to hand in his weapons leaving Jane alone – but assertively so – in the middle of the Pod Bay.

An hour later Team Weird were assembled in Briefing Room 3. Luke had presented his bruised face in MedCen and been dismissed with contempt. The word 'girl' had been used and not in a good way.

Major Ellis surveyed his team. 'Good work, everyone.'

'What will happen now?' enquired Jane.

'Well, you'll hand in your reports. Yes, you will, Parrish, and by 1800 hours today, and then . . .'

'She won't do time,' said Luke, confidently.

'I'm afraid she will.'

'Hay and her mother will do a deal.'

'Commander Hay and Mrs Farnborough have indeed done a deal and Imogen will still go to prison.'

'But,' said Luke, suddenly concerned, 'I told her . . .'

'The matter's out of our hands now she's been arrested. There'll be a hearing and the length of her custodial sentence determined.'

'But her cooperation will be taken into account?' said Jane, anxiously.

'Of course. And they'll be very anxious to hear what she has to tell them. Names, places and so on.'

'But she'll still go to prison.'

'Yes – that's how it works.' Ellis paused, suddenly. 'You are aware of how this works, aren't you? You covered this in training?'

'You mean the Narnia effect, don't you?' said Jane.

'The what?' said Luke, twisting in his seat to look at her.

'Well, that's what some people call it,' said Ellis. 'After the Narnia stories. In the book the children step into a wardrobe, enjoy a lifetime's adventures and then return through the wardrobe door to find they haven't aged and no time at all has elapsed. If they'd come back any sooner, then they'd actually have caught themselves stepping through the door – with all the problems that would entail. It's the same thing here. Say Imogen gets ten years. She will serve those ten years in one of our special establishments – with possible time off for good behaviour . . .'

'Not too optimistic about that,' muttered Matthew.

'On release, however, she will find she's only been out of circulation for, say, six months.'

'But she's still served ten years?'

'Yes.'

'How is that a punishment?' asked Jane.

'Imagine a young man of twenty-five and serving forty years – which is the usual sentence for this type of offence. He's released. Technically his punishment is over but it's not. His punishment really begins when he realises he's now an old man who can't get his knees to work properly any longer. His hair's fallen out – because the Time Police won't have made it an easy forty years for him. He returns to the outside world to find he's older than his parents. His kids don't recognise him. His wife and all his friends are still twenty-five and on their way to the pub for a piss-up. Without him. Because he's in bed. With his Horlicks. His life is drawing to an end but everyone else is just beginning theirs. His youth has gone forever and he'll never get those years back. He may have been released but he'll be isolated for the rest of his life. Think about it.'

They did. The room was very quiet.

'On another subject,' said Ellis, jolting them from their thoughts, 'you have just over three weeks left of your grunt-work. One of my few remaining duties to this team is to ask you for your preferences. So – have any of you given any thought to where you want to work next?'

They shook their heads.

Ellis sighed. Lt Grint's team, organised, enthusiastic and conventional, had completed and submitted their Form D12s a week ago.

He pulled up a Time Police data stack and spread it out in front of them. 'Let's start with the many things you can't do, shall we? You can't be Hunters, of course. Not yet, anyway. Get some experience under your belt first. You can't be mechs – none of you has the technical know-how. And trust me, you don't want to join the clean-up crews. You're eligible – on paper, at least – but you don't want to. I'm required to remain neutral – my responsibility is to provide you with enough information for you to make an informed choice – but I'm guessing from what you've seen so far, you don't want to become a member of the clean-up crews.'

They shook their heads.

'Then there are the security teams.' He sighed. 'You've all – for one reason or another – already come to the attention of our security team. I don't know if any of you find the idea of poacher turned gamekeeper particularly attractive, but security is one of your options.

'Then there's Recruitment and Training. They usually prefer articulate and good-looking people who can be a positive image for the Time Police, but they're fairly desperate at the moment so they'd probably be prepared to consider you three. The job also includes stints downstairs on Reception, a lot of which is dealing with idiots who've made a complete dog's breakfast of their lives and think they'll join the Time Police and lie low for a bit until everything blows over.'

He was very careful not to look at Jane as he said this, wondering if she was aware the Time Police always carried out very thorough background checks. Did she really think they were ignorant of the circumstances that had led her to enlist?

'Next on the list is the section dealing with Big Business and Organised Crime. BeeBOC. Probably the most interesting field to work in. Lots of variety. Obviously, everyone wants that one but be aware there are challenges. Organised crime is considerably more organised than national governments. Better funded, too. The threat to the future is Temporal Tourism and big business attempting to loot the past. It'll all come at you thick and fast in that section.'

And Lt Grint was headed there, too, although that was common knowledge now. Parrish, in particular, would have to think very hard about whether to choose BeeBOC.

'Moving on – the Religious Nutters section.' He sighed. 'I hardly know where to begin with this one. You'll get people who can't believe the things their religion has done in the past and want to put it right. They mean well but – well, you can imagine.

'Then there are those convinced theirs is the only true religion and their mission is to bring the light and compassion of that religion to those who don't realise how unfortunate they are. Conversion techniques generally include every weapon you care to name from pointy sticks upwards. It's an unpopular section staffed mostly by atheists. There are moral choices involved and not everyone is comfortable with that. But, as I say, it's your decision.'

He manipulated the data stack again.

'Ah – speaking of nutters, here's Hitler's Little Helpers. Unfortunately for us here in the Time Police, the world is full of people who think they can save millions of lives by offing Hitler. That they're subsequently ending even more millions of lives never seems to occur to them. You'd be dealing with people whose mental states range from the tearfully fragile to the screamingly insane. And that's just your colleagues. Be aware.'

He rotated the stack again. 'What's next? Ah yes – Records and Information.' He looked up. 'Supposedly the soft option for those who can't hack things in the real world.'

Again, he didn't look at Jane.

'They're wrong. This is vital work. You'll need an ordered mind, a good memory and the ability to transmit a lot of data fast. And accurately. Where do you think the info for each mission comes from, sometimes at very short notice? Who flashes the relevant facts to your scratchpads before you even know you need them? You never stop to think about it, do you, which just shows what a good job they must be doing.

'The rest – MedCen, IT and so on – have no vacancies at the moment.' He began to shut down the data stack.

'What about working with the Time Map?' asked Luke.

'Again, technical abilities are required. Or, of course, for the lucky few – a natural aptitude is enough.'

Jane looked across at Matthew, who stared straight ahead.

'Those are your options, people. I've flashed full info packs and the appropriate D12s to your scratchpads. Completed forms to be returned to me within seven days. I advise you all to think carefully. And include second and third choices as well because not everyone gets what they want.'

'So we're able to choose our future section?' asked Luke.

'No. You apply. The section head will survey your form, attempt to reconcile the information there to what they already know about you, and approve or disapprove accordingly. If you don't get what you want, you get passed down the line until someone accepts you.'

'What if . . . ?' said Jane nervously, almost unable to put such a humiliating future into words lest it happen to her. 'What if *no one* wants . . . ?'

'It's never happened yet,' said Ellis reassuringly. 'Most people get their first choice. And you can transfer out after six months if you're really unhappy. Although that doesn't make you popular, so you usually end up even more unhappy.'

He perched on the edge of his desk. 'It is my duty to make you aware of the final option. As trainees, you can leave at any point during your training. For free. This offer extends until midnight on your last day of training. After that, you belong to the Time Police, body and soul – and trust me, we will extract our pound of flesh.'

Silence.

'Well, don't just sit there. Dismissed.'

10

Imogen Farnborough was interviewed four times in all. The first was a preliminary – to establish what she could know and to establish the best interview technique for her personality type. The second drilled down to dates, names and places, and began to build up a structure for the Time Police to work with. The third dealt with every snippet of information in the minutest detail. Line by line. The fourth – the toughest – tested every fact to destruction. Imogen's destruction.

By the time they'd finished with her, she was tearful and exhausted. She was then permitted one short interview with her mother. From the Time Police point of view, nothing useful emerged from that exchange.

'So many tears,' remarked one officer. 'It's a miracle neither of them went rusty.'

All reports were forwarded directly to Commander Hay, who made herself a coffee and settled down to read.

The main fact leaping off the page was that Imogen, either deliberately or otherwise, knew hardly anything about Temporal Tourism. No, she never heard the name of the organisation that had offered her the opportunity to time travel. No, she had no idea who ran it. Despite careful questioning,

121

security had been unable to decide whether she'd deliberately been kept in the dark or was simply too self-obsessed to absorb anything that didn't relate directly to herself. If asked, they'd be inclined to say the latter. Stripped of Imogen's complaints, self-pity and indiscriminate recrimination, the story ran thusly:

Imogen had been sitting in a bar with Eric. No, she couldn't remember the name. She'd been complaining about something – no, she couldn't remember what – when a friend of Eric's had said did she fancy trying something different? There were these people, he said, and they can take you to some pretty weird places. It was the latest thing. Everyone was doing it. Yes, all right, it was time travel and for God's sake, don't tell anyone and yes, it was the teeniest bit illegal but that was only to stop people doing it. This friend had it on very good authority that the law was going to be relaxed any day now. Of course, once that happened the whole world would be at it, but this was a chance for them to be in ahead of the crowd.

According to Imogen's statement, she had initially been quite horrified at the thought of breaking the law in such spectacular fashion, declaring several times, quite vehemently, that she wouldn't dream of doing such a thing. It was Eric who had reassured her that it wasn't really illegal – sort of like getting a parking ticket and no one worried about those, did they? she said.

An enclosed note from Officer Varma indicated that, after discreet investigations, security rather thought the boots had been on the other feet and that it had been Eric who had been the cautious one. When challenged on her statement, Farnborough appeared gobsmacked they hadn't just taken her word for everything, and there had been tearful accusations – firstly of invasions of privacy and secondly of police brutality. Officer Varma had noted, rather wistfully, that the latter was almost completely untrue.

Another note informed Commander Hay that Eric's friend from the bar, the original contact, had disappeared without trace.

Imogen eventually admitted that she'd been persuaded to partake of the experience. No, she couldn't remember by whom, exactly. The friend – whose name she didn't think she'd ever known, let alone could remember because she knew so many people – you know how it is – had said it was all great fun. Perfectly safe. They'd never lost a client yet. And all right, not quite legal, but they'd been operating for some time and the authorities had never even had a whiff of them.

Depressingly true, thought Hay, flicking to the next page.

According to the still-unnamed friend, time travel couldn't possibly be classed as a crime because there were no victims, were there? Simples.

And so, somehow – Imogen was a little hazy on this point – she and Eric had found themselves at a restaurant on the river – the King's something or other – Arsenal, that was it. The King's Arsenal. It was apparently *the* place at which to be seen, so obviously Imogen should be seen there. She'd talked about it for some time while the long-suffering Officer Varma had probably decided she wasn't paid enough for this and wondered what to have for lunch.

Prolonged and penetrating questioning, however, had elicited a contact at the King's Arsenal. Geoffrey. Whether this was a first or second name was unknown because he,

Geoffrey, was so awful that she, Imogen, had been unable to bring herself to listen to a word he said.

Anyway, they'd had dinner and Geoffrey had been a bit of an oily git, but an appointment had been made for the next day. Somewhere by the canal, Imogen had said vaguely. The travel arrangements had been left for Eric to arrange while Imogen appeared to have concentrated on other issues. No, she couldn't quite remember what they were.

They'd found the place easily enough the following day. Some sort of industrial unit, she'd said, which covered just about every building in the area. Pressed for details of the interior, she remembered it had been dark. No, not night-time – it had been dark inside and she couldn't make a guess as to how big it was – it was just big.

Yes, there were other people. No, no idea how many.

More than five?

Yes. But less than a hundred. No, she didn't know exactly. Because it was dark, wasn't it? For security or something.

She and Eric had sat in some sort of box. There was champagne and canapés. It was all very nicely done. There were attendants and other passengers. No, she couldn't remember how many.

More than five?

Yes. Definitely less than a hundred. Probably about twelve. Or seven. Or nine, perhaps.

Commander Hay imagined Officer Varma, an experienced and intelligent officer, sitting in a tiny, claustrophobic interrogation room, with the headache-inducing lights, gritting her teeth as she struggled to pin the prisoner down on the details and getting almost nothing.

And then what?

Well, it was all very exciting – the lights dimmed – like in one of the old cinemas, you know – and off they went. No, she had no idea how long the trip – sorry, jump – had taken. She was talking to Eric when it happened but suddenly the big window things – which weren't windows at all, it seemed – lit up and there they were. In Ancient Rome. There were buildings and people everywhere. No gladiators or lions or people being stabbed. One of the attendants had droned out facts and figures – as if anyone was interested in that sort of thing. No, they weren't allowed outside. No one was. Not on a first jump. Apparently, there were germs and things.

Varma had queried 'first jump' and Imogen had happily replied that for regular customers, arrangements could always be made, which she'd thought to be some sort of frequent-flyer scheme. Like the air-travel people do.

Anyway, the whole thing had – from Imogen's point of view – been rather underwhelming. Varma had the impression if it hadn't been for the secret frisson of law-breaking, Imogen wouldn't have been inclined to proceed any further. A fact she had restated on several occasions in the mistaken assumption it would help her defence.

Eric, however, had quite enjoyed himself, joining one of the attendants at the screen and having landmarks and buildings pointed out to him, leaving her, Imogen, completely abandoned.

At this point, Commander Hay began to flick through Imogen's really rather lengthy statement, picking out the salient points as they struggled to emerge from the narrowness of Imogen's Imogencentric world view.

It would seem that she and Eric had allowed themselves to

be tempted into a return visit to the dark industrial unit. Tudor England had been their next destination. No, she hadn't seen the queen – although since it appeared Imogen had based her romantic image of Elizabeth on the film-maker Calvin Cutter's legendarily inaccurate view of the Virgin Queen, and since the real monarch was a short, badly pockmarked, overly made-up woman with bad teeth and an obvious wig, it seemed likely to Commander Hay that Imogen had seen the queen but failed to recognise her.

She and Eric had also gone waltzing in romantic, snowy, 19th-century Vienna which Imogen had thoroughly enjoyed – even her failure to exchange Eric for a handsome European prince had not marred her pleasure. Why she might be looking for a prince was an area Varma had inexplicably failed to explore – although by now Commander Hay couldn't find it in her heart to blame her officer. European princes tend not to be bright, but even the dimmest specimen would have taken one look at Imogen, enlisted in the military and volunteered for distant parts.

Over the weeks, however, Imogen – according to Imogen – became aware of a cooling in her feelings towards Eric. Unfortunately for everyone – as it turned out – Eric was warming up nicely and unbeknown to her was in conjunction with that sad sack, Geoffrey, and organising some sort of surprise.

Unfortunately, 17th-century England had not impressed her and Eric's so-called proposal even less so. Hay was amused to see that Imogen's version of Eric's proposal differed considerably from Eric's. There were several pages justifying her rejection – hairy toes, snoring, and not remembering people didn't like smoked salmon appeared to be the most serious

– and several more pages devoted to justifying her decision to have a look around London without Eric whinging on, or that oily git Geoffrey breathing on her.

Commander Hay fought her way through several more tear-splattered pages concerning Time Police brutality, which led her to believe the more old-fashioned method of shoot first, torture the survivors, and destroy anything else in sight had more merit than she had previously perceived.

Geoffrey and the King's Arsenal were, however, the meat of Imogen's statement. The remainder was all self-justification, self-pity and a confident expectation of being allowed to go free.

Jane knew that Luke had visited Imogen on several occasions before her final transferral from security to one of the Time Police's special detention centres.

'I've encouraged her to cooperate,' Luke said to Jane in the bar one evening. It was still early and they were almost the only people there. It would fill up soon and such girlie pastimes as a quiet drink would be drowned in a sea of testosterone and beer. 'I told her to tell us everything she knows in return for a light – a lighter – sentence.'

Jane toyed with her orange juice. Neither the taste nor the look of beer had led Jane to believe she would, in any way, ever *fancy a quick pint*. 'What do you think will happen to her?'

He shrugged. 'I don't know. Depends on the intel she can give them, I suppose. If it's valuable they're likely to be more lenient.'

'But she's definitely going to prison?'

'I was convinced she wouldn't – because of her mother – but

now, yes, Commander Hay has spoken – she'll definitely serve time.' He paused. 'I'm still not sure *she* believes it though.'

'How do you think she'll handle it?'

He shook his head. 'Dunno.'

Jane shivered. 'It's such a cruel system.'

'Do you think so?'

She nodded. 'Well, yes, imagine it's you, Luke. You come back after all those years only to find that Matthew and I haven't aged a bit. We're still young and fit . . . fit-ish, anyway. Everything's exactly the same. The same notices on the board. The same day-to-day concerns. Your name might even still be on the team lists. Except you're an old man. Too old to serve. Too old to do anything except come to terms, as best you can, with the knowledge of a wasted life.'

Luke frowned. 'Imogen's not likely to get a long prison sentence.'

'Do you think so?'

He shrugged. 'Well, say what you will, Mummy's an important figure. It might only be two years.'

'Which means she could be back in circulation in a month or so.'

'That's the whole point, Jane. It's the criminal who serves the time – not the family or other innocents.'

Still unaccustomed to maintaining her point of view in the face of opposition, Jane gritted her teeth and prepared to argue. 'No, you misunderstand. She could be back in a matter of weeks. What will this mean for you? She knows your past. Could she make trouble for you? With your dad?'

'Well, he knows I'm with the Time Police because he's the one who abandoned me here.'

'Your friends then?'

'I don't have any friends, Jane. I knew lots of people and they liked me because I was rich. Now I'm not and they've forgotten I exist, so I don't see how Imogen could possibly cause me any problems. Besides, I'm certain the Time Police must have some way of dealing with threats of that nature. You know the sort of thing.' He deepened his voice. *Make trouble for us, Farnborough, and we'll make trouble for you. The first sign of misbehaviour and we'll rescind your time off for good behaviour and pack you off back to prison for the remaining thirty years of your sentence. To one of our special units this time.* I suspect the threat alone would keep her quiet.'

Jane shivered. 'I think the whole idea of imprisoning someone outside their own Time is rather barbaric, don't you?'

'I suppose I've never really thought about it before. As Major Ellis says – it's not our concern. No one makes them break the law. And you know what they say – you do the crime, you do the time. We catch them and we hand them over. That's our job. What happens next is not our affair. It can't be. We can't afford to get involved or we'd never be able to do our job properly. It's separation – like church and state.'

She looked at him. 'It's not like you to be such a deep thinker.'

'No, it's not, is it? And it's not as if I feel any better for it. Shan't do that again. Here's Matthew.'

11

Three days later, the results of Imogen's hearing were flying around the building.

'What did she get?' asked Jane.

'Eight years,' said Luke quietly, burying his face in a mug of coffee.

'Well,' Jane said, trying to find the positive, 'that's a very lenient sentence. And she won't serve all of that, surely. They'll take her cooperation into account.'

'That *was* taking her cooperation into account, Jane. The official sentence was seventeen years reduced to eight.'

'How did she take it?' asked Matthew.

Luke shook his head. 'I don't think it sank in to begin with. I know she thought I could somehow speak up for her and that my words would carry weight. She thought after she'd told us everything she knew that they'd let her go. Perhaps with just a fine. Which, obviously, would be settled by Mummy. So, then she blamed me. Then she lost her temper. Then she cried. Then, when none of that worked, she just sat there. I think that was the worst bit.'

Luke's mind went back to the small room. A table, two

chairs and the inevitable cameras. Imogen, already in her prison uniform, white-faced and shocked.

'*Eight years, Luke.*'

'You might not serve it all, Immy. There might be more time off for good behaviour. So, don't go thumping anyone. And your mother's got influence, remember.'

'If she cares to use it.' She rocked backwards and forwards. 'I'm being abandoned, Luke.'

'No, you're not, Immy.'

'You promised me you'd get me off.' Words spilled from her in her panic. 'I cooperated! I told them everything I knew. Names, dates, places. Everything they wanted. And I spoke up for you. Why didn't you do the same?'

'I did, as far as I could, but I don't have that sort of power and . . .'

'You told me to tell them everything they wanted to know. And I did. I did everything they – you – wanted. And look where it got me.'

'It got your sentence more than halved.'

She thumped the table in frustration. 'I should never have listened to you. I should have known you'd lie to me. I should have stayed there. Eric would have come for me and everything would have been all right again.'

'Immy, that's not true. He wouldn't . . .'

'I *loved* him.'

'You're just telling yourself that.'

'This is your fault, Luke Parrish. This is all your fault. You did this to me.'

'No – I'm sorry to say you did this to yourself. Please – try to look on the positive side. Without your mother's influence you'd never have been rescued at all. You'd have been picked up by 17th-century thief-takers and probably hanged. Compared to that, your sentence is lenient. Comparatively lenient. Immy, we could have left you there. Or, you could have got the death sentence.'

'I wish I had.'

'Immy . . .'

She was crying now, tears streaming down her face. 'You betrayed me, Luke Parrish. Letting people down is what you do. You said cooperating with the Time Police would save me and now you're sending me to prison. *Eight years, Luke.* And when I come out no one will remember who I am.'

'Yes, they will. It'll only be a couple of months for everyone here. You can pick up your life again as if nothing has happened. You can even make some changes. Go back to uni and get your degree. That sort of thing.'

'And where do I tell people I've been for a whole couple of months?'

'We talked about this,' said Luke. 'You and I have . . .'

'There is no you and I,' flared Imogen.

'All right,' said Luke, steadily. 'When I had lost time to account for, I generally told people I'd been in rehab. It sounds a bit glamorous and has the added bonus of a good reason for you looking so rough when you are released.'

She stared at him. 'Is that the best you've got?' but before he could reply, the security officer, Varma, appeared at the door, saying, appropriately, 'Time,' and he'd had to leave with Imogen's sobs ringing in his ears.

* * *

132

Twenty-four hours later, Commander Hay called an emergency meeting, consisting solely of herself, Major Callen and Captain Farenden. Imogen had – to use a phrase currently popular among the Time Police – sung like a cassowary. The info might have been sparse, but there were dates, names and a location.

Strict security was essential. 'Let's keep a lid on this one. Charlie, don't minute anything, please. Let's keep things as simple and discreet as possible. Major, your people will report directly to you and you report directly to me.'

Major Callen nodded. As usual his face showed nothing. 'Understood, Commander.'

She pushed a file across her desk. The red cover denoted 'Eyes Only'.

'You should find everything you need in there. You can read it in Captain Farenden's office.'

Major Callen nodded and left.

Commander Hay watched the door close behind him. 'When he's finished, Charlie, get that file back off him. Keep it in here. Don't send it down to Records.'

'No, ma'am.'

'In fact, lock it away unless it's actually in use.'

'Yes, ma'am.'

Twelve hours later, Major Callen despatched two of his best Hunters, Officers Nuñez and Klein, to pick up the trail at the King's Arsenal. No one saw them go. So unobtrusive was their departure that most people were unaware they'd gone until their return.

Life went on. Luke devised a countdown calendar showing the number of days remaining until Team Weird would complete their gruntwork and become fully qualified officers. He pinned it to the inside of his door with the intention that he, Jane and Matthew would congregate for the 'Crossing Off Another Day' ceremony every morning, before going down to breakfast.

If Major Ellis was struck by the lack of enthusiasm for their future shown by all three members of Team 236, he said nothing. The deadline was approaching but, so far, not one of the D12 application forms for their permanent section had been returned.

On the plus side, there had been enormous improvements in the dynamics of Team 236 in that they could now communicate with each other without arguing – mostly – and had even been known to socialise together. Jane's favourite occupation was still reading in her room, Luke was still juggling precarious relationships with the blonde from Logistics and the brunette from IT – and Matthew, solitary and silent as ever, took every opportunity to commune with the Time Map.

The Time Police's representation of Time involved a giant sphere built around two axes, one horizontal and one vertical, representing space and Time. Where the two axes intersected represented the ever-changing 'now'. Everything above 'now' was the future, and everything below it, the past. It was a colossal structure housed in a correspondingly colossal chamber over three storeys high.

There was a general feeling among those who spent their working days racing around the timeline that it was good to spend some time with the Map occasionally, grounding them-selves – *This is where I am in the scheme of things. This is my place. This is where I belong* – because it was a well-known phenomenon that those who made too many jumps too quickly could suffer unfortunate side effects. The sensation that part of oneself had been left behind somehow. A feeling of disorientation – something akin to vertigo. Falling through Time, as one slightly more articulate officer had described it. Not knowing which way was up or down, had said another. Lost, was another frequently used word.

For most officers, a trip to the Time Map – to see Time as a whole and be able to find their own place in the universe – was usually enough to sort them out. Until the day when it wasn't and that was the day to quit. And there was no doubt the Time Map exercised a strange fascination for many people and Matthew was one of them, although as Luke had often remarked, only Matthew Farrell was peculiar enough to bond with an inanimate object and no wonder people called them Team Weird. He was often to be found on the observation deck, leaning on the railing, watching the giant Map slowly evolve before his eyes. Countless streamers set into walls, floor and ceilings beamed millions of tiny mosaics of information, all to be put together by a sophisticated computer system to form the giant holosphere slowly rotating in this vast space.

Matthew would watch as thousands and thousands of tiny, glowing points formed a complex filigree of fine shimmering silver lines that he could almost reach out and touch. Although past experience had taught him this was not a good idea.

Scattered throughout this intricate network he could see twinkling blue, purple and green dots, denoting every jump of which the Time Police were aware – their own legal jumps, illegal jumps by other people, and those of St Mary's, which could be either legal or illegal depending on what that erratic organisation was up to at that particular Time.

Superimposed over everything were large red dots denoting major events in history. Not that the Time Police cared about major historical events – they were there solely for the purposes of navigation and finding one's way around the Time Map. Because, according to the Time Police, it was Time that was important. History – less so. Without Time, history could not exist. Time was the structure – history simply the furniture therein. According to St Mary's, however, without History, time is pointless. A bit like the Time Police, they would go on to say. And then run away.

Flickering red lines connected each red dot to others nearby – and sometimes as far away as the other side of the Map as well, because, as anyone from St Mary's will tell you – and there's a significant portion of your life you'll never get back again – nothing ever happens in isolation. Every event is connected to every other event and the Map reflected this.

The enormous room was dimly lit – the centrepiece was the Map, hanging in space, humming gently as it rotated. The Song of the Time Map, as it was known. Small groups of officers stood around the observation ring which had been built about halfway up the Map Room, almost level with the ever-changing now. There were always people there, watching the Time Map slowly evolve, silver light playing softly on their upturned faces.

The Map Master and her similarly obsessed team worked on the ground floor, crouching over their consoles, managing the vast amounts of information that flowed into the Time Map in their never-ending efforts to keep it as up to date as possible. Tiny silver lines extended to form new pathways, growing imperceptibly as they inched their way across the Map.

Whether they were reflecting this information or whether the Map was actually sentient enough to grow itself was the subject of lively, sometimes vigorous and occasionally overenthusiastic debate in the bar.

According to the Time Police, Map technicians were instantly recognisable by their weedy frames and unhealthy complexions, being physically unable to cope with long periods of daylight and then only with protective clothing and a safety net. By nature solitary and sad, they lived in the shadows with only each other and a lifetime's supply of energy drinks to sustain them.

There were eleven of them altogether, although, looking down into the well of the chamber, Matthew could see only six were actually present. One would be on leave – which was Time Map-speak for spending time in his darkened room in the company of magazines of a very specific nature. No, not that sort of specific nature.

Two were on a training course – continuing professional development being a big part of the new Time Police ethos.

Two were off sick – one with an improbable and much discussed groin strain and the other suffering some kind of skin complaint that caused people to approach him wearing a rubber apron, face mask and tongs.

It goes without saying that all members of the section – other than the Map Master herself – were male. Popular opinion maintained she'd accidentally wandered in one day while looking for the Battersea Dogs Home. 'Looking for something to adopt,' said someone – and in lieu of something with a cold wet nose that crapped on the carpet, had taken on the Time Map Maintenance section – TiMMs – instead.

Looking down from the observation ring, Matthew could see two rows of three consoles, drawn up in a semicircle to face the Map. The Map Master's workstation – which apparently made the controls of the Mars lander look like a Lego model – stood on a slightly raised platform behind them. Matthew was only too well aware that nothing escaped her vigilant eye – especially where he was concerned. To one side stood another row of three seldom-manned consoles, which was where they dumped trainees, incompetents and Matthew Farrell.

Alone among Time Police departments, this was not a paper-free zone. Each chaotic workstation benefitted from its own free-form filing system. No food or drink, however. Anyone caught eating or drinking at their workstation could rely on their already slim chances of reproduction being eliminated altogether by a vengeful and dog-deprived Map Master.

On this particular morning Matthew was standing alone on the observation ring watching the Map shimmer. Several other groups of people were also present, walking around the Map, pointing. No one spoke much. The Map usually engendered a respectful silence.

Time passed – as it tends to do, especially with a Time Map – and still Matthew stood and stared. Stillness can attract its own attention and after a while, he began to attract that attention.

Completely unaware others were watching him, Matthew frowned. The light played on his face as he gazed down at the Map, his strange golden eyes gleaming like a hawk looking down from a great height searching for its prey in a distant cornfield. Narrowing it down. Focusing. Homing further and further in. Still as a statue. Concentrating. Finally, he had it.

Turning on his heel, he trotted along the observation ring,

disappearing through a door and reappearing several seconds later in the well of the Map Room itself, a forbidden area inhabited only by the Map Master and her team.

The Map Master turned from the console at which she was working. 'Farrell – what are you doing down here? You know you're banned.'

Matthew's eyes glittered with reflected light from the Map. 'It's happening again.'

'What is?'

Matthew gestured. 'There. Can you see?'

'No.'

'There – that section there.'

The Map Master regarded him thoughtfully. The rules demanded she chuck him out. And it wasn't as if he didn't have form. Sometimes, in her worst nightmares, especially after too much cheese too late at night, she remembered Matthew Farrell, his eyes glowing gold as the Time Map darkened and disintegrated around him. He'd been a child at the time, however, and her instinct told her to listen to him now. She hesitated for only a moment and then held out her gauntlets. 'Show me. Carefully.'

Slowly, never once looking away from the Map, Matthew drew on the gauntlets and moved closer. Looking up, he moved his right arm, isolating a particular section. This he enlarged, his movements confident and sure, digging deeper and deeper into the cat's cradle of glowing silver lights, until, finally, 'There.'

The Map Master moved to stand beside him, squinting up at the Map. 'Where? I can't see – yes, I can. Wait – don't touch anything. Don't change anything.'

She turned to her second in charge. 'Connor – replicate

this section. Detach the replica from the original and isolate. Enlarge and enhance.'

With a deeper hum, a giant segment of the Time Map replicated itself and appeared before them. A 3D representation at eye level. People left their consoles to walk around it, staring. 'Where? Yes – there – look. Shit.'

A riot of comment broke out.

'Bloody hell.'

'Not again.'

The Map Master issued a barrage of instructions. 'Connor – isolate Area 4b. Magnify. More . . . more . . . Hennessy, slave the replica to the original. I want a moment-by-moment track. Khouri – set up a series of replicas. I want forward projections. And a specific location. Above all, I want to know if it looks like it's deviating from its normal path. All of you – move.'

Techs swept the debris from their workstations and began to fire up additional screens, shouting to each other. Above them, the Song of the Time Map faltered.

The Map Master's voice rose above the clamour. 'Don't just stand there. Someone get me the duty officer. Move.'

In a considerably less stressed part of the building, Captain Farenden was frowning at a report from one of the clean-up crews that would lead anyone not actually acquainted with a clean-up crew to assume they had the literary levels of a haystack, when Major Ellis entered.

There was no preamble. 'Sorry, Charlie, I need to speak to Commander Hay immediately.'

'She has the Principal Management Team with her.'

'Chuck them out.'

Some people might wait for anything from thirty minutes to thirty days to see Commander Hay. Major Ellis was not one of those people.

Captain Farenden got to his feet and limped to the door. Tapping, he entered.

'Ma'am, your urgent attention is required.'

Commander Hay and Captain Farenden had worked together for a long time. They'd been field officers in the Time Wars. Over the years they'd developed a code. Certain phrases said more than the actual words. She rose to her feet. 'My apologies, everyone. I'm afraid we'll have to postpone the rest of this meeting. Charlie will reschedule.'

They filed out.

Major Ellis stood aside for the PMT – frequently described by Commander Hay as something unpleasant and unavoidable that happened every month – to file past him, then strode into her office, saying, 'You might want to come in as well, Charlie. We have a problem.'

Commander Hay was closing down her data stack. 'Well, Major?'

'I'm duty officer today, ma'am. I've just received this from the Map Master.' He passed over his scratchpad. 'Time-slip at Versailles.'

'Again?' She flicked through the scratchpad and looked up, saying sharply, 'It says here that Farrell was involved. Tell me he didn't initiate it.'

A trifle defensively, Major Ellis informed her that no, Trainee Farrell had discovered the anomaly, not caused it.

'I thought he was banned from the Map Room.'

'I believe the Map Master has relented, ma'am. Somewhat.'

'Really? I didn't know she had it in her. Not where her precious Map's concerned.'

He pointed at the scratchpad. 'As the Map Master herself admits, ma'am, Farrell was able to identify and isolate this anomaly long before anyone else even had a whiff of it.'

'Good to see his old skills haven't deserted him.' She passed him back his scratchpad. 'Now you're no longer signed off, I want you on this one, Major. Time-slips are always tricky and we need to shut it down as soon as possible. Who do we have available at the moment?'

'There's my team, ma'am, Lt Chigozie's team and Lt Grint's team. Ten people altogether, plus any Hunters Major Callen can spare.'

'Is it spreading?'

'Unknown as yet, ma'am. The Map Master has two teams monitoring the time-slip, but it is moving. One end appears relatively stable in 1901. The other end, in 1789, for some reason, is not.'

'Because . . . ?'

'Unknown as yet, ma'am. It could be anything.'

She drummed her fingers. 'Something must be different this time. Something perhaps trying to send events down a different course. I don't need to tell you how serious that could be, Major. Take whoever and whatever you need and check it out immediately. You'll need to be quick, but most of all, you'll need to be discreet. There are contemporaries involved. No one must be aware of your presence. Whatever you do – get it shut down. Charlie, can you designate a replacement duty officer, please.'

Team 236 were yanked out of the dining room. At least one third of them was not happy about this.

'How can we be having an emergency?' complained Parrish. 'They keep telling us – it's not when you depart, it's when you arrive, and we can arrive at any time we like.'

Jane and Matthew pushed him, alternately chewing and protesting, out of the dining room.

On his way to the briefing, Ellis encountered Officer North.

'Are you on this one, Celia?'

She fell in beside him. 'I've been asked to provide an historical briefing, sir.'

'Excellent. I've been meaning to ask – how are you enjoying Hunter Division?'

'Quite a lot, actually.'

'Are you working alone these days?'

'Mostly. Although Lt Bower roped me in on Project Bluebird.'

'Yes, I hear that was very successfully concluded.'

'He went in the front – I was waiting around the back . . .'

'Dressed as a homeless person, I hear.'

'Yes,' she said briefly.

'And you got both of them as they climbed out of the window.'

'The clothes were uncomfortable and smelled so I was anxious to conclude the mission as quickly as possible.'

Already present in Briefing Room 2 were Lt Grint and his team, consisting of Trainees Hansen, Kohl and Rossi – Team 235. Team 236 arranged themselves untidily behind them. No one looked at anyone else.

An uninformed observer would find it hard to believe these two teams had done their basic training together. Since then they had gone their separate ways. Team 235 had followed the traditional Time Police path – a strong team of four officers, well-disciplined and integrated. Their views of the slightly more unconventional Team 236 were well known and inter-team relations had been poor, culminating in the recent unfortunate incident in the Pod Bay when former 235 member Alek Anders had been shot dead. An event never mentioned by anyone. And now Team 235 was down to three men as well. Hostile glances were exchanged.

'I'm surprised to see you here,' said Luke chattily to Grint, still seemingly unaware of the respect due to higher-ranking officers. 'This must be your last mission before your transfer out to BeeBOC.'

Grint wasn't the world's fastest learner but in his book only an idiot engaged Parrish in conversation. He busied himself, meaty fingers bashing away at his scratchpad and ignored him.

North sat slightly off to one side in no man's land. There had been a time when, as a member of Team 236, Trainee Parrish's disrespect would have been very much her concern, but not any longer. Now she was a Hunter and Trainee Parrish was someone else's problem. Her days with Team 236 were behind her. A fact pointed out by Lt Grint, to whom the social graces were things that happened to other people. 'So why are *you* here?'

She closed her notes and replied, 'To provide an historical context.'

'What for? This isn't bloody St Mary's, you know. All we have to do is get in there, sort it out and come home. Basically, this whole panic is just about making sure a couple of old women get through a time-slip safely.'

North took a deep breath and spoke calmly. 'Time-slips are fragile, sir. It's important to ensure nothing happens to change history.'

He shrugged. 'Not a priority for me.'

Sitting back, he folded his arms. The matter was obviously closed. North sighed. Clearly a very light touch would be required for this one. To say nothing of an adequate briefing. Although whether adequate listening would occur was debatable.

Major Ellis opened the batting.

'Pay attention, everyone. Today's minor problem is a time-slip. I don't think any of you have been with us long enough to have experienced one of these. It's relatively straightforward, but time-slips can be nasty so we need to get on to it as soon as possible, so prep for immediate departure.'

Luke sighed, 'Really? Is that necessary? Is there really any reason why we couldn't rise gently at half past nine, and then when everyone's quite ready, we could assemble here, quietly and without all the shouting – definitely no shouting – while someone gently explains what's going on and . . .'

Grint twisted in his chair to look at him. 'Shut up, Parrish.'

'I'm just saying . . .'

'Well, don't.'

'But . . .'

'Shut up, Parrish, before I put you on report.'

'But . . .'

'You're on report.'

'But . . .'

'You're on report *again*.'

'Is that the same report?'

Lt Grint blinked. 'What?'

145

'Are these two separate reports I'm on, or am I on the same report twice?'

'You're nanoseconds away from a third report,' said Ellis, without looking up. 'A record even for you.'

'I should get danger money for doing this,' muttered Jane, nudging Luke to another seat well removed from Lt Grint's blast zone.

Ellis began again. 'Another time-slip has been discovered.' He looked around the room. 'You will all have covered this in your basic training, but a time-slip is an area where some people – usually quite unwittingly – appear to be able to enter another time period as easily as entering another room. Sometimes, they don't even know they've done it until it's all over. Sometimes they never know they've done it at all.

'Many people offer time-slips as an explanation of ghosts – a person moving from A to B, often in strange clothes and repeating the same actions over and over again. Are they trapped, unable to escape until some circumstance changes and they are able to break out? Or does some external event somehow release them? As you can imagine, a great deal of work has been done on this subject and it would be fair to say we're no wiser now than when we started.'

Grint sighed. 'It's not Bold Street again, is it? I thought that had finally been plugged.'

'No, not Bold Street again, and incidentally, that particular plug isn't working so I'm guessing we'll be back there before long. This time I'm afraid it's the Versailles time-slip. The year 1789 is a key point in history which is why I've asked Officer North to join us today. Officer North, a little context, if you please.'

North brought up a map of the Palace of Versailles and its grounds. As usual she spoke without referring to her notes.

'I want to take you through events as they occur within the slip so you'll recognise anything unexpected.'

Grint sighed loudly.

'The first reported instance of this particular time-slip is at the beginning of the 20th century.'

Luke Parrish sat up, alarmed. The 20th century was not his favourite century.

'In 1901, two English academics, Charlotte Moberly and Eleanor Jourdain, visit Versailles. Somehow, they become lost. On their way to the Petit Trianon, they miss their turning and find themselves in a deserted part of the gardens, where they begin to experience what their contemporaries have called either a shared delusion or the inadvertent participation in the recreation of an historical event, but which we know now is a genuine, recurring time-slip.

'The *Petit Trianon* is a small palace, located in the gardens of the larger Palace of Versailles. It was given to Marie Antoinette by her husband, King Louis XVI. The palace was for her use exclusively. Only her very close friends were ever admitted.

'Our two English ladies have a guidebook – a Baedeker – but somehow they will miss the turning to the Avenue de Trianon here,' North pointed to an area on the map, 'and take a more minor path. They wander around between the Petit Trianon and the Temple de l'Amour . . .' she highlighted another area of the map, 'a pretty area of woodland and water. They report seeing other buildings and other people as they wander the paths. Importantly – and this does seem to be a common feature of time-slips – they both experience feelings of depression and

147

hopelessness. Afterwards they rather fancifully ascribe these feelings as somehow being telepathically projected by Marie Antoinette, whom they are convinced they encounter. We now know that tightness of the chest, feelings of panic and so on are typical time-slip features and probably *not* due to telepathically picking up the queen's feelings of despair on the day of her arrest.

'They will say they encounter gardeners, together with an old woman and a child outside a cottage, which, at the time, they thought was a *tableau vivant*.'

'What's a . . . ?' said Grint, managing to make his feelings about time-slips, Team 236, poncey briefings, the French language and female officers known to all present in just two short words.

'*Tableau vivant*,' said Luke. 'Think Madame Tussauds.'

'Another foreigner?'

'As are so many of us,' Luke said, brightly. 'The Grints, I believe, hail from darkest Scotland.'

North swept on before the situation could deteriorate any further. 'Both ladies also comment on the lifelessness of everything around them, describing their surroundings as flat – like being in a tapestry. At the edge of the wood, close to the Temple de l'Amour, they encounter a man. A sinister individual, according to them, ugly and with dark, pockmarked skin. We now think this might be the Comte de Vaudreuil, whose mistress was Gabrielle de Polignac, one of the queen's favourites.'

Grint sighed at the Frenchness of these names.

'Both ladies feel a great reluctance to pass him but fortunately another man turns up and is able to direct them to the Petit Trianon. A little further on they will encounter a solitary lady, sketching. Moberly particularly notices her old-fashioned dress, and later, firmly believes she has seen the queen, Marie Antoinette. They will pass her by and shortly afterwards, walk out of the time-slip, return to 1901 and join another party of travellers, without really realising what has happened.' She shut down the map, saying briskly, 'And that, lady and gentlemen, is what you can expect to encounter within this particular time-slip.'

Ellis stood up. 'Thank you, Officer North. Now, we know this is not the first time this time-slip has appeared, and this one is well-documented so we won't be working in the dark. We know exactly what should occur and when, so it's just a case of ensuring that it does.'

Jane raised her hand. 'Sir, how often does this particular time-slip materialise?'

'I think this is its fifth appearance to date and the first one for about seven years. It's a recurring problem. Not as bad as Liverpool, of course, but nothing is as bad as Liverpool. Apparently, it is now almost impossible to arrive at the end of Bold Street and still be in the same century in which you set out. For some reason there was a lot of activity there in the Time Wars, which has substantially damaged the fabric of Time, and if we had our way, the whole area would be a no-go zone but, apparently, we're not allowed to shut down a large chunk of Liverpool. Or so they tell us. To some extent I can see their point – it would only draw attention to the time-slip, and every nutter, conspiracy theorist, new-age weirdo, mad scientist, teenager, and historian in the world would be all over it.

'What marks *this* occurrence as a genuine time-slip event, however, is not what the women in question saw, but the feelings they experienced. Those of us who've had the misfortune to encounter a time-slip will be well aware of the . . . flat . . . nature of events inside. It's been likened to being inside a picture. There is no sound. No wind. No light and shade. Everything is lifeless. You will also experience feelings of nausea very similar to travel sickness. Be aware of how easily you can lose your sense of direction. If the slip closes with you still inside, you're stuck for good until either it opens by itself or we can force it to do so. So stick together and don't get lost.

'You will also find yourselves subject to feelings of despair and hopelessness. Live with it. It's not as if you don't encounter despair and hopelessness every day in the Time Police. You might also find difficulty in concentrating, but since in my experience this is your default state, I encourage you to work around it.

'Lt Chigozie's team are already in 1789, unobtrusively keeping an eye on things at the Versailles end. Your two teams will both be in 1901. Lt Grint's team will set up an unobtrusive perimeter to ensure no one else can be involved. Usually, this is a very well-behaved time-slip. Nothing ever changes. The women enter, wander around for a couple of hours and then exit. On this occasion, however, the slip is generating anomalous readings, as observed by Trainee Farrell.'

He turned to Grint. 'You'll need to be vigilant, Lieutenant.'

Grint nodded. 'No problems there.'

'My team will enter the time-slip to keep an eye on our two intrepid English ladies. At a discreet distance, people. Our only purpose is to ensure nothing befalls them, that they tread the familiar path and emerge safely back in 1901. The time-slip usually seals itself once they're out. Any questions so far?'

'Yes,' said North. 'I'd like to be included, sir. I speak excellent French and an historical perspective might be useful.'

'Doubt it,' said Grint. 'The old biddies wander in and then wander back out again. It's always the same.'

'Nevertheless . . .' said North, managing in just one word to convey her misgivings at Grint's attitude. Major Ellis nodded his understanding.

'Agreed,' he said. 'You probably won't be needed, North, but it'll be useful to have you around. Unless you object, Lieutenant?'

Grint scowled and shook his head.

'You're with me then, North. Standard operating procedures for this one, everyone. And don't bother with weapons — anything not contemporary with that particular period will work in a time-slip. Nor your coms. Be aware.'

'Sir, do we know what triggered this particular time-slip?' asked Jane, scribbling in her notebook.

'No one ever knows what sets them off. We haven't yet discovered whether they work to a timetable, or just randomly occur. I suspect, given the date and location of this one, it's something to do with the period in which time travel was legal, and we're looking at a recurring phenomenon caused by too many would-be time travellers all trying to catch a glimpse of Marie Antoinette as she's arrested at Versailles, and this has made the entire area unstable. All attempts to fix this one have, so far, proved unsuccessful, and we usually just deploy a team to keep an eye on things. Today, however, our priority will be to identify the source of the anomaly before it escalates into anything major. Once we've dealt with that and if it follows its own rules, the time-slip should spontaneously shut itself down once the Englishwomen emerge and then we can all come home.'

Ellis sighed heavily. 'Please also keep your eyes peeled for any time-travelling lunatics from St Mary's who, with our luck, are almost certain to turn up and make a bad situation considerably worse.'

No one looked at Matthew. Matthew continued to stare at his scratchpad.

Everyone else sighed in unison. The Time Police and St Mary's had, on several occasions, been forced to work together and that had rarely ended well. Standing orders forbade the Time Police to shoot St Mary's dead on sight and this was a recurring grievance. Several officers had offered to forgo their next pay rise in return for the privilege of eliminating every member of that cursed organisation who unwisely crossed their path. Commander Hay, with some regret, had declined these kind offers.

Luke put up his hand. 'We won't have to wear those daft clothes, will we? They had mice living in their wigs, you know.'

'Our presence will be discreet and unobtrusive. If it isn't, you'll be answering to me afterwards. You will keep an exceedingly low profile, so no daft clothes, no mice. And be aware that anyone inadvertently preventing the French Revolution from occurring as it should can expect to find themselves explaining to a deeply unhappy Commander Hay – together with all the unpleasantness that usually entails. Any other questions?'

Luke raised his hand again. Without even looking, Jane pulled it back down.

Ellis wound up the briefing. 'Remember, people – this is a time-slip. There will be a certain amount of confusion and disorientation. You'll be jumping to 1901 but you'll be operating in 1789. Keep your wits about you. That's it, everyone. Dismissed.'

12

'Versailles, August 1901,' said Luke, appreciatively, sniffing the air. 'Nice. A gentle stroll on a summer's afternoon. This is going to be a piece of doddle.'

'Don't you ever learn?' said Matthew, checking his utility belt.

'Oh, come on. We're following a couple of women in a garden. What could possibly go wrong?'

'Do you want it alphabetically or chronologically?'

'Actually, I'm quite optimistic about this one, as well,' said Jane. 'Not only do we not have to do *anything*, but today we have a proper team leader who can competently supervise us not doing anything. And it's a lovely day.'

It was indeed a beautiful day. Wispy white clouds decorated a clear blue sky. A gentle breeze rustled the leaves on the trees. Everything was peaceful and quiet. In the distance, however, ominous storm clouds were gathering.

A bit of a metaphor, thought Jane. Violent thunderstorms had been reported that day. The jury was still out on whether heavy electrical activity was a cause or a by-product of time-slips.

Grint and his team appeared. 'Pod secured, sir.'

'Right,' said Ellis, because they were all officially still under training, 'does anyone know exactly where we are?'

'The Plaine Saint-Antoine,' said Jane, pulling out her note-book. Scratchpads might not work in a time-slip but her trusty notebook would never let her down. She flicked to a sketch map. 'The palace of Versailles itself is over there.' She gestured to their left. 'That wide path is the Allée Saint-Antoine. On the other side is the Petit Trianon. Moberly and Jourdain will miss the turning to the Avenue de Trianon and end up in the vicinity of the Temple de l'Amour, which is just over there.'

'Well done, Lockland,' said Ellis, 'good groundwork,' and she blushed.

'Still not got that licked, then?' remarked Bolshy Jane.

Jane ignored her.

'There are a lot of people about,' said Luke, looking around.

There were indeed a lot of people about. Most were in pairs or small groups. There were very few single women and no children – this being an era when, presumably, children were neither seen nor heard until their early thirties. Nearly all the women were accompanied by men wearing dark suits with small lapels. Everyone – men and women – wore hats.

'We're going to stand out a bit,' said Jane, gesturing to their hatless state.

'It shouldn't matter too much,' said North. 'There's always something going on here – re-enactments, or *tableaux vivants* – with luck they will assume we're part of the entertainment.'

'What's a tabloo vivorn again?' asked Grint.

'A living picture. People dress up in the appropriate costumes and pose. Often for photographs. A very popular pastime.'

Silence implied Lt Grint was never going to be that desperate for something to do. 'With your permission, sir, I'll take my team and check things out before establishing the perimeter.'

Ellis nodded. 'Disperse your team as you think fit. Just make sure everything proceeds as normal. Other than us, no one in and no one out. Be aware, Lieutenant, there's something different about this one so keep your wits about you.'

Grint nodded, signalled to his team, and they set off down one of the wide paths.

Jane resumed her scrutiny of her surroundings. The women were all similarly dressed in variations of frilly, puffed blouses – usually white – and dark, fluted skirts that flared from the hip.

'Very elegant,' said Jane. Many carried parasols to protect themselves from the complexion-wrecking sunshine. The slightly higher waistlines plumped out their chests.

'They look like pigeons,' said Luke, critically.

'And the men look hairy,' said Jane, which was perfectly true. Nearly all the men wore facial hair of some kind. Beards of all shapes and sizes on the older men and luxuriant moustaches for the younger. Jane glanced at her cleanly-shaven colleagues with misgivings.

Everyone around them was walking slowly – partly because of the hot sunshine, she supposed, and partly because of the weight of all that clothing.

'Right,' said Ellis. 'Lockland, you have the map – you lead. Officer North, if you would be good enough to bring up the rear, please – and off we go.'

Pulling their cloaks around them, Team 236 set off. They'd had worse assignments, reflected Jane. Much worse. The formal gardens were bright with summer flowers and the wide gravel paths well-raked. Somewhere nearby, she could hear the hum of busy bees. Everything was immaculate. Yes, they'd definitely had worse assignments.

'Do we know what they were wearing?' asked Luke, as they made their way down the Allée Saint-Antoine.

North spoke from behind him. 'According to our records, both ladies are wearing light-coloured blouses. Moberly has a dark blue skirt and Jourdain's is grey. Moberly has a light veil attached to her hat and Jourdain is rocking a frivolously pink parasol. No reason they should be wearing anything different on this occasion.'

'I can't believe this keeps happening. Don't we have any idea what triggers it?'

'Not that we can discover. There's the electrical factor, of course,' she looked up at the sky, 'but Time – all Time here is . . .' She paused for the right word.

'Wobbly?' suggested Luke.

'Unstable,' said Ellis. 'July 1789 was a very popular destination before the Time Police started cracking down. People wanted to see Marie Antoinette in her last hours of freedom and they were jumping in and out on a regular basis and, of course, people being what they are, there were any number of idiots who thought they could improve on the original events. Before my time, but from what I can gather, there was a lot of activity here and it didn't do the fabric of Time any good at all. Don't ask me any technical questions – perhaps it's something Farrell here will be able to explain after a year or so working with the Time Map.'

His eye fell on Matthew as he spoke, quite casually, and he was surprised to see a shadow cross his face. Ellis said nothing – this was not the time or place – but made a mental note to find time for a quick word on their return. He remembered Matthew's lack of enthusiasm when discussing Team Weird's

157

future roles within the Time Police. Something was not quite right here.

The gardens were exquisite. Jane could easily see why Marie Antoinette preferred to spend her time here, rather than the stifling formality of the French court. Unfortunately, stifling formality was the price to be paid for being queen. Along with rigid protocols rooted in Time and tradition, and carried out to the letter, no matter how irrelevant. The French Revolution did not happen overnight. It had taken decades, possibly centuries, of bad political decisions, mismanagement and general all-round incompetence before the Revolution finally kicked off.

Daisies, rarely seen in Jane's modern world of pesticides and weedkillers, dotted the grass, although how such pretty flowers could be classed as weeds was a mystery to her. The grass was short – sheep-cropped, she guessed – and not the green velvet favoured by modern gardeners. To their left, the cultivated areas were very formal with precise geometric designs, all enclosed by tiny, immaculate hedges, while on their right, carefully planted groups of trees played at being proper countryside.

Everything was quiet and orderly. The air felt heavy and sleepy.

'Are we in the right place?' said Luke, looking around.

North nodded. 'Yes.'

'Only I thought there would be more . . .'

'More what?'

'Consternation.'

Ellis shook his head. 'No one here has any idea a time-slip is about to open up. Not even the two ladies concerned. Remember, it's just a normal day for everyone here except us.'

Jane had never stopped scanning their surroundings. 'There they are. That must be them. Over there.'

Two women appeared on the gravel path, walking slowly towards them. And yes, there was the pink parasol. Jane blessed Miss Jourdain's daring choice of fashion accessory. The older lady in front, Miss Moberly, was consulting a book, while the other had fallen a little behind, walking slowly and looking about her.

They watched both ladies halt, consult their Baedeker, come to some sort of a decision and set off with purpose into the wooded area.

'Here we go,' said Luke.

Ellis quickened the pace. 'They're off to find the Petit Trianon. After them. Whatever happens, do not let them out of your sight. Everything *must* happen exactly as it always does.'

The Time Police had a procedure for this sort of thing. Automatically, they divided themselves into two groups. Ellis, North and Luke stepped off the path and moved to their left, meandering casually across the grass. Jane and Matthew followed on behind the ladies, looking everywhere except at their targets. Matthew went so far as to embrace the prevailing practice of the times and point out various landmarks Jane was perfectly capable of noticing for herself.

Neither women were hurrying, strolling along and admiring the scenery. Neither showed any signs of triggering a time-slip.

'I suppose . . .' said Jane, hesitantly.

'No,' said Matthew with certainty. 'There's definitely a time-slip about to occur. I know it.'

'*How* do you know it?'

'How do you know when you're thirsty? How do you know

when someone is standing behind you? How do you know when there's going to be a thunderstorm?'

'I don't know – I just do, I suppose.'

'Same with me. In the same way that you know today is hot, I know a time-slip is about to kick off.'

'Matthew . . .'

He was watching the women ahead of them. 'Mm?'

She tried to pick her words carefully. 'Are you aware of the time-slip . . . ?' She took the plunge. 'Or are you *causing* the time-slip?'

He stopped and stared into space. 'That's a thought, isn't it?'

'What is?'

'That you could artificially manufacture a time-slip. There have been rumours . . .'

Jane glanced at him. His eyes looked very bright. 'Are you all right?'

'Yes. Fine. Why wouldn't I be?'

'No reason. You just look a bit heated.'

'It's very muggy, don't you think?'

'Yes, quite oppressive. Perhaps we're going to have a storm after all.'

Ahead of them, the women were meandering from path to path, through the woods and along the bank of a pretty stream. Ellis signalled the teams to catch up.

'They're lost,' said Luke. 'Typical female sense of direction.'

The two females regarded him without expression.

'It was a joke.'

Their expressions did not change.

'All right, children – no fighting,' said Ellis, suddenly feeling extremely old.

'Wait,' said Matthew. 'Something's happening. I knew it would.' He took a few steps off to the side.

'Just a moment,' said Ellis. 'We need to stay together.'

Ahead of them, the air began to shimmer. Jane felt the faint touch of electricity. The short hairs on her arms bristled. Matthew was right.

'Is that it?' said Luke, peering over her shoulder. 'Just looks like a heat haze.'

'That's it,' said Matthew, his eyes glowing.

'I expected more. Some sort of Dread Portal. Spectral voices warning us not to approach. The Trumpet of Doom . . .'

'Move,' said Ellis. 'We do not lose sight of those two women. Now, you know what to expect. I've done this before. It's not pleasant but it won't kill you. Ready, everyone. Follow me.'

Heart thumping, Jane lined up with Luke. Matthew and North brought up the rear.

Ellis led the way. For a moment his silhouette was outlined against the shimmer and then he disappeared. Jane paused. Suppose something went wrong. Suppose she ended up in a different Time to everyone else. Suppose she was torn to pieces in some sort of temporal vortex.

'Come on,' said Bolshy Jane, scornfully. 'What are you waiting for?'

A very good question, thought Jane, and stepped into the time-slip.

13

Ellis was right. Stepping into a time-slip was not pleasant. Not pleasant at all.

The transition was abrupt. Between one step and the next Jane passed from summer 1901 to autumn 1789. There was no warning – no fanfare. Nothing to show they had left their own Time, but the effects on all of them were perceptible.

Jane felt a shortness of breath. As if someone had passed a band around her chest and was twisting it more tightly every second. She stood for a moment, trying not to panic. It was important not to panic. She couldn't breathe out. It wasn't a case of gulping for breath – she just found it impossible to exhale.

'Steady, everyone,' said Ellis's voice. 'Just stay calm. Remember there are two middle-aged ladies over there who are coping with exactly the same symptoms so let's not embarrass ourselves, eh?'

The pain was easing even as he spoke. Jane drew in a trembling breath. And then another one. Every breath grew easier. Wiping the sweat from her forehead, she looked around.

Nothing was quite right. The landscape was more or less the same – there were different trees in different places and the grass was longer and coarser, but Versailles 1789 wasn't that much different from Versailles 1901. That they weren't in 1901 any longer was clear, however. Nothing seemed to have any substance. The world was flat. There was no depth. The sun was still in the sky but there were no shadows. Colours were muted. The blue sky had faded to a milky white. Green trees had a very washed-out appearance.

When she had been at school, Jane had once experienced an eclipse of the sun when the light had dimmed and birds had ceased to sing. The air had cooled rapidly but she could still feel the heat coming up from the ground. This was very similar. She stared around. It's like a picture. I'm trapped in a picture. Oh my God, I'm trapped in a picture and I'll never get out. I'm here forever. I'll never even get back to 1901, let alone my own Time. I'm going to die here. We're all going to die here.

This feeling of panic was followed by a massive wave of depression. Of hopelessness. What did it matter anyway? They should get out. They should retrace their steps and return to the safety of the pod and think again. Or should they? Perhaps they should follow their original plan. But was that the best approach? What should they do?

She stared around. Which way should they go? Which was the way out? She couldn't even remember which was their path. And the landscape had changed. They'd never be able to find their way out. She could see them running up and down first one path and then another and never ever being able to find their way out of the gardens that were now their prison. Completely and utterly lost.

She drew another deep shuddering breath. Luke stood

163

alongside her, his eyes flickering left and right. Sweat lined his upper lip. She put a trembling hand on his shoulder. 'Luke. Come back.'

He gasped, seemed to return from wherever he'd been, stared for a moment and then nodded. Beside her, Ellis said, 'All right, Lockland?'

Calming Luke had calmed her. 'Yes. Yes, I am now. That was . . . unpleasant.'

'It always is. Welcome to 1789, everyone. All of you just take a moment. Get yourselves together again.'

Matthew looked back. 'So we just walked here? From 1901 to 1789? We walked?'

'Correct.'

'Can we get out that way?'

'No. We can only go forwards. If we walk back along that path, it's just a path.'

'Suppose we need to pull out in a hurry?' asked Luke.

'Then we're buggered, aren't we? Now then, Moberly and Jourdain are just over there. You can see her parasol.'

'Are they all right?'

'Perfectly. Both ladies experienced similar symptoms but only mentioned it afterwards. Don't get too close to them. We know they'll wander around this area, see a few people and then return harmlessly to their own Time. The time-slip always closes behind them. We follow them out, back to 1901, make sure that happens, pick up our pod and return home to well-earned applause and admiration.'

The two ladies had paused to sit on a rustic bench and recover themselves. One was fanning herself with her handkerchief. Otherwise they looked perfectly normal.

164

'There are differences,' said Jane, looking about her. 'More trees. Longer grass.'

Luke pointed. 'Oh my God. Look at the sheep.'

On the other side of the stream, some ten or twelve sheep had gathered at the foot of a tree. Luke stared. 'I've never seen sheep like those. Have you? Has anyone?'

Fully expecting green-glowing, radioactive, two-headed sheep at the very least, Jane looked. Twelve snowy-white, perfectly presented sheep wore pretty blue ribbons round their necks.

'It's like the white rabbit all over again,' said Luke, rubbing his eyes.

'Marie Antoinette liked to amuse herself with rural pursuits,' explained North, quietly. 'She and her friends played at being farmers.'

'That would explain those picturesquely poor cottages over there.'

Jane nodded. 'You can see why people got upset.'

'Says Jane the Republican.'

'Did she never stop to consider the feelings of people who had no choice but to live like that?'

'Not even for a second, I should imagine.'

'There's nothing picturesque about poverty,' said Matthew, who had spent his childhood on the receiving end of poverty of the worst kind. 'No wonder people thought she was just taking the piss.'

'They're on the move,' said Ellis. 'Remember, don't get too close.'

The area was by no means deserted. Following the women round a bend, they came across another quaintly derelict cottage with an old woman and a young girl standing by the open front door. The garden was stuffed full of flowers, Jane noticed, but unlike normal cottage gardens with their traditional mix of medicinal flowers, fruit and veg, nothing here was edible. Everything was immaculate, beautifully maintained and slightly unreal.

The Englishwomen waved but neither woman nor child responded, staring suspiciously after the women. As Ellis and his team passed them, they scowled and backed into the cottage and closed the door. Jane suspected they knew trouble when they saw it.

Still at a discreet distance behind the women, they headed towards a small wood. The air closed in around them. Jane could feel sweat in her hair. Here was silence. No buzz of insects, no breeze, no rustling leaves. Just silence and stillness. She wondered if this was how ghost stories began.

'We should have a checklist,' said Luke, his voice sounding oddly muffled. 'So we can tick off the sightings as they occur.'

'Already ahead of you,' said Jane smugly, ticking off something in her notebook.

'Jane, I'm sure I've told you this before. No one likes a smart arse.'

'You're just annoyed because, finally, my notebook is more useful than your scratchpads. Where are our ladies off to now?'

'They're still lost,' said North, 'but from our point of view everything is proceeding perfectly normally.'

'Normal?' said Wimpy Jane, as they moved off after the women. 'There's nothing normal about any of this.'

'Right, two more interactions just up ahead,' said Ellis. 'The pockmarked man followed by the sketching woman.'

'Pockmarked man coming up on our right,' announced Luke.

Beside the path, a man was seated next to a small, painted wooden hut, its purpose unknown. Jane slowed, uneasy for some reason. Something was wrong. She stared, unable to put her finger on it. And then she had it. She turned to Ellis. 'Sir, he's dressed like us.'

Jourdain and Moberly were approaching the seated man who, as Jane had pointed out, wore an all-muffling long cloak very similar to their own, except that his was dark red in colour.

Ellis slowed. 'Stay alert.'

'Lockland's right,' said North, from the rear. 'He should be wearing a hat – not a cloak. There's no record of him ever wearing a cloak before.'

Hearing their voices, the man looked up.

Jane, whose research had led her to believe the Comte de Vaudreuil was, in fact, an ugly, middle-aged man, was very surprised to find herself looking at a youth, barely out of his teens. Watery hazel eyes peered out of a long, pale face. His forehead was beaded with sweat. Another one affected by the time-slip.

Matthew blinked. 'Who is he?'

Luke automatically groped in his pocket.

'Your scratchpad won't work in a time-slip,' said Jane. 'Remember?'

'Nothing not from this period will work,' said Ellis. 'That was the whole point of the historical briefing.'

'And because history is important,' said Matthew.

Everyone politely ignored this plainly inaccurate statement.

Luke patted his shoulder. 'It's your upbringing,' he said. 'You can't help yourself. Just breathe deeply and this embarrassing moment will pass.'

'Pay attention,' said Ellis, sharply. 'This isn't a game.'

Jane had dragged out her notebook. 'I can tell you who it's not,' she said, flicking through the pages. 'It's not the Comte de Vaudreuil. He's older, dark-skinned and with a badly scarred face.'

Ellis nodded. 'Then I think we need a word with this person, don't you?'

As if he had overheard them, the young man got slowly to his feet, staring at them in alarm.

'This isn't right,' said Luke, suddenly uneasy. 'Something's gone horribly wrong.'

'He's the anomaly,' said North, suddenly. 'He's the one causing the instability. He shouldn't be here.'

Jane stood, momentarily petrified. There was someone else here in the time-slip who shouldn't be. Ellis had been very clear. The time-slip must proceed exactly as normal. No – wrong word. Usual. Things must proceed as usual. The slightest deviation could cause instability and shut it down. Leaving them inside. Or the other end could wander. The technical people had mentioned it was unstable. It could dump them anywhere. And they had no pod. They'd be trapped there. Forever.

'Oh, for God's sake,' said Bolshy Jane, exasperated. 'You don't get any better, do you? You're a very nearly qualified Time Police officer. You've got Ellis with you and he's the best there is. As is North. You couldn't be in better hands. Just calm down and try to contribute something positive.'

Yes, thought Jane. Thanks.

'You're welcome. Now get on with it.'

'Stay calm, everyone,' said Ellis. 'We have a teeny-tiny situation here. Move forwards slowly and stay alert.'

The young man, seemingly completely unperturbed by the Englishwomen nearby, had taken one glance at the Time Police, realised exactly how much trouble he was looking at, and stared wildly about him as if unsure what to do next.

'He knows who we are,' whispered North.

'Gun,' said Luke, suddenly, catching sight of a weapon. Instinctively he reached for his useless sonic. 'Some sort of flintlock, I think. Long-barrelled. Beneath his cloak. If it's contemporary – it will work.'

Barely had he spoken than the cloaked figure began, slowly, to edge away. That he wasn't an experienced assassin was apparent as he struggled to extricate the long barrel from the clinging folds of his cloak.

Ellis pushed back his own cloak. 'Parrish – you stay with Moberly and Jourdain. Keep them on track. North and Lockland – find Marie Antoinette. Protect the queen at all costs. Farrell – with me. After him.'

North took off through the trees with Jane close behind. There was a picturesquely winding path which made progress easier. North, with her conscientiously completed hours in the gym, ran like the wind. Jane, less conscientious but equally keen, was not that far behind. Her cloak hampered her movements, but she dared not shrug it off and leave it. This was a time-slip – the smallest anomaly could derail the whole thing, which was why it was so important to ensure nothing happened to Marie Antoinette.

Being the meticulously cared-for property of the French crown, this wasn't a real wood. Designer trees stood prettily grouped. There was no untidy undergrowth. No unsightly scrub. And no queen, either.

Jane panted along in North's wake. The air was hot and strangely oppressive. All sounds seemed muffled and distant. She couldn't even hear the sound of her own footfalls. There were no woodland noises – no birdsong. Whether the lack of wildlife was due to the excessive tidy nature of their surroundings or the time-slip itself, she had no way of knowing.

Ahead of her, North halted. Jane crept to her side. They stood at the edge of the wood, peering out over an impossibly pretty landscape. About fifty feet away, on the other side of the stream, a woman in a pale blue gown sat among a pile of matching cushions underneath a willow tree. She seemed to be sketching a late flower, concentrating hard on her task. There was no one else around. Was this her? How likely was a queen to be without servants? Surely someone would be within call in case she needed her nose scratched or something.

Jane counted herself lucky to have once caught a glimpse of Julius Caesar. And lately Charles II, of course, the Merry Monarch himself. Many Time Police officers went through their entire service without seeing even a semi-famous historical personage. Now, she was pretty sure she was looking at Marie Antoinette. The woman who, when told the people of Paris had no bread, probably didn't say, 'Let them eat cake.'

The queen's face was shaded by a very pretty Bergère hat. Her full-skirted pale blue polonaise gown billowed around her while, either by accident or design, her white fichu drew attention to the shape of her breasts rather than concealing them. A royal shepherdess dressed in finest silks and lace. Which would account for another small flock of beautifully presented, carefully coiffured, snowy white sheep with the usual matching blue ribbons around their necks grazing tidily nearby.

She was not as beautiful as Jane had been led to believe. Nothing could disguise the typical Habsburg face – big-chinned and with heavily-lidded eyes and full lips. She had pale skin, carefully shaded by her wide hat, and light eyes. Long curls of reddish blonde fell to her shoulders.

Abruptly – whether she was bored, or whether she had suddenly lost concentration was not clear – she sighed, tossed her drawing materials to one side and stood up, shaking out her petticoats. Her blue overskirt was looped up in the manner of peasant girls – presumably to protect it while she worked. Had she ever actually done any work? – and the colour was exactly the same as the ribbons around the sheep's necks. Matching sheep and shepherdess. Jane could just imagine how that went down with real shepherdesses. And real sheep, come to that. She knew she shouldn't let her mind wander, but she couldn't help wondering: if the queen had chosen another gown – yellow, perhaps, or rose – would they change the ribbons on the sheep or bring in a whole new flock? A yellow flock for a yellow dress. Was there a man employed to ascertain the colour of the queen's gown and proceed accordingly? 'OK, guys, bring out the blue flock today.'

Jane pulled herself up because this was irrelevant specula-tion. There was another side to the story. There was always another side and the truth usually lay somewhere between the two. That was what St Mary's always claimed to be about – discovering the truth. As well as buggering up the timeline and making life difficult for honest, hard-working Time Police officers, of course.

How misunderstood was Marie Antoinette? These beautiful surroundings were her refuge from the oppressive ceremony of the French court, where she never had even a moment to herself. Where everyone was out for what they could get and viewed the queen as a shortcut to getting it. Where every word must be carefully analysed for hidden meanings. Where every smile was false and they all watched her like hawks, waiting for the tiniest error – something that would give them personal leverage in the never-ending and often deadly game of court intrigue. How exhausting must that be?

Here, at the Petit Trianon, Marie Antoinette herself was in control. This was where she could relax. Only a few of her closest friends were ever allowed in. Here was where she led, what was to her, a simple life. To outsiders, however, this must seem like the rich playing at being poor. That their queen was deliberately mocking them.

She wasn't relaxed now. Despite the tranquillity of her rural surroundings, Jane could see she was obviously in an agitated state. She paced. She wrung her hands. Every now and then she would stop and anxiously scan the meadow around her. Was she waiting for news? Or was something about to happen?

Jane drew back behind a convenient tree and consulted her notebook. On 5th October 1789, the mob came to arrest the king and queen and any members of the court they could find, to take them to the Tuileries Palace. Jane looked at the yellow and gold leaves just beginning to show among the green. If this wasn't actually the 5th it must be very close. What must it have been like for the queen? One moment so remote from her subjects that they were barely even in the same world, and the next being ordered from her home by them. To be so powerful one moment and so powerless the next. Was this the moment when she had an inkling of how things would turn out? Or was she encased in disbelief and denial right up until the very end?

Jane knew suddenly and with certainty: Marie Antoinette was waiting for news. She was waiting to be told the armed mob was on its way. Did she know these were the last free hours of her life? Freedom being relative, of course. A cage is a cage, even when provided with every luxury. But how desirable would a gilded cage seem to the starving poor in Paris?

North, having located the queen, wisely saw no reason to approach her. She crouched at the foot of a wide-trunked tree and gestured for Jane to do the same.

The Time Police had a procedure for this. North watched Marie Antoinette and Jane faced the other way, watching their backs and scanning the silent wood around them, the sunlight slanting dusty gold through the trees, the empty path. What was happening to the others? Had Ellis and Matthew been able to capture the young man with the gun? Who was he? Why was he here? And Luke? How was he faring with those two formidable Englishwomen, either one of whom could easily eat him for breakfast? Where were they at this very moment? And where was the Comte de Vaudreuil, who should be here and wasn't?

As if in answer to her question, Moberly and Jourdain both appeared to her right, strolling along the path following the course of the stream. Catching sight of the queen, still standing beneath the willows, Moberly paused for a moment in surprise and then, drawing level with the motionless Marie Antoinette, she acknowledged her presence with a small curtsey which Marie Antoinette acknowledged with an inclination of her head.

Obviously not having a clue who either of these women could be, she'd fallen back on court etiquette.

Jane breathed a sigh of relief. Whatever was going on elsewhere, everything here was occurring exactly as it should. The ladies walked on. Marie Antoinette watched them for a moment and then turned away.

Someone hissed quietly to Jane's right. Luke peered from behind a tree, gestured to the two women and gave North a thumbs-up.

Jane nodded at him. So far, so good.

He grinned at them and then set off again. Eventually Moberly and Jourdain would exit the time-slip as easily as they had entered, the time-slip would shut down, everyone's life would continue as it should and the Time Police could go home.

Jane shifted her position to ease her legs. The queen was here and apparently alone. Ellis and Matthew must surely have the intruder under control by now. She could understand North's instinct to leave well alone. In Jane's experience, interfering rarely ended well. There was no immediate peril. They would wait here behind the tree and keep an unobtrusive eye on the queen until Major Ellis gave them the all-clear. Everything was in hand.

The red-cloaked figure crashed noisily through the trees. Sweat was pouring down his face and his eyes bulged in fear. Panic was written all over him. He appeared to be running quite blindly. Matthew and Ellis were directly behind him. There had obviously been some sort of confrontation already – the assailant was festooned with hardened pieces of yellow string. So for some reason, their liquid string aerosols worked. She would discover later that aerosols had been invented in this very year. Who knew?

Brandishing his pistol and shouting incoherently, the young man ran towards the startled Marie Antoinette, who, very sensibly, took one look at the wild-eyed man heading directly towards her and fled. Picking up her skirts, she ran along the stream, calling for help.

Jane leaped to her feet and followed North who, in turn, had set off after the queen.

'So that's all of us chasing her now,' said Bolshy Jane, cheerfully.

No one came to the queen's aid. No Swiss Guards, no servants, no courtiers – no friends. Whether they were already under arrest or whether, knowing what was about to happen, they'd abandoned their queen, Jane had no idea. Nor should she allow it to distract her. She'd been ordered to protect Marie Antoinette and protect the queen she would.

Queens, in general, do not run – as a child, Jane had wondered if their wide skirts meant they were on wheels – and Marie Antoinette was even more rubbish at running than most. Jane and North splashed through the stream and headed after her. They didn't have far to go. Hampered by her clothing and a complete ignorance of how to perambulate at speed, Marie Antoinette had not got very far. She leaned against a tree with her hand on her heaving bosom.

Jane was unable to decide whether she was just unfit because queens never did anything more strenuous than look at themselves in mirrors, or whether women in general just didn't exert themselves in this day and age. It seemed safe to assume her role as shepherdess had not been particularly arduous.

The intruder leaped the stream, brandished his pistol and shouted incoherently.

North stepped between the man and the queen and held up her hand, palm out. Her voice was strong and clear. 'Halt. Time Police. By the authority vested in me, I order you to lay down your weapon and submit to questioning.'

Strangely, the man failed to comply. Jane was unsure what to do next because – as Luke had frequently remarked during training – 'The official warning is so long the suspect has usually taken the opportunity to shoot us and escape before we've finished, so what to do next is not usually a concern.'

Fumbling at her belt for string and baton, she began to move very slowly to her left. To get behind him. Because North, for some reason, had delivered the warning in English. The assailant wouldn't have understood her.

She was wrong.

He backed away, one arm outstretched, palm outwards in a warning gesture, very similar to North's own, shouting, 'No, no. Stay back. Keep back. I have to . . .'

Surprised, Jane halted fractionally. Because he too had spoken in English.

There was no time to think about that now. Time Police procedures were clear about this sort of thing. Secure the situation and await reinforcements.

North was still standing between him and the queen. 'Stand still. My colleagues are behind you. Slowly – lay down your weapon and you won't be harmed.'

Ellis and Matthew were behind him. Jane was quietly moving off to one side. The man was surrounded. A sensible assassin would give up at this point.

He was shaking his head. Sweat was running down his face and his eyes were wild. 'No. You don't understand. I've come to save her. You have to let me go. Time is short. They're on their way. I have to get her out of here before they arrive.'

He turned to Marie Antoinette, whose bosoms were still having behavioural problems, and began to shout. In French this time, but the queen wasn't listening in any language. She was already turning to run away. Or as close as she could get to running.

Jane sighed. Fire-truckity fire truck. It was so much effort to chase after her. Too much effort. Her chest felt tight. She couldn't catch her breath. How pleasant would it be to just sit on the banks of the cool stream and doze the afternoon away? Let someone else sort it all out. Mentally, she shook herself. She shouldn't be feeling like this. A child could catch Marie Antoinette. What was the matter with her?

The young man – and he was very young – gave a cry of despair. 'You've ruined it. I'm trying to save her. Take her to Switzerland. She doesn't have to die. She can live.' He paused. 'With me.'

'Oh,' said North, unimpressed. 'You're one of those.'

The timeline is full of romantic young men endeavouring to rescue tragic young women from their inevitable ends. Joan of Arc, Helen of Troy, Mary Stuart, Marie Antoinette . . .

'Think of all the good they could still do,' they say, closing their minds to all the harm removing these unfortunate women from their own Time will cause.

And it works both ways. Attempts to kill Adolf Hitler had become so frequent and widespread that Commander Hay had found it necessary to increase the staffing levels of the

177

Hitler's Little Helpers department by nearly twenty per cent, thus ensuring a significant number of Time Police officers spent their days ensuring he lived long enough to fulfil his evil destiny. And not just Hitler – their services extended to other despots, as well – Rasputin, Attila the Hun, Nero, Stalin, Pol Pot, Genghis Khan. There were any number of well-meaning lunatics out there, all determined to thwart these tyrants' evil plans for world domination and bring good to the world instead. For the continued well-being of the timeline, this could not be allowed to happen, hence the creation of this perpetually overworked department within the Time Police dedicated to ensuring the world could stagger on with its full complement of unbalanced megalomaniacs, psychotic despots, brutal tyrants and politicians.

The queen was on the move again. For someone hampered by tradition, by her clothes and by lack of practice, she was still managing to cover the ground. Jane suspected she was just running blindly because somehow – and Jane had never thought this description would apply to her – she had mistaken them for the armed mob that history was sending her way.

North was shouting at her. 'Lockland – I've got him. You get after her.'

Jane was already moving. Behind her, the young man was shouting in French. Jane had no idea what he was yelling but it didn't appear to be having any helpful effect. Actually, she couldn't help feeling that if he was bombarding the queen with declarations of undying love and his determination to whip her off to Switzerland to live a simple life halfway up an Alp, she didn't altogether blame her for running away. She, Jane, would have been far over the horizon by now.

From the corner of her eye she saw Matthew, small and light and their fastest sprinter, race past them both. Ellis had sent him ahead to try to cut the queen off before she inadvertently ran straight out of the time-slip.

The young man appeared in her side vision with North hot on his heels, stringing him as she ran. They drew level with the queen. Now they were all in a tight group together with Matthew just ahead, moving in to cut her off. The air around them began to shimmer again. Fire truck. They'd nearly run out of Time. Swerving, Jane fired her own string at the young man. North went for the queen, pinning her arms to her sides because string would be useless against those voluminous skirts. Whether the queen was so outraged at this awful breach of royal protocol that her legs gave way, or she tripped over her own dress was never clear.

To Jane, it all happened in slow motion. The queen began to fall forwards, her momentum taking North with her. They both toppled into the shimmer. The young man panicked, tore one arm free of the hardening string and aimed his long-barrelled flintlock at North.

Everyone and everything happened just a fraction of a second too late.

Jane was still festooning the young man with liquid string but he was running so fast it didn't have time to harden. She fumbled for her baton and as she did so, there was a blinding flash, a bang and a strong smell of gunpowder.

North, Marie Antoinette, Matthew and the bullet disappeared into the shimmer. With a cry, the young man hurled himself after them.

Fire-trucking fire truck! Jane hurled herself after him and

they all stumbled through together. Back to 1901. Back into the real world where their tech would work. Coms, scratchpads, sonics – the lot.

And a camera. Only one. But one was all it took.

14

The first indication Jane had that they were out of the time-slip was that she could breathe properly again. The tightness had disappeared. Life and colour had come back. She knew that because there was Matthew, sprawled on the brilliant green grass with bright red blood oozing from his arm. The young man's bullet had found a victim after all.

And sound had returned as well. Around them, women screamed hysterically. Marie Antoinette, on the ground and entangled equally in her own clothing and Officer North, was also screaming hysterically. The young man, now being competently zipped by Ellis and Luke, was sobbing – hysterically – hiccupping and trying to speak. In fact, chaos reigned. As it frequently did on a Team 236 assignment.

North, focused as always, disregarded everything going on around them. Seizing the queen's arm, she pulled her to her feet, because the most important thing was to secure the queen. Everything else, including Matthew bleeding on the ground, was secondary.

Luke rolled the young man over. 'You're under arrest, buster,' which wasn't the correct Time Police procedure but close enough for Team 236's purposes.

Jane knelt beside Matthew. Ellis and Luke had the young man, North had the queen, and crowd control was down to Grint and his team, who should be around here somewhere, which left Matthew up to her. The wound was high up on his right arm. She ripped at his sleeve, exposing a ragged and bloody gash.

Groups of people stood around, obviously stunned at the sudden appearance of these strangely clad people. Jane couldn't blame them. One minute they'd been enjoying a summer's afternoon stroll in beautiful and peaceful gardens and the next moment there were bleeding men, hysterical queens, and sinister black-clad figures sprawling on the ground in front of them. Discretion and caution were conspicuous by their absence.

Several women were still screaming in the approved manner. It would appear that in 1901, women were required to scream and faint at every opportunity. Jane ignored everything around her. Grint and his team would have her back.

She realised later, when she had time to think properly, that that was when it must have happened. At the time, she was too busy to notice. Blame would fly in all directions and at least one life would be changed forever, but that was for the future.

Major Ellis, leaving Luke to deal with the prisoner, took in the confusion around him and moved smoothly into damage limitation mode.

Discreetly, he opened his com. 'Grint, where the hell are you?'

'Approaching your position, sir. About a hundred yards to your right.'

It was on the tip of Ellis's tongue to ask why he wasn't here, dealing with the situation right now, but he refrained. Time for that later when Lt Grint would be subject to some very stringent questioning, and Ellis fully intended to be the one doing the stringent questioning.

Stepping forwards, he assumed what he hoped was a reassuring smile, summoned up as much of the French language as he could remember, and said, 'Please, *mesdames et messieurs*, relax yourselves. These ladies are actresses. Today they re-enact the part of Queen Marie Antoinette as she is seized by the brave citizens of France.'

Taking the hint, North pulled her cloak around her and endeavoured, very unsuccessfully, to look like a common citizen.

'The young man you see before you,' he gestured to Matthew, 'has been injured in his brave attempts to secure the rights of the citizens of France. His gallant comrade tends his wounds.'

Jane looked up from applying pressure and smiled as gallantly as she could.

'Please, I ask you all to compose yourselves and move on, that others may enjoy this . . .' he paused.

'*Tableau vivant*,' supplied North.

'Yes. This *tableau vivant*.' In English, 'Smile and wave, everyone. Smile and wave.'

They smiled and waved. With the exception of Jane, who couldn't feel that displaying her bloody paws would allay anyone's fears.

'Thank you, ladies and gentlemen, for your cooperation.'

Grint and his team arrived, skidding to a halt.

'Where the hell have you been?'

Grint was defensive. 'We got here as quick as we could.'

It wasn't Ellis's normal policy to argue in public, especially with another officer, but he was still suffering from the effects of the time-slip, he'd seen a member of his team shot, his assignment had fallen apart under his nose and he was very angry.

'As quickly as you could? We've located and identified the two Englishwomen. Lockland and North have managed to protect the queen from an assailant who shouldn't have been here. Yes, that's him there. The one who went on to shoot a member of my team. What's your info? Was he working alone? He's not a contemporary – where's his pod? What exactly have you been doing all afternoon?'

'Sir,' said North, very quietly.

The crowd, recognising angry authority when they saw it, obeyed the command to disperse, and the two teams soon found themselves more or less alone.

'All right?' said Jane to Matthew.

He tried to sit up, wincing with pain. 'Yeah. Stings like hell. Was it his flintlock?'

'It was.'

'Oh God, if the shot doesn't kill me then gangrene probably will.' He nodded over her shoulder. 'Trouble. You may have to utilise your Parrish-saving skills again.'

Luke was in Grint's face. 'Where the fire truck was our back up?'

Luke's fury cooled Ellis's temper. Someone should remain calm. 'Thank you, Mr Parrish. It's a little late to establish a perimeter, Lt Grint, but if you could check for possible accomplices, please. Thank you. Lockland, how's Farrell?'

'Conscious and complaining, sir.'

'Typical Time Police officer.' He turned his attention to

North, still supporting a white and shocked Marie Antoinette. 'We need to get her back as soon as possible.'

'Agreed, sir, and we can't go back the way we came. The time-slip has closed. We'll need to do it manually. Grint . . . where's your pod?'

Wordlessly, Grint gestured. Ellis turned to North, saying in a low voice, 'Get the queen out of here. You and Lockland. Quick as you can. Leave her where you first found her. She has to be arrested – it's a key point in history. Besides, if we don't get it sorted, then we'll have those clowns from St Mary's knocking on the door and no one wants that. I'll deal with things here.'

She turned an anxious face towards him. 'De Vaudreuil, sir? Is he alive?'

'Yes. We found him in a ditch not too far away. He was coming around on his own so we left him to recover and came to join you. Too late, it would seem. Off you go now.'

Between them, North and Lockland helped Marie Antoinette to adjust her dress. She was staring around in a bewildered, confused manner, obviously without any idea of what was happening to her. North spoke quietly to her in French, and she consented to be led away.

With Matthew in no immediate danger, Ellis turned his attention to the young man, now securely zipped and on his knees sobbing. Luke stood over him, making the flintlock pistol safe. Ellis nodded his approval. 'Keep an eye on him.'

With the situation secured, he gazed around. Apart from a few small blood spots on the grass, nothing remained to show a time-slip had occurred or that a temporally displaced member of the French royal family had ever been here. The site was clear.

All officers were aware that missions didn't always go to plan. Everyone had a bad assignment every now and then. There were occasions when the Time Police had no choice but to reveal themselves. Sometimes things could be glossed over with a plausible explanation – as now. Sometimes they had no choice but to send in a clean-up crew. That rarely ended well for anyone. Clean-up crews do what it says on the tin. Ellis sighed. This shambolic mission might well lead to his team's period of gruntwork being extended – at least until they'd expunged their sin. God, what a cluster-fire truck. A useful lesson in how things could go wrong at the very last moment.

Arriving back at TPHQ, the first thing Ellis saw was North and Lockland waiting for him. Both looked dusty and weary.

The second thing was Grint and his team.

The third was the medical team waiting to attend to Matthew.

Wiping his brow, he motioned for Grint and his team to remove the prisoner to the security department where he could expect to spend some quality time in their tender care.

Luke, supporting a bloody Matthew, volunteered to go with him to MedCen for treatment.

'Thank you, Parrish, if you would, please. I'll be along later.'

He turned to North. 'Tell me you got her back safely. That someone did something right today.'

'Yes, sir. She was in shock, I think. Probably no one's ever caught hold of her like that before. We were just in time. We could hear voices in the distance. Whether it was alarmed courtiers coming to warn her or the mob on its way to arrest her, we didn't stop to find out. Whichever it was, she's home and safe. For the time being.'

Ellis sighed and wiped his face again. 'Well, given what's about to happen to her, I think we were probably the least of her problems today. Well done, you two. Go and get yourselves cleaned up. I'd like your reports as quickly as possible, please.'

'How's Matthew, sir?' asked Jane, anxiously.

'His wound didn't look serious and I'm sure he'll be back with us in a day or two. Off you go, now.'

An hour later, enjoying a quiet drink by himself in the bar, he became aware of North approaching him. He sighed and put down his drink. 'Do we have a problem, Celia?'

'Just a very small one, sir.' She nodded over to where Grint and his team were enjoying a self-congratulatory drink. 'Are you aware Lt Grint appears to be taking the credit for capturing the young man at Versailles?'

He frowned. 'I haven't seen his report yet.'

'You won't, sir. His and his team's reports have gone straight to Commander Hay.'

He shrugged. 'Credit usually goes to the officer handing in the prisoner. And how much do we actually want to be associated with this one?'

She frowned. 'The perimeter was his responsibility. We should have been free to act without having to worry about the effect on contemporaries. Sir, I feel compelled to say his contempt for the historical aspect of our missions is beginning to affect his judgement. In my opinion. Sir.'

He nodded. 'Your opinion is duly noted, Officer North.'

One of the bar staff approached. He raised his voice to include them all. 'Message from Captain Farenden, sir. Could you, Lt Grint and Officer North please report to Commander Hay's office as quickly as possible, please.'

Grint looked pleased. Possibly he thought a commendation was in order.

'My compliments to Commander Hay,' said Ellis. 'I have a wounded team member to check on again. I'll be there in a moment.'

'Captain Farenden was explicit, sir. Immediately, please.'

Ellis and North exchanged glances. This sounded serious.

Captain Farenden stood up as they entered his office and gestured towards the commander's door. 'This way, please.'

They filed in and he closed the door quietly behind them.

Ellis, Grint and North were all field officers. Over the years they had all developed certain instincts. Quite a few of them were kicking in right now.

Without preamble, Commander Hay turned her screen for them to see. 'I'd like an explanation of this, please.'

The screen showed an enormous picture of Officer North wrestling with a particularly frantic-looking Marie Antoinette. Jane's legs were in there somewhere, but the star of the show was definitely Officer North. The headline screamed, '*Did Time Cops Cause French Revolution?*'

The only slightly smaller headline read, '*Undercover Cop Exposed in Time Cop Cock-up,*' with North's head carefully ringed so that less gifted readers could be in no doubt as to which of the two figures was the undercover cop in question.

North had gone white.

'Where did this come from?' demanded Ellis.

'Exactly my first question,' said Hay, coldly. 'My second was – who ran the perimeter?'

There was silence. North was unable and Ellis unwilling to speak. The silence dragged on and then Grint said, very reluctantly, 'That would have been me, ma'am.'

'How could you allow this to happen, Grint?'

'It was a very public spot, ma'am. There were a lot of people around. We weren't expecting a non-contemporary to come through. And I didn't know they had cameras in those days.'

'Did you run the scan? Did you locate his pod?'

'Eventually, ma'am, yes.'

'And? Where is it?'

'Gone, ma'am. By the time we arrived . . . We were delayed by events with the queen.'

'There must have been at least two of them. Because someone got that pod out of there.'

Grint had the sense to say nothing.

'Who took this image? The one now plastered all over the media.'

'I do not have that information, ma'am.'

'At what point, Lieutenant, did you run the scan to locate the pod?'

'After visual identification of the non-contemporary, ma'am. Once we realised he was also in the time-slip, we proceeded according to protocol.'

'So he was actually standing in front of you before you were aware of his presence? Despite the importance of ensuring no detail of the time-slip was changed, you failed to take basic precautions. Your first action on arrival should have been to run the scan. Which would have located the pod. Which would have alerted you to the fact there were illegals present. Which should have initiated stringent perimeter procedures. You should have cleared the area. You should have identified and neutralised the accomplice before he could do any harm. You did none of that. Basic procedures, Lieutenant, and you neglected every single one of them.'

Grint was rigid, staring at the wall over her shoulder.

Captain Farenden said sharply, 'Look at the commander when she is speaking to you.'

Grint swallowed audibly. 'Yes, ma'am. But as soon as he appeared . . .'

She slammed a drawer shut. 'Have you any idea what would have happened had his intention not been to save Marie Antoinette? That he was, in fact, nothing more than a romantic boy hell-bent on rescuing his goddess was good fortune we did nothing to deserve. Suppose he had shot her?'

Well, she died anyway so what does it matter? was what Grint was visibly refraining from saying.

Commander Hay drew a long breath. 'This, however, is not the most serious blow we have sustained today.'

Ellis looked down at the still silent North and felt his stomach lurch. He had a very good idea he knew what was coming and there was nothing he could do to lessen the blow.

There was a tap at the door and Captain Farenden ushered in Major Callen, North's immediate boss. Ellis now knew for certain what was to happen next.

'Lieutenant, you are dismissed.'

'Ma'am . . .'

'I said, dismissed. I now have to deal with the consequences of your carelessness and . . .'

'With respect, ma'am, no harm was done. The queen was saved. The time-slip closed.'

190

Hay slapped her desk and he jumped a mile. 'Get out of my office.'

The words reverberated around the room. Grint marched stiffly out through the door.

Commander Hay looked suddenly very tired. 'Shall we sit down?'

Wordlessly they sat.

Almost gently, she said, 'Celia, you know why you're here, don't you?'

North nodded.

Hay gestured to the screen, her voice grim. 'Someone, somewhere, was an accomplice. Waiting for Marie Antoinette to emerge from the time-slip and step into their pod. They'd saved her and they had a recorder to capture that special moment. Unfortunately, it wasn't quite the image they'd hoped for, but it was easily good enough to ruin the career of one of my most promising officers.'

Ellis sighed. Of course there would have been an accomplice. Someone standing by with the pod. Someone who wanted to record the moment of their success in saving the queen. Only there hadn't been a success, so there had been revenge instead.

North was still staring at the image, seemingly unable to tear her eyes away. Major Callen leaned across and blanked the screen.

Commander Hay continued. 'This picture was taken by the accomplice of the young man currently enjoying our hospitality downstairs. I received a message from him offering it to us in exchange for our prisoner. I'm sorry, Celia, I had no choice but to refuse. As you can see, he has taken his revenge.'

North nodded. Ellis could see her throat working.

'You know what this means, don't you?'

She swallowed audibly. 'It means I'm finished as a Hunter, doesn't it?'

'I'm afraid so, yes.' She turned to Callen. 'Major, I've tried every way I can to avoid taking this action, but I have no choice. Thanks to this image, Officer North's career as a Hunter is finished. The world has seen her face. Spectacularly so. Her value as an undercover officer is gone. It's not her fault and I'm desperately sorry, but from this moment on, anyone has only to run her image through facial recognition software to be able to identify her as a member of the Time Police. I would be allowing her to endanger herself and others if I permitted her to continue as a Hunter.'

If Major Ellis had been angry, Callen was furious. 'Commander, this is a . . .'

He stopped, apparently unable to find words.

'A waste. A massive, unnecessary waste of an exceptional officer. You're right. It is. A promising career has been stopped in its tracks.'

'Not necessarily,' said Ellis, angrily. 'This only means North can't continue as a Hunter. It doesn't mean she can't remain in the Time Police. I, for one, would be proud to have her back in my team. Anyone would.'

'Well, that is Officer North's decision, don't you think?' said Hay, gently. 'As far as I can remember, no one has ever returned to the ranks after serving as a Hunter. If Officer North chooses not to do so, then that is her decision. Perhaps we should leave her to consider her future in peace and quiet. Majors – if you could leave us for a moment, please. Yes, and you too, Charlie.'

She escorted them to the door.

Ellis turned, saying quietly, 'Ma'am, I'd like to remain, please.'

'No, Major, I don't think so. I think Officer North would prefer to be alone for a while.'

'I understand, ma'am, but . . .'

She glanced back at North, still sitting at the table, white and unmoving. 'The best thing you can do for her, at this moment, is give her the time and space to regain the face she likes to show the world, Major.'

He nodded and closed the door behind him.

Commander Hay said gently, 'Well, Celia? Tell me what you're thinking.'

For possibly the first time in her life, Celia North appeared uncertain what to do. 'Ma'am, I . . . I . . .' She stopped, swallowed, and tried again, more firmly this time. 'Commander, I can't . . .'

'Celia, be aware, it is only your time as a Hunter that is ended. There is still a place for you here in the Time Police. I would be extremely reluctant to lose an officer of your calibre – especially for such a reason as this. I know you must be devastated but . . .'

'Ma'am, I can't . . . I don't want to . . .'

Hay put her hand on her arm. 'No – I think I know what you're going to say, so please allow me to speak first. No matter what it is, I will not accept any decision from you for seventy-two hours. Go away. Calm down, because you're not as calm as you think you are. Try to think constructively. Don't brood. Come and see me in three days' time and we'll talk then.'

'I don't think I will change my mind.'

'Then that will be a decision taken calmly and rationally and after due consideration and I shall accept it.'

North focused hard on a small chip on the briefing table. 'No officer has ever commanded the Time Police without at least a short stint as a Hunter. Although not as short a stint as mine. My career is stalled. I'll never go anywhere now. Logically I should remove myself from the Time Police. I'll be an embarrassment to you and other officers. I don't want officers trapped behind me, unable to advance simply because I can't move on. I think it's best for everyone if I leave.'

Hay was silent for a moment and then said, 'I will accept your resignation when you make it for the right reasons. Those are not the right reasons. And for your information – there will be no pity. A great deal of sympathy, yes, but sympathy is not pity and I'd like you to remember that.'

North's numbness was wearing away. There was a great pain in her heart as if it had been dealt a heavy physical blow.

She made a huge attempt at a smile. 'Actually, ma'am, I was thinking it's rather like Kipling, isn't it?'

Commander Hay blinked. 'Is it?'

'"If you can meet with Triumph and Disaster / And treat those two imposters just the same." When you promoted me to the Hunter section, I thanked you politely and carried on with my day.' She stood up. 'With your permission, now that I've been demoted, I'll thank you politely and carry on with my day. If you'll excuse me now.'

'Three days, Officer North.'

'Yes, ma'am.'

*　　*　　*

194

On the other side of the door, Captain Farenden was speaking to Major Ellis. 'I've reserved Briefing Room 3 for you, Matthew. You won't be disturbed there. And I've arranged for some coffee to be sent up.'

'Thanks.'

Captain Farenden folded his arms. 'This is a shit business. What will she do, do you think?'

'I don't know. I suspect her instinct will be to get as far away from us as possible.'

'Will she go back to St Mary's?'

'That's what I'm afraid of.'

'Try to talk her out of it.'

'I will, but this has got to hurt, Charlie. And it's not her fault, but people won't know that. I can just hear some of them saying they always knew female officers couldn't hack the Hunter Division. It's all so unjust. That stupid bastard Grint . . .'

Ellis looked up as the door opened and she emerged. 'This way, please, Officer North.'

She still had that strange, blind look about her. 'If it's all the same to you, sir . . .'

'It is not. This way, please.'

Once in the briefing room, he poured her some coffee. 'Here, drink this. You're looking very shaken and I'm concerned for you.'

She made a huge effort that was painful to watch.

'Coffee? This is very kind of you, sir. Every mission should end with senior officers bringing coffee to the other ranks. Are there any biscuits?'

The hand holding her cup was very nearly steady.

'I'm so sorry, Celia. This happened while you were serving on my team and I feel responsible.'

To someone who didn't know her well she was almost back together again, functioning nearly normally, but he could see the lost look in her eyes. She shrugged, saying lightly, 'My life has always gone exactly as I've planned. I've never actually experienced a setback before. It will be quite interesting to see how I deal with it, don't you think?'

He sipped his own coffee. 'Listen, I've had some thoughts about what you could do next. It's not exciting or glamorous, but I think, after today, that's not what you need.'

'What is it?'

'Well, I wondered if I could, perhaps, welcome you back into my team. I know that this all happened while you were out with us, but we would all be very pleased to have you back again.'

'They'll be qualified in less than three weeks and then no more team.'

'Well, that's the beauty of it. It'll give everyone a few weeks for things to settle down a bit because there's going to be a lot of bad feeling flying around – mostly directed against Grint. You'll have had a chance to think and make your decisions when you're less . . . stressed.'

North made no response.

'And,' he added, well aware he was at risk of overselling, 'you did once say you were becoming fond of them. Like pets, I think was the expression you used.'

She very nearly laughed. 'Yes, I believe that was what I said.'

'There you are. And this is the Time Police. Who knows what could happen in a few weeks?'

'Yes, indeed,' she said brightly. 'If whole careers can go down the tubes in a single afternoon, who knows what could happen in a few weeks?'

'Celia, if you want to talk, then I'm available. If you don't want to talk, I'm still available to sit in silence for as long as you like. You are not alone in this. Please promise me you'll think carefully before coming to a decision.'

She nodded and Ellis could see she very much wanted to be alone. 'I shall. And thank you for the coffee, sir. If you'll excuse me now . . .'

Back in Commander Hay's office, Captain Farenden was also pouring out coffee. Commander Hay was looking out of the window, her back to the room. Without turning, she said, 'Did I make a mistake when I gave Grint a second chance? Go on, Charlie, say I told you so.'

'I would never do anything so dangerous, ma'am. Although I wish I'd been wrong.'

'So do I,' she said shortly. 'And it's not me who's paying the price for my bad judgement. He's lost me a valuable officer.'

'You think she'll leave?'

'Oh yes. Her pride won't allow her to stay.'

'Will she go back to St Mary's?'

'I don't know. What reason could she give?'

'They wouldn't care. Anyone leaving the Time Police would be welcomed as a hero by St Mary's.'

'Damn and blast Grint.'

'What will you do with him?'

She sighed. 'I think . . . I shall leave him to the mercy of his peers.'

'You're throwing him to the wolves, ma'am? He won't have an easy time. North isn't loved but people respect her. She'll get a lot of sympathy.' He considered. 'Whether she wants it or not.'

15

No one ever knew how the details of North's misfortune got out, but get out they did. As Captain Farenden had said, North was not loved, but she was respected, whereas Grint was neither loved nor respected. Nor was he socially sensitive. It took him a while before he noticed that no one wanted to eat or drink with him. That people were blanking him in the corridors. That conversations died away as he approached and then started up again when he'd passed. North, on the other hand, was surprised to find people nodding at her as she passed, or shunting up to make room for her in the bar.

Luke in particular was furious, railing against Grint and vowing retribution.

'And keep Kohl, Rossi and Hansen out of my way as well,' he said to Jane, viciously kicking a shoe across his tiny room. 'Fire-trucking pillocks.'

Even Jane was conscious of a slow, boiling anger within her. That this should happen to North, of all people. Word on the street was that she would leave, and there were few enough women in the Time Police these days. And North was Jane's role model. North had forced the Time Police to accept her on her own terms, and they had. She was respected. People listened when she spoke. She was everything Jane wanted to be, and if this could happen to strong, resourceful North, then what could happen to Jane?

Unofficially, every member of a team had a specific function. Luke was their usual team leader – for which both Jane and Matthew were grateful. Matthew handled the more technical side of the mission and Jane, following in North's footsteps, had taken it upon herself to provide the background and historical details. For which, Luke had informed her, no one would thank her, but it had given her an identity – a place in the team. And, occasionally, it was useful – as in identifying the Apostle spoons Imogen had stolen.

Now, it seemed to Jane, the Time Police had demonstrated very definitely that historical background and scholarly details had no part in their assignments. That was not their function. If that was indeed the case, then what was Jane's role here? What other aspect could she make her own? She wasn't the muscle – the thought was laughable. She wasn't a particularly good shot and she had no combat skills. She felt the familiar stir of anxiety. She had no discernible abilities bar one and that one did not appear to be valued in any way by her colleagues.

TPHQ, situated in the former Battersea Power Station, was a big building with a large footprint, containing many floors. It should be perfectly possible for someone to avoid someone else for a considerable period of time, should they choose to do so. Jane could only regard it as bad luck when, the very next day, Team 236 rounded a corner to find themselves face to face with Grint and his team. All of them. There was a moment's silence as each team took stock of the other. Luke, Jane and Matthew were outnumbered and outgunned, but as Luke explained later to Major Ellis, they had right on their side.

To help fullfill the professional needs of the Time Police, there are any number of private rooms where disputes could be settled in a measured and constructive manner. It seems odd, therefore, that so many confrontations should take place in the corridors, but they do.

'Well, this is new,' said Luke chattily as the two teams glowered at each other. 'Normally it's us that gets set on. Makes a change for us to be doing the actual ambushing.'

'How far we've come,' said Matthew, his arm still in a sling but willing to work around that.

'Yes,' said Jane, nervous but resolute. 'Our trainers will be so proud.'

The three of them stood shoulder to shoulder.

'We're not looking for trouble,' said Grint.

'Well, you've found it, nevertheless,' said Luke. 'You should set up a perimeter – you know, so we're not disturbed. Oh, wait – you don't know how, do you?'

Grint bristled. 'What's that supposed to mean?'

'Exactly what you think it does. Everyone knows to keep things simple for Grint and his team.'

'That's Lieutenant Grint to us,' said Jane. 'He's an officer.'

'Yeah?' said Luke. 'Well, other things float to the surface besides the cream.'

Grint's face was suffused with colour. 'Parrish, you're on a charge.'

Luke shoved his hands in his pockets. The very picture of privileged insolence. 'If it's all the same to you, I'd rather be charged by a proper officer.'

201

Here we go, thought Jane, keeping her weight on the balls of her feet in the Time Police-approved manner and wishing very much that the next twenty minutes were over with.

Grint drew himself up, making an attempt at authority. Fixing Team 236 with a glare that significantly failed to intimidate them, he said, 'I don't know what's going on here but I'm ordering you men to disperse immediately.' His gaze fell on Jane. 'And non-men too.'

No one took any notice. Both groups moved closer and Jane found herself face to face with Grint himself.

He loomed over her. 'Push off, Lockland, before I make you cry.'

'Really?' said Jane, vibrating with equal terror and righteous belligerence, and as much in his face as she could manage, given that he was nearly twelve inches taller than her. 'You really want word to get out that you've been flattened by a non-man?'

He smirked. 'I don't think so, Lockland. You can barely reach . . . oof.'

His knees sagged.

'Oh, nice one, Jane,' said Luke in admiration. 'Good to see someone else on the receiving end of your signature knee.'

There was no time to say any more. Jane found herself dragged out of the fray by Rossi. 'You're going to get hurt. Stick with me. We'll do a little light grappling and honour will be satisfied on both sides.'

'I don't think so,' said Jane, thoroughly fired up by now and with that strange feeling of invincibility often experienced by those about to encounter a splashy and painful death.

'Jane, I'm not going to hit a wo—'

'Really? I have no problems hitting a man.'

'Yes, and everyone starts calling me *Wife-beater Rossi*. I don't think so.'

Grint straightened up and pushed Luke against a wall. 'Right – that's enough. Team Two-Three-Six is on a disciplinary charge. All of you.'

Luke pushed him back. 'Great. Our chance to tell everyone officially what really happened at Versailles.'

Grint hesitated.

'Yeah,' said Luke. 'Now what are you going to do?'

Grint stared for a moment and then turned on his heel and limped away. 'That's right,' yelled Luke. 'Walk away. Do a half-arsed job. Again.'

'Parrish, what's all this noise about?' North appeared around the corner. 'What's going on here?'

'Nothing,' said six voices in unison.

'Where's Lt Grint?'

'He had to leave,' said Jane, hastily.

North eyed them all. Team 235 shuffled their feet. Team 236, bloody and pugnacious, stared back. One wrong word . . .

She looked around to make sure no one else was in earshot. 'I understand this situation, but remember this – Lt Grint is a good officer and anyone can make a mistake.' She looked at both teams. 'One day it will be one of you. Treat him as you would expect to be treated yourselves and have some compassion. That's all I'm going to say. I don't want to see any of you still here by the time I've finished this senten—'

She was talking to herself.

*   *   *

203

That evening, North sat alone in her room, staring at a piece of paper with two columns – one neatly headed 'Leave' and the other, 'Remain'. The rest of the sheet was blank.

Someone knocked at her door. She ignored it. They knocked again. More loudly this time.

Opening the door, she sighed. Her evening was about to become even worse. Standing before her was Luke Parrish – a little battered from the day's activities but otherwise looking quite normal. For the Team 236 value of normal.

They looked at each other.

'We clubbed together and bought you a present,' he said, offering a small wrapped box. 'Or a bribe, if that's what you're more comfortable with.'

Automatically, she took it. 'Thank you.'

He waited, smiling hopefully, and so she unwrapped it. And stared.

'It's a mug,' he said, helpfully.

'So I see. Why does it say Two-Three-Six?'

'Not just Two-Three-Six. If you turn it around it says 2^2 x 59. Look.'

'Yes.'

'That's Two-Three-Six.'

'Yes.'

'And just here, look. 11101100. That's binary for . . .'

'Two-Three-Six. I think I'm beginning to get it. And this Greek bit here?'

'δύο τρείς έξι means Two-Three-Six.'

'And look – CCXXXVI . . .'

'Let me guess . . .'

He pointed. 'They all mean Two-Three-Six.'

204

'I see. And the significance of Two-Three-Six?'

'Aha – glad you asked me that,' said Luke, who had been hoping to avoid this part of the conversation. 'Two-Three-Six is a happy number.'

'I know I'll regret this. A what?'

'A happy number. You know – a happy number is a natural number in a given number base that eventually reaches one when iterated over the perfect digital invariant. Those that don't are known as unhappy numbers. I'm really surprised you didn't know that,' said Luke, who had spent most of the afternoon memorising that particular snippet.

North raised an eyebrow. 'I challenge you to say that again.'

'Actually, I don't think I could.'

'I'm disappointed you didn't have all that happy number stuff put on the mug as well.'

'Well, we considered it, but the bloke said it would have to be the size of a cauldron to get it all on.'

She regarded the mug. 'This is . . .'

'Surprising?'

'Lovely.'

'You still sound surprised.'

'Well, I am.'

'No need to be. This mug is just what you needed. Trust me, if anyone's an authority on what disappointed women want, it's me.'

'Ah – do I deduce you and the blonde in Logistics have reached a parting of the ways?'

'Alas . . .'

'You do tend to leave a trail of broken hearts in your wake, don't you?'

'I don't know why you're assuming it's her heart that's broken. If you want to know the truth, she ditched me. I gave her my heart and she's pushed off with a Records clerk. Can you believe it? I'm devastated.'

North held out the mug. 'Do you want it back? Your need sounds much greater than mine.'

He laughed. 'You should hang on to that. I'm not noted for gift giving. It'll be worth a bit one day.'

'After your demise, presumably.'

'Well, obviously we'll have to wait a while for that.'

'Not too long, we can only hope.'

'That rather depends on whether you're going to rejoin our little team, doesn't it?'

'And why would I want to rejoin your little team?'

'So that you can devote yourself to my preservation. A fit and proper ambition for any right-thinking woman.'

She opened her com. 'Lockland, where are you? I need you to save a life.'

'Oh,' said Jane. 'He's with you, is he, ma'am? On my way.'

Parrish took himself off, grinning in a manner that made normal people want to kick him. North closed her door. Casually she shoved the mug on to a shelf out of the way, reseated herself at the table and picked up her pen again. Thirty seconds later, she screwed up the paper, reached up for the mug, placed it carefully next to her kettle and gazed at it for a moment. Then she grabbed her jacket and left, because, for some reason, unexpectedly becoming the owner of the world's most 236-themed mug had enabled her to come to a decision. She headed for the bar and the first person she saw was Lt Grint. She slid on to a bar stool next to him. 'There you are.'

He scowled and made to move past her.

'Let me buy you a drink.'

Grint's fragile social skills proved not fit for purpose. 'I . . . um . . . no.'

North ignored him. 'A single malt for me and whatever he's having.'

The barman moved away.

'Smile,' she said, smiling. 'Everyone's watching us.'

'I don't want your pity.'

'I don't have any pity. In fact, I'm famed for it.'

'Look, I . . . you must know I didn't . . .'

'No, I know.'

'Is this some St Mary's thing? You know . . . *loving your enemy.*'

'Categorically not. Enemies of St Mary's tend to have horrible things happen to them. As I'm sure you're aware.'

'Then why?'

Their drinks arrived. She clinked his glass. 'You're about

to start a new job in a new department. It would be fatal for you to go into it with half the people there feeling they can't trust you to watch their backs. Fatal for you and for them as well. As Time Police, we can't afford not to trust each other with our lives.'

'I've been thinking about that and . . .'

'You've been thinking about declining the position.'

'Well . . .'

'That would be a mistake.'

'I . . .'

'You are an excellent officer. The Time Police need people like you.'

'Actually, I was wondering . . .'

'Yes?'

'Whether I'd ever get to finish a sentence?'

'Unlikely – and that is a St Mary's thing.'

'Look . . .'

She sipped. 'No need to thank me.'

He frowned, perplexed. 'Why are you doing this?'

She leaned towards him. 'Because here I am, drinking with you, and everyone is watching us – and believe me, they are watching us – and thinking we're good friends. But mostly because now you owe me a solid. And one day I will remind you of it.'

She smiled, finished her drink and walked away.

16

It would appear everyone considered the incident closed and Jane could only regard it as bad luck when, two days later, while waiting for the lift, the doors opened and she found herself face to face with Lt Grint.

They stared at each other, mountains of guilt quietly accumulating on either side. Social etiquette books are mysteriously silent on the correct form of greeting one whose male dangly bits had unexpectedly encountered the female knee. Specifically, his dangly bits and her knee. The silence stretched on. Jane was very conscious her eyeline was only around his chest area. And also, that she was alone.

Staring at him, it suddenly dawned on her that Grint was waiting for her to step aside so he could exit the lift. As normal people would do. Her brain threw out the appropriate commands to her feet but these appeared to have taken the scenic route because nothing happened.

Eventually, with an exasperated sigh, Grint leaned down, clamped her upper arms tightly to her body, picked her up and deposited her in the lift. Remembering her training, Jane immediately assumed Defensive Position 2.

He stared at her in astonishment. 'What are you doing?'

'Defending myself,' she said in her best *bring it on, buster* voice which, to everyone else, was almost indistinguishable from her normal voice.

Grint sighed. 'In that case, untuck your thumb, straighten your wrist and remember your left arm is supposed to be an iron bar protecting your upper chest . . .' he glanced quickly away from Jane's upper chest, 'throat and face. You're not looking at your watch. And your feet are too far apart. Other than that, the rest of it was rubbish too.'

Jane slowly drew herself up which meant her eyes were now level with Grint's nipples.

He stared at the control panel. 'Which floor?'

'Oh. Um. Four.'

He stabbed at the button and the doors closed.

'I'm going to the library,' she said, because she'd been brought up always to be polite and considerate of other people's feelings. How this reconciled with the recent dangly bits incident she had no idea.

Grint grunted.

'You're very lucky, you know,' she said.

He scowled at her. 'How's that?'

'You could be sharing an enclosed space with Luke Parrish.'

He shrugged. Jane decided her social commitments had been met and abandoned further attempts at social intercourse.

The silence became painful. Watching Grint from the corner of her eye, she could see he was working up to saying something. Luke would have made a comment about hearing the gears engage. Matthew would have watched with bright-eyed interest. Jane stared at her feet.

'Sorry.'

She jumped. 'What?'

'Sorry.'

'What for?'

'North.'

'Well . . .' Jane fumbled for words. 'That's very . . . good of you, but surely North is the one . . .'

'Done it,' he said, staring at the doors.

'Well . . .' said Jane again. 'Good.' And wondered how it could take a modern lift so long to get from the ground floor to the fourth. She'd been in here for *years*.

The lift juddered to a halt. The doors opened. Two officers, about to step inside, took one look at the occupants and remembered stairs were the healthier option. In more ways than one. They stepped back and the lift resumed its interminable ascent.

'Anyway,' mumbled Grint. 'Just wanted to say . . .'

'No,' said Jane, adrift on a social sea. 'I . . . um . . .'

'*You* are an embarrassment,' said Bolshy Jane.

She pulled herself together. 'Apology happily accepted, sir. No need to say any more.'

And then, having said to say no more, she found herself saying, 'Did it hurt?'

Grint grinned. 'Like buggery.'

'Sorry,' she whispered.

He nodded.

Finally . . . finally . . . the lift halted and the doors opened. A long corridor stretched ahead of them. Neither moved.

Eventually Grint sighed and lifted Jane out into the corridor, setting her gently on her feet.

She said, 'Um . . .'

He nodded.

She turned and walked away. One hand holding the doors open, Grint watched her go.

Ellis reported that Officer North had put in a request to rejoin his team and he was happy to welcome her.

'I know it won't be for long, ma'am, but I think she'll be more able to make rational decisions about her future by then.'

Commander Hay was dubious. 'I suspect her instinct will still be to leave us. I shall rely on you to nip that in the bud, Major. Speaking of making decisions concerning the future, I don't appear to have received any Form D12s from your team. Time is getting on, so if you can let me have them as soon as possible . . .'

'I haven't had them myself, ma'am.'

'Oh? Is there a problem?'

'Absolutely not, ma'am. I'll get on to it right away.'

'No rush. I'm giving everyone a weekend pass. I don't think either team has had much in the way of leave since they joined up.'

Ellis had to acknowledge the truth of this. On paper, every officer was entitled to twenty-four hours after every jump to reset their internal clock. If operational requirements permitted, of course. Mostly they didn't.

She was still speaking. 'Both teams – yours and Grint's. I think time and space for a little calm reflection would be good for everyone. Starts 1700 hours Friday evening and ends at 0800 Monday morning. Where and when people go is not an issue – just don't let them start any wars.'

'An excellent idea, ma'am. I'll go and spread the good news.'

*   *   *

212

'Where will you go?' he asked North.

'Home, I think,' she said. 'Spend some time rethinking my life and making some decisions.'

'That sounds drastic.'

She held his gaze. 'I wondered if you would care to join me. For the weekend.'

It was on the tip of his tongue to say, 'No, thank you. It's probably not appropriate,' when he had a second thought. Hay had said that where and when people went was not an issue. And she'd more or less ordered him to order Celia to stay. And – the tiny thought came from nowhere – how would he feel if she left the Time Police altogether . . . ?

He played for time. 'I'll need to check where and when my team intend to spend their leave, of course . . .'

'They'll need to do without you sometime, you know.'

He sighed. 'Yes, I know.'

'Your chicks will leave home. Do you think you might be developing empty-nest syndrome?'

He grinned. 'Something like that. Half of me looks forward to returning to more conventional teams, but the other half . . .'

'Is it because of Matthew? You were his mentor when he was young.'

'No, not really. He's growing up fast and seems to be able to hold his own these days. Have you noticed – he's even quite chatty sometimes? Two, sometimes three sentences.'

'Still hasn't had his hair cut.'

'And soon not to be my responsibility. And it won't be a problem if he goes to work with the Time Map. He'll be tucked away out of public view and it won't matter so much.'

'Very true. So – would you like to?'

'Oh . . . um . . . yes . . . thank you. I would. Care to join you, I mean.'

Team 236's plans were simple. Matthew was returning to St Mary's to visit his parents and Lockland was to accompany him. This was not her first visit to St Mary's. Ellis had paused before signing her request but Hay had said people could go where they liked. At least Parrish was remaining on the premises. He had, apparently, an exciting weekend planned for the brunette from IT. Bets were being placed around the building. And no one cared about Grint's team. Yes, he, Ellis, could enjoy a guilt-free weekend.

He and North were dropped off in a small wood on the Blackbourne estate. Emerging from the trees, he experienced a small shock. He knew that North was actually Lady Celia North, daughter of the late Earl of Blackbourne and sister of the current Earl of Blackbourne, and should therefore have been prepared for the stately pile sprawling haphazardly in front of him.

North was watching him.

'Got to love a house with its own turrets,' he said, hoisting his bag on his shoulder.

'And a bell tower,' she said, pointing.

'Does it still work?'

'Of course. It's to warn of invasion. You know – the Scots, the French, the parliamentarians, the Jacobites and so on. Archie's currently locked in mortal combat with the Inland Revenue and we'll use it to warn of their approach.'

'So you can start heating the boiling oil and winding up the trebuchet.'

She frowned severely. 'You can't fire missiles at the Inland Revenue.'

'Sorry.'

'You can't get clearance over the walls. The angles are wrong.'

She spoke with authority and for some reason, he had the feeling this had already been tried.

'Sorry,' he said meekly. 'My parents live in a semi in the Midlands and hardly anyone ever besieges them.'

'Lucky devils. This way,' she said, leading him up the drive to the front door.

There was a strong family resemblance between all of them.

'And this is Archie,' said North, introducing the individual known to the rest of the world as the Earl of Blackbourne. 'And Davey, my other brother.'

They all shook hands. Both brothers regarded him in silence. Ellis braced himself.

'Do you ride?' asked Archie.

'Yes.'

'Do you shoot?' asked Davey.

'Yes.'

'Do you hunt?' asked Archie.

'Yes.'

'What do you hunt?' asked Davey.

'People.'

They stared at him. 'And how do you do that?' asked Archie in disbelief.

'Very successfully,' said Ellis, answering a slightly different question. 'You?'

There was a bit of a silence.

'Don't make me come over there,' said North, without even looking up from saying hello to the dogs.

'What exactly *do* you do, Mr Ellis?'

It occurred to Ellis he hadn't asked North what she'd said her job was.

'It's major,' said North. 'Same as you, Davey.'

'So what *do* you do, Major Ellis?'

'Pest control,' he said, and folded his arms.

'So I'd watch my backs if I were you,' said North.

They turned back to Ellis. 'Do we need to watch our backs?' enquired Davey.

'No,' said Ellis. 'You don't really register on my pest radar.'

There was a long silence and then they both burst out laughing.

'Better than the last one,' said Davey over his shoulder as they strolled away.

'Do you have brothers?' asked North.

He shook his head.

'Would you like some?'

'Everyone does as they like here,' said North, after he'd unpacked. 'Ride, read, eat, sleep, shoot rats round the back of the barn, take up flower arranging – whatever floats your boat.'

They were in the small family sitting room. A room about twice the size of Ellis's parents' entire house. He wondered about the dimensions of the large family sitting room. The room was shabby but comfortable, furnished with saggy furniture, overstuffed bookshelves and what seemed like hundreds of family photographs and images. Everything was slightly dusty and most horizontal surfaces wore a thin coating of dog hair.

On the mantelpiece stood a picture of a young boy, grinning gap-toothed at the camera. A small vase of flowers stood nearby. Something in its positioning told him it was important.

'Who's that?'

She turned to look. 'Oh, that's my other brother. Charles – known as Chuffy. He's not here. Shall we go outside and have a drink in the garden?'

She produced a bottle of wine and two glasses, and trailed by what, to Ellis, seemed like every Labrador in the northern counties, they walked out through the French windows and across the terrace. Crossing the lawn, they found a battered-looking wooden table with four mismatched chairs set under a shady tree and made themselves comfortable. The dogs found a patch of shade, collectively retracted their undercarriages and fell deeply and doggily asleep.

'This is very nice,' said Ellis, looking up at the rambling building around them and thinking nice must be the understatement of the year. The building had surely passed 'nice' about six hundred years ago.

'Originally built in the late fourteen hundreds,' said North, unconsciously confirming his thoughts. 'Then again in the fifteen hundreds. And again in the sixteen hundreds. Then added to in the seventeen and eighteen hundreds. Mostly rebuilding because the family invariably backed the wrong side in whatever wars were going on at the time. We were for Mathilda, not Stephen, until it was too late. We were Yorkists under the Henrys and then Lancastrians under Edward. We backed the northern Catholics against Elizabeth, and declared for the king against Cromwell. We stood solidly behind both the Young and Old Pretenders and just generally got it wrong every time. The only time we did get it right was against Hitler. Fortunately, the then countess couldn't stand either Edward or Wallis Simpson so there was no danger of us becoming embroiled with the Nazis. Oh, and we were a first-aid post and hospital during the Civil Uprisings so the east wing took a bit of a bashing. Thirsk sent a lot of their people here to recover so we did at least get it right that time. Otherwise, we're a bit of a disaster when it comes to picking winners. Most of us have to take a blood oath never to back horses. Archie says that even today most of the aristocracy look to see what the Norths are doing, then head firmly in the opposite direction.'

She sipped her wine, staring up at the building. 'It's not huge, but it seems so because it rambles about all over the place – that's because usually not only could the earls and their spouses not stand each other, but they never liked their offspring either, so everyone wanted as much space as possible between themselves and the rest of their family. Half the house is practically in the next county. Anyway, picturesque makes up for grand, or so they tell me.'

Major Ellis was very fond of his parents and the three-bedroomed semi-detached house they'd lived in all their married life. Not grand, nor rambling, nor picturesque. If, for some reason, his parents weren't speaking to each other, then his father sat in the garden shed for half an hour. Or until his mother took him out a cup of tea – whichever came first – but it was as warm and welcoming as his parents could make it. He remembered the sacrifices they'd made to give him an education. How they'd struggled to give him as good a start in life as they could manage.

'You're very lucky to live here.'

'I am, yes. The boys, less so. Especially Archie.'

He sipped his wine. 'How so?'

'He was born to be Earl of Blackbourne, but he really wants to be an architect. He did the training. He even worked in London for a couple of years. He was good. He enjoyed it. Then our father died, and like it or not, he wasn't an architect any longer – he was officially the Earl of Blackbourne, with everything that entails.'

Ellis gestured around. 'Living here, for example.'

'Yes. Living here. Attending to estate duties. The social round. Obligations. Responsibilities. Some people like that sort of thing. Archie just wants to design buildings.'

'What does Davey do?'

'Davey was in the army. He loved it but he had to leave.'

'Why?'

'He served – all the boys do – but he's the spare. Until Archie marries and has a son, Davey's next in line. We can't afford to have anything happen to him until the succession is assured, so out he came.'

'What will he do?'

'I don't know. He certainly doesn't.'

'What about Chuffy?'

She twisted her glass on the table. 'Chuffy's dead.'

He sat up with a jerk. 'Celia, I'm so sorry. Why . . . ? How . . . ?'

'He died . . . oh . . . about twelve years ago now.'

'How?'

She nodded across the green lawns. 'Drowned in the lake.'

He followed her gaze. 'That one?' and then kicked himself

for his stupidity. How many lakes could one family possibly have?

'Yes, that one. There's another smaller one on the other side of the Rose Garden, but no – that one. You'll notice, when Mama comes home this evening, she'll always sit with her back to it. And she rarely ventures around this side of the house at all. She sits in the White Garden when she's home.'

'What happened? If you want to tell me.'

'He fell in. She ran to save him. Everyone ran. She just didn't get to him in time. She swam and dived for hours looking for him. Convinced he'd bob to the surface at any moment – and of course, he never did. They recovered his body a day later.'

'I'm so sorry.'

'I wasn't home at the time. I was at school.'

'How old was he?'

'Nine years old. Oh, he could swim. He was quite good. But not that day.'

She fell silent.

'Would you like me to make a clumsy effort to change the subject?'

She smiled. 'That would be a very good idea.'

'So, Archie the earl, Davey the . . . ?'

'Ex-Major.'

'What about you, Celia . . . ?'

'I'm not sure. I have no calling. I don't want to be an architect or a soldier. I especially don't want to be an earl.'

The words, 'And now I'm not going to be a Hunter,' hung unspoken.

She seemed to shake herself. 'But we can't walk away, can we? Living here is painful for Mama – because of Chuffy

– that's why she spends most of her time in London. But we can't sell up and move. We don't own the house – it's entailed so the house owns us and we must do our duty – that's what we're bred to do.'

He considered this for a while. 'Where do you see yourself ending up, Celia?'

She smiled suddenly. 'Wherever I like. There's no pre-ordained path for me – for which I am extremely grateful. It used to be that it was the girls whose lives were so restricted. There would be a little light schooling – certainly not enough to clog up their tiny brains – then they'd be presented at court and dynastically married off to some chinless oik. A year later they'd produce the heir and then two years after that, the spare. Duty done, they'd be permitted a couple of discreet affairs, then a spot of drug or alcohol addiction, followed up shortly afterwards with death by boredom. Now, thank God, we can do as we please. Look at Mama – I'm not too sure what she gets up to in London – it's classified – but I know she's something big at Whitehall. No, these days it's the boys who have the short end of the stick.'

He stepped out on to thin ice. 'Will you stay in the Time Police?'

She smiled. 'If I want to.'

'The smart money says you'll be running the place one day.' And could have kicked himself again. That might now never happen.

She changed the subject for him. 'And what about you, sir?'

'Celia, if I have to call you Celia then I'm sure you can call me Matthew.'

'All right. What about you, Matthew? Do you want to run the Time Police?'

'Well, possibly. One day. Although I look at what Hay goes through every day and I'm not sure I could handle it. The urge to make stupidity a capital offense would be overwhelming. And as for dealing with all those politicians and other idiots . . .'

He broke off, remembering, possibly slightly too late, that Miss North's mother was an important if undisclosed member of the government of this Time, and slightly changed the subject. 'We could approach the top job by different paths. It could be interesting, don't you think, to find ourselves competing for Hay's job one day?'

She looked at him speculatively. 'Yes, one day I may have to consider the necessity of moving you out of my path.'

'I look forward to seeing you try.'

They both smiled at each other.

Seeing the smile, he was content to leave the subject, saying, 'Do you feel sorry for them? Your brothers, I mean.'

'No – Archie is hard-working and conscientious. He'll make the best of it and be an excellent Earl of Blackbourne. Davey will turn his energies to something constructive – Mama will see to that. It all seems a bit gloomy at the moment but they'll survive. I'll survive. We all do, don't we?'

'We do,' he said, putting his glass down. 'And speaking of surviving, I've had an idea.'

She threw him an amused look. 'Not "a brilliant idea"?'

'Well, modesty forbids me saying "yes", but yes.'

She laughed. 'Go on then, tell me this brilliant idea.'

'Well, not so long ago – before you joined the TP – we enjoyed – or endured, however you want to describe it – the presence of a certain Dr Maxwell from St Mary's. She was with us for another reason completely, but her cover was to provide us with historical context. Surprisingly, the cover proved quite successful. She remembered her audience and kept things brief and punchy – a quick resumé of the circumstances leading up to whatever particular event we were about to investigate – what we could expect to find when we got there – and even a quick "what happened afterwards", just to give us some perspective. There was a certain amount of resistance – we're the Time Police, after all – but there's no doubt that the more thoughtful officers found it very useful. I was wondering – and feel free to say no if you want to, because it's only an idea – whether you couldn't do something very similar. Provide historical briefings. You've done it before and I think it would be of enormous benefit to the organisation as a whole and something you could make your very own. It's something you're uniquely qualified to do.'

He picked up his glass again and peered into the depths. 'And having planted the idea in your mind, I shall leave you to think about it.'

'Clever.'

'I did the *How to Get Your Own Way Without Leaving a Pile of Bleeding Corpses in Your Wake* course last year. And, I have to say, continuing the modesty theme – I aced it.'

She laughed. 'The irony is that I always said I'd get Maxwell's job one day.'

'Seriously, Celia, think about it.'

She nodded. 'I will.'

She wasn't given the time. Her two brothers appeared from the French windows and crossed the grass towards them.

Archie folded his arms and stared down at them. 'There's a sinister, black-clad individual at the front door who I feel sure is something to do with you two,' he said. 'He wants a word with Major Ellis.'

Ellis looked up in surprise. 'He asked for me by name?'

'He did. Davey will show you the way.'

Ellis put down his glass and got to his feet.

'I left him in the hall,' said Davey.

'Unwise,' said Ellis. 'He'll have had half your silver by now.'

Archie watched them walk away and then sat down in Ellis's seat. 'Want to tell me what's going on?'

North shook her head. 'Can't. Sorry.'

'No, not about the job, stupid. About what brought you here.'

'Oh. Bit of a thing at work.'

'No, not about the thing at work.' He nodded meaningfully after Ellis. 'Him.'

'Oh. No, not really.'

'OK, have it your own way, but you've been recalled, haven't you?'

'Looks like it.'

'You'll miss Mama this evening.'

'Yes, tell her I'm sorry I didn't get to see her this time.'

'Are you in trouble?'

'If you mean have I done something wrong, then no. I have a series of decisions to make, and I thought, heaven knows why, that a little peace and quiet might make things easier.'

'And has it?'

She sighed. 'I suspect I'm not going to get the chance to find out.'

Emerging ten minutes later, Ellis looked for North, who was still in the garden. 'We've been recalled.'

'Now?'

'Immediately. No messing. They're waiting for us.'

'So,' said Archie, to North. 'You're someone important.'

She headed towards the house. 'Not really.'

The brothers looked at Ellis.

'She is extremely important,' said Ellis. 'To many people. In many different ways. If you'll excuse me, I must get my gear together.'

As he and Officer North walked back towards the woods he said, 'I'm sorry I won't get to meet your mother.'

'Yes – given Parrish's remarks on the advisability of meeting the mother before committing with the daughter – the missed opportunity is regrettable. From your point of view, of course.'

He said nothing. The jury was still out on the extent or even the existence of North's sense of humour.

17

In just a few short hours, life at TPHQ had taken an abrupt turn for the worse.

'Well now,' said Commander Hay brightly, endeavouring to generate some enthusiasm for her second PMT in a week. 'Our last meeting was interrupted, for which I apologise. Let's see if we can get this finished today, shall we?'

Captain Farenden, making ready to take notes, glanced at his scratchpad, stiffened and quietly left the room.

Commander Hay watched him from the corner of her eye. 'Now then, shall we start with individual departmental budgets? I believe we're looking at a carry-forward of . . .'

'Ma'am,' said Captain Farenden, returning, 'your urgent attention is required.'

She glanced at his face and then said, 'It would appear we are fated, gentlemen.' She began to shut down her data stack. 'If you would all excuse me, please.'

Once again, the PMT officers gathered their papers and filed out.

She leaned back in her chair. 'Go on then, Charlie, hit me with the bad news.'

'It's very bad, ma'am. A friend of mine is in the River Police. Sometimes she's in a position to give me a heads-up.'

Commander Hay was seized with a sudden foreboding. Leaning forwards, she said, 'Go on.'

'This morning, two naked bodies were taken from the river at Vauxhall.'

'Go on.'

'They've been knocked about. Whether that was the river or . . .'

'Just say it, Charlie,' she said wearily.

'Ma'am, from the preliminary descriptions – I think it's Klein and Nuñez.'

'Were they found at the same location?'

'Handcuffed together, ma'am.'

'Sending a message.'

He was silent.

'Give me a moment, will you?'

'Of course, ma'am.'

He left the room. Commander Hay rose stiffly from her seat, turned and looked out of the window. The shining Thames flowed as it always had, thick with shipping. A River Police launch raced downriver, bouncing across the water. A long line of laden barges was being towed slowly in the opposite direction. On the north bank, almost directly opposite, a water taxi cast off and followed them upriver. The sun shone – the Madrid airship chugged sedately overhead. Business as usual for the rest of the world.

For a long time, she stood motionless, looking but not seeing, until she drew a long breath and turned back to her desk. 'Could you come in, please, Charlie.'

They both seated themselves and looked at each other.

'Shall I set things in motion, ma'am? Body recovery procedures, notifying relatives, section heads, paperwork and so on?'

She said flatly, 'No.'

'Ma'am?'

'It's not going to make any difference to them, poor beggars. Let's keep a lid on things while I implement our next move.'

'Which is?'

'I want two more people in the field as quickly as possible. Before we're officially notified of the deaths of our two officers.'

'Who? Who else have we got? They were Hunters, ma'am. Among the best we had to offer.'

She regarded him grimly. 'Exactly. I think that's the problem, Charlie. All our Time Police officers look like Time Police officers. There's something about us that is instantly recognisable.'

'Well, yes, ma'am. That's the whole point.'

She stood up and began to pace. 'I don't want you to do anything, Charlie. Don't claim the bodies. Don't start the wheels turning. Officially, we know nothing. We'll wait until we're formally notified that the bodies of two of our officers have been recovered. However long that takes. Can you trust your friend to say nothing?'

'I can, ma'am, yes.'

'Then we'll wait before taking any action regarding Nuñez and Klein. Once we know officially, Major Callen and I will contact the relatives. We'll formally express our sympathies and send the appropriate people to assist with funerals and financial arrangements. All the usual stuff. Do they have any relatives?'

He looked up from his scratchpad. 'Klein lists an aunt in Stuttgart and Nuñez has a father and sister. Both in this country.'

She nodded. 'Now – we need to move quickly. For the time being, this is between the two of us, Charlie.'

'Not even Major Callen?'

'No.'

'They're his people, ma'am.'

'I know.'

There was a delicate pause. 'Is this because of the incident in the Pod Bay? When he pulled a gun on you?'

'At this point, I'm not trusting anyone. Either Nuñez and Klein betrayed themselves – a possibility but not likely – or someone betrayed them. I know we joke about it, Charlie, but there are still a lot of people in this building who don't like the way I do things.'

'Not to the extent of betraying their own, surely?'

'We're the Time Police. We're brutal and ruthless and we do things the Time Police way. No – I'm not taking any chances with this one. And I'm already thinking about their replacements.'

Farenden sighed and stretched his bad leg in front of him. 'It's a pity we can't utilise Imogen Farnborough in some way. She already had the entrée. She was rich, well-connected, selfish, out for a good time, heedless of consequences – and did I say rich? She would have been ideal bait. But, she's in prison, and we, as the ones who put her there, are unlikely to be her favourite people at the moment.'

Hay regarded him enigmatically. 'Oh, I think we can go one better than Imogen Farnborough, don't you?'

It took him a second to grasp her point. 'Ma'am, you cannot be serious.'

'Ask yourself, Captain. Who have we got who still don't look like real Time Police officers? And probably never will?'

They looked at each other. Captain Farenden consulted his scratchpad again. 'We sent them on leave, ma'am. Before someone got hurt.'

'Recall them. And Ellis as well. He'll have to know what's going on, but I have no doubts about him.' She sat up and began to move files around her desk.

'I thought you didn't want to draw any attention.'

'I want new people in place before we're officially informed of our two officers' deaths. I want these illegals – whoever they are – to be so busy looking for our replacement agents that they don't notice the two already under their noses. And then I want their balls in my blender. Get on it, Charlie.'

Luke was outraged. 'Worst timing ever. I was so nearly there. We'd had dinner – which was not cheap, let me tell you. My wit and sparkling conversation were just about to pay off, and then some bloody great hairy officer comes barging into her room *at the very worst possible moment*. She screamed. He knocked over some ornament she was apparently most fond of in all the world. She screamed again. For a completely different reason that time, and I was the one who got my ears boxed. I didn't even have any trousers on. How is that right?'

'Commander Hay wants to see us,' said Ellis, ignoring this. 'Now.'

'Oh God, she hasn't received a formal complaint about me, has she? It's not my fault the bloody vase-thing went flying. And it can't possibly be valuable – it was the ugliest thing I've . . .'

'Is there the very faintest possibility you could ever think of someone other than yourself, Parrish?'

'Well, no, I shouldn't think so.'

'Find Farrell and Lockland and meet me in Commander Hay's office.'

Jane panicked immediately. 'Are we being discharged? Is it because of the thing with Grint? I'm sorry if I hurt him. I did apologi—?'

Luke raised his finger before she could dig herself any deeper. 'Lockland, a couple of points. Never admit anything until you're directly accused. And not even then if you can help it. Always let everyone else do the talking until you know exactly what's going on and how much trouble you're in. Once that's established, issue a blanket denial.' He turned back to Ellis. 'My apologies. Lack of experience on the part of Lockland here.'

Ellis shifted his weight. 'Parrish, shut up. This way,' and ushered them into Hay's office.

On the point of saying, 'Shutting up now, sir,' Luke paused. The atmosphere in the room was heavy. He looked around. No one appeared angry or irritated or retribution-seeking. They looked serious.

'Shall we sit down,' said Hay, and they sat at her briefing table. Jane pulled out her trusty and by now quite dilapidated notebook.

'No notes,' said Captain Farenden. 'Not for this one.'

Jane looked around. Ellis, North, Luke and Matthew. The whole team was here. What could they possibly have done that would warrant a confidential interview with Commander Hay?

Captain Farenden began. 'This is for your ears only. Nothing is to be discussed outside this room. Acting on intel provided by Imogen Farnborough, we sent in two Hunters.' He hesitated and looked at Hay.

'Full disclosure, Captain.'

'Their task was to pose as the sort of people who might be tempted into indulging in a little Temporal Tourism, infiltrate the organisation, report back here and be on the inside when we eventually took them down.'

He stopped. Jane looked at Hay's impassive face.

'This morning, we received unofficial word that two bodies found at Vauxhall are probably Nuñez and Klein. They've been murdered.'

The room was very silent.

Luke shifted, uneasily. 'May I ask a question?'

Commander Hay nodded.

'Vauxhall – not that far away.'

'No. Under the bridge.'

Luke frowned. 'You could say, almost on our doorstep.'

'You could.'

'Could it be – is it possible – they were intended to wash up around here?'

'That is a possibility, yes.'

'Someone wanted to send the Time Police a message.'

'Perhaps, yes.'

Parrish nodded and said no more.

Under the table, Jane clasped her hands in her lap. They were very cold.

'What exactly do you require from my team?' asked Ellis, softly.

Farenden closed his file and pushed it slightly to one side.

'Imogen Farnborough was just what they were looking for. Rich, heedless, irresponsible, a bit of an adrenalin junkie . . .'

'Shame we banged her up, then,' said Luke, bitterly.

'Not really,' said Farenden. He looked directly at Luke. 'Here in the Time Police, we have our very own rich, heedless, irresponsible adrenalin junkie. Someone we feel they would be unable to resist targeting.' He looked at Jane. 'And his girlfriend.'

Jane filled the silence by turning scarlet.

'What about me?' said Matthew.

'Two points,' said Farenden. 'Your wound isn't yet healed, and you will have another part to play in this operation.'

'Which is?'

Ellis sighed. Briefings and their conduct had been covered during his team's basic training. There was a form to be followed. The mission statement, allocation of personnel and resources, programme of events, individual responsibilities, questions at the end. A rigid format. It wasn't supposed to be . . . a chat.

Commander Hay spoke. 'Trainee Farrell, it is essential you continue with your gruntwork as if your teammates are still in place. You'll be seconded to work on the Time Map because of your injury. You must maintain the fiction that this team is still functioning normally – a fiction Major Ellis and Officer North will also do their best to support. Your names will continue to appear on all appropriate rotas, staff lists. To all intents and purposes, you are all still here, still working, and everything is normal.'

Ellis cleared his throat and said carefully, 'Ma'am, while I myself consider my team equal to any situation they may encounter, in this instance . . . and yes, I do realise it's their inexperience and generally . . . informal . . . approach that makes them so ideal for this assignment, I . . .' He stopped, lost in the complexities of his own sentence, and finished with, 'They haven't even completed their gruntwork yet.'

'Actually,' said Luke, leaning forwards, 'can we assume that accepting this mission will automatically conclude our gruntwork? We'll be fully-fledged Time Police officers at the end of it?'

'Yes,' said Hay, without hesitation. 'You may assume that.'

'Would that be,' said Jane, 'because we probably won't survive, so the question is academic?' and then realised, to her immense relief, that she hadn't actually asked the question out loud. Fine undercover agent I'm going to make, she thought. No training, no skills, no hope. My one talent is that I look so useless no one will ever suspect who I am.

'So play to your strengths,' said Bolshy Jane, who seemed more and more inclined to shove her oar in these days. 'Everyone agrees you're not a proper officer. You don't look like a proper officer . . .'

'. . . And now you'll never live long enough to become a proper officer,' said Wimpy Jane.

Bolshy Jane regarded her severely. 'Oh, *you're* back, are you?'

'I'm just saying.'

'Well, don't. This is grown-up stuff and the last thing Jane needs is a wimp like you inside her head. Go away and embroider something.'

I had my quarterly medical last week, thought Jane. Why has no one ever picked up on my schizophrenia?

'The upside,' continued Bolshy Jane, 'is that you'll be able to spend a few extra weeks with your team.'

'And Luke,' said Wimpy Jane, slyly. Jane wouldn't have believed it of her, but it was true. A couple of extra weeks with Luke and Matthew, doing the job she liked before shuffling off into the Slough of Despond. Or Records, as the Time Police had designated it.

'Well, at least get some information before imperilling your life,' said Wimpy Jane, and she was right. Jane tuned back in again.

'So,' Luke was saying, and Jane could see the glitter in his eyes. 'I've been handpicked for this mission because I'm rich, selfish, entitled and irresponsible. Do I understand that these qualities – the ones the Time Police have been trying so hard to thump out of me over the last six months – have now suddenly rendered me your favourite person?'

'Parrish,' said Ellis, warningly.

'No,' said Hay, 'it's a valid point. Yes. The very things that make you such a pain in the arse also make you perfect for this mission. Nuñez and Klein were excellent officers but they didn't have the advantages of your background. Luke Parrish is already well known as . . . as someone who enjoys a good time and is prepared to pay for it.'

'And Jane – she's been selected because she looks the very opposite of a good Time Police officer – as you're always telling her. Suddenly, that's a good thing?'

'Yes. Can you do it?'

'I *can* do it,' he said angrily, 'but you're asking the wrong question – *will* I do it?'

'Parrish,' said Ellis, sharply this time.

Commander Hay raised her hand. 'No, Trainee Parrish is perfectly correct. The qualities that make him – both of you,' she nodded at Jane, 'so imperfect for the Time Police render you perfect for this assignment. And yes, I am as aware of the irony as you. And while we're speaking so frankly to each other . . .' she drew a breath, 'please do not forget that the last officers assigned are almost certainly in a morgue somewhere. They were Hunters. They were the best. And now they're dead.'

'Do we have any choice?' demanded Luke.

'In this case, yes. You might struggle to believe this, Parrish, but sending young officers to their deaths is my least favourite thing.'

'And if I . . . we . . . say no?'

'Then I'll simply have to come at the problem from another direction.'

'Can you do that?'

'Yes, of course. We are the Time Police.' She paused. 'But somewhere out there is an organisation – possibly more than one – which preys on the rich, the bored, the mentally fragile, the obsessed – and is none too fussy about bringing them home again. Imogen Farnborough was an idiot, but no one deserves to die just because they're an idiot. How long would she have lasted in the 17th century? Without her mother's intervention – if we hadn't pulled her out – what sort of life would she have had to endure? How many more Imogens are out there, do you think? And how many of them have powerful mothers like the Right Honourable Mrs Farnborough? How many do we never know about? How many never come home?'

'Like Klein and Nuñez?'

Ellis intervened. 'Parrish, that's enough.'

Jane sat welded to her seat, listening to the argument rage around her. She saw Imogen, bloody, battered, humiliated. Hay was right. How many more were out there? Abandoned once they'd paid the money. Or left behind on purpose. She could imagine the conversation.

'Here's a lot of money. It would be really useful if so-and-so could just . . . disappear. You know? No mess. No fuss. No questions. *No evidence.*'

'I'll do it,' she said suddenly, sitting up straighter in her chair. 'You're right, Commander. They must be stopped. It's our job. If Luke doesn't want to do it then I'll work with someone else.' Honesty compelled her to add, 'Although I'd prefer to work with Luke.'

She stopped speaking, her face a flaming red.

Commander Hay nodded. 'Thank you, Lockland.' She turned to Parrish. 'And what about you? Will you do it?'

He smiled his charming smile. 'How gratifying to note the Time Police are finally coming around to our way of doing things.'

Ellis stirred. 'Parrish.'

Luke smiled. 'Yes, I know. I'm on report. If I live that long. I'll think about it and let you know.'

Commander Hay narrowed her eyes. 'Parrish – this is the Time Police. You'll do as you're bloody well told.'

'No, I won't. Not in this instance. I'm still under training.'

Commander Hay leaned menacingly over the table. 'This is not the moment for your particular brand of insolence, Parrish.'

He sat his ground. 'Commander, I am simply requesting a moment to consider whether this team, out of everyone in

237

this huge organisation you command, are the proper people for the job, and if I feel we are not, then it is my duty to inform you.'

She turned to Ellis. 'Get them out. Get them out now before I hurl him from this building myself.'

They left. Rather more speedily than they had entered.

North followed them out but Ellis lingered.

'Well,' Hay said, raising an eyebrow, 'will they do it?'

'I think so, ma'am.'

'Make sure they do.'

Ellis frowned. 'I'll arrange a tail they'll never know anything about.'

'No.'

'No tail?'

'No tail, no back-up, no communication, no anything. They must appear to be completely what they are: two young people out looking for a good time. I won't have anything connecting them to us.'

'Ma'am, I must protest. They don't have a clue what they're getting into. They'll be completely exposed.'

'What would you have me do, Major? They're Time Police officers. As am I. As are you. And we get the job done.'

Ellis was angry. 'Whatever it takes.'

'Yes, Major. Whatever it takes.'

He turned on his heel and strode from the room.

Captain Farenden followed him out and closed the door firmly behind him. 'Well, thanks for that, Matthew,' he said, seating himself at his desk.

On his way out, Ellis paused. 'What did *I* do?'

'I was planning to present next year's budget figures to her this afternoon and now I'll have to put that off for at least a week. I've got an entire in-tray of things I was going to quietly slip past her this week. Half an hour ago she was perfectly calm – ten minutes with you and your team and she's threatening to fling people off the battlements.'

'Parrish had a point. Basically, she was saying, "You're a waste of space, Parrish, but we need you to go out and die for us."'

'I don't think that was quite the message she intended.'

'Intended or not, that was my understanding. I'm pretty sure it's his as well.'

'Well, you can't deny they're all a bit weird.'

'I don't deny it at all. I also know they get beaten up in the corridors more often than any team we've ever had. I know they're regularly scorned, laughed at, despised and underrated. And now, suddenly, the very virtues that the Time Police have been trying to eradicate – and not gently – are the very virtues the Time Police suddenly need. You can't blame my team for being a touch on the stroppy side.'

He turned to go.

'Where are you going?'

'To find my team and calm them down. You might want to do the same with your boss.'

North was waiting for him in the corridor.

He looked around. 'Where have they gone?'

She indicated with her head. 'To the park, I think. I thought it best to let them have some time to themselves.'

'Good call.'

'So – my particular role?'

He shook his head. 'To stand back and let them get on with it.

239

And before you give me that whole *mess with me and I'll drag your bollocks out through your left ear* thing, it's my role, too.'

'Sir, at the very least I assumed you and I would be the tail they didn't know they had.'

'No.'

'No? But . . .'

'No. To quote Commander Hay – they're completely on their own.'

'But . . . reporting back to us . . . safe extraction . . .'

'No contact of any kind.'

'So . . . what *is* our role in all this?'

'The most difficult. Yours will be to keep an eye on young Farrell and mine . . . mine, I suspect, will be to bite my finger-nails until all this is over.'

18

Major Ellis eventually found Team 236 in Battersea Park Zoo, just a little further along the river, standing in front of a large paddock full of rabbits, miniature donkeys, guinea pigs and some dismayingly ferocious South American chickens.

'There she is,' said Jane, pointing to a truly vast white rabbit. 'She's had her litter, then.'

'Are you sure? She's still looking enormous,' said Matthew, peering through the fence.

There was a lot of counting on fingers.

'Yes,' said Jane. 'She must surely have had it by now.'

'I tell you she hasn't,' said Luke. 'Look at the size of her.'

'There you are,' said Ellis, behind them. He flourished a take-out tray. 'Fancy a coffee? My treat.'

Luke turned, his eyes hard and a new determination around his mouth. Jane and Matthew lined up at his shoulders.

Ellis sighed. *Now* they decided to become a proper team. And with a proper leader, too. He led them to a quiet area and they sat under a tree.

'Before you start,' he said, pulling the heating tab on his coffee, 'Commander Hay has just lost two good officers. And you can't just wander around shouting, "Look at us – we do things differently," and then be surprised when she recruits you because you do things differently.'

'Is she very angry?' asked Jane, apprehensively.

'Well, she didn't pick up her paper knife. That's always a bad sign. Charlie Farenden would have had you out of the door like a shot. Yes, she's angry, but she was angry before and not all of it was directed at you. Parrish, promise me you'll never volunteer for diplomatic work.'

'I doubt I'm going to live long enough for that to become an option.'

'You'll do it then?'

He looked at Jane and Matthew. 'Yes – we'll all do it.'

'Right. Finish your coffees, then let's go back and get started.'

Back at TPHQ they ensconced themselves in a briefing room.

'So how does this work?' asked Luke. 'What's the plan? Do we come up with something or do we have something imposed upon us? Because I have to say, I don't think traditional Time Police tactics have worked so well up to now, have they?'

Ellis looked at him. 'I rather suspect Commander Hay will want to have an input but I see no reason why you shouldn't come up with your own game plan. It'll be good experience for you, even if it's not used.'

'Who usually devises this sort of thing?'

'Well, Hunters usually sort themselves out. Other teams have their officers draw up a plan of action, which they then implement. If you'd paid attention during your training, you'd know there are set procedures for set situations. However, you've been selected because you're unconventional officers, so you may as well come up with an unconventional way forwards as well.'

Luke looked at the other two, who nodded their consent.

'Something I should mention,' said Ellis quietly, 'you'll be on your own. No back-up and no lines of communication. Nuñez and Klein were reporting in and we suspect something might have been intercepted.'

Matthew frowned. 'Either that or they gave themselves away somehow.'

'That is also a possibility.'

'So we're really on our own,' said Luke.

'I'm afraid so. Does this change anything? Speak now and I'll cover you as far as Hay's concerned.'

They looked at each other and then shook their heads. 'We'll sort ourselves out,' said Luke. 'Like Hunters.'

'Have at it,' said Ellis, getting up. 'Just watch where and when you discuss things. Nothing outside of this room, and nothing beyond the three of you, me and Officer North, for obvious reasons. Run everything by me when you've got something and I'll run it past Hay.'

'Why?' said Luke, bristling. 'You just said we could sort ourselves out.'

'Because – and again, I'm sure we covered this during training – she commands the Time Police and anyone attempting to implement any course of action without her knowledge, let alone her consent, will have an excellent opportunity to observe just how unpleasant she can be when she really puts her mind to it. And remember – keep it under your hats.'

'Yes, we know,' said Luke. 'After all, it will be our lives on the line.'

'Let's hope it doesn't come to that,' said Ellis.

The door closed behind him. Team 236 looked at each other.

'We need sandwiches,' said Luke. 'And coffee. Lots of paper and things to write with. In different colours. Not your notebook, Jane, because we'll have to shred everything afterwards.'

'Or burn it ourselves,' said Matthew.

'Yes, a better idea. We certainly won't be shoving any of this down the corridor incineration chute.'

'And we only work here in Briefing Room 3,' said Jane. 'If anyone asks, we've been tasked with analysing the Versailles time-slip and what went wrong. Part punishment, part training.'

'Yes,' said Matthew, 'then when I trot off to the Time Map to do some theoretical work on time-slips no one will be surprised.'

'I don't think anyone's surprised by us any longer anyway,' said Jane, gloomily. 'Did you know there's a sweepstake running on exactly how we'll manage to screw up our next assignment?'

'We don't screw up,' said Matthew, annoyed. 'That's what's so unjust. We get the job done. They just don't like it because we don't get it done the way they think we should get it done.'

There was a short silence as they considered this last sentence. 'Yeah,' said Luke. 'And look where that's got us.'

Gloom descended again.

'Right,' said Luke, rousing himself. 'We play to our strengths. Matthew, you're in charge of refreshments. Jane, you're in charge of writing everything down, and I'll tell everyone what to do. We'll make a list of our assets, our talents and so forth. Then we'll make a probably very much longer list of all the things we don't have and can't do – so we know what to avoid.

Remember, nothing is too weird or too stupid to be considered. And . . . go.'

And go they did. They started after breakfast each morning, covering every flat surface in Briefing Room 3 with at least two layers of planning notes, all of which was to be carefully burned at the end of each day. A procedure which, they discovered, was not the best way to dispose of vast amounts of secure paperwork.

Major Ellis, watching them attempt to dry themselves out, gave them to understand that they were never, ever to do that again and a portable shredding machine would be made available for their use immediately, because attempting to burn huge quantities of paper in an indoor environment was now absolutely forbidden by order of Commander Hay and what the hell had they been thinking and were they aware they'd managed to set off the fire alarms and activate the automatic sprinkler system for the entire floor? People were looking for them, he added, menacingly. And not in a good way. He ended his bollocking with the observation that he would not have thought they could possibly make themselves any less popular, but, against all the odds, they'd managed it somehow, and look at this mess, and a hundred yards of sodden corridor carpet would have to be taken up and replaced because it smelled as if every cat in Battersea had pissed on it. And then died.

Jane sighed. 'Are we on report again, sir?'

'Almost certainly, but not until after your mission.'

'Well, there's an incentive to return safely,' said Luke.

Ellis paused. 'You will return safely. I wouldn't let you do this if I didn't think you could pull it off.'

'And because Hay told you to.'

'No.' He sighed and sat on the edge of a table. 'Believe it or not, there have been several instances where a team leader has declined an assignment with thanks.'

'On what grounds?'

'Grounds they have felt justified their actions.'

'And she had them shot, presumably.'

'No. Hay is a first-rate commander. She trusts her officers and it's a two-way process. It has to be. If I didn't think you could do this, I would have said no. On your behalf.'

'So if we fail . . .'

'If you fail then address your complaints to me.'

'Posthumously, presumably.'

He sighed. 'I have a horrible suspicion the silence of the grave will have no more success keeping you quiet than I've been able to achieve, Parrish, so yes, feel free.'

Two days after the unfortunate incident with the automatic sprinklers, Team 236 waited outside Major Ellis's office, ostensibly to hand over the results of their time-slip investigations.

'I'll do the presenting,' Luke had said to Jane and Matthew. 'Because in public situations, Matthew has a vocabulary of four words and Jane's cheeks will set the sprinklers off again.' No one disagreed.

They filed in to face Commander Hay and Major Ellis.

'Here's our idea,' said Luke, without any preamble. 'Jane and I will occupy my old flat on the river. It's still empty and tailor-made for our plans.'

'And where have you been for the last six months, as far as the outside world is concerned?'

'Rehab,' said Luke, promptly. 'That old standby. And it will make sense to everyone. Obviously dear old Dad shoved me into rehab after I was involved in an unfortunate incident and someone . . . died. Everyone knows about it. No one will be surprised. They always said I was just rehab waiting to happen.'

'Some people might think you've been in prison.'

He shrugged. 'Still not a problem.'

'And was Lockland in rehab with you?'

Everyone looked at the world's most unlikely rehab occupant.

'Actually,' said Luke. 'We've been rather brilliant. Since Jane has unaccountably refused to assume the role of girlfriend . . .' he paused for comment but none was made, 'she will be my sober counsellor.'

'Your what?'

'Sober counsellor. That's a person who monitors someone who's been in rehab and is now ready for the outside world but can't quite be trusted. Jane will be providing me with much needed moral strength and guidance and keeping me out of trouble. So not a huge change for her.'

Jane swallowed and spoke. 'It's a good reason for not letting him out of my sight, sir. And ma'am. I'm not glamorous enough to be his girlfriend – no one would believe that for a second – but I could easily be mistaken for some sort of chaperone.'

'And brains of the outfit,' said Matthew.

Hay turned to Matthew. 'And your particular role will be?'

'Just what you suggested, ma'am. Keeping the home fires burning. Carrying on as if Luke and Jane are still in the building somewhere. And working with the Time Map.'

Luke picked up the thread again. 'Jane and I move in to my

247

old flat and indulge in a period of conspicuous consumption. You know – *here I am* – *back on the street and looking for a good time* sort of thing.'

'And you think you'll be contacted by these illegals?'

'Well, Eric Portman was. And they allowed him to involve Imogen, so I don't see why they wouldn't jump at Jane and me. No pun intended. That's our plan, anyway.'

Ellis and Hay waited but it was apparent no more was forthcoming.

'Is that it?' demanded Hay.

They nodded.

'It's very loose,' complained Ellis.

'It needs to be,' said Luke. 'We don't want to tie ourselves down to a course of action that may not be appropriate.'

He sighed. 'You are still aware your lines of communication will be non-existent? You will be completely on your own.'

'Yes. We'll be exactly what we appear to be – a recently released playboy looking for something to spend his money on and his conscientious and long-suffering sober counsellor.'

'And if you do manage to secure the information we need – what is your exit strategy?'

He shook his head. 'There's no reason why, having obtained everything you need, Jane and I can't just jump into a water taxi and come home.'

Ellis made no comment at Luke's use of the word 'home'. He looked at Jane. 'Lockland?'

'We won't be going anywhere near the King's Arsenal, sir. Or any of the places mentioned by Imogen Farnborough. Too suspicious for words. We're going to make ourselves accessible and wait for them to come to us.'

Hay looked dubious.

'As you said, ma'am,' said Jane, feeling the flush start, 'if Luke hadn't joined the Time Police, then with his track record he would probably already have been contacted. He's exactly the sort of heedless, selfish, not very bright but extremely rich person they're looking for.'

Matthew grinned at Luke who said, 'Yes, there's been a lot of discussion along those lines over the last forty-eight hours.' He looked at his teammates. 'No one held back.'

'So, other than that, you have nothing further. No contingency plans, no exit plans . . .'

'No fixed plans of any kind,' said Luke. 'We will respond to circumstances as they arise.'

'What about Lockland's employment records and so forth?'

Matthew produced a data stick. 'I've had that covered. Jane has been working at the Tall Trees Clinic for the last six months. Her work is exemplary; she's regarded as quiet but effective. Luke is her first major client. Before she was at Tall Trees, she was with a psychiatric unit in Herefordshire for six months, and before that at Thirsk University doing post-grad work. There's lots of other more personal stuff on there – exam results, links to friends and family social pages, awards, school prizes, holiday holos – enough to establish Jane as a real person.'

Major Ellis took the data stick. 'And what do you expect me to do with this?'

'Have it all uploaded, sir, including to the Tall Trees personnel database.'

'You omitted the word "illegally" from that sentence.'

'We are the Time Police,' intoned Luke. 'We do whatever it takes.'

'Including involving the Time Police in criminal acts.'

'Because we're utter bastards, sir.'

Ellis sighed. 'You think it will pass muster?'

'Depends how well IT can do it, sir.'

Ellis slipped it into his pocket. 'Anything else?'

Luke delved into his pocket. 'Yes – for that added authenticity, Jane and I will be wearing these.'

He produced a pair of proximity bracelets.

Proximity bracelets are commonly used when two or more people are required to remain in close . . . well, proximity . . . to each other. Parents disentangling their giggling toddlers for the umpteenth time after they had chosen a separate route around a lamp post had discarded leading reins and adopted proximity bracelets with huge relief. Rumours they could be adapted to give a mild electric shock have, so far, remained unfounded. They were also in use in such establishments as rehab units as discreet monitoring devices.

Commander Hay poked one with her paper knife. 'Where did you get these?'

'Anonymously through the online ordering service – Orinoco.' He picked them up and put them back in his pocket.

Commander Hay looked at them. 'I'm going to give you one last chance to step back from this. You're young, you're inexperienced, and no one will blame you in any way if you've had second thoughts now you've had a chance to discuss the mission in more detail. I'm going to ask each of you – Parrish and Lockland, do you have confidence in your plan – such as it is?'

Luke nodded. 'I do, ma'am.'

'And Lockland? You're quite happy to do this? If you're not, then say so now. Please speak honestly.'

If Jane had been flushed before, she was quite composed now. 'Thank you, ma'am, but I have complete confidence in our plan and my colleagues.'

'Good for you,' said Bolshy Jane.

'You're going to die,' said Wimpy Jane.

Shut up the pair of you, thought Actual Jane.

'Farrell?'

'Well, obviously I wish I was going with them, but we're all playing to our strengths and mine is the Time Map. Besides, I'm wounded.' He flourished his sling. 'No one will notice we're not around as usual – it's not as if we have any close friends here – or even any friends at all – so I don't see a problem.'

Commander Hay regarded him. 'And you're all right with your colleagues out there, on their own, out of touch . . .'

Matthew shrugged. 'I'm not happy about it at all, ma'am, but any sort of contact with us increases their chances of being discovered.'

She nodded. 'Any questions, Major?'

Ellis shook his head. 'Let me make one thing perfectly clear: you are responsible for your own extraction. I trust you to choose your perfect moment. Be aware of the implications of outstaying your welcome.'

They nodded.

'You are completely on your own.'

'The strength of our plan,' said Luke.

'And its weakness. One more time – you are aware of and accept the implications of being out of touch with this organisation?'

Luke nodded. 'We are.'

'Very well. Be ready to go at a moment's notice. And good luck.'

Twelve hours later, Matthew had been drafted to the Time Map and Luke and Jane were out of the building.

19

'And here we are,' said Luke, flinging open the front door. 'Home sweet home.'

Jane stared around. After her tiny cubicle at TPHQ, Luke's flat was vaster than a very vast thing. She stood on the threshold, completely overwhelmed.

Nearly every outside wall was a series of gigantic windows. Light streamed through the apartment, illuminating gleaming wood, fabulous textiles, brilliantly coloured rugs in all shapes and sizes, original art – even books. And not the *books by the yard provided by the interior designer* books but proper books, with colourful jackets and creased spines. Luke Parrish read books. Who'd have thought?

She looked down at her feet, reluctant to sully the beautiful floor with her unworthy shoes.

'Let me show you around,' he said, taking her arm and urging her inside. 'Hall.' He gestured about him so she could appreciate the hallness of her surroundings.

'Mm,' she said, politely. 'Very nice.'

'You ain't seen nothin' yet. This way.' He led her down the hall, casually dropping his backpack on the way. Trees *died* for this floor, thought Jane. 'Living room over there . . .' Jane looked at the three massive sofas. One each and one left over for Matthew – if they survived the next few weeks. And they were cream. Who has cream sofas? And more importantly – who has *three* cream sofas?

Someone who didn't have to keep them clean, obviously. And not a red wine stain in sight.

Jane stood, almost too petrified to move.

'And here we have the kitchen-diner . . .'

Jane tried hard not to be knocked sideways and failed. Dismally.

'Not bad, is it? Then through here . . .' he guided her through an arch into another hall she hadn't seen yet, 'the bedrooms.'

'Ah,' said Jane, feeling her usual blush coming on. Until this moment the sleeping arrangements were not something she'd given any thought to.

'Mine's through there . . .' He pointed to two massive oak doors at the end of the passage.

Jane stopped. The word 'mine' implied there would be a 'yours' which was reassuring, but she couldn't help feeling he could at least have made a small effort to lure her into his lair.

'But you don't want to share his room,' objected Wimpy Jane.

'But *she* wanted to be able to reject him, not the other way around,' said Bolshy Jane.

'Will you two shut up,' cried Actual Jane.

'Eh?' said Luke, startled.

'Nothing.'

'You worry me sometimes, Jane,' he said. 'Anyway, the guest room,' he opened a door, not as big and imposing as his

254

own bedroom door but biggish and imposing-ish nevertheless, 'is here. Nice view of the river.'

'I had a nice view of the river before,' said Jane, determined not to be impressed. 'We all did, remember?'

'Yes, but now you'll have time to look at it occasionally. From your very own wrap-around veranda.'

She looked at the giant bed. 'Is this where you put your . . . friends?'

He grinned at her. 'Don't be silly, Jane. My friends are usually in with me. Being friendly.'

She blushed again. 'Exactly how many . . .' The words were out before she could stop herself.

He grinned again. 'Hard to say.'

She put her hands on her hips. 'Try.'

'This passion for numbers, Jane. OK. Less than a hundred.'

'*A hundred?*'

'*Less* than a hundred,' he said reprovingly. 'You weren't listening.'

'So I'm number . . . what?'

'I've really no idea but since you're so set on it . . . how about number fifty?'

'*Fifty?*'

'All right, calm down – you'll have the neighbours banging on the walls again. How about forty-four? A good solid number. You can be Luke's Female Friend Forty-Four. Who could possibly quarrel with that?'

'I'm the forty-fourth woman in this room?'

'We've covered this, Jane. At least forty-two and a half of them would have been next door with me. Although not all at once, before you form an inflated idea of my talents. Now, in the interests of full and frank disclosure, I've answered all your questions and the time has come for us to move on. As North would say – accentuate the positive.' He whipped open a door. 'Look at all the wardrobe space here.'

With the enormity of the task before her suddenly brought home by her surroundings, Jane was determined to be grumpy. 'I don't have anything to put in any wardrobe, big or small. We left with practically nothing, remember?'

'Jane, you considerably underestimate me.' He indicated a built-in data table. 'Shop away.'

She hesitated. 'I don't have a lot of money . . .'

'You don't need any money at all. Just order and it will come.'

'I . . .'

'It's charged to the apartment, dummy. Now, just stand in front of the screen and it'll scan you for size and colouring. Simply select the stuff you like the look of and it'll be delivered. Correct size and everything.'

'But . . .'

'The concierge will bring it up to you. Get cracking.'

He disappeared. Left alone, Jane sat on the most expensive bed of her life and looked around her. This was easily the most high-end establishment she had ever been inside. The floor was a vast, honey-coloured wooden acreage, randomly scattered with expensive rugs. Huge windows opened on to her own personal veranda together with the roof garden and hot tub Luke had forgotten to mention. This terrace, together with the view of London and the river, had almost certainly added three noughts to the asking price.

Her bathroom had passed luxurious and was approaching

256

sumptuous. There were fixtures and fittings in there of whose purpose she had no idea. Her bed was huge. She could sleep in it for a week and there would still be regions of it she hadn't yet occupied. The room had everything, including all the electronics – climate control, SmartGlass, and the very latest in entertainment walls. Drawers and wardrobe doors opened smoothly in a manner that was quite unknown to her. And closed themselves when they sensed she'd finished with them.

The doors to the terrace swished silently open as she approached. Stepping outside, London lay before her. Luke's apartment was in the fashionable Carmelite area with Black-friars Bridge to her left and Waterloo Bridge to her right.

The sky was low and dark, bulging with rain. She stood for a long time, letting the cold wind blow her hair, just taking everything in. Events had moved so quickly. Just over a week ago, she'd been at Versailles. Then North's personal disaster. Then the confrontation with Grint's team. Then a few welcome – although not completely peaceful – hours at St Mary's with Matthew, where she'd spent most of her time sitting in the sun with a geriatric chicken on her lap and trying to read. Without success, until she'd accidentally discovered that a sleeping chicken makes an ideal bookrest. Now she was here – a stranger in a strange new world. And she missed Angus, whose company was gentle and affectionate and who only occasionally pecked at her or pooed on her jeans.

She'd enjoyed the peace and serenity of St Mary's – marred only by the brief unpleasantness of Matthew's dad's Power-Point presentation, prepared specifically for the benefit of Matthew's mother, on the correct way to manipulate a tube of toothpaste. This had not been well-received. Views had been expressed and the tube of toothpaste, carefully marked Visual Aid One had, apparently, been the first, but not the most serious, casualty. As Matthew had said – the toothpaste had really hit the fan. Jane was content to have missed it.

And now . . . she was here. She wandered back into the bedroom. The glass doors automatically closed behind her. She didn't have to do a thing. All the fixtures and fittings were quiet, understated and very, very expensive. And immaculate. Jane looked down at her modest top and jeans. She was lowering property values simply by being here.

Somewhat nervously she approached the data table, which fired itself up as she sat down.

'Welcome, insert name here.'

Jane couldn't resist. 'Luke's Female Friend Forty-Four.'

'Welcome, Luke's Female Friend Forty-Four. What can I show you today?'

'Um . . . women's clothing,' said Jane tentatively.

'Please specify.'

Jane took a deep breath. 'Everything.'

Emerging some forty-five minutes later, she found Luke in the kitchen.

'There's nothing to eat,' he announced, 'obviously, but I'm ordering some stuff in. Anything in particular you want?'

Jane, whose pre-Time Police days had largely consisted of lugging home vast amounts of food as demanded by her grandmother, sighed. Obviously not that much had changed. 'Something light.'

'What? What does that mean?'

'Something not too heavy to carry back. Do you know how much two melons and five pounds of potatoes weigh?'

He stared at her. 'What are you talking about?'

'Heavy food. Lugging it uphill. Every day. About the only good thing about the Time Police is that they provide food and we don't have to go out and get it ourselves.'

'I also provide food,' said Luke, striking his chest. 'I am the alpha male of food provision. The ultimate hunter-gatherer.'

'Oh God, I've set you off again, haven't I?'

Wearing his *I'm Luke Parrish and I'm wonderful* smirk, he waved his arm in front of the fridge. The door lit up with many, many symbols.

'Right,' he said. 'I'll order you potatoes if that's what you want, Jane, but mostly I was thinking wine . . .' he tapped the fridge door, 'some cheese; some nice French bread; ooh yes, croissants for breakfast, I think; eggs and bacon for midnight sandwiches; chocolate, obviously; more wine because they're having a special; German beer; my favourite paté; coffee; more coffee . . . and some wine.'

The fridge door was chirping and lighting up – a real sound and light show, thought Jane. 'But you haven't ordered any real food. There's nothing to make a meal from.'

He stared around the kitchen. 'Jane, I am pleased and proud to announce no meal – and I repeat, *no meal* – has ever been cooked in this kitchen. This is a cooking-free zone.'

'So how do you eat?'

'I go out. Like a normal person. Seriously, Jane, who cooks any more?'

'I do,' said Jane. 'Or rather, I did.' She looked at the giant fridge that was almost certainly more intelligent than she was. 'I had no idea about any of this.'

'No, I gathered that. Look, sit down a moment. I want to talk to you.'

They sat at the kitchen table. Luke ran his hands over the surface. 'I joined the Time Police at this very table.'

'We should have it inscribed. What did you want to talk to me about?'

'I've been thinking. Specifically, how we should go about this. We deliberately kept things loose. We don't have any formal plan. We certainly don't have any formal instructions from Hay – just a general *go out there and get them* command – but I've been thinking.'

'Yes?'

'We have to get into our roles. Complete immersion.'

'Agreed.'

'So, from tomorrow onwards we never, ever mention the Time Police. Not even here in this apartment. If we're going to be targeted, they'll find some way of bugging us, I'm sure, so we stay in character at all times. No matter where we are, we always assume someone's listening.'

'Agreed.'

'And I'll start inferring I've been in rehab.'

She frowned. 'Actually, I don't think you should infer. I think rehab is the sort of thing you'd fling at people. "Hey, look at me. I'm Luke Parrish and I've been in rehab for six months. In your face, buster."'

'An excellent idea. Moving along . . . Are you sure you don't want to be my girlfriend?'

'Luke, it's very kind of you, but no one's going to believe that in a million years. No one who's seen Imogen Farnborough could possibly believe I'm your girlfriend. I'll be your sober companion, chaperone, gaoler and general party-pooper. That was the whole plan – we all play to our strengths and those are mine.'

'But how does this fit in with our hitting the town and having a good time? That's the part of my plan, Jane, to which I am particularly wedded.'

'I can imagine. If you like, we can have a number of very public arguments as I endeavour to keep you off the booze. Which I will win, because I'm not at all sure having you lurch from one alcoholic session to the next will be particularly helpful within the context of this mission.'

He gazed at her. 'I don't know . . .'

The apartment was far too grand to have a doorbell.

'You have a visitor,' announced the AI.

'Show me.' He squinted at the screen. 'Oh God, I suppose I should have guessed.'

'Not an ex on the doorstep already?' said Jane, impressed. 'That didn't take long.'

'I should be so lucky. This is Ms Steel. PA to dear old Dad. I can't tell you the number of advances I've made in that direction and she's ignored me every time. I don't know if she doesn't like men in general or just me, unbelievable though that seems. The two of you should get on well.' He addressed himself to the screen. 'Ask her to come in, please.'

He got up and went to greet his guest.

'Ms Steel – how are you?'

Jane saw a tall, striking woman, dark-skinned with silver hair, wearing a severely cut business suit and a very serious expression. Efficiency oozed from every pore.

She wasted no time on preliminaries. 'Why are you here, Mr Parrish?'

'Never mind that – how did you know I was here?'

'This apartment is monitored for security purposes. You triggered the alarm . . .' she glanced at her watch, 'one hour and twenty-three minutes ago. I contacted the concierge and he reported that Mr Luke Parrish and a companion appear to have resumed occupation.'

'Of *my* apartment, yes.'

'Again, Mr Parrish, why?'

'Because it's my home.'

'Do I understand you have left the Time Police?'

'No.'

'No, you haven't left the Time Police? Or no, I don't understand?'

'No.'

She stared at him for a moment and then turned to Jane. 'We haven't been introduced. I am Lucinda Steel.'

'Hello,' said Jane. 'I'm Jane. Won't you sit down?'

Ms Steel pulled out a chair and frowned. It was obvious she was measuring Jane against previous occupants and finding her . . . different.

Luke leaned forwards and placed his hands on the table. 'You'll be pleased to learn, Ms Steel, that I've been released from the extremely expensive and luxurious rehab facility into which dear old Dad had dumped me.'

Ms Steel sat very still. As the person who had presided over Luke's enforced enlistment in the Time Police, no one knew better that Luke had been nowhere near rehab – expensive and luxurious or otherwise. 'Have you, indeed?'

Luke beamed. 'Yes. Apparently, I've made such stupendous progress that I can now be trusted in the outside world. Although not without my sober counsellor here to look after me.'

Another long silence fell. Ms Steel's face did not change.

'For how long do you contemplate remaining here, Mr Parrish?'

'Well, I can't give you any timescale, but certainly until a resolution is arrived at.'

'Have we any idea when that resolution will be?'

'Not at this stage, no. But please be assured the terms and conditions of our original deal remain unchanged.'

She stood up. 'I understand you, I think. Is there anything you require?'

'Access to my bank accounts, but only for the period of my . . . rehabilitation.'

'I'll see what I can do.'

'And I'd be grateful if you didn't bother anyone else with this, Ms Steel. Too much attention is often counter-productive to . . . rehabilitation.'

'I understand the need for discretion, however, my original instructions from Mr Parrish senior have not changed.'

He said nothing. They regarded each other in silence.

'Very well, Mr Parrish. I will unfreeze one account. Will I be wasting my time if I request you exercise at least a modicum of restraint?'

'Oh God, yes,' said Luke, happily.

20

It would appear that Jane had not exercised a modicum of restraint, either. Well, not for Jane, anyway. Some ten minutes after Ms Steel's departure, the AI announced a delivery. Jane's order had arrived.

Luke opened the door to a smartly dressed concierge.

'Good afternoon, sir. A delivery for . . .' he ostentatiously consulted his palmpad and continued straight-faced, 'Luke's Female Friend Forty-Four.' Apparently oblivious to Jane's sunset-style blush, he continued. 'If you can indicate the room, please, madam,' and wheeled the rail into the flat.

Wordlessly, Jane indicated her bedroom. The concierge opened the wardrobe door and began to transfer the contents from the hanging rail, carefully removing the wrappings. A small box containing personal toiletries was handed over with all the reverence of a religious icon.

'For you,' said Luke, waving his card over the concierge's palmpad.

'Thank you, sir. Please contact us downstairs should there be anything you're not happy with, madam.'

He backed out of the door.

Luke turned to her, his hands on his hips. 'Luke's Female

Friend Forty-Four? You know that's all over the building by now, don't you?'

Jane was very nearly incandescent.

'I didn't,' she said, indignantly. 'Well, yes, I might have said that to the AI but I thought the stuff would come in your name. After all, you're paying for it. I've never done anything like this before. You should have explained.'

'Yes, well, never mind all that right now. Let's see what you've got.'

He surveyed the garments now hanging in the wardrobe. 'Not a lot here, Jane.'

Jane, who thought that actually there was rather a lot there, prevaricated. 'No, well, it was a bit pricey.'

'You really haven't got the hang of being rich at all, have you?'

'Nor ever likely to.'

He was rifling through the clothes. 'It's all a bit . . . black.'

'It's my style,' she said, struck with sudden inspiration.

'The safe option?'

'No – understated and classical.'

'Don't use the word classical, Jane. It's fashion shorthand for frumpy.'

'Nothing that expensive could be frumpy.'

The AI announced yet another caller.

'That'll be my stuff,' said Luke. 'This is fun, isn't it? Are you enjoying yourself? There's nothing like a bit of conspic-uous consumption, is there? You get yourself ready and then we'll go out for something to eat.' He cast a glance out of the window. 'It's chucking it down out there. There's a restaurant on the top floor. We'll go there.'

'Really?' said Jane, sarcastically. 'I thought the swimming pool would be up there.'

'In the basement,' he said seriously. 'With the gym, the spa and the cinema. Get a move on, now.'

The hour was unfashionably early and there weren't that many diners in the penthouse restaurant.

The head waiter seemed overjoyed at Luke's reappearance. 'Mr Parrish, welcome back.'

'Thank you, Giles.'

'Table for two, sir?'

'Please. By the window, I think. Jane likes to look at the rain.'

'Certainly, sir.'

They were escorted to an appropriate table. Jane obediently looked out at the rain.

'What do you fancy?' asked Luke, passing his hand over the virtual tablecloth. The menu appeared in glowing copperplate.

'Oh . . . um . . .' She stared at Luke helplessly. 'I don't think I'm cut out to be rich.'

'Well, don't start blushing again. Oh – too late. Look, when the waiter comes back, I'll order for you because you're too bored and sophisticated to do it for yourself. How about that? And don't forget to tell me I can't have any wine. Now, apparently, I'm talking to you but in reality, I'm scanning the room for anyone I know.'

Jane poured them both some water. The ice clinked expensively. Jane sighed. Her ice never did that. 'And is there? Anyone you know?'

'No, don't think so. Wait, actually, yes. I'm not going to

catch his eye. I'll wait for him to come to me. Which he will because he's easily the nosiest, most gossipy blabbermouth in town and just what we're looking for. Could you gaze adoringly at me, please, Jane, and hang on my every word. Yes, that's very good.'

'You do know it's only because we're both playing a part that I haven't thrown this very expensive water over you, don't you?'

'Actually, I'm banking on it. And here he comes.'

'Luke? Luke Parrish? Is that you? Dear boy, wherever have you been?'

'Oh,' said Luke, 'I think we both know the answer to that one.'

'No!' he exclaimed in delighted concern.

''Fraid so. Courtesy of dear old Dad.' He assumed a very creditable impression of his father's voice. 'Pull yourself together, Luke. Stop wasting your life. Can't go on like this. Sort yourself out or I'll do it for you.'

'Dear boy!'

Luke shrugged. 'Not the first time. Probably won't be the last either. Although I shouldn't say that with Little Miss Gaoler here. Jane, meet Alphonse. Alphonse, meet Jane. And for God's sake don't look cheerful or she'll be searching you for happy pills, because that's what you do, isn't it, Jane, dear?'

Jane sat back and smiled politely, giving, she hoped, the impression of someone with a job to do and determined to do it whatever the provocation.

'Delighted to meet you,' said Alphonse, smiling too brightly and too briefly. He transferred his attention back to Luke. 'So what are your plans, dear boy, as you pick up the reins again?'

'Not sure,' said Luke, frowning at the table. 'Why can't I access the wine menu?'

'Guess,' said Jane, accepting her cue and feeling it was time she flexed her sober-counsellor muscles.

He sighed. 'You know what it's like when you've been . . . away . . . Alphonse, the world moves on. So do tell me – where's hot and where's not these days?'

'Ah well . . .' and he launched into a sea of names, none of which meant anything to Jane. Nor did he mention the King's Arsenal. She studied him as he talked. Not as young as he looked. Not as wealthy as he looked, either. She looked down at his shoes. Shiny but worn. Which just about summed up Alphonse, she thought. A nasty little man who earned a living enticing young people into things they probably shouldn't allow themselves to be enticed into. For a fee, obviously. Exactly the sort of person someone fresh from rehab should avoid and definitely someone Luke should cultivate. She should let him get on with it.

'Do excuse me a moment,' she said. She smiled at them both and headed for the Ladies, where she washed her hands extremely slowly in the most luxurious restroom she had ever seen. And there were the products to sample, as well. She worked her way slowly down the line. Soap, hand cream, a different type of hand cream, a light perfume . . . Jane anointed herself with everything in sight and then, considering she'd given Luke enough time, made her way slowly back into the restaurant.

Alphonse had gone but she was just in time to catch Luke hastily stowing an empty glass under the table. 'Did I see that?' she said, sitting down.

'Not this time. I really needed that. Actually, ten minutes with Alphonse and I usually feel the need to immerse myself in the nearest sheep dip.'

'Yes,' she said. 'He is a little . . . unwholesome . . . don't you think?'

'I've known him for years,' said Luke, 'and he's a nasty piece of work. Always on the lookout for someone young and vulnerable to leech off. But he knows everyone and everything. In half an hour, most of London will know I'm back in circulation, that I've been in rehab, that I have a minder, and that I'm up for anything going. And we didn't even have to go out in the rain. I'm really good at this, aren't I?'

'Did you get anything useful?'

'I did. A whole list of new places recently opened up.'

'Did he mention . . . ? You know . . . ?'

'He slipped it in but didn't make a big thing of it and neither did I. Apparently it offers gambling, gaming, dancing, free drink and good food. Just the sort of place I like. We'll check it out sometime.'

'Not tomorrow, surely?'

'No. I thought early next week. We don't want to seem too eager.'

'Do you think they're still operating from there?'

'We'll go and look.'

'It's a bit public, isn't it? A fashionable restaurant on the river?'

'That's the point, I think. If the Time Police come calling, then it's just what it appears to be. A nice place on the river. Always heaving until the fashionable crowd discovers the next Big Thing and moves on.'

'Will we even get in?'

He blinked in genuine astonishment. 'Why wouldn't we?'

'It's always heaving?'

'Oh, I'll get the concierge to make reservations. It won't be a problem. Drink your water, Jane, and stop fretting.'

They ambled through the next few days. Hundreds of people seemed pleased to see Luke again. He was greeted ecstatically wherever he went. And he appeared equally pleased to see them. There were hugs, kisses and high-fives as Luke enthusiastically skidded from group to group of welcoming friends.

To Jane, however, it was a cacophony of dark places, loud music, shouting men and shrieking women. And a waste of time. No one made any effort to entice them into illegal activities. 'Well, not that *you* can see, Jane,' said Luke, sitting himself opposite her. 'However, I've just had an interesting ten minutes in the Gents.'

He uncurled his hand to show her a couple of small white tablets.

She kept her face very still.

'Oh, don't worry.' He dropped them to the floor and crushed them underfoot. 'It was only for the look of the thing. Sending out all the right messages, don't you think? For our purposes, I mean.' He frowned. 'Because drugs are *bad*.'

She looked at him. His face was flushed and his eyes too bright. 'Luke . . .'

'Jane, I'm joking.'

She held his eye. 'I'm beginning to wonder if this wasn't a big mistake on your part.'

'In what way?'

'I'm not sure if you're pretending to embrace your old ways or pretending you're not.'

'What does that mean?'

'Luke, all you had to do was swallow those pills and for you, it would be as if the last six months in . . . rehab . . . had never existed. How easy would it be for you to pick up your old life where you left off?' She reached across the table and took his hands. 'I fear for you.'

He stared at her for a long while, making no attempt to take his hands away. Around them, the music thumped and people danced and swung their way past, faces flushed with excitement, screaming at each other to be heard.

She stared back, forcing herself to retain eye contact and all the while thinking, I've gone too far. I shouldn't have said it. I've risked the mission. I risked the team. I've risked us. Stupid, stupid Jane.

'Hang on,' said Bolshy Jane. 'Don't panic yet. Give it a moment.'

He pulled his hands free and her world felt suddenly colder. Passing his hand over the paypoint on the table, he said, 'Come outside, Jane.'

Here we go, she thought miserably. Or here I go, anyway.

They were somewhere in Chelsea, she knew that. The pavements were thronged with people. Bright lights winked and flashed, reflected in the wet pavement. She saw none of it. A dark fear gnawed at her.

They were being jostled by late-night revellers. She pushed him into a doorway. Someone shouted at them to get a room. Jane wondered whether she did actually go to the trouble of blushing in the dark or whether some mechanism inside her

271

brain decided it would be a waste of time and therefore didn't bother.

Lights flicked across Luke's face – yellow, red and white. She waited for him to shove past her and disappear into the night. Without her. To fall prey to whatever might be waiting for him out there. She fully expected his next words to be 'Just bugger off, Jane, will you?'

She gripped his jacket. 'Luke, will you do something for me?'

She watched his eyes harden as they frequently did when someone tried to tell him what to do.

Deliberately, she stepped back and made her voice calm.

'Look . . . I've had a thought. We've been making it abundantly clear you're back in town and up for a good time but I'm guessing enough people are talking about you by now and you don't actually need to be here physically. Let's go away somewhere. Even if only for a day or so. Get you out of this environment for a little while. Is there perhaps somewhere you've always wanted to visit? We could go there.'

Luke stared at her for a moment, eyes unfocused, and then said, 'Actually . . . yes.'

She waited.

'I want to find Birgitte. Will you help me?'

'Yes, of course,' she said unhesitatingly. 'Um . . . who's Birgitte? And why?'

He ignored the first question. 'Because you're right. I am at risk here. And it'll probably be because of something trivial and stupid and I won't be able to help myself and then I'll be right back where I was before I . . . entered rehab. Only worse, this time. So, you're right. Let's get out of here.'

272

'Where to?'

'I don't know. I'll have to find out where she's living now.'

'Birgitte?'

'Yes.'

'Why?'

'Why not?' he said, lightly.

'No, I mean – why now?'

'Well . . . for some time now . . . there's something I've been thinking of doing. I didn't – no, that's not right – I felt I *shouldn't* do it before because, as you may know, I made a bit of a mess of my life and I didn't – I suppose I didn't want to face her with all that going on – you know, Jane – gambling, drink, women, drugs . . . not a lot of drugs,' he said quickly, seeing her face. 'But now I have a job, and it seems to me – here we are – happily in the wind and with no responsibilities to anyone – yet – that this would be a good time. Do you remember – when we were in Egypt . . .'

Jane experienced a jagged flash of memory. '*You will not fear the terror of the night* – you said she taught you that.'

Luke took a deep breath. 'Birgitte is the only person in the world – apart from you – who has ever held my hand and said she feared for me. I've spent years thinking about her. So let's find her. Shouldn't be a problem for two resourceful people like us.'

'But who is she?'

He looked around. There was a café across the road. The Greasy Spoon. 'Come on, I'll buy you a coffee.'

'And tell me about Birgitte.'

'And tell you all about Birgitte.'

273

21

The café was warm and steamy. Since this was Chelsea, and despite the name over the window, the establishment was only playing at being a greasy spoon. The inside was bright and cheerful with red gingham tablecloths and travel posters on the walls.

'I'm going for coffee and a sausage sarnie, Jane. You?'

'Coffee and a bacon roll, please.'

Luke typed their order into the table and then paused with his hand over the paypoint.

'While I think of it, I got you one of these.' He handed her a paycard.

'Thank you.' She turned it over. 'What's the limit?'

'Sorry?'

'How much can I spend?'

'Sorry?'

Jane enunciated slowly but clearly. 'What is the amount of money I can spend on this card?'

'As much as you like. It's unlimited.'

Her jaw dropped. 'What?'

'Well, what's the point otherwise? Suppose you suddenly decided to buy your own helicopter?'

She sat back and stared in astonishment. 'How likely am I to buy my own helicopter?'

'I've known you six months and I can honestly say you're the only person I've ever known who's been arrested for murder or destroyed a seagull, so how should I know what you'll do next? Seriously, Jane, you've got a bit of a rep, you know.'

'Have I?' she said, suddenly feeling quite proud of herself.

'You do, yes. I think one or two people at rehab have got their eye on you. For what reasons, of course, I've no idea.'

She tucked the card away. 'Bit of a risk, isn't it, then? Giving this to me?'

He smiled at her. 'No, Jane. No risk at all.'

'Is that a compliment?'

'No.'

Their food arrived and Luke got stuck in. Jane stared at her coffee, still stunned at the prospect of unlimited credit. 'Tell me about Birgitte.'

He chewed and swallowed.

'Birgitte was what they used to call an au pair. Don't know what they call them now. This was a long time ago.' He sighed. 'I had a lot of nannies when I was little. They were all much the same. They lasted as long as it took Dad to get them into bed. The next day there would be Ms Steel on the doorstep – payoff in one hand, NDA in the other. It wasn't actually a case of out through the back door as the new one came in through the front, but near enough.'

He sipped some coffee.

'Right from the start, Birgitte was different. She was with me for over a year – easily the longest any of them ever lasted, so Dad must really have had to work for it.'

Luke was silent for a while, staring into space and then continued.

'I liked her. She didn't just lie around doing her nails or talking to her friends on the phone. I was at a local school then but we did things together at weekends. She was a design student. We went all over London looking at houses, gardens, parks and so on. We went to the zoo, the Natural History Museum – things like that. During the school holidays I used to wake up every morning wondering where we'd go that day and what I'd see when we got there. We read books together and she actually talked to me about them – what I was thinking when I looked at this or that. She was about the only person who ever actually spoke to me properly. My father just issued a set of instructions – usually by proxy – but Birgitte was different.'

He gazed back into his past. 'She loved to sketch. She taught me about colours and perspective and so on. She bought me my own sketchpad and paints so I could experiment. That summer seemed endless. It must have rained, I suppose, but I only recall long, hot days. After a while I couldn't remember a time when she hadn't been with me. I thought it would go on forever. As you do when you're too young to know these things don't last.'

He pushed his empty coffee cup across the table. 'It didn't, of course. Last, I mean. One day I woke up and she was gone. No warning. Two days later I was off to a new school, full of utter bastards, where I had to learn to be an utter bastard myself pretty damned quick. I didn't know what had happened or why she'd gone, of course. I only knew it was connected to Dad somehow. I think I thought I'd done something really bad and

276

he'd held her responsible. Although what . . . And that school was brutal. I hated it. I sometimes have a bit of a problem with discipline, as you well know. But trust me, there was no holding me back then. I lost count of the number of schools I was expelled from after that. The number of girls I left behind me. Broken friendships and so on. Before long no one halfway decent would have anything to do with me. I don't blame them now. In fact, it was only when I went to rehab that I realised just how close I was to becoming my father.'

Jane stirred her cold coffee and said carefully, 'Are you going to tell her you're coming?'

'I don't know. Uncharacteristic indecision on my part. What do you think?'

'I think you should. You've guessed at why she left, but you might be wrong. It might be painful for her to see you again. I think, hard though it might be, you should give her the option to refuse. Just turning up on her doorstep could be upsetting for her.'

He nodded. 'Good point.'

'How will we set about it?'

'Well, if we were still in . . . rehab . . . it might not be so difficult, but we no longer have access to those resources.' He brooded.

'How about . . . it's just a thought . . . but how about asking Ms Steel? I mean, obviously, I don't know her, but she seemed very . . . competent.'

'Oh, she is. She had me trapped, trussed and delivered to rehab before I even knew what was happening.'

'Really?'

'Trust me, Jane – I barely had time to grab a toothbrush

and a clean pair of kecks before I was on the rehab centre doorstep wondering what the hell was going on. The woman is shit-hot.'

'Do you think she could find Birgitte then?'

'Oh, she could – it's whether she would.'

'Well,' said Jane, 'if she won't, then we'll have a go ourselves. And to return to the original point – we did rather pitchfork ourselves into this. Let's ease back for a while.'

'Good thought. I'll fire off a message to Ms Steel when we get back. *And* . . . if we are attracting the right sort of attention – which we will be because we're so good at this – then it will make bugging our apartment so much easier. Really, you know, I think they should be grateful, don't you think?'

Jane closed her eyes and shook her head.

He brought up the bill. 'Your treat, I believe.'

Jane could not believe the speed with which Ms Steel acted. She'd always thought the Time Police to be reasonably efficient – although life hadn't exactly given her much to compare them with – but this brought home to her Commander Hay's oft-repeated assertion that big business was considerably better funded, better equipped, better staffed and infinitely more efficient than the public sector. Not twenty-four hours later, Luke was in possession of a name and address.

'You're sure that's her?' said Jane, peering over his shoulder at the screen. 'Birgitte von Essendorf.'

'Well, Ms Steel is sure and that's good enough for me.'

'How did she find her so quickly?'

'She had her employment details from when she worked for Dad, I expect. And women don't change their names with

278

marriage any longer so that makes everything much easier. Shall we go?'

'Now?'

'Well, pack, obviously, but yes.' He scanned the screen. 'Tickets, travel permits and visas all waiting for us.'

'I don't have a passport,' said Jane, panicking. 'And I can't travel on my rehab docs. Even if I'd brought them with me. Which I haven't.'

'It's just Scotland, Jane. A visa is sufficient. Especially now they've abolished the Tartan Tolls.'

'Ten minutes,' said Jane, disappearing into her room.

They took the Glasgow airship from Croydon. The *Billy Connolly* floated serenely overhead, moored fore and aft to its tethering posts. Jane looked up, swallowed hard and told herself everything would be just fine.

'Four hundred and twenty-eight miles,' said Luke, consulting his itinerary as they sat in the airship's comfortable lounge waiting to de-tether. 'About six hours, they reckon. Weather permitting, we should arrive around 1730 hours.' He considered the rigid Jane sitting opposite. 'Which means, in terms of journey comfort, that we get lunch *and* afternoon tea.'

'Is that good?' asked Jane, apprehensively.

'Afternoon tea on board any ship of the Glasgow Line is worth having, so don't go stuffing yourself on lunch. Why are you gripping the arms of your seat like that?'

'I'm bracing myself for take-off.'

'Sweetie, look out of the window.'

'What? Oh. Oh my God. What's happening?'

'We took off four or five minutes ago.'

279

'I never noticed. And don't call me sweetie.'

'Your eyes were shut.'

'I thought there would be a surge or a jolt or something.'

'And was there?'

'I don't know – unusually, you were talking.'

'I was taking your mind off things. An act of compassion on my part.'

'I've never flown before. Was that supposed to happen or have we just accidentally become untied and drifted away?'

'Jane, how can you expose yourself to all the dangers of . . . transportation rehab-style and yet be rigid with fear on the safest method of travel yet invented?'

She risked a glance out of the window. 'We're so high up.'

'Sweetie, you never noticed.'

'You could have said. And don't call me sweetie.'

'Shall we have a look round and then go in for lunch?'

She hesitated.

'It's perfectly safe to stand up. You won't make us tip up, or anything. Come on.'

Very much against her will and certainly against her better judgement, Jane was impressed. Although prior to joining the Time Police, her only experience of travel of any kind had been journeying to London to join the Time Police, so there wasn't much to compare it to. Those not rich enough – i.e. Jane – were exposed to the dubious delights of cross-channel ferries, the public hyperloops and the decaying motorway system.

The Promenade Deck was spectacular. Giant windows set down each side gave a far more panoramic view than Jane was happy with. At one end was the dining room, large enough to seat all seventy passengers simultaneously, and at the other, the public lounge with its own grand piano and conference rooms beyond. The well-appointed cabins occupied an entire deck above them. Most of them had no windows, but as Luke said, who would want to spend time in their cabins with views like these to marvel at. Jane, who hadn't yet been able to bring herself to marvel at the view, nodded and kept her eyes firmly on the carpet.

The décor was 1920s style, harking back to previous centuries of gracious travel. Groups of people stood or sat around, reading and talking together. White-coated waiters carried trays of drinks. Mindful they were in public, Luke stuck to orange juice.

On the lower deck, a specific area had been set aside for those psychologically incapable of separating themselves from their personal electronics and communication devices, partly because they were inconsistent with the carefully contrived 1920s ambience and partly so the electronic beeping couldn't annoy the other passengers.

There was no smoking lounge. Popular rumour had it that anyone caught with a naked flame would be pitched overboard from seven hundred feet.

The brochure informed them the airship supported a crew of fifty. 'One and a half passengers to each crew member,' said Luke.

No wonder it's expensive, thought Jane. She calculated her return ticket was the equivalent of four months' pay.

'You'll enjoy lunch,' said Luke, seating them at a table. 'We're only flying at about seven hundred feet so the food will taste good.'

Jane shuddered. 'There is nothing *only* about seven hundred feet.'

Lunch was followed almost immediately by afternoon tea. Jane drank a cup of tea and nibbled a tiny, crustless, triangular-shaped sandwich. Luke, obviously regarding the laden tiers of sandwiches, scones and dainty cakes as a personal challenge, got stuck in. 'Shame Matthew's not here. Even with his appetite I think he'd have had trouble with this lot.'

Matthew Farrell's capacity for food was legendary. No one could ever remember an occasion on which he had not cleared his own plate. And everyone else's as well if they didn't get a move on.

'I wonder how he is.'

'He'll be fine,' said Luke, inaccurately. 'He'll be making love to that big silver Map thing and probably hasn't even noticed we've gone.'

They arrived so promptly at seventeen thirty that Luke felt compelled to ask if Jane thought they'd circled Glasgow until it was time to land.

Jane wasn't listening. 'Oh my God, we're going down.'

'It's quite hard to land if you don't. You can't just park in mid-air and step out, you know.'

'Don't call me sweetie.'

'I didn't.'

'You usually do.'

'Not this time I didn't.' He stood up.

'Where are you going?'

'We've landed. I'm getting off. Don't know what you're doing.'

Jane picked up her expensive new handbag. 'Next time we go anywhere together you go alone.'

'Excellent trip, don't you think?' said Luke as they made

their way down the airbridge, both of them so stuffed with good food they could barely walk. Smiling staff checked their entry documents and indicated the appropriate customs channels.

'Do we know where we're going?' asked Jane as they emerged from the terminal.

'Yes, I have the address.'

'Does she know we're coming?'

'I messaged her. No reply as yet.'

'Where are we going?'

'She teaches at the Design Centre. A water taxi to Clyde-bank should get us there. I thought her place of work might be less threatening than turning up on her doorstep. You know – neutral territory.'

Luke had worried unnecessarily. A tall woman with faded blonde hair and very blue eyes was waiting for them outside the Design Centre.

'Luke? Oh my God, Luke – is that you? Look at you. Oh, my lovely boy, how are you?'

She did not hold back. Luke was enveloped in huge hugs and kisses. Jane took a few paces to the side and looked away.

Birgitte was beside herself. 'It is so good to see you again. And welcome to your friend Jane, too. I am so happy to meet you. We will go to my apartment straight away. We've so much to talk about.'

'What about . . . ?'

'My wife? Ilse is away on business in Sweden. We will have the whole place to ourselves. Come. Come.'

Glasgow was not as warm as London but much less muggy. Green roofs were much more in evidence here. As they walked briskly through the city, Jane was particularly struck by the imaginative placing of trees some fifty feet in the air. And Glasgow was much easier to get around. The much less crowded streets meant the use of energy-generating pavements produced more credits. Luke handsomely donated his and Jane's to Birgitte. For which she thanked them.

Her flat was tiny with minimal furnishings but very comfortable. Everything was in Scandinavian colours, all muted blues and greys. Jane wondered if the art on the walls was Birgitte's own.

She served excellent coffee in tiny cups and they sat down. 'It's so wonderful to see you again, Luke, but what are you doing here?'

He put down his coffee untasted. 'I wanted to talk to you.'

She nodded encouragingly.

Being Luke, he got straight to it.

'What did I do that was so bad?'

22

There was complete silence in the room. Not even the background creaks of an old house. Just complete silence.

Jane froze, wondering if she should leave, give Luke and Birgitte some privacy. But they were between her and the door. Had they forgotten she was here? Better to sit back in her quiet corner and keep quiet.

Birgitte put down her cup. Genuine astonishment was written all over her face. 'Nothing. You did nothing. Whatever made you think that?'

'Well, I must have done something to make my father sack you. I know that. You left so quickly. And then I was bundled off to that awful school – it was like a prison – a punishment – and . . .'

'No, no, Luke. This is all wrong. Did your father not talk to you after I left?'

'No. Not a word. One minute my world was . . . normal . . . and the next moment . . . it wasn't. Why? What happened? Why did you leave me? And don't tell me you can't reveal anything because the old man made you sign an NDA.'

'I'll willingly tell you what I know. I would have done so years ago if I'd known you had no idea . . . Although I'm not

285

sure how helpful I can be because I don't really know what happened, either.'

Luke visibly braced himself. 'Tell me.'

'It was a Saturday like any other. I think we'd been to look at the Tower, you and me.'

He nodded. 'I remember that. You wore a red scarf.'

She frowned. 'I did, didn't I? I had forgotten. Anyway, we came home and I made . . .'

'Fish finger wraps,' interrupted Luke. 'And then we had strawberries.'

'That's right. You went to bed and I wrote up my notes for my workbook. You remember my workbook?'

'I do. With the blue and green cover.'

'It was just a normal night. I went to bed. I vaguely heard your father come home late. I went back to sleep. And then . . . and then there was shouting. Lots of men shouting. And a door slamming. And something smashed. I heard the pieces shatter. It was that big blue vase that stood at the top of the stairs . . .'

Luke nodded.

'I ran out on to the landing. It was dark. I couldn't see anything. I heard your father shouting at someone. At whom, I don't know. What he was saying I couldn't make out. My thoughts were for you. I ran into your room. You were awake but very sleepy. I don't think you quite knew where you were. I sat on your bed and we said that little prayer I taught you.'

'You will not fear the terror of the night,' said Luke unsteadily.

'You remember that still? The noises downstairs died away. I heard vehicles outside and men running in and out of the house. Your father opened your bedroom door to ask if we were both all right and I said yes, you were asleep. The house fell silent.

286

I stayed with you all night. I could hear your father pacing around the house, talking to people on the phone. Several times he put his head around the door to check on you. He brought me up a coffee. I was shocked, Luke, when I saw him. He was so altered, his face seemed to have fallen in on itself. Such a big change in such a short time. He walked the house all night but there were no more disturbances.'

Jane wondered what that must have been like for her. Sitting in the dark with a little boy, wondering what was happening as men ran through the house shouting. Who were they? What could they have wanted? Was it a break-in? Or – and this seemed likely, given Luke's immediate removal to a new school – had it been a kidnap attempt? He was the son of a wealthy industrialist. Had there been a ransom planned?

She thought back to her one sight of Luke's father. A big, powerful man. In every sense of the word. It was hard to imagine him showing any signs of agitation, and yet . . . Was he fonder of Luke than he liked to show? And, having heard this, would Luke feel more kindly disposed towards his father?

'The next day Ms Steel called to see me,' Birgitte continued. 'She was very pleasant, Luke. She apologised for bringing bad news but my employment was terminated immediately. Mr Parrish wished to express his gratitude for my services. I would be paid up to the end of the year. There would be a bonus as well.'

'Contingent on your silence.'

'Contingent on nothing. Nothing like that was ever mentioned. I've never told anyone about that night because no one has ever asked.'

'So that was it. He just . . . cut you off?'

'Not at all. A small apartment had been found for me so I could continue my studies in London and a sum of money set aside should I wish to start up on my own afterwards. He was extraordinarily generous.'

'He bought you off.'

'That may be so, but why would he do that? He was perfectly entitled to dismiss me at any time.'

'He just cast you adrift.'

'No, Luke. I moved out, of course, and about two weeks later I received a very nice letter from him, apologising for curtailing my employment so abruptly, thanking me for my care of you, assuring me you were well, and wishing me all the best for the future.'

'You mean Ms Steel sent you a nice letter in his name.'

'Again, Luke, no. It was handwritten. By him. I recognised his writing.'

Luke was bewildered. 'So – all the shouting – what was that about?'

She shrugged. 'I don't know. I wondered afterwards if perhaps an attempt had been made to break in and your father had decided you would be safer at a boarding school rather than the one around the corner. Whatever it was, I can assure you he was most concerned for your welfare. Indeed, it was the only time I ever saw him not in complete control of himself.'

'But you just vanished out of my life. Why didn't you write?'

'I tried, but I didn't have an address, Luke. Your father sold the house – my letters were returned. I didn't know to which school you'd been sent. I had no electronic address for you. I assumed your father was concerned for your safety and this was part of the increased security. I thought it best to leave you be. But it's wonderful to see you all grown up now.'

For Jane, the rest of the evening was a blur. Luke and Birgitte talked and talked, reminiscing over days long gone. Jane dozed, listening to their voices coming and going. Eventually, they both wound down. A short silence fell and then Luke stood up to go and saw Jane still curled up in her chair.

'Jane, I . . .'

'It's OK. You've had other things on your mind. But now I think we need to find our hotel.'

'I am sorry I cannot put you up here,' said Birgitte. 'My other bedroom is Ilse's studio.'

'No, no,' said Jane. 'It's fine.' She regarded Luke for a moment and then extended her hand. 'It was nice to meet you, Birgitte.'

'And you too. Luke, I hope now you will stay in touch. I have often thought of you over the years.'

'Yes, I will,' said Luke vaguely. His eyes were unfocused. Jane suspected he was operating on automatic pilot. 'That would be nice. I have your address.' He appeared to pull himself together. 'It was so good to see you again.'

'For me too.' She looked at him closely. 'I think you need to take better care of yourself.'

He nodded at Jane. 'Already in hand.'

She smiled. 'I think you could not be in better hands.'

Jane glowed. For the right reasons. Just for once.

Back out in the street, he turned to her. 'Jane, how tired are you?'

'I'm fine. I've slept for most of the evening.'

'Would you mind if we went straight back to London? I

know we were supposed to be here for a few days but . . . I have some things to think about.'

'No, of course not. Here's our taxi.'

Luke said very little on the journey back to London. Attendants brought pillows and blankets for those who hadn't booked a cabin. Luke stared out at the darkness on the other side of the window and Jane stared at Luke staring at the darkness and wondered just how helpful this trip had been. Did his old life still have such a hold on him? And, now he'd heard Birgitte's story, Jane wondered whether Luke might, just might, harbour more friendly feelings towards his father.

Looking at the reflection of his face in the window, it seemed unlikely.

Back in Glasgow, the sounds of the city had died away. A tall man, muffled against the night chill, emerged from the shadows and crossed the street. He paused before knocking, looked up and down the street and rang the bell.

Birgitte's voice sounded through the intercom. 'Yes?'

'Ms von Essendorf. This is Raymond Parrish. I wonder if I could come in for a moment.'

23

The return journey was not so smooth. Strong winds added an extra hour to the flight time and they missed their slot at Croydon. Consequently, it was around mid-morning when Luke and Jane finally returned to the apartment. Only to find Alphonse waiting for them in the foyer and looking very dapper in an overdesigned suit that made him appear to be exactly what he was.

He laid down his newspaper and rose from the armchair. 'Luke, my dear boy, we missed you at Maisie's the other night.'

'Oh, yeah,' said Luke, sourly, tired and not in the best mood. 'I was dragged out of temptation's way by someone professing to have my best interests at heart.'

'Anywhere interesting?' enquired Alphonse, skilfully inserting himself between Jane and Luke.

'Glasgow,' said Luke shortly.

Alphonse was severely shocked. 'Dear boy!'

'Yeah . . . well . . . What do you want, Alphonse? Got to say I'm not feeling my best at the moment.'

'No, no, I can see. Take a day, dear boy. Take two. I'll be in touch.' His eyes slid sideways to Jane, waiting by the lift. 'Or perhaps we could meet somewhere . . . discreet.'

Luke scowled at Jane and then back to Alphonse. 'Yeah, well, if you can arrange something then I'll be there.'

'Shall we say lunch tomorrow?'

'Say anything you like, Alphonse, I don't really care.'

Alphonse turned slightly so his back was to Jane.

Does he think I can read lips? she thought, wearily.

'Maxwell's then,' he said softly. 'One o'clock.'

Luke blinked. 'You're a member?'

'No, dear boy, but you are.'

He passed on, nodding at the expressionless concierge on his way out.

Luke joined Jane in the lift.

'And what did he want?' she said, with a tartness not altogether assumed.

'Lunch. Tomorrow. Maxwell's.'

'Where's Maxwell's?'

'My club,' he said shortly, not quite answering the question.

'Why there?'

'Two reasons.' The lift pinged and they exited. 'No women allowed, so you can't come. And secondly, and probably as importantly, it gives him an entrée. He can't get in unless I sign him in, of course, but it gives him something to drop into future conversations.' He pursed his mouth and mimicked Alphonse's slightly too refined accents, '"As I said to Luke Parrish at Maxwell's . . . Do you know Maxwell's at all? Excellent food there and a very passable cellar." That sort of thing. I probably haven't done his next victims any favours at all.'

He opened the door and Jane made a mental note that whatever happened, she, personally, would make sure Alphonse was never again in a position to prey on vulnerable young people.

Because Luke was vulnerable. Far more so than he realised. She glanced at him, wearily dropping his bag in the hall.

'Don't worry,' he said. 'I'm feeling fine. Everything's going well, don't you think?'

As he spoke, he raised his eyes to the ceiling and then back at Jane. Was it possible? she wondered. Could they – whoever *they* were – actually have taken advantage of their absence to bug the place? The presence of Alphonse downstairs made that very easy to believe. Easy enough to find out if they had a box of Time Police tricks with them, but they didn't, so it seemed sensible to assume they had.

'Yes,' she said. 'You're making excellent progress. I'm very pleased with you. You're working hard at this, Luke, and deserve success.'

He grimaced at her. 'I'm for a shower.'

'I'm for a bacon sandwich,' said Jane, firmly. 'I'm starving.'

'Brilliant idea,' he said. 'Make mine crispy.'

'I am not your housekeeper,' she shouted after him.

'And no sauce.'

He slammed his bedroom door and Jane stamped off into the kitchen.

On his return from Maxwell's the next afternoon, Jane could see immediately that things had gone well.

'There's a new place on the river,' he announced loudly, kicking off his shoes in the certain knowledge the shoe fairy would pick them up later. 'Well, new to me, anyway. I've got us an invite.'

'What sort of place?' she asked, raising her eyes from her book. 'Is it a bar?'

'King's Arsenal – heard of it?'

She shook her head.

'Well, that doesn't surprise me in the slightest. One day we must make a list of all the places you haven't heard of.'

'When?'

'As soon as we can't think of anything better to do.'

She sighed patiently. 'I meant – when is this invite for?'

'Tomorrow evening.'

'Luke – do I have to remind you of the rules? Every week you get one solo session or event or whatever you want to call it and you've just had it. At all other times you are to be accompanied. You know that. You agreed to it.'

He sighed impatiently. 'You're not listening, Jane. I said "us".'

'Oh.'

'Dinner by the river. Very pleasant. Nice treat for you. Any chance of a coffee?'

'None whatsoever, I would think,' she said, turning a page. 'But you can make me one while you're at it.'

Alphonse had not just made the reservations at King's Arsenal – he'd arranged a private water taxi as well.

'Not the public clipper?'

Luke shook his head. 'Not for the likes of us, sweetie.'

'I wish I was rich,' said Jane, as they made their way down to the river.

'So do I,' said Luke.

Jane raised a disbelieving eyebrow and gestured behind them to their apartment block.

Luke shook his head. 'It all belongs to dear old Dad, I'm afraid.'

'But surely you'll . . . well . . . inherit?'

'Depends where I am in our relationship cycle. He changes his will every six months or so to accommodate me being in or out of favour. If he dies now, I'm in dead trouble because he's not even speaking to me after –' Jane nudged him and he remembered – 'after that bad business with Orduroy Tann-hauser, so it's in my interests to ensure he lives long enough to put me back in the will again. And here we are.'

The yellow and black water taxi was waiting for them. They walked along the wooden jetty and were assisted into the boat.

'Inside or out, Jane?' enquired Luke.

'Oh, outside,' said Jane, for whom this was a huge adventure.

'Outside it is. Don't blame me if your hair gets blown off.'

Nothing so drastic occurred as the boat pulled away and they set off downriver.

This was not the public clipper, chugging sedately down the Thames with frequent stops. This was a slim, neat little craft that would take full advantage of the high-speed zone between Tower Bridge and the Thames Barrier.

As far as Jane was concerned, she'd entered into a fairyland. The river was a path of light weaving through a canyon of illu-minated buildings on either bank. They whipped under softly lighted bridges. A cold wind blew into her face and whipped at her hair. Occasionally another lighted boat zipped past going in the other direction. Snatches of music or shouting floated across the water.

She turned a shining face towards him, shouting to make

herself heard over the noise of the wind and the engine. 'Luke, this is *amazing*.'

He laughed. 'You must have done this before?'

'I was never in London until . . . I took this job. And now there's never much time off and if there is, then I either walk or take the public clipper. This is wonderful. How long until we get there?'

He shrugged. 'Not long at this rate.'

She settled back to enjoy the trip.

Tower Bridge was magnificent. As was the floodlit Tower of London on their left.

They passed the Brunel Museum where the young Brunel had nearly drowned in the Grand Entrance Hall and through Canary Wharf. Ahead of them, Jane could see the Cutty Sark, brilliantly spotlit.

'Will we see the Naval College?' she asked.

Luke shook his head. 'Another time. We're nearly there.'

The King's Arsenal at Greenwich was set back from the river slightly and completely dwarfed by the tall, modern buildings around. 'The highest thing here will be the price,' said Luke, winking. 'Let's hope we can afford it.'

Originally a small stone building erected by Charles I for the purpose of storing powder and cannonballs outside the city, the arsenal was garrisoned by a small platoon under the command of one Captain Fley, who, on observing the approaching parliamentarians, issued instructions to his men to fight to the death, grabbed the nearest horse and fled. He was subsequently discovered hiding in a cellar at Rotherhithe and executed on the spot.

After that brief moment of fame, the King's Arsenal sank

back into obscurity, emerging briefly to join the nation's fight against the monster Bonaparte, and then again in 1941 to provide a home for two anti-aircraft guns, after which it became a warehouse, after which it became a public house of dubious reputation, after which it sidled into a related trade and became a house of extremely ill repute, after which it provided a rallying point in the Civil Uprisings, during which it was bombed almost out of existence, after which it was rebuilt and entered its current incarnation as a smart riverside venue.

A small plaque in the entrance hall proudly asserted there had been a building on this spot since 1641.

The river frontage was narrow, but the building seemed to go back a long way. The front was brightly lit and the four trees in the front garden were a mass of golden fairy lights.

A large crowd of mostly young people were sitting at the tables or sprawled on the grass chatting. Some wore evening dress, others were more casually kitted out. The whole set-up was bright and welcoming but a massive doorman waited on the jetty, all ready to tell those not making the social grade that they'd got off at the wrong stop.

'And the clipper doesn't stop here, either,' said Luke. 'If you're coming by river – which most people do – you can only get in by private water taxi – the cost of which tends to separate the princes from the paupers. Come on. Let's see if we're socially acceptable, shall we?'

There were no problems of any kind. The doorman recognised Luke instantly.

'Not sure if that's good or bad,' said Jane, as he waved them through.

'Yes, when you think I've been out of circulation for six months, it's a bit disconcerting, isn't it?'

The doorman not only recognised them, but spoke into his lapel, and a fraction of a second later, as if by magic, a Mr Geoffrey appeared. Jane could only put his rapid response and smooth arrival down to an excess of grease. He certainly possessed the most supercilious nostrils Jane had ever encountered in her admittedly sheltered life. Mr Geoffrey was suave, handsome, well-groomed and smooth. And shiny. Everything was shiny – his skin, his hair, even his shirt, which was manufactured of some unpleasantly slippery material. His black shoes shone. His tie looked military but probably wasn't, fastened with a shiny tie-pin.

'As if he'd been put together by a committee,' said Bolshy Jane. 'A bunch of idiots who sat down and said, "What makes a man look trustworthy?"'

Mr Geoffrey produced a plain business card – also shiny – bearing nothing but his name, greeted Luke effusively and even remembered to nod politely in Jane's direction.

Luke swung into action.

'Sweetie, I think you need to freshen up a little,' he said. 'That windswept look is so passé these days.'

Jane was flustered. 'Oh. Yes. Of course. Um . . . where . . . ?'

'Just down the corridor,' said Mr Geoffrey, extending an immaculately suited arm with an immaculately manicured finger on the end of it.

Jane disappeared, the thick carpet rendering her footsteps soundless.

Mr Geoffrey turned to Luke. 'Welcome to the King's Arsenal, Mr Parrish. How can we amuse you this evening?'

298

'Well, just a quiet dinner, I think. You know, still easing myself back into the swing of things.' He paused and then said, 'Alphonse recommended the place so I thought I'd check it out.'

'Of course, sir. He has mentioned you.'

Luke lowered his head confidentially. 'Um . . . not sure if he'll have mentioned it, but it's a bit of a no-no as far as alcohol is concerned. Well, so Jane thinks, of course.'

'Say no more, I understand perfectly.'

'I thought perhaps you could stick something clear in a long glass and call it lemonade.'

'Such as?'

'Anything. I don't care. Just as long as it gets past Jane the Gaoler.'

Jane, meanwhile, was bimbling around a maze of corridors. Lost while looking for the loo, would be her explanation. There were several closed doors behind which she could hear chatter, laughter, music, and once, the clatter of what she thought might be a roulette wheel.

Thick carpet and expensive curtains rendered the corridors soundless. Jane assumed the slightly desperate expression of one who can't find the Ladies and meandered slowly from door to door. As far as she could make out, there were two or three bars of differing sizes and intimacy, and a restaurant, from which she could hear the hum of conversation and the clatter of crockery. A pair of large double doors denoted the Entertainment Room – whatever that was.

Eventually, Jane ran out of corridor. Two large swing doors marked Private lay ahead. Even as she stared, they swung open and a waiter appeared.

'Can I help you, madam?'

Jane fluttered. Officer North had once told her to play to her strengths and fluttering was definitely one of those. 'He said it was on the left,' she said, infusing just a tiny note of panic into her voice, 'but it's not.'

'Ah. You've come too far. Just down here.'

He escorted her to the door clearly labelled Ladies.

Jane fluttered a little more. 'Oh. Um . . . thank you.'

'My pleasure.'

Given everything she'd anticipated, Jane was somewhat disappointed to find the restroom empty. No one was snorting anything white and sinister through rolled up banknotes. All the cubicle doors were ajar and no one was engaging in anything . . . unusual. She sighed. There was a whole sex, drugs and rock and roll revolution going on out there and all of it had passed her by completely. She tried not to feel disappointed. Not that she wanted . . . obviously . . . but the opportunity to decline the opportunity would have been good.

She stared at herself in the mirror, saw what Luke had meant about her hair and dragged out a comb. She also took the opportunity once again to anoint herself with all the free products on offer and set off to find Luke, preceded by a cloud of fragrance that was very nearly tangible.

Luke and Mr Geoffrey had obviously bonded in her absence. They stood together, laughing at something. Almost certainly me, she thought. As she approached, she heard Mr Geoffrey say, 'Yes, she is rather sweet, isn't she?'

Jane's bright smile never faltered for one moment.

'Proud of you, sweetie,' whispered Luke in her ear as they

followed Mr Geoffrey into the restaurant. 'I was worried Mrs Knee might be making the acquaintance of Mr Todger again.'

'Oh, no,' she said quietly. She patted his arm, reassuringly. 'But one night . . . and you'll never know when that night will come . . . I will smother you in your sleep.'

'Eh?'

But Mr Geoffrey was showing them into the restaurant.

For someone supposedly on lemonade, Luke was enjoying himself enormously. His cheeks were flushed, his eyes sparkled. As the meal progressed, and ignoring Jane's mounting discomfort, his voice became louder and louder.

Jane leaned across the table. 'For heaven's sake, Luke, how am I not supposed to notice you're as drunk as a newt?'

'As a what?'

'Newt.'

He wagged a finger. 'Jane – pay more attention to the world around you. The expression is either *drunk as a skunk* or *pissed as a newt*. Pick one and go with it.'

'How am I supposed to get you home?'

'Dunno, but I'm really looking forward to seeing you try.'

'How do I know you won't throw up all over the boat?'

'You don't. And I probably will. I've got form in that area. You're in for an embarrassing ride home, Jane. Unless, of course . . .'

He winked heavily across the table.

Jane held his gaze, filled with misgivings. Was this handsome, charming Luke Parrish looking for another notch on his bedpost? Or was this Officer Parrish playing his part to the best of his considerable ability? There really was no way to tell. She should give him the benefit of the doubt.

She scowled. 'Unless what? Unless I walk off and leave you here to fall in the river and drown? Because trust me, I don't think I'm going to be able to resist the temptation. In fact, I might even throw you in myself.'

'If I might be allowed to insinuate myself, I wonder if I might offer up a solution to this . . . er . . . dilemma.' Mr Geoffrey was back. Heroically, Jane's flesh refrained from creeping.

'Perhaps you may not be aware, but we are residential. I am certain we could provide appropriate accommodation.'

'You hear that, Jane? They're residential. Solves all your problems. Not mine, of course, because I don't have any. Problems, that is. Yes, we'll have a room, please.'

'Two rooms,' said Jane swiftly.

'Jane, Jane, Jane,' he said, swaying slightly as he smiled down at her in what he probably imagined was a winning way. 'You know you don't mean that.'

Jane smiled back and fluttered her eyelashes. 'He's right, Mr Geoffrey. Just the one room, please. And a sleeping bag in the garden for Mr Parrish here.'

Mr Geoffrey smiled whitely. 'I shall arrange your rooms immediately,' and oozed from the room.

Luke lifted his glass in a defiant toast. 'Nice one, Jane.'

Jane was not entirely surprised when Luke didn't appear for breakfast the next morning. She found herself a quiet table and, secure in the knowledge that whoever was paying for this, it wouldn't be her, proceeded to breakfast heartily.

There was no sign of the gelatinous Mr Geoffrey, either.

Finishing her breakfast – scrambled eggs, smoked salmon, sourdough toast, fresh fruit and yoghurt, all washed down with the best coffee she'd ever tasted – and armed with her complimentary newspaper, Jane retired to the sunny garden and prepared to enjoy a Parrish-free morning. She told herself she was very fond of Luke, but there was no doubt he could be an unexpected item in the bagging area of life. Occasionally a passing waiter would refill her coffee cup, but otherwise she was content just to watch the river go by and enjoy a rare moment of peace. There hadn't been many of those since she'd joined the Time Police.

As he was bringing her another fresh cup, the waiter enquired whether she would like him to take something up to Mr Parrish?

'Oh. Please. No.'

'I understand perfectly, madam. May I send you out some pastries?'

'You certainly may. Thank you.'

It was very pleasant, sitting in the sun. Jane selected something flaky and chocolatey and rather thought she could get the hang of this undercover stuff.

The morning wore on. The lunchtime trade turned up, laughing and shouting, and with a bedraggled Luke Parrish in their wake. Someone had taken pity on him and provided him with a pair of dark glasses.

'Fine sober counsellor you turned out to be,' he moaned, carefully seating himself with his back to the sun.

She looked up from her newspaper. 'How is this my fault?'

He winced. 'For God's sake, Jane. Stop booming at me.'

Her anxieties flooded back. Was he acting or, after the excesses of last night, had he really crashed? How reliable was he at the moment?

303

She lowered her voice. 'And just to add to your woes, here comes your new BFF.'

Mr Geoffrey was crossing the grass, as shiny as ever.

'Oh God,' groaned Luke.

'Luke, you've emerged.'

It was 'Luke' now, Jane noticed.

'Do allow me to offer you lunch – on us, of course. Between you and me, the King's Arsenal does feel just the tiniest bit responsible for you feeling a fraction under the weather this morning. And you too, of course, Miss . . . um.'

He flashed Jane a wide smile obviously intended to compensate for not remembering her name. Jane tried to feel compensated and failed.

She looked at her watch. 'Well, actually . . . Mr . . . er . . . I think it's time we were . . .'

'Oh, surely not. And I really think Luke should have something to settle his stomach before attempting the return journey.'

Luke paled and groaned and Jane allowed herself to be persuaded. She didn't want to put herself in the position of being deliberately excluded in any future conversations.

They dined privately in Mr Geoffrey's office behind the restaurant. Mr Geoffrey really was rather good, thought Jane. The conversation was perfectly choreographed. Nothing was rushed or forced. Nothing could have been more natural than his enquiry as to Luke's plans for the future.

Luke shrugged. 'I've been a bit out of things recently. Plus, of course, I'm avoiding the old man before he starts on about my spending habits again. You know how it goes. Same old, same old. Not a penny if I don't start behaving myself. Thinking of taking myself out of London for a while. Away from the Eye of Sauron, so to speak. Might take Jane on a cruise. Between you and me,' he continued in a hoarse whisper audible not only to Jane but to the two waiters standing over by the door, 'she's a bit of a challenge, that one, but I'm quietly confident. Might even leave the country altogether. Dunno. I'll have to have a bit of a think. According to the rehab people, it's always important to have a plan. Apparently drifting aimlessly through life, though pleasant, is not the right way to go. They even talked about getting a job and I think they meant me. Anyway, mustn't trespass any longer. Thanks v much for lunch and hospitality. Nice place, this. You can rely on me to put the word out to the right people.'

Mr Geoffrey pulled his chair closer. Jane tried not to edge away. Leaning forwards, he said confidentially, 'You know, Mr Parrish, I think you and I might be in a position to help each other out a little.'

Luke smiled politely. 'Oh yes?'

'I think I know some people who might like to meet you and the lovely Miss .., erm ... if you'd be amenable.'

Luke shook his head. 'You know me, Geoffrey – I really don't do hard work and discipline.'

'I think we could spare you that, Mr Parrish. I see you in a more ambassadorial role. You know . . . representing us to some very exclusive clients. A couple of days a month, perhaps.'

'Really? Well, yeah, I expect I could do that. Yeah – why not? Although I've got to ask – what would I be touting? I tell you now – if it's women or drugs, I don't do that.'

'No. Oh, no, no, no. Nothing like that. This is a very high-class outfit. I'll see if I can arrange a taster session, if you like.'

'Sounds interesting, but not this morning. Sorry – this

afternoon. Bit of a head at the moment. And, as I say – lots of threads to pick up. Bit busy these next few weeks.'

'Of course. We'll be in touch in a week or so.' He looked out of the window. 'I believe your taxi is here.'

Luke stood up, wobbly but resolute. 'That reminds me – how much do I owe you?'

Mr Geoffrey waved the offer aside.

Yes, thought Jane. The obligation is beginning. Slowly, imperceptibly, the net will tighten.

'On the house, Luke. Our gift. We think this might be the beginning of a very profitable partnership.'

Luke nodded, hauled himself to his feet and swayed. Jane made absolutely no effort to render assistance. Groaning, Luke set off for the jetty.

They boarded the taxi. On their return, Luke had a bit of a lie-down and Jane had a long hot bath to remove the residue of Mr Geoffrey.

24

Four days passed during which nothing happened. Jane was unsure whether this was good or bad. She knew Mr Geoffrey had said about a week, but even so . . .

Still, Luke seemed relaxed and so should she be. This was just how they'd planned it. Make them do all the work. And, as Luke said, as they strolled around the Serpentine one day, dodging the feral ducks, Geoffrey and his gang – whoever they were – would be busy checking them out. Ensuring Luke and Jane were exactly who they said they were.

Another week passed which included more socialising than Jane had ever done in her entire life. Until she joined the Time Police, Jane's entire social life had consisted of catering to acquaintances of her grandmother – you couldn't call them friends – all of whom were grandmother clones when it came to sucking the life out of those around them.

And then – finally – a personal invitation arrived at the apartment from the oleaginous Mr Geoffrey. For lunch and, if Mr Parrish was agreeable, to meet some people.

'I don't think you should go alone,' said Jane, giving voice to her role as sober counsellor, chaperone, fun-spoiler and inconvenient appendage. A role at which, Luke had informed her several times, she excelled.

'I don't have to,' he said. 'You're included in the invite.'

'Me? Why?'

'Heaven only knows,' he said, without thinking, and was surprised to receive a cushion round the side of his head.

'Well, face it, Jane, you're not the most frivolous person on the planet.'

'I know how to have fun,' she said, furiously.

'I'm sure you do – it's just that your idea of fun is completely different to the rest of the world's.'

'Go by yourself then,' she replied huffily. 'I don't care.'

'Jane, you know very well that the terms of my release state very firmly that I must be accompanied to social events. I'm going – therefore you must too. But don't worry – enjoying yourself is optional.'

'When?'

'Day after tomorrow.'

'That's a bit sudden, isn't it?'

'It is. I think I shall decline but offer an alternative date. What are you doing next Friday?'

'Absolutely nothing, as you well know.'

'I'll offer next Friday then.'

'Same place?'

'Yes.'

Jane poured herself more coffee. 'Um . . .' She stopped, mindful of Luke's warning about bugging. 'Will we need to book a private boat? You know – so the concierge knows where we're going.'

'Well, they've offered to send transport, which I think we'll ask to wait – in case we want to go on somewhere afterwards.'

She smiled at him. 'That's a very good thought.'

'Not just a pretty face, you know.'

'Hmm.'

'Any plans for today?'

'Not really.'

'I thought I'd put in some time at the gym downstairs and then go for a run.'

Jane blinked. 'You?'

'Look.' He gestured at himself. 'This level of perfection has to be maintained, you know. It doesn't happen by accident. What about you?'

'I need to send my usual report on you and then I'll just read a book on the balcony and enjoy the view. I know it's not exciting, but it's a bit of a luxury for me.'

'Whatever floats your boat, Jane. I'll see you at lunchtime.'

'Where you'll replace the calories you worked off in the morning.'

'Absolutely. Try and stay out of trouble.'

He disappeared and Jane went to get her book.

Settling herself in the surprisingly comfortable recliner, she found, for once, that her book had lost its charms. For someone who, until she joined the Time Police, had never had time to read at all, picking up a book was still an almost unknown luxury and yet, today, she found it hard to concentrate. Sighing, she let the book fall and stared out over the river, thinking about what she would be doing now if she was still living with her grandmother.

Well, today was Wednesday so there would be lots of

complaints about yesterday's trip to the social centre – the venue, the other visitors, the staff, the facilities, the meal, the transportation arrangements, use and misuse of her monthly subscription, the government, foreigners in this country (bad), foreigners in their own country (not quite so bad but still not good), Jane and her uselessness, standards these days and the falling thereof, Europe – in whichever incarnation it happened to be that week – and a general all-purpose criticism aimed at everything not previously covered by her rambling monologue, by which time Jane's ears would be bleeding and her brain numb.

Her grandmother, however, having talked herself into a good humour, would drop off to dream of an England where everyone was the same age, colour and religion as herself, young people had mysteriously disappeared from the planet, and the country perpetually dozed in the afternoon sunshine sometime around 1937. A time when the butcher's boy delivered on his bicycle, shops shut on Thursday afternoons and bank managers were real men in morning suits and not some twelve-year-old sapling with GCSEs in Economics and Woodwork, who would spend two years in the job before going on to break the world again and embezzle her life savings. For Jane, the rain would run down the windows and her life would stretch ahead of her with no respite or relief until merciful death came to claim her.

'Dear God,' said Bolshy Jane, breaking into these doleful imaginings.

Good to see you being useful for once, thought Jane. She tossed aside her book and went off to write her illegal and completely forbidden by Commander Hay daily progress report to Matthew. There had been considerable Team Weird discussion over this, with Jane quite horrified at the thought of so comprehensively disobeying instructions, Matthew maintaining it was a sensible course of action and Luke saying it would be fun. The report would be sent via the perfectly genuine rehab centre that had, until very recently, supposedly enjoyed the dubious pleasure of Mr Parrish's company. Thudding into their spam box, it would pause for a microsecond and then reroute itself to a certain M Farrell Esq., where it would sit quietly until read and then self-destruct in five seconds.

Patient LP/105/6331/JL

The patient's behaviour remains erratic but no more so than usual. I have been unable to dissuade him from re-engaging in some of his normal pursuits. Alcohol continues to be an issue he makes very little effort to combat. He does, however, speak of a more structured future and there is the possibility of a job being offered in the next few days, which I consider encouraging. I do consider this to be an important development in his rehabilitation and will encourage him to see employment and a structured use of his time in a positive light.

Otherwise, the patient continues cheerful and positive, although whether this can be maintained given his predilection for taking the easy option remains to be seen.

She read it through with a grin, auto-signed it, and hit send.

25

'Fun day ahead,' said Luke at breakfast on the appropriate Friday. 'Are you sure you want to come?'

'If you think I'm letting you out of my sight . . .'

'No, I'm just saying,' said Luke, pouring himself a coffee. 'After all, you don't really do fun, do you?'

'I can do fun,' said Jane defensively.

'Name one occasion on which you've done fun.'

'I'm not being paid to enjoy myself.'

'No, you're being paid to prevent me enjoying myself.'

'And don't you forget it,' said Jane.

Luke poured himself a coffee. 'Don't stuff yourself today,' he said, provocatively. 'Free lunch coming up.'

Jane helped herself to more toast she didn't want.

'It'll be interesting to see how they deal with you, though, don't you think?' continued Death-Wish Parrish. 'I'm certain you won't be included in any discussions, so perhaps they'll just give you a few ribbons to play with while the men do the thinking.'

'Kill him now,' said Bolshy Jane. 'No court in the world will convict you.'

Come up with a foolproof plan and I'll certainly consider it, thought Jane.

They spent the rest of the morning in icy silence until the concierge rang through to say their water taxi had arrived.

'Are you going to sulk all the way there?' enquired Luke.

'Do it,' said Bolshy Jane. 'Do it now. You know what to do. Elbow to the kidneys, swift shove into the Thames and club him to death if he tries to climb out. You can do it.'

I'm going mad, thought Jane. He's actually driven me over the edge.

She halted on the jetty. 'You have a choice. You can shut up and live, or continue talking and find yourself taking your chances with Old Man Thames. Choose now.'

They continued on in silence. At the water taxi, Luke cleared his throat. Jane wheeled on him.

He raised his hands in surrender. 'I was only about to ask whether you wanted to be inside or out?'

'Inside,' said Jane stiffly, remembering the damage to her hair the last time.

'Right,' he said, steering her towards the cabin.

'I'm inside,' she said. 'You're outside.'

'Jane . . .'

She shut the door in his face. Because he needed to be reminded of her role in all this. And of his, too. And they were getting close and neither of them could afford to slip up now. And then spent the rest of the trip feeling guilty.

'Wuss,' said Bolshy Jane, but mercifully left it at that.

Mr Geoffrey was waiting on the jetty to greet them.

'Just as well,' said Luke, helping Jane off the boat. 'I didn't really fancy my chances of disembarking without incident. Fortunately, Mr Geoffrey here has saved me.'

Mr Geoffrey wore the bright smile of one who knows a joke has been made but hasn't quite managed to spot it.

'Luke, how pleasant to see you again. And Miss . . .'

'Sober counsellor,' announced Luke without embarrassment. 'You want me – you get Jane too. Until I get signed off as a responsible adult and frankly, no one's holding their breath over that one.'

Mr Geoffrey recovered well. 'Nevertheless, it is delightful to see you again.'

'Thank you,' said Jane. 'And obviously I don't want to embarrass anyone, but that old vodka-in-a-lemonade-glass trick isn't going to work this time. Perhaps I should also inform you that Mr Parrish's legal status is, at the moment, uncertain, and anything signed by the aforesaid Mr Parrish could almost certainly be successfully challenged in a court of law. Just in case anyone had any thoughts of taking advantage.'

'Most amusing,' said Mr Geoffrey, hugely unamused. 'Shall we go in?'

After that, Jane was completely unsurprised to find herself being shepherded into the smallest bar and ensconced at a quiet table with a view out over the river, where she was plied with newspapers, magazines and coffees. A very young man, obviously detailed to keep an eye on her, unconvincingly polished glasses behind his bar and studiously avoided looking at her. It was apparent that there would be no getting lost on the way to the loo this time. It was all up to Luke. Who was doing rather well.

'May we offer you some refreshment, Luke?'

'Thank you, just some water, please.'

'As you wish.'

'So, Mr Geoffrey, what did you want to speak to me about?'

'I believe, when we last spoke, we touched on the subject of offering you . . . a position.'

'We did indeed, but I believe we also touched on the subject of my extreme reluctance to undertake anything that would seriously cut into my leisure time.'

'I think we could undertake not to do so.'

Luke laughed. 'And still pay me?'

'And still pay you.'

'By results? Or a salary?'

'Well, it wouldn't be a salary. We strive to avoid . . .'

'Paper trails?' suggested Luke.

'Unnecessary bureaucracy.'

'Ah.'

'This is a cash environment.'

'I could live with that.'

'We rather thought you might.'

Luke shifted in his chair. 'In the interests of full disclosure, I'm assuming you've checked me out.'

'We have, indeed. You will be reassured to hear you are exactly who you say you are.'

'Well, that's a relief. I was rather getting to the stage where I was beginning to wonder.'

'Except for the last six months, Mr Parrish.'

'Ah. Yes. Well, I've made no secret about it – rehab.' Mentally crossing his fingers, he continued. 'I'm sure you have all the details. When, where, why and so forth.' He nodded through the wall in the rough direction he assumed Jane to be. 'Hence the old ball and chain, of course.'

'Tough regime?'

Luke rolled his eyes. 'You have absolutely no idea. Up at the crack of dawn. Shit food. Some of my fellow inmates were literally the dregs of the earth. Bells going off at all hours. Massive fixation on physical fitness – as if anyone cared. Lectures, homework, everyone in uniform – it was ghastly.'

'Have you seen Mr Parrish senior recently?'

'Not since he deposited me on their doorstep. There was a moment when he tried to remind me that I was his son, which went down about as well as it usually does.'

'So he's not speaking to you after rehab?'

'No, but to be fair, he wasn't really speaking to me before rehab, so no great change there.'

'Well, we're happy to be able to offer you this opportunity, Luke. I think this will benefit both of us.'

'I'm sure it would,' said Luke, 'had I any idea of the opportunity being offered.'

Mr Geoffrey clasped his hands on the table and assumed his sincere but discreet expression. Unnecessarily lowering his voice, he said, 'We have identified a niche market that is turning out to be rather lucrative.'

'Well, good for you.'

'The start-up costs were enormous but we are now at the point where we are beginning to see a return.'

'That's nice.'

'We now feel we are in a position to enlarge our customer base. To the right sort of people, of course.'

'To people who can afford it.'

'Yes . . . obviously . . . but also to the sort of people who would appreciate not only the opportunity but the overwhelming need for discretion.'

'Sorry,' said Luke, putting down his glass. 'As I said before, I don't do trafficking. Women *or* drugs. Thanks for the opportunity – but no.'

He made to get up.

'It's neither.'

Luke regarded him with what he hoped was his best shrewd expression. 'I get the feeling we're talking about something not strictly legal.'

'Not strictly, no – although we're hoping that will change soon. Some very important people are right behind us on this – and as soon as things change – well, we'll be ideally placed to lead the field.'

'And what is the field? I should say I'm probably in enough trouble these days without breaking the law as well. I think that would just about finish me with Dad and I really don't fancy swelling the ranks of the unemployed. And probably the unemployable, too.'

'I think you underestimate your talents, Mr Parrish. Luke. All we require from you is that you pursue your usual vibrant social life and should you come across someone you think might benefit from our service, that you simply pass their details on to us.'

Luke shook his head. 'If it's moneylending – I'm still out. I've once or twice been on the receiving end of people who were cross with me over money and I'm not inflicting that on anyone else.'

Mr Geoffrey shook his head. 'Let me reassure you on that point. Obviously, our customers will pay for our services, and we shall be offering you a substantial percentage of every fee.'

Luke stared suspiciously. As he said afterwards to Jane, he

could feel his father's genes lifting their long dormant heads. 'How substantial?'

'Ten per cent.'

'Twelve and a half,' he said, automatically.

'Agreed,' said Mr Geoffrey with a promptitude that made Luke wish he'd asked for fifteen.

'You still haven't told me what the product I'm supposed to be promoting actually is.'

Mr Geoffrey smiled.

'Not a product – a service. We are in the business of offering a very select clientele the opportunity to . . . travel in time.'

Luke was conscious of a feeling of deep satisfaction. However, the time for him to cartwheel across the floor would come later. At the moment there was still a job to do.

He leaped to his feet. 'Are you insane?' He apparently remembered to lower his voice and sat down again, saying urgently, 'Are you completely out of your minds? What about those thugs in the Time Police? They're utter bastards, you know. Have you heard of some of the things they've done?'

'Please be calm, Luke. I don't think I'm giving too much away when I say we've been operating for some time now to various exclusive historical locations and the Time Police have not the slightest inkling of our existence.'

Luke visibly refrained from looking over his shoulder. 'Are you sure?'

'Well, we're still in business. Very profitably, I might add. Luke, we are offering you an unparalleled opportunity here. This enterprise will make you rich. And at absolutely no risk to yourself. All you have to do is circulate as you would usually do, put out a few subtle feelers, send us the details, and we'll do the rest. As soon as our clients make their initial disbursement, twelve and a half per cent will come your way. For very little effort – although, obviously the more customers you manage to find for us, the more you will earn. We could be talking about very substantial amounts of money. With our assistance – investment advice and so on – you might even earn enough one day to render yourself independent of your father.'

Luke paused – his attention apparently caught by this. 'Even so,' he said, allowing a little uncertainty to enter his voice, 'it's illegal.'

'It's a *victimless crime*, Luke. No one is hurt. In fact, many have said it's a life-enhancing experience. Some say their lives have been changed forever. For the better, of course. And you would be an integral part of this. And I mean it when I say there is no risk. No one will expect you to join our clients. You need never go anywhere near our centre of operations should you wish not to do so.'

'Oh no,' said Luke. 'You don't get me promoting something I haven't experienced for myself. How do I know you can do what you actually say you can do?'

'A very good point. We would be very happy to arrange a taster session.'

'And suppose I go blabbing about it afterwards?'

Suddenly, Mr Geoffrey was considerably less oily. 'Oh, my dear boy, I don't think that's something we need concern ourselves with – do you?'

Luke felt his stomach slide. 'No,' he said, carefully. 'I understand, I think.'

'I knew you would.'

'In that case, yes, I'm willing to give it a go. It's actually quite exciting, isn't it?'

'That's the spirit,' said Mr Geoffrey, completely restored to his gelatinous self. 'I am completely convinced we will all find this mutually beneficial.'

'Um . . . I'll have to bring Jane along.'

Mr Geoffrey appeared surprised. 'Oh . . . well . . . obviously I don't want to cause any offence but . . .'

'I don't have any choice.' He held up his wrist to reveal a bracelet. 'Jane and I are electronically linked. It's part of the terms of my release. I'm allowed one Jane-free treat per week – as long as I stay within a two-mile radius of her, but otherwise, if we're more than a hundred yards apart, then an alarm goes off somewhere. If Jane can't account for the discrepancy, then back I go to rehab. I only get three strikes and I've accidentally had one already.'

Luke sipped his water. 'I'll tell you straight – I am *not* going back to that place again – ever – so if we can't come to an arrangement then I'm sorry, but I'll be unable to avail myself of your kind offer. Jane and I have been through a lot together. I have great confidence in her judgement. I want her opinion on this. The nature of her job renders her legally bound to confidentiality – a right recognised by the courts – but I quite understand she's an unknown quantity to you and if you're not happy for her to be included, then obviously there's no more to be said and this conversation never happened.'

Mr Geoffrey hesitated. 'I must consult others.'

'Of course.'

'Someone will contact you.'

'OK. And now – if you don't mind – I'm famished.'

'Allow us to offer you lunch here.'

'That would be delightful, but I think we're going on some-where else. Thank you, anyway.'

Until he stood up, Luke had been unaware of his own tension. His shirt was sticking to the small of his back and for a moment he felt almost light-headed.

Mr Geoffrey, seemingly aware that a little of him went a long way, shook hands and escorted him to the door. On legs of rubber, Luke went off to find Jane.

She shot him one sharp look as he appeared. Without a word, she picked up her bag and the two of them walked slowly down to the river and their waiting taxi.

Once on board, he seated himself, leaned back and closed his eyes.

Jane said nothing, just squeezed his cold hand and spent the rest of the return journey looking out of the window.

They disembarked and paid off the driver.

'Let's not go inside,' said Luke and so they went for a walk, strolling slowly along the embankment in the sunshine, watching the boats go by.

Jane waited for him to open the conversation. Luke's warning about constantly listening ears was always with her. They walked very slowly but it was nearly half an hour before he finally spoke.

Guiding her to an empty bench, he said, 'Jane, I've just received the most extraordinary offer.'

She turned to face him. 'Really – how exciting. What is it?'

Luke detailed the conversation.

'Wow – Luke – I can hardly believe it. A job, at last. Will you say yes?'

'Well, I think I will. It's a fantastic opportunity – don't you think?'

Jane was watching an elderly council worker make a bit of a business about emptying a nearby bin and said carefully, 'I do – but – isn't it against the law?'

'Yes, it is, at the moment. But Geoffrey seems to think that's all about to change and if it is, then I'd be right in on the ground floor, Jane.' He paused. 'If they'll have me.'

'Why wouldn't they? Surely they just made you an offer.'

'Yes, but I said I wanted your opinion. They're going to arrange what Geoffrey refers to as a little taster and I told him I wanted you along as well.'

'Oh, my goodness, Luke. What did he say?'

'They'll let us know.'

The elderly man was now struggling to get his bin bag knotted. 'Well, I'm flattered, of course, but if they say no, then I don't think you should let it stand in your way.'

'Well,' he said, standing up, and she was pleased to see a little more colour in his cheeks. 'We'll see.'

'Luke,' she said, suddenly. 'You are on board with all this, aren't you? You know – your rehabilitation? You are aware of the . . . the pitfalls awaiting you?'

He took her hand and smiled. 'Yes, Jane. I promise you – I am completely on board with my rehabilitation. You don't need to fear for me.'

They set off homewards. As far as she could see, the elderly man took no notice of their departure at all.

26

Jane's private opinion, given as they enjoyed dinner in the penthouse restaurant, was that they would never hear anything again. While she appreciated Luke's attempts to include her, she was convinced her presence would be a step too far for an organisation which must, for its own survival, remain as invisible as possible.

Luke, on the other hand, maintained that something like that would be expected of him. 'I'm rich, Jane,' he explained, gesturing around them in case she had failed to notice the luxury of their surroundings. 'I'm spoiled. I'm accustomed to getting what I want and it's entirely likely I'd want my own way on this. And besides, what good would you be stuck here while I'm encountering peril and danger out there? I need you with me. As my sober counsellor.'

'Gratifying,' she said, 'but taking me along might be the straw that breaks the camel's back and we'll never hear from them again.'

'No,' he said smugly. 'You're wrong. They won't let me go now. I'm a catch. Trust me – I used to play cards a lot and I watch people's faces.'

'Are you sure? I don't want to jeopardise . . .'

'I am very sure. And just think – if you're not with me and anything happens, then you'll never know anything about it until it's too late and you'll spend the remainder of your life in a downward spiral of regret and alcohol until you die young and alone.'

'Still not too late to kill him,' said Bolshy Jane. 'Shove him off the balcony and swear it was an accident.'

Jane sighed. He is very irritating, isn't he?

He was even more irritating when, two days later, and far more quickly than they had anticipated, they received a simple message. Just a date, a time and a location, together with what Jane maintained was the extremely sinister phrase 'Admits Two'.

'Hand-delivered,' reported the concierge when Luke queried its origin. 'Sorry, Mr Parrish, we were busy and I just looked up and there it was. I brought it straight up.'

'Well, thanks anyway,' said Luke, crossing his palm with plastic. Turning to Jane, he announced he'd been right.

'I know,' said Jane. 'Who'd have thought? Where and when?'

'This afternoon. Somewhere in Shoreditch.'

'Presumably, the short notice is so we don't have time to notify the authorities.'

'Jane, I've never notified an authority in my life and I'm not going to start now. Grab your coat – we've pulled.'

'Just a tiny shove,' pleaded Bolshy Jane. 'It wouldn't take much.'

The address turned out to be a light industrial estate within walking distance of Shoreditch Park.

'Easy to get to,' said Luke. 'Along the Haggerston stretch of

Regent's Canal, somewhere between the mosque and the site of the old Hackney Brewery, I think.'

He was right.

'I was right,' he announced, bouncing from the public clipper.

'Again,' said Jane sourly.

'I know. I don't really know why I'm surprised because I usually am. Right, I mean.'

'Push him into the canal,' said Bolshy Jane. 'With luck he might get sucked into someone's propeller. Messy but satisfying.'

'Do narrow boats have propellers?'

'What?' said Luke.

'Sorry – I was just wondering whether narrow boats have propellers.'

'Good to see you focused on the job in hand. Over here, I think.'

They crossed a patch of waste ground and found themselves outside a medium-sized industrial unit painted in a rather pretty shade of pastel green.

'No logos, no names, no signs,' said Jane, looking around. 'Nothing to identify it in any way.'

A small door was the only entrance they could see. A polite notice instructed them to ring and wait.

They rang and waited.

Luke stepped back, looked up, smiled and waved.

'What are you doing?'

'Smile for the camera, Jane.'

'Shouldn't you be taking this a little more seriously?'

'Will that change the outcome?'

'Probably not.'

'Then smile, Jane, and have a little confidence.'

The door opened and there stood Mr Geoffrey.

'Good God,' said Luke. 'Are you cloned?'

They were once again treated to Mr Geoffrey's blindingly insincere smile.

If anyone goes down over this, thought Jane, stepping over the threshold, you will, Mr Geoffrey, if I have to fake the evidence myself.

They found themselves in a small waiting room. Comfortable chairs were arranged in several small groups and a low table held all the latest newspapers and periodicals. Nothing electronic. Several other people were already seated and perfunctory introductions were performed. First names only. No one shook hands and there was very little eye contact. They'd been thrown together for something illegal and would go their separate ways immediately afterwards, presumably hoping never to see each other again.

There was a single man in a shabby suit, keeping himself slightly apart, who introduced himself as Terence. He had an academic look about him and was quivering with what Jane could only hope was suppressed excitement as he pored over a dog-eared notebook. Jane could relate.

A young couple – well dressed, late twenties – whispered excitedly together. Ali and Giselle. Thrill-seekers, she guessed, just like herself and Luke.

They were followed by a small family group consisting of two adults – Heather and George – together with their slightly overweight teenager, seemingly immersed in her hand-held device.

The two other women were possibly together – possibly

not. The darker one was Helga – she didn't catch the other's name. Ten of them altogether. Jane feverishly committed them all to memory and wished for her own trusty notebook – that never-failing barrier between herself and the outside world, left behind in her room at TPHQ and sadly missed. She tried to memorise names and facial details as best she could.

'Now then,' said Mr Geoffrey brightly, 'just a little house-keeping before we begin. You will pass through this door here,' he gestured to a door in the right-hand wall, 'and through our security portal. You will appreciate we must ask you to sur-render all electronic devices beforehand. Failure to do so will result in irrevocable damage to said devices and so . . .' He gestured at the tray on the table. 'Together with any bags the ladies may be carrying.'

There was a slight struggle in separating the young person from her device, but Mr Geoffrey's smile was invincible and eventually this was achieved.

'Everything will be locked safely away here,' he said, per-forming this action. 'You have my personal guarantee all your property will remain secure and undisturbed until you return.'

If they believe that . . . thought Jane, convinced someone would be hacking their devices as soon as their backs were turned.

Mr Geoffrey held open the door. 'Shall we go?'

'Through the Dread Portal of Doom,' whispered Luke. 'And beyond.'

Jane nudged him sharply.

One by one they stepped through the security arch. Both Jane and Luke bleeped. Two rather large men emerged from the gloom.

'Ah,' said Luke, before Jane could panic. He held up his wrist. 'Jane and I are linked.'

The two men stiffened. 'Trackers?'

'Oh God, no,' said Luke, easily. 'We're linked, that's all. We can't be more than a hundred yards apart or Jane will lose her job and I'll lose my head.'

'Do they come off?'

'Of course.' He slipped his over his wrist. 'Jane?'

Remembering her role as sober counsellor, Jane was properly reluctant. 'I don't know . . .'

Luke picked up her wrist and removed her bracelet, handing them to Mr Geoffrey. 'Just keep them together and it shouldn't be a problem. Not for a couple of hours, anyway – will it, Jane?'

'I don't know . . .' said Jane again and was ignored.

Once through the Dread Portal of Doom they found themselves in a large, echoing space.

'Could we have the lights on?' said someone behind her. 'I can't see a thing.'

'Just follow the lighted path, please,' said Mr Geoffrey from the rear.

Jane looked down. Red guidelights set into the concrete floor illuminated their path. Like a runway. Everything else was dark. A cool current of air wafted past her. She was conscious of larger, darker shapes around them and she could hear voices somewhere off to her left. Someone dropped something metallic and cursed. She followed Luke as they made their way, single file, deeper into this unknown space.

It's a pod bay, she thought. The smell, the chilly air, the echo, the feeling of something hidden . . . a pod bay. She squinted, trying to pierce the gloom. What did this darkness conceal?

As if in answer, overhead lights flicked on, white and blinding. Several people cried out and shaded their eyes. Remembering her training, Jane closed her eyes, counted to five and then opened them again.

Ahead of her stood a big, dark, solid-looking shape silhouetted against a blaze of dazzling lights. She felt Luke take her hand and squeeze hard which was about the only way they could congratulate each other. They were in the right place.

'Keep walking, please,' said Mr Geoffrey from behind them.

They continued in single file. Jane remembered to look up but could see nothing. The bright lights blinded her to everything else around them. Sounds were magnified and distorted past identification. Even with her training she was disoriented and confused. And awed. How must her fellow passengers feel? She could feel her heart thumping, and her palms were sweaty, but half of her couldn't help admiring this build-up. Dramatic, spectacular and impressive, but not so much as to scare the pants off the punters.

I'm a punter, she thought, and tried not to laugh.

The bright lights went off and for a moment everything was solid blackness. Before they had time to panic, however, ahead of them, someone opened a door and a smartly dressed woman, silhouetted against a warm, golden light, said, 'Welcome. Welcome, everyone. Please, enter.'

She stepped back. Luke, who was first in line, entered, looking around him, and Jane followed him inside, remembering to move up to give the others room to enter.

After the chilly gloom of the pod bay outside, this room was warm and well lit. Jane found herself a quiet space against the wall and looked about her. She was standing in a space about twenty feet by twenty feet and her first impression was of a nicely appointed waiting room. That of an up-market solicitor, perhaps. Or a dentist. Respectable, reassuring and slightly dull. Jane, who hadn't been quite sure what to expect – dramatically flashing lights and banks of high-tech equipment perhaps – found this nice mixture unexpectedly reassuring after the drama outside. As was probably intended.

Comfortable seats – more like armchairs – were arranged in three outward-facing rows – each facing a wall fitted with a large screen, currently blank. So, thought Jane, looking around and trying to take everything in, seating for twelve and there's ten of us. Not fully booked then. Even without Luke and me.

The fourth wall had two doors. One, ajar, led to what looked like a luxurious bathroom facility. Standing in front of the second door were two attendants. One male, one female, both wearing smart navy and white uniforms vaguely resembling that of airship pilots.

'Good afternoon, everyone,' said Mr Geoffrey rather in the manner of an infant teacher calling his class together. 'Please let me present myself. I think most of us have met before, but for those who haven't, my name is Geoffrey and I'm your host this afternoon. Now, as you can see, this is our transportation vehicle. The popular description is "pod", I believe. We have two in our fleet – if two vehicles can be called a fleet, of course.' He laughed deprecatingly.

Jane's flesh gave up the unequal struggle and crept.

'We're in Capricorn today. Our sister vehicle is called – as you will probably have guessed – Cancer. The door to my left leads to our facilities – and yes, to revive an old joke – you

330

can flush the toilet while the pod is standing in the station.'
He laughed again.

'Another one who's got to go,' muttered Bolshy Jane. 'Shall
we do a list? You like lists.'

'Behind the second door here are what we like to term *the
working bits*. There's the kitchen and crew facilities and beyond
them – you'll be relieved to hear – the cockpit. If I might introduce you to our pilot and first officer. They are among our most
experienced members of staff. We don't need two pilots – we
often joke our pod could fly itself – but for us, passenger safety
is always paramount.'

He clasped his hands and moved towards them. 'Now, if
you'll take your seats, please – sit anywhere you like – all the
seats have an excellent view of at least one screen. We'll be
departing in a very few minutes.'

'Where are we going?' asked one of the women.

Mr Geoffrey waved a finger. 'Ah, dear lady . . .'

'Kill me now,' said Bolshy Jane.

'. . . you're asking the wrong question. You should be asking
"*When* are we going?"' His teeth nearly blinded them all.

'We'll sit here, Jane,' said Luke, pulling her down. 'Good view
of everything going on. We wouldn't want to miss anything.'

He was right. From here they could see two screens, together
with the doors to the crew area and toilet. The chair was indeed
very comfortable – she could feel it adapting itself to her
form. She looked around. The colour scheme was neutral –
shades of grey and lavender with the occasional accent of deep
purple – very carefully neither male- nor female-oriented. The
temperature was just right and there was a sharp but pleasant
smell of lemons.

'There don't seem to be any seat belts,' said Jane, fumbling away and fully embracing her role as nervous passenger.

The first officer moved forwards, setting a small table at her elbow. 'Not necessary, madam.' His voice was hoarse and with a strong London accent. 'I do assure you. In fact, if you close your eyes it is unlikely you will even be aware of the jump.'

'Just like you and the airship, Jane,' said Luke, cheerfully. 'We were halfway to Scotland before you even realised we'd taken off.'

'We have not become leaders in our field by endangering our guests,' said Mr Geoffrey, effortlessly impeding the first officer's efforts to provide a similar table for Luke.

'So you're the best, are you?' said Luke in his *I'm Luke Parrish and I deserve the best of everything* voice. The one that always made lesser mortals want to punch him in the throat. 'Exactly how many other companies deliver this type of service?'

But the first officer was not to be drawn. 'As far as I am aware, sir, we are the *only* people in this field worth bothering with and we offer a first-class service. Now, may I direct your attention to your call button here. You have only to ring and I shall be with you immediately.'

'Excellent,' said Luke. 'Can you bring me something alcoholic, please?'

Jane shook her head. 'Later, perhaps.'

The first officer departed to serve the other passengers.

'Wow,' whispered Jane, gazing around at all this never-before-dreamed-of pod luxury.

Luke grinned, looked around and risked it, whispering, 'Jane – we're in the wrong job.'

'I'm sorry?' said Geoffrey, disconcertingly materialising behind them.

Luke leaned back, very much at his ease. 'Just saying – this is so exciting. I never dreamed the operation would be this classy.'

'Well,' said Mr Geoffrey, 'we're thrilled you're so impressed.' He drifted away to nauseate another guest.

The captain was still hovering nearby. 'Are *you* able to tell us?' asked Jane. 'When are we going?'

'Today, madam, our destination is Ancient Egypt.' Her voice was as upper class as the first officer's definitely wasn't.

'Oh,' said Luke, his voice hovering on the verge of disappointment. 'Rather a safe choice, isn't it?'

'We labour under a number of constraints, sir. We need to avoid anything religious, obviously. Close examination of major religious events is rarely without distress. We also need to avoid placing our valued guests in any danger, which means no battlefields, no natural disasters, no epidemics or social upheavals. But we still have to show you something spectacular and we feel things can't get much more magnificent than Ancient Egypt. It also needs to be recognisable and familiar. We need to protect ourselves against charges of fakery – holos, mass hallucinations, trickery and so on – so we generally go for the dramatic but well-known. Ancient Egypt, Ancient Greece or Ancient Rome.' She smiled. 'Today is Egypt day.'

Jane was conscious of a cold feeling in the pit of her stomach. Both she and Luke had already jumped to Ancient Egypt. True, the Egyptian empire lasted thousands of years, but there is only one unbreakable rule in time travel – you can't be in the same

Time twice. Luke's face showed nothing at all and she could only hope hers was equally obedient.

'How interesting,' he said lightly. 'Are we by any chance to see Tutankhamun?'

'A very popular choice, sir, but not today. Today we are visiting the Temple at Abu Simbel during the reign of Ramses the Great, which we hope very much you will enjoy. Might I fetch you a glass of prosecco, madam?'

'Orange juice,' said Luke firmly. A recent team night out had left him with a very low opinion of Jane's alcohol-metabolising talents. 'But I'll have one.'

'No,' said Jane, equally firmly. 'He will not. Two orange juices, please.'

Mr Geoffrey had claimed the floor again.

'Ladies and gentlemen, I know you're all anxious to learn our destination so I'd like to inform you that any moment now we'll be off to Ancient Egypt. More specifically, the Temple of Abu Simbel at sunrise. Now, I have just one or two things to say. Spectacular though the sight may be, you must remain inside at all times. There are all sorts of quarantine controls and procedures that would enable you to step outside, but many of them are rigorous and unpleasant and obviously we can't do that to our guests because we'd like them to join us again in the future – so I'm afraid none of us can leave this pod. And, of course, we mustn't contaminate ancient people with modern germs and start an epidemic ourselves. It behoves us to act responsibly and these are obligations we take very seriously.

'So, we offer you comfy seats, and a first-class view of something unique, together with an official historian – our multi-talented captain – to guide you through your exciting afternoon.

'I'd like to take this opportunity to reassure you – both our hosts today are fully trained medics in whom you can repose complete confidence should any unfortunate situations arise.'

'Do they?' asked Jane.

'Do they what, madam?'

'Arise.'

'Not so far,' he said, 'but medical training is mandatory for at least two staff on each trip. Company rules.'

'Whose company?' asked Luke idly, apparently studying the nearest screen.

'This company,' Mr Geoffrey replied blandly but the message was clear.

Luke smiled and left it. Idle curiosity was only natural. Persistent curiosity could have unpleasant results. It certainly wasn't his plan to rouse suspicions in the opening stages of this operation.

A discreet chime sounded and both pilots smilingly whisked themselves into the crew area.

The lights dimmed dramatically. A cosmetic effect, thought both Luke and Jane, each aware there was no technical reason why the lights should dim. It was, Luke had to admit, all very nicely staged. They'd managed to introduce just enough drama to excite their customers without frightening the living daylights out of them, just as they'd intended.

Mr Geoffrey cocked his head. 'Our captain informs me we are about to depart.'

There was a stir among the passengers.

Luke put his hand on Jane's forearm. 'All right?'

She nodded, hardly having to fake apprehensive passenger at all.

The academic man, Terence, opened his notebook and sat, pen raised expectantly. The air of excitement increased. A stir ran through the passengers as they waited . . . in the dark . . .

'How long will it take?' asked someone off to Jane's left.

'Actually, madam,' said Mr Geoffrey with the air of a conjuror producing an extra-large rabbit. 'We have arrived.'

27

In a slightly less highly-charged atmosphere, Matthew Farrell had duly presented himself at the Map Room. The Map Master regarded him without enthusiasm. Matthew peered at her from under his shock of dark hair but refrained from smiling because he'd been told that could be irritating.

She folded her arms. 'What are you doing here, Farrell?'

'Temporary transfer, ma'am. I do have permission from Commander Hay.' He flourished his scratchpad. She ignored it.

'Yes, I know, but I'm the Map Master here, Farrell. It's my permission you need.'

'Yes, ma'am.'

'Why are you here?'

'Because Commander Hay told me to.'

'No,' she said, patiently, because this was not their first encounter. 'What is your purpose here?'

He beamed – all bright enthusiasm. 'To study the Time Map, ma'am.'

When dealing with Trainee Farrell, the Map Master had learned to be specific in her questioning, otherwise they could both be there all day. 'For what purpose do you wish to study the Time Map?'

He assumed his earnest expression. 'Time-slips, ma'am. After our recent assignment to Versailles, it occurred to me that if we could identify and isolate . . .'

She held up her hand because, again, they could both be there all day. 'Connor?'

Her second in charge looked up from his console. 'Yes, ma'am?'

'Which console have you set aside for Farrell's use?'

'G14, ma'am.' He stood up. 'This way.'

G14 was at the end of the spare consoles. About as far from the centre of operations as possible. Which suited him just fine. Matthew seated himself, wriggled his bum on his seat to get comfortable and entered his access code.

The Map Master, however, hadn't finished with him. 'Ground rules, Farrell. You're here under sufferance. You're not yet qualified so you'll undertake no independent work.'

Matthew sighed. You break one Time Map . . .

The Map Master hadn't finished. 'I shall want to see a work plan from you every morning. You'll define your goals and outline your methodology. In other words, you show me your workings. How do you intend to start?'

'With two major time-slips,' he said, allowing the words to tumble over themselves in his enthusiasm. It was well known that only the Time Map could rouse him from his habitual taciturnity. 'Bold Street and Versailles. I want to run a compare-and-contrast program. Identify similarities and anomalies. I particularly want to consider meteorological conditions at the time. Both sites reported imminent thunderstorms prior to the time-slips occurring. Are they a by-product or do they in some way trigger . . . ?'

'Good start,' she said, stemming the flow in self-defence. 'It's been done before but there's no harm following in other people's footsteps. Obviously, you'll need a control. A time-slip-free period for comparison. Have you given that any thought?'

Matthew stared at his blank screen, apparently thinking deeply. 'Well, there's nothing happening at the moment, time-slip-wise, so how about the here and now? Easy to monitor as well.'

She nodded. 'Makes sense. Connor – replicate and remove the appropriate sections and send to Farrell's console.' She turned to Matthew. 'Your console is receive-only, Farrell. You'll be able to tinker to your heart's content but you won't be able to damage the real Map.' She scowled at him. 'This time.'

Matthew ducked his head. It would seem that wrecking the Time Map was, for the Map Master anyway, the defining moment of his life. On the other hand, the memory of the Map slowly darkening, the silver lines coming adrift and waving aimlessly as it slowly disintegrated around him was not something he ever wanted to repeat. Besides, work on time-slips wasn't the real reason he was here. Bold Street and Versailles were only for show. It was the present that inter-ested him most. Luke and Jane were out there somewhere. In the here and now.

The Map Master was continuing. 'I'll check on you regu-larly and I'll want a short update on your progress at the end of every day.'

Matthew nodded obediently, fired up his console and got to work.

* * *

In response to a request from Major Ellis, the Map Master was able to report that Farrell appeared to have settled in well and was taking an *innovative and unorthodox* approach to time-slip study. Since *innovative and unorthodox* was Time Police-speak for downright weird, Ellis grinned and left him to it.

Inasmuch as Matthew could be while his teammates were out there – as Luke had put it, encountering peril during their every waking moment – he was enjoying himself. The Map towered high above him, glowing silver in the semi-darkness of the Map Room, and he found its continual hum quite soothing.

While his time-slip C&C program was running as camouflage, he had . . . let's go with the word *acquired* . . . a program very similar to the planet-hunting software employed by the European Space Agency. This program was designed to take a series of rapid images of a complex subject – the Time Map, for example – and compare them, looking for minute changes undetectable to the human eye, and use these to locate possible planets. Or in Matthew's case – minute irregularities with the Time Map. Because if Luke Parrish was out there and anywhere near a pod, there would be irregularities, he was convinced of it.

With his perfectly legitimate C&C program chugging away in the background and knowingly in direct contravention of Commander Hay's instructions, he initiated his third program, the one he and Jane had set up to monitor all email addressed to an entirely legitimate rehab unit. Or the *Tall Trees Clinic for Rich Inadequates Perpetually Bombed Out of Their Brains*, as Luke referred to it. Any email from Jane with a particular line of code would immediately be intercepted and rerouted to Matthew's scratchpad, currently located in a bag under his console. All he had to do now was wait.

Each day he would report for duty at the allotted time, fire up his console, and from that moment onwards, no one, not even the Map Master herself, could get a word out of him as he sat hunched, his face illuminated by screen light, fingers flying, not even taking a few minutes to ease his eyes and chat with his neighbour. On the other hand, it was well known that many social skills still eluded him – and at least he wasn't doing any harm – so he was left alone.

True to her word, the Map Master dropped by at irregular intervals to monitor his work. He knew better than to try to conceal anything from her, laying ninety per cent of his work out in front of her and talking her through his progress, step by step, confident she would cut him short before her ears started to bleed. But to be fair to her, she was encouraging for the most part.

'Interesting approach, Farrell. Keep it up. I'm just over there if you want me. Or talk to Officer Connor if I'm not around.'

Matthew would nod, his attention already back on his work.

There were regular messages from Jane – ostensibly to her supervisor. The one reporting a prospective job offer for Luke was interesting. Reading the sting between the lines, he grinned – so typically Jane – and deleted it immediately. He was surprised to find he missed her. He even missed Luke.

His childhood had been non-existent. No one employed as a chimney boy in 19th-century London had had that luxury. No games. None of them ever had enough strength left at the end of the day when they were locked in their shed with a crust between them. And between the hunger, the cold and the rats, not much sleep either. No one ever spoke to the boys – commands were relayed by boot or fist – so none of them had a vocabulary of more than a few words.

And then his dad had taken him away and he'd lived at St Mary's. It was good there. He'd liked it but they were all adults. There had been very few opportunities to mix with people his own age.

Now, however, there was a place for him here, however small that place was. There were people his own age. Whatever that age was. No one was quite sure. He had friends. Jane and Luke were his friends. They were away from the safety of TPHQ and he was covering their backs. Disobeying his instructions, of course, but Matthew was his mother's son. He'd often seen her shrug and ask why she should care. They weren't her rules. Well, these weren't his rules. His part was to keep his friends safe and, so far, things were going well.

28

While Matthew was beavering away back at TPHQ, Jane and Luke were up to their necks in illegal time travel and rather enjoying every moment of it. Luke was steadily working his way through an entire tray of canapés and wondering if similar refreshments couldn't be introduced on future Time Police jumps.

Jane, slightly more focused on the job in hand, was doing her best to memorise details of the pod interior and who was doing what, when suddenly, the screens began to break up. Someone gasped in the dark. Jane just had time to be reluctantly impressed at the softness of the jump – really, when you thought about the many things that could go wrong in the hands of amateurs, this had been as smooth as silk – when the screens suddenly cleared, showing a night sky. The brilliant Milky Way was just about to disappear beneath the horizon. Something black and solid reared up in front of them. A darker hole in the dark sky.

The captain spoke from directly behind her.

'Every day – every single day since Amun created the world – the great Sun God Ra sails his solar barge across the sky, to bring light and warmth into the world. And every night – every single night since Amun created the world – he does battle with the giant serpent Apophis, God of Evil, Chaos and Darkness. And unless the Sun God wins that fight – every single night – the giant serpent will consume the sun. It will not rise in the morning. Not this morning. Not any morning. Ever again.

'In time, the two gods – Amun and Ra – merged to become Amun-Ra, greatest of all the gods, and to show his gratitude and respect to the great god, the pharaoh, mighty Ramses II, has built the Temple of Amun-Ra, here at Abu Simbel.

'Ladies and gentlemen, as you can see, the sun has not yet risen. The world waits. Will it rise or will it not? Have we had our last day? Has the Sun God failed at last? For our survival, mighty Ra must triumph every night. The God of Chaos has only to triumph once. Look outside. All is dark. We, along with the people of Egypt – of the world – can only wait. Has the Sun God finally been defeated? Are we all doomed to eternal darkness? Until the end of time itself?'

There was no sound inside the pod. Everyone was staring at the screens, straining their eyes, waiting to see if the sun would rise. Even Luke had forgotten to eat.

Someone said, 'There – look.' A faint glimmer showed on the horizon. Someone cheered and there was a brief round of applause. It would seem that Apophis had not triumphed this night. The glimmer swelled. Gold replaced pink and then light flooded across the screen, dazzling their eyes as the great god Amun-Ra rose triumphantly over the horizon.

The cameras must be aligned directly into the sun, thought Jane, blinking.

'Ladies and gentlemen – behold.'

The cameras swung dizzyingly. There was a moment's

disorientation and then, with a crashing musical chord that made everyone jump, the purple shadows were swept away and a massive stone face filled the screens.

The captain moved round to stand in front of them. 'Ladies and gentlemen, the year is 1248BC. Today we have brought you to the country of Nubia. Or Kush, as it was known at the time. We have landed near the Second Nile Cataract. This is the site of the Great Temple of Ramses II. Over to our right stands the Small Temple of Nefertari, his chief wife.'

She gave them a moment to take it all in. The mountain, the temple, the four massive statues of Ramses the Great – a pharaoh who never knowingly sold himself or his achievements short.

There was no soundtrack to the screen, Jane noticed. No noises filtered through from the outside. The images were impressive but somehow sterile. Almost unreal. Jane had never before realised how much her senses of sound and smell contributed to the world around her. In the background, a speaker played what Mr Geoffrey and his colleagues no doubt considered to be 'Egyptian music'. Discordant pipes and clashing cymbals rose to a dramatic crescendo and then died away. Jane made a mental note never to let anyone from St Mary's near this.

The captain continued. 'You might not perhaps have noticed, but this is not the temple we see in our own time. In 1960, reacting to the threat of flooding from the newly built Aswan High Dam, the decision was taken to move both temples out of harm's way.'

Her voice swelled. 'What you see before you today, however, is the original site, and the temple, as you can see, is still under construction. I think it's worth mentioning that *no one else in all the world* has seen what you are seeing today. This is the sort of very unique, very special experience we aim to bring to you, our customers.'

She gestured at the screen, her voice becoming more businesslike. 'So, to get down to basics – the temple complex at Abu Simbel is being built by Ramses II to commemorate his supposed victory at the Battle of Kadesh. The construction will take around twenty years – between 1264 and 1244BC. As you can see, the façade is almost completed and most of the work is now taking place within the temple.

'Each of the statues you see before you is of Ramses himself, wearing the double crown of Egypt. Each is sixty-six feet high. You will see that all four are intact – in our time the statue to the left of the entrance is damaged and the upper part lies on the ground.'

She continued with more statistics – details of the façade and the names of the king's immediate family, depicted as the tiny figures clustered around his legs. Jane let most of it wash over her. She wasn't here for this. She sipped her orange juice and watched those around her, their faces illuminated only by the light from the screens.

'Most of the masons have departed – the workmen you see now are the artists and painters. Today, we are accustomed to the bare, undecorated stone, but as you can see, when they were built, Egyptian monuments were a riot of colour. Red, blue, yellow, green, white and black.'

The cameras were sweeping across the temple façade, operated, Jane assumed, by the unseen first officer.

'The Great Temple is dedicated to the gods Amun-Ra,

Ra-Horakhty and Ptah. The Small Temple is dedicated to the goddess Hathor.

'Unlike the pyramids, these temples weren't built block by block. They were actually carved out of the living rock. Not an easy task, I think you'll agree – especially since the early Egyptians had very little iron. Working almost entirely with stone and soft copper tools, they carved this marvel out of the mountainside.'

She took a sip of water. 'You might ask why here? Well, this site was carefully chosen. Twice a year, on the 22nd February and 22nd October, the sun penetrates the doorway, sweeps deep into the Great Temple and illuminates the statues of Ramses, Amun-Ra and Ra-Horakhty. The statue of Ptah, however, remains in shadow as befits the Lord of the Underworld. The significance of the dates is unknown but it is thought they could possibly commemorate the dates of Ramses's birthday or coronation.'

The camera was panning around. 'As you can see, the Great Temple faces the east and the sun is rising and the work gangs are mustering, so I shall leave you a moment to enjoy this magnificent spectacle.'

Obediently, Luke peered at the screen. The dark shapes he had seen earlier were now revealed as men. Just ordinary men. No supernatural entities of any kind. Brilliant sunshine dazzled his eyes as the Sun God rose enthusiastically into the sky. No jackal-headed god stood atop the mountain, starlight winking off his golden kilt and collar. Egypt by day was a very different place from Egypt by night.

The busy scene was not as chaotic as Jane had first supposed. They were organising themselves, receiving their instructions for the day and being issued with their tools and equipment. Foremen pointed and one by one, the gangs dispersed to their allotted tasks. There were no whips. No one was being flogged to within an inch of their life. The whole scene was one of professional tradesmen who knew exactly what they were doing and were getting on with it.

'Why isn't it finished?' enquired the teenager, twisting in her seat to address the captain.

'Because, as I just said, it takes them twenty years to build.'

The teenager's mouth twisted petulantly. 'Why can't we see it when it's finished?'

The captain's bright smile never faltered. 'You can. Your parents have only to book a return trip for you to see the completed complex as the Great Pharaoh Ramses himself would have seen it.'

Clever, thought Jane. Engage people's interest now and then get them booked for the return trip to see the completed building. She wondered how many trips Imogen and Eric had taken. And, come to think of it, whether anyone back at TPHQ was chasing up Eric Portman. He shouldn't be allowed to escape. Or would Hay wait until this particular mission was over with? He would almost certainly be under observation, but the Time Police wouldn't want to frighten him off. They'd leave him where he was. For the time being.

She sighed and sank deeper into her seat, feeling the tiredness wash over her. Sitting in the warm darkness brought home to her how completely she'd underestimated the strain of undercover work. The constant vigilance. They'd had weeks of it. The never-ending need to watch everything they said and did. Always behaving as another character. Her job was exhausting.

Speaking of which, she sighed again and pulled herself back into the present. Or rather, the past.

'Um . . .' she said, feeling her face take on its familiar flush. Nearly six months in the Time Police and they still hadn't cured her of that. It looked as if she were stuck with it for life. She assumed a hopeful expression. 'Um . . . would we ever be able to go outside and experience another Time for ourselves?'

Mr Geoffrey beamed at her with rare approval. She'd obviously asked the right question. 'Yes, perhaps, but obviously we have to take very great care of our valued clients. We never take any chances on their first jumps. We have our three periods – Ancient Greece, Ancient Rome and Ancient Egypt. We offer a glimpse of Cleopatra, or the victory parade of Ramses after the Battle of Kadesh, or an opportunity to explore the mysteries of the Sphinx. We know the safe times and places and we stick to those. We don't, for instance, want to drop our guests in the middle of the St Bartholomew's Day massacre or the Crusaders sacking Constantinople in 1204 or the early 20th-century Boxer Rebellion. And for some people – many people – this is enough. I should also mention that although it is still early morning out there, it is already very hot. Temperatures will climb to around forty degrees, which I think everyone will agree is not pleasant. Much nicer to stay inside and watch others sweat. Time travel isn't for everyone, you know, but for anyone who's still interested, there are many options available.' He smiled again. 'Everything is possible.'

At a price, thought Jane.

'This is so wonderful,' she said, hoping she was giving the impression of someone whose qualms had been overcome big time. 'I've always been interested in Elizabeth Tudor. Do you do requests?'

Mr Geoffrey smiled. 'We do offer tailored packages. Something to round off a celebration, perhaps, or to mark a special occasion.' His glance flicked disparagingly over Jane. 'It's not cheap, of course.'

'You're going to die, you bile-boiling, scum-sodden globule of grease,' said Bolshy Jane, amiably. 'Slowly and painfully.'

'*Do* people come back for more?' asked Luke, apparently dragging his eyes from the screen with great difficulty and entering the conversation.

Mr Geoffrey smirked. 'It *is* addictive. After a while some people can't help themselves.'

That would account for the nutjobs at St Mary's, thought Jane, fondly.

'We're a very exclusive company,' Mr Geoffrey continued. 'Nor do we pretend to be anything else. We are always very clear about this, Luke. Yes, we come at a price but we offer our clients extremely good value for money.'

'Do you have competitors?' asked Luke. A legitimate question, he thought.

Mr Geoffrey glanced around at the other passengers and then edged Luke gently to one side. Jane pulled herself out of her seat and followed them.

'I won't lie,' said Mr Geoffrey, secreting discretion and sincerity. 'There are other companies out there, but none of them – and I say this with the utmost confidence – none of them can hold a candle to us. We are the leaders in our field.

And as we grow our business, these other, lesser companies will simply . . . cease to exist.' He lowered his voice even further. 'You can promote us with a clear conscience, Luke.'

He appeared unaware of the irony of his words. Jane stared hard at the screen, hoping she was giving the impression of someone very willing to become completely addicted to this sort of thing.

Luke's attention span, not something for which he'd ever been famous, appeared to be dissolving fast. He was looking at something over Mr Geoffrey's shoulder. 'I think you might have a problem.'

The academic – Jane remembered his name was Terence – had discarded his notebook and was sitting back in his chair, gripping the arms. Even from where she was sitting, she could see his chest rise and fall with agitation. His face was pale and sweat lined his top lip.

'Sir, are you all right? Can I be of any assistance?' The captain was bending over him. From the corner of her eye, Jane noticed the first officer pull out a medkit and take out what looked like a small hypo.

So far, no one else seemed to have noticed anything wrong. Ali and Giselle were excitedly pointing things out to each other. The two women also appeared to be engrossed in whatever was happening on the screen and almost completely oblivious to everything going on around them. The great Ramses himself could have emerged from the toilet and it was very likely they would never have noticed.

Heather and George, the parents, appeared mildly interested, seemingly regarding this as an old-fashioned TV programme. Their teenage daughter – whose birthday treat this was supposed to be – was completely unengaged, staring blank-faced at the screen.

'Not enough boy bands probably,' said Bolshy Jane, uncharitably. Jane was beginning to think Bolshy Jane was having all the fun these days.

With surprising speed, Terence leaped to his feet. 'I must get out. I have to have air. Let me out.'

His seat was in the row nearest the door and he was there before anyone knew what he intended, scrabbling with his fingernails. Failing to find any sort of door handle, he began to pound on the door switch.

'Stop him,' shouted Mr Geoffrey, his face suddenly quite white. 'Don't let him . . .'

Rather foolishly he moved between the first officer and his quarry. In a move of which Jane could only approve, the officer stiff-armed Mr Geoffrey to one side. He bounced off the refreshment table in a very satisfactory manner before sliding down to the floor, accompanied by a plate of vol-au-vents.

No one moved to help Mr Geoffrey. The other passengers appeared paralysed either in shock or fear. The mother had her arm around her daughter, who had finally woken up at the prospect of excitement at last.

Terence was screaming now. 'You have to let me out. Please let me go.'

Heather was screaming too. As was the young woman who wasn't Helga. Hysteria was in the air. The situation was skidding out of control.

The door chirped and slowly began to open. Mr Geoffrey's alarmed shouts were added to the din. Jane felt Luke slip his arm through hers and gently ease her out of the way as the two crew members struggled with a frantic Terence.

The first officer pulled him away from the door and applied the hypo as the captain smacked the switch and the door closed.

Together, they heaved Terence into a chair, where he continued to thrash around for a few seconds until finally whatever was in the hypo took hold and he slowly subsided.

Jane pulled herself free of Luke and joined the captain who was still bending over Terence. No one was assisting Mr Geoffrey to his feet.

The situation was not yet under complete control. Heather was crying and everyone was talking at once. Panic hovered in the corners of this suddenly tiny space – all ready to pounce.

'I've got this,' said Jane. 'You see to the other passengers.'

The captain's solution was to break out more alcohol. 'Because in a crisis alcohol is definitely the way to go,' said Luke, approvingly.

Jane pretended not to hear.

Bottle after bottle was opened. Drinks were poured and passed around. There was no stinting on the hospitality. Jane suspected a deliberate policy to get them tipsy.

Gradually everyone settled down. At some point they'd turned down the thermostat. The temperature dropped. Fresh air circulated, along with vast quantities of food and drink. Especially drink.

Despite sedation, Terence was still not calm. His chest rose and fell and his eyes were flickering wildly from side to side. Jane bent down and picked up his notebook which had fallen to the floor. 'Is this yours, sir?'

He nodded.

'It looks fascinating. May I see?'

He nodded again. Sitting next to him, Jane slowly leafed through the book. Most of his handwriting – in true academic style – was unreadable, but Jane could see sketches of sphinxes, hieroglyphs, and what looked like a stele. For one mad moment she wondered how he would react if she told him she'd been inside the tomb of Tutankhamun.

'This is so interesting,' she said, pointing. 'What's this?'

He sat up a little straighter and pushed his glasses up his nose. 'That? That's a gateway pylon. Outside the temple of Karnak.'

'Fascinating,' said Jane. 'Have you actually seen it?'

'Not in . . . in contemporary time,' he said sadly. 'I saved so very hard for this trip and I had great hopes but . . . but now I'm not sure I'm cut out for this type of . . . travel.'

'Oh no,' said Jane. 'That would be such a shame. Should you arrange a second trip, you might find you experience no difficulties at all. You've got it out of your system, so to speak. And next time, of course, you'll know what to expect. I really wouldn't give up if I were you.'

'Do you think so?' he said, pathetically eager.

'I do indeed. Oh, this is a beautiful drawing. What is it, exactly?'

They worked their way slowly through his notebook and after a while his breathing and colour returned to normal.

'That was so . . . embarrassing,' he said.

Jane felt very sorry for him. 'No, no,' she said. 'I must admit, for a moment, I too felt a little . . . strange.'

'Really?'

'Yes. I expect this sort of thing affects people in different

354

ways.' She raised her voice. 'For example, my companion is making valiant efforts to drink this pod dry. It's his way of ensuring he never has to face up to life's difficulties. I find the way he thinks I haven't noticed particularly amusing.'

Across the pod, Luke pulled a face at her and then turned back to Mr Geoffrey.

Terence had turned his attention back to the screen.

Jane said, 'May I watch with you? And will you mind if I ask questions?'

He blushed. 'Oh, no, no. I mean, yes. I mean, no.'

They both laughed.

'I would be honoured,' he said.

They settled down to watch the scene outside. All the Egyptians were male, Jane noticed. No women anywhere. Small boys, almost naked, scampered around with waterskins and a wooden cup. All the men wore either kilts or loincloths. Many were bare-headed which, given the sunshine, she found surprising. One man did wear a headdress and he stood apart. He performed no labour, but simply watched. He carried a staff – some sort of badge of office, she assumed. He had been burned brown by the sun and his linen tunic was crisp and white.

'I think he must be an overseer,' murmured Terence. 'Because of the khat – his headdress.'

'Is he holding his staff of office?' asked Jane.

'I think so. It's so exciting to see actual people . . . in the flesh . . . such a wonderful opportunity . . . to compare what we thought we knew to what we can actually see. We've got so much wrong, you know.'

By now, however, he and Jane appeared to be the only people

still paying attention to the outside. The captain was dispensing alcohol on a heroic scale.

Jane smiled and glanced at the screen again. She leaned forwards in her seat, staring. And then she frowned. With a murmured apology to Terence, still scribbling in his notebook, she got up to join Luke. Who was also staring at the screen. She wondered if they were looking at the same thing.

Mr Geoffrey had oozed away on damage limitation duties.

Jane said softly, 'Luke . . .'

'Yeah,' he said. 'I saw it.'

'I wondered,' she whispered. 'Something was missing. Couldn't put my finger on it. It seems . . . sterile.'

'That's because we're not actually here,' he said. 'When you do this for a living, Jane . . .'

'It was only for a moment – I don't think anyone else noticed.'

'Yeah.' He nodded at the screen. 'It's gone now.'

Under cover of pointing at something on the screen she leaned in close and breathed, 'We know they're genuine, so why?'

He shrugged. 'Something else for us to find out.'

Now that calm had been restored, Mr Geoffrey judged it time to return home. Rightly judging that however fascinating the subject, interest would wane either after about ninety minutes or when the drink ran out – whichever came first – he tinkled his glass and informed everyone they would be leaving Ancient Egypt in five minutes.

'Are we allowed on the . . . er . . . flight deck?' Luke asked the first officer, who was just clearing away the last of the refreshments. 'I'd love to see.'

356

'I'm afraid not, sir. Our security procedures require us to keep the flight deck completely separate from the rest of the pod.'

'Understood,' said Luke. 'Given our little incident just now, rather sensible when you think about it.'

'Indeed, sir.'

Geoffrey tinkled his glass again. 'Ladies and gentlemen, if you could take your seats for our return trip, please. Thank you.'

Jane sat motionless, her eyes still glued to the screen. Around her, the two attendants were whisking themselves into the cockpit. A musical chime sounded a warning and the lights dimmed again.

For those accustomed to the frequently bowel-loosening landings of their colleagues, this again was surprisingly imperceptible.

Mr Geoffrey stood up. 'Ladies and gentlemen, we have landed. Please take a moment to gather yourselves together and then make your way towards the exit.'

Jane glanced at Luke, who was making no move to get up, sighed, and sat back in her seat.

Mr Geoffrey glanced across. 'When you're ready, Luke.'

Luke stretched his legs out in front of him. 'Oh, I don't think you'll want me to say this in front of the punters.'

Mr Geoffrey's smile vanished. 'I beg your pardon.'

Luke watched the last tourists leave the pod and then turned back to Mr Geoffrey. 'It was very well done, I grant you. I'm impressed – especially with the build-up to take-off – but you really need to check over your people more carefully.'

'I'm sorry?'

'You should be. How stupid do you think I am?'

'I'm not sure I . . .'

'The overseer, for example.'

'What about him?'

'The one with the pretty staff.'

'Yes?'

'And the khat.'

'I don't . . .'

'And the wristwatch.'

There was complete silence in the pod.

29

For the life of her, Jane couldn't imagine what would happen
next. To her complete surprise, Mr Geoffrey laughed.

'Well done. Well done, both of you.'

He seated himself alongside Jane. Because he thinks I'm the
weakest link, she thought, and he can use me to bargain his
way out of this. Well, he's got that wrong.

She braced herself for action but, disappointingly, Mr Geoffrey showed no inclination to use her as a human shield while
he fought his way to freedom.

'Allow me to explain.'

'Not sure we want to hear,' said Luke. 'It's not as if we
paid for this charade, but they did.' He nodded his head in the
direction of the departed passengers.

Mr Geoffrey dismissed his valued customers with a contemptuous flick of the wrist. 'Camouflage.'

'You mean they're your people?'

'Oh no, they're genuine enough. It's just that they're the sort
of people who apply but aren't quite . . . you know.'

'So if we turned out to be not quite who you thought . . .'

'Then no one important would ever know and our credibility
remains intact.'

Oh, thought Jane. Yes. Of course.

'You see, even though you checked out, we still weren't too sure about you. Either of you,' he said, with a glance at Jane. 'And so, we offered you this . . . alternative . . .'

'So,' said Luke slowly. 'You don't do time travel after all. Well, that's disappointing.' Jane was already on her feet.

'Yes, we do,' said Mr Geoffrey.

'Complete with holos, wristwatches, man-made fabrics, tattoos and so forth.'

Mr Geoffrey didn't do sarcasm. 'Well, hardly.'

'Dear God, no wonder you panicked when that Terence guy tried to open the door. That would have given everything away, wouldn't it? Heaving open the door to reveal – what? People sitting around drinking coffee while a holo played out on the screens? Just a normal afternoon in the fraud and deception business?'

To say nothing of two highly pissed-off Time Police officers who had expended a great deal of time and effort on pursuing the wrong people, thought Jane.

'And what about your customers?' she demanded, righteously indignant. 'Those people just paid a lot of money and . . .'

'Come with me, please.'

Jane took Luke's arm to hold him back. 'I don't think so.'

'Yes,' said Mr Geoffrey, thoughtfully. 'I always suspected you have the brains.'

'Hey,' said Luke indignantly. 'I have brains too.'

'Of course you do,' said Jane soothingly.

Mr Geoffrey led them out of the door and back into the hangar. The other passengers had disappeared. She stood, puzzled. This looked completely genuine. Now that the lights were

360

on, she could see a number of other pods standing around the edges of the hangar. One large one – Cancer, she assumed, sister to Capricorn behind her, and two or three smaller ones. Jane noticed they used the old-fashioned plinths, like St Mary's. She could see the thick, black umbilicals running up into the walls because these pods would need regular charging. This was a proper, working pod bay.

Mr Geoffrey was continuing. 'This is standard procedure for everyone's first jump. There have been occasions when some of our customers have not been quite who they claimed to be.'

'Shit,' said Luke, looking around as if he expected to see the door explode off its hinges at any moment. 'Not Time Police.'

'Oh no,' said Mr Geoffrey, comfortably. 'No, they have no idea. Trust me.'

'So,' said Jane, 'you set this up as a kind of . . .'

'Firewall,' supplied Mr Geoffrey.

Jane nodded. 'Yes. This way the worst thing you could be charged with is fraud. Just a few years in prison. If that.' She looked at Mr Geoffrey. 'For which, I am assuming, those affected and their families are more than adequately compensated.'

Mr Geoffrey smiled at her. Jane's flesh stopped creeping and positively bolted.

'I find myself quite impressed by you, Miss um . . . and I suspect you have more influence over our Mr Parrish here than either of you realise. We would be more than willing to incorporate you, too, if you wish. At a suitable remuneration, of course.'

'How suitable?' said Jane, with a swiftness that surprised even her.

'Considerably more than you are remunerated at the moment, I am certain,' he said, attempting a joke.

'And if I don't want to? What will you do to me then? Kill me?'

'Dear lady, nothing like that. We're not monsters. Just businesspeople making money. We'll simply deposit a large sum of money into your bank account and leave you to try to explain it away at your trial.'

'You mean from this moment on, I'm as implicated as the rest of you,' said Jane, flatly.

'Well, yes, obviously.'

'I won't accept the money.'

He tapped at a sleek scratchpad. 'Too late. That is your bank account, I believe?' He showed the screen to Jane, whose eyes bulged at the new balance. 'So, Luke – are you in or out?'

'Fifteen per cent,' said Luke, who could never be accused of not learning from past mistakes.

'Agreed,' said Mr Geoffrey. 'But I would council you against pushing things too far, Mr Parrish.'

'No need,' said Luke cheerfully. 'I've got what I want. What about you, Jane?'

She hung back. 'I don't know. I'd like to think about it.'

'Again, my dear. Too late. I suspect that, even now, an astonished bank clerk is staring at the really very generous stipend we've just paid you. May I advise you to accept gracefully and just go with the flow.'

Jane closed her eyes – a picture of indecision – and then sighed and opened them, injecting a newer, stronger note into her voice.

'Of course I'll do it. Have you any idea what it's like nannying morons with more privilege than sense through their pointless lives? Watching them drop more at the gambling tables in one night than I earn in a year? Listening to them talking about themselves for hour after hour after endless hour? About how difficult their lives are? About their perceived problems? None of which involve how they're going to pay the rent at the end of the month. It's all about how Daddy's a money-obsessed megalomaniac and Mummy's a drug-addled wreck? Or the other way around,' she added, in the interests of equality. 'And nothing is ever their fault? Do you know how hard it is not to slap them senseless ten times a day? Try holding me back from making myself some decent money.'

Luke blinked. 'Think you and I need a quick chat when we get home, Jane.'

'Fire truck that, Parrish. We're equals now. Pay someone else to listen to your incessant whining.'

'Well, who'd have thought?' said Bolshy Jane. 'Well done, you.'

Luke appeared genuinely shocked. 'Jane . . .'

'What?' She wheeled on him.

He stepped back. 'Nothing.'

Jane nodded towards the door. 'We need to get our bracelets back. I'll tell the clinic we've been swimming and then the spa, but they've been a couple of hours without movement and it'll show up somewhere.'

'Of course,' said Mr Geoffrey. 'This way.'

Luke gestured around. 'So this – all of this – is actually genuine.'

'Oh yes. We are exactly who we say we are.'

As they exited the pod bay, the captain detained Jane briefly.

'Thank you for your assistance. Your handling of Terence was spot on.'

'It's my job,' said Jane, modestly. 'And I don't want to criticise in any way, but I do think some sort of discreet psychological evaluation might be useful in future.'

'Well,' the captain said, 'I always think you have to be a little bit bonkers to do this in the first place, but I shall certainly recommend it. Again, thank you.'

'I'm sure you would have had Terence well in hand without me.'

'It's kind of you to say so, but most of my time would probably have been occupied with preventing Pennyroyal solving the problem by shooting him.'

Jane blinked. 'Well, in that case, I was very happy to help.'

'Yes, good work with the notebook.'

'Thank you, but his academic nature didn't take long to reassert itself, did it?'

'No. I've often noticed how one's true employment reveals itself in a crisis, haven't you?'

Jane stared.

She smiled. 'Sober counsellor? Dealing with unstable people?'

Jane stared. A rabbit exposed in car headlights. 'Oh. Yes.'

The first officer appeared at her elbow. 'Captain Smallhope, we need to upload the cargo for the afternoon drop.'

'Yes, of course. Coming now.'

Luke called to Jane from the door. When she looked back, both first officer and captain had melted away.

They were escorted back to the waiting room. The other customers had long since departed. Their belongings were ready for them on the table. There was an expectant pause as they slipped on their bracelets and then Luke said to Mr Geoffrey, 'Well, I'm very happy to promote you. In fact, I'm quite enthusiastic. I know loads of people who'd be interested. And would happily pay for the privilege.' He stopped for a moment, looking thoughtful. 'In fact, if an opportunity presents itself, I might not mind reinvesting some of my own commission.'

Mr Geoffrey beamed. His teeth gleamed like a supernova. Jane could feel her retinas shrivel. 'Excellent, Luke. I shall certainly talk to some people about that. Now, initially, we'd like you to spend some time socialising. At which you are so good. Just chat generally – it's very important you say nothing too specific at this early stage. Just pass on the names of anyone you think might be interested. We'll carry out suitable checks, of course, both personal and financial, and if they pass muster, then we'll ask you to introduce us – and that really is all you have to do. As you can see – no risk to you whatsoever.'

Jane was thinking – had this been Eric Portman's role? As another young, rich, single man he would have been ideal. Were they considering replacing Eric Portman with Luke? Or were they still unaware of Imogen's betrayal and Luke was simply a normal addition to the team? Hay would almost certainly have people on Portman at this moment. If they – whoever they were – had associated Nuñez and Klein with Eric and Imogen then Eric might no longer be alive. What happened to people who were no longer useful to them?

Luke nodded. 'But – and I don't think you can blame me for wanting absolute confirmation – you really do . . .'

'We really do time travel, yes.' Geoffrey paused. 'Would it help if you actually saw the real thing?'

'*Real* time travel?'

'Oh, we offer so much more than just time travel.'

'My God, do you?'

Jane blinked. 'What could be more exciting than . . . ?'

Mr Geoffrey smiled at them. And not in a good way. 'I could show you. If you like.'

'Of course we'd like to see. Wouldn't we, Jane?'

Jane was none too sure. They had what they needed. They had King's Arsenal and they had Shoreditch. They could take a water taxi back to TPHQ. In two hours, this could all be over with. Job done. They could go home.

Before she could speak, however, Luke turned back to Mr Geoffrey and nodded. 'Lead on,' and the opportunity was gone. They'd never let her leave on her own. She forced a smile, took off her bracelet, and nodded.

Luke followed suit. They dropped their bracelets on the table.

For once, Mr Geoffrey wasn't smiling. 'Are you sure? Because there'll be no going back afterwards. What we're doing is much too big and much too important for you to back out of. There's big money involved and once you see what I'm going to show you . . .'

Luke was conscious of his heart thumping in his chest. By Geoffrey's own admission this was bigger than the Time Police had thought. They had to go on. They couldn't possibly stop now.

'What? What could be even bigger and more important than what we've just seen?'

Mr Geoffrey smirked. 'Come and see.'

30

The second jump was very different. For a start, there were no other passengers and their surroundings were considerably less luxurious than before.

This is a working pod, thought Luke as they crossed the pod bay towards something much smaller and much less imposing than the Capricorn. Very similar to their own Time Police pods. And, from the little he'd heard about St Mary's pods, very similar to their stinky little boxes, too.

Two people were waiting inside the pod. Luke recognised Smallhope and Pennyroyal from their previous jump. They'd changed out of their smart uniforms into something more comfortable but less impressive. Simple black jumpsuits with no badges, no insignia and no logo. Smallhope looked younger with her hair pulled back into a ponytail. Pennyroyal continued to project barely controlled menace.

Everything in the pod was a functional grey. From the small console with a screen above it, to the lockers, to the metal seats bolted to the wall. Two-thirds of the floor area was taken up with what looked like crates of supplies and equipment. A shuttle pod, thought Jane.

Mr Geoffrey waved them to their seats. The door closed

behind them. Jane gripped her armrests, still every inch the terrified passenger.

And I don't even have to pretend, she thought. Time Police pods were carefully built and rigorously tested. Probably even those pod jockeys at St Mary's had basic standards of pod building to which they probably adhered. Most of the time. But this pod was unknown. Untried – by reputable sources, anyway. Anything could go wrong. She'd never seen a pod disaster – although Commander Hay was a walking demonstration – but the word on the street said there usually wasn't much left standing afterwards.

Luke's concerns were less pod-based. This could go one of two ways. Either they were about to be initiated into something important and all they had to do was survive long enough to report back to TPHQ, or they'd been rumbled and this was just an elaborate charade to dispose of their bodies.

'Please do not be alarmed,' said Mr Geoffrey. He patted Jane's hand and now she could add revulsion to fear, apprehension, regret and a general wish she'd stayed in bed that day.

He addressed the two people at the console. 'Site X. Now.'

'Hold on a minute,' said Luke. 'I'm not time travelling to some unknown destination. No one would.'

Another smooth smile wormed its way across Mr Geoffrey's face. 'I must ask you to trust me, Luke. I promise you your trust will be more than adequately rewarded.'

His smile was long past its best-before date. He turned back to the pilots. 'I gave you an order. Get on with it.'

Jane was watching Pennyroyal. Not a muscle moved on his always inexpressive face but Jane had the definite impression that one day, Mr Geoffrey might regret that.

This was more like it. There was no doubt they were actually making a jump this time. Luke felt his stomach slide away. There was a second or two of darkness and then a bump that jarred his spine. The lights came back on.

'So sorry,' said Mr Geoffrey, smiling only with his mouth. Not looking at either of the pilots, he added, 'We are working on our landings. This is just an ordinary transport pod and we haven't paid much attention to customer comfort.'

'How many of these pods do you have altogether?' asked Luke, feeling that now he was a prospective investor, this was a perfectly reasonable question to ask.

'I know of five. Two "public" pods, Cancer and Capricorn, and the three transportation pods, which are our workhorses.'

'There might be others?'

He shrugged. 'I only know what I know.'

'So the very impressive pod back at the hangar was real? Not a mock-up?'

'Yes. That's our public face. For impressing people.' He raised his voice. 'Could you turn on the screen, please, and one of you talk our passengers through what we're seeing?'

'Of course,' said Smallhope. She fiddled with the screen for a moment and then stepped back.

'This is the Pleistocene period.'

The screen showed a white landscape. A few humps denoted boulders or snow-smothered small trees. The wind was whipping the snow into small dust devils. In the middle distance a rocky cliff reared up, dark against the white sky, and at its foot, as if for protection, huddled more snow-covered trees.

'Is it?' said Luke sceptically. 'Only we've been caught like this once before.'

Smallhope shook her head. 'I can assure you, sir, this is the Pleistocene period. Approximately forty thousand years ago, give or take a few millennia. This whole period is one of constantly moving ice sheets – advancing and retreating and then advancing again. They're advancing at the moment, rendering large areas of Europe inhospitable.

'The continents are in their familiar position. We are located in what will be Doggerland – the land bridge between England and France – an area now beneath the North Sea. The temperature rarely rises above freezing and anyone imprudently stepping outside without cold weather gear will not last very long. And when the temperature drops at night and the wind gets up – even less long.'

At a nudge from Luke, he and Jane left their seats and drew closer to the screen. 'Wow,' said Jane. 'Do people actually live here?'

'Other than us, you mean? Yes, this area is populated. Small groups of Neanders are dotted around. The population here is comparatively dense. They're nomadic but we estimate there are usually between twenty and fifty of them within a twenty-mile radius.'

'Never mind people,' said Luke, leaning forwards in excitement. 'Mammoths! Are there any mammoths?'

'Probably. You will appreciate that they are migratory and therefore their provision is not something over which we have any control. Nor is it the primary function of this organisation.'

'What is the . . . ?'

'Thank you,' said Geoffrey, cutting everyone off.

'All very impressive,' said Luke, straightening up from the screen, 'but frankly, this could be anywhere. I've seen parts of Scotland that look as if they've never emerged from the Pleistocene. When exactly are we?'

'I'm sure you won't mind if we keep that to ourselves for the time being. But rest assured, we are exactly where and when our captain said we were.'

'But unfortunately,' said Luke, scanning the hard, white, empty landscape on the screen, 'massively underwhelming. I can't see the punters being excited by this.'

'Oh, trust me, those in the know are very excited by this.'

'In the know?'

'Temporal tourism – very lucrative though it is – is just a front.'

Luke was conscious of his heart beginning to pound. Together with the all too familiar feeling of having bitten off considerably more than he could chew. 'And what exactly is it fronting? What could be more lucrative than charging people the earth to do something illegal and about which they can never complain or demand their money back?'

Geoffrey gestured. 'Well, if you'll step this way then I'll show you.'

'We're going outside?' said Jane, remembering to be alarmed. 'I didn't think that was allowed.'

Luke patted her arm. 'Jane, Jane, we're fully-fledged law-breakers now. We can do things which aren't allowed. In fact, it's rather expected of us. Although – and I'm experiencing the same misgivings as Jane but being braver about it – are we really going outside? Is it safe? I'm not sure what's required in the way of shots but I'm certain I haven't had any of them.'

'You won't need them. You are about to enter a sterile area.'

Luke was openly scornful. 'Here?'

'Yes.' Mr Geoffrey leaned over and manipulated the screen. The camera panned sharply and both Luke and Jane experienced a moment's disorientation. Mr Geoffrey was obviously not an expert.

The screen now showed a very large, flat-roofed, prefabricated complex. Circular modules had all been bolted together to form a building of some considerable size. Some units were single and some two storeys, which gave the whole building a random, higgledy-piggledy look. As if the modules had been bolted on as required rather than being planned as a whole. All the units were painted in shades of camouflage grey and white, which rendered them almost invisible in this landscape. Snow covered the roof and was piled up in steep drifts around the sides.

'No electric fence?' asked Luke, mockingly.

'Power is a continuing problem here. Batteries are unwieldy. Wind power is too unreliable, and even though the sun does shine, it's not for long enough.'

Luke, who hadn't expected a reply, stared at Mr Geoffrey. 'You mean this is an actual working building?'

'Of course.'

'People live here?'

'Many people live here.'

'And work here?'

'Of course.'

'How many?'

'I can't say at the moment – it fluctuates, you understand – but there are usually around thirty people on site. We're very proud of what we've achieved here.'

Luke squinted at the screen. 'What exactly have you achieved here? What is this?'

Mr Geoffrey was clearly enjoying himself. '*This* is what is making us all very rich. Shall we go?'

The two pilots had opened a locker stuffed full of grey and white cold weather gear.

'Boots,' said Smallhope, pulling out a pair for Jane. 'They fit over your normal footwear.' She regarded Jane's sensible shoes with approval. 'One size fits just about everyone. Trousers first, obviously, then boots, then jacket. You'll find gloves in the pocket, and keep your hood up if you don't want to lose your ears. It's very cold out there and the wind-chill factor makes it even worse.'

Luke opened another locker and began to pull out a set of clothing. About to take out his boots, he stopped suddenly and stared at the locker. Casting a swift glance at Mr Geoffrey, who was making a bit of a meal of getting into his gear, he stepped closer, squinting for a long time until Mr Geoffrey zipped up his jacket and got to his feet. 'Are we ready?'

'Nearly,' said Luke, sitting down and grappling with his own clothing.

'How far are we going?' said Jane, regarding the snowy landscape with a not entirely assumed lack of enthusiasm.

'It's only a short walk to the facility,' said Mr Geoffrey, pulling on his gloves. 'I'm sorry about the inconvenience but we really don't want to land too close to our operations. We certainly don't want to materialise inside.'

'Why not?'

'We don't have the space and then there's all the problems of contamination, that sort of thing.'

'What sort of contamination? What is this place?'

'It's a sort of medical facility.'

'Sort of?'

'Yes. If you're quite ready . . .'

The two pilots had been pulling on their own gear. Now they lined up at the door.

Geoffrey turned abruptly. 'We don't need you.'

'We don't need you either, mate,' said Pennyroyal, 'but we have supplies to deliver and empties to take back.' He gestured at the crates.

Mr Geoffrey's attempt to gain lost authority was pathetic. 'Very well, carry on.'

The two pilots were, in fact, already carrying on regardless. Luke winked at Jane and they all stepped out into the cold. The icy, biting cold. The shock of it nearly took her breath away. She'd never been so cold in her life. She was certain she could feel the hairs in her nostrils freezing over. Beside her, Luke was doubled over, coughing.

The pilots turned back. 'Here,' said Pennyroyal. Straightening Luke up, he zipped his hood up over his chin until only his eyes showed. Smallhope was doing the same for Jane.

'You should have warned them,' she said reprovingly to Geoffrey.

'Just get on with your job.'

They shrugged and turned away.

Bad mistake, thought Jane, without quite knowing why.

This world was quite silent. No birds sang here. There were no black specks wheeling around the thick grey sky. Although they could see drifts of snow piled everywhere, there was, at this moment, no wind. The clouds above were bulging with more snow. A few flakes drifted silently down. The world was utterly still and utterly silent and, as far as Jane could see, apart from themselves, utterly empty.

They trudged through the snow, Mr Geoffrey in particular finding it heavy going.

This is the real stuff, thought Jane, looking back at their foot-prints. Not the girlie snow we get in England. This is real snow. Thick and white and deadly. You wouldn't build a snowman out of this stuff. It would turn on you and rip your throat out.

The ground was rough under the snow and several times they staggered and nearly fell.

'We keep putting down a walkway,' panted Mr Geoffrey, struggling on, 'but it gets buried in only a few hours. Some-times even before we're back inside again. We have plans to build a proper landing area and install a tunnel that would run from the pod to the facility. With airlocks, of course. Easier for everyone. We've had to dig pods out before now.' He attempted another joke. 'Good job it's the summer season at the moment.'

No one laughed.

The two pilots had reached the facility and were holding the door open for them. Gratefully, Jane and Luke stepped inside and found themselves in some kind of locker room. Jane sus-pected the temperature in here was only just above freezing but it seemed almost tropical compared with outside.

Luke stamped his feet free of snow and sniffed the air appre-ciatively. 'Ah, this takes me back. Locker room lilac. I should perhaps inform everyone now that my fagging days are long gone.' He grinned at Jane. 'Don't look so panic-stricken, Jane. It's not what you think.'

Following Mr Geoffrey's example, he sat down on a bench and began to divest himself of his outer clothing. Jane followed suit. Mr Geoffrey indicated convenient lockers behind them for storing their cold weather gear.

They struggled out of their thick clothes. Jane, who had dressed for a London summer, began to shiver.

'This way, please,' said Mr Geoffrey, indicating another door. 'Luke?'

'Mm?' said Luke, all his attention inside his locker. Shielded by the open door, he slowly reached out and touched the logo stamped in the top left-hand corner. A small diamond enclosing the letter 'P'.

'Luke?'

'What? Oh, sorry, didn't realise you were waiting for me.' He slammed the door. 'Ready when you are.'

Pennyroyal was holding the door open for them. A blast of warm air swept over them.

'Does anyone else think it's all rather like a supervillain's lair?' asked Luke chattily. 'Will there be henchmen, do you think, Jane? Or a pool of piranha, possibly?'

'Alas,' said Mr Geoffrey, again venturing into the unfamiliar world of humour, 'the temperatures are not conducive to piranha.'

Complete silence followed this remark. Luke winked at Jane and followed her through the door into another small area, empty apart from a rack of shelving against one wall.

'Please put these on.' Mr Geoffrey pulled down a number of shrink-wrapped packages containing what looked like sterile wear.

'What's this?'

'Sterile coveralls. You can pop them on over your own clothes. And the overshoes, please.'

'Why?'

'We can't take any risks.'

'Any risks with what?'

'The livestock. Come this way.'

Behind them, the two pilots, slowly removing their own gear, watched them go. As soon as the door closed behind them . . .

'Quickly,' said Smallhope. Wrenching open a locker she seized Jane's cold weather gear and boots. Bundling it all up, she opened the outer door. Cold air snapped at her lungs. A few snowflakes whirled around her head. She carefully placed it all against the wall a few feet away from the door. Pennyroyal did the same with Luke's. Then they both stepped back inside and closed the door behind them.

The wind moaned again. The snow fell gently, slowly covering two piles of cold weather clothing.

Jane and Luke emerged into a long white corridor which curved away from them to the left and right.

'This way,' said Mr Geoffrey, setting off left.

'What is that smell?' asked Jane, wrinkling her nose against the pervasive, musty animal smell with its overtones of faeces. 'It's like the zoo.'

'My apologies. We keep the facility as clean as we can but I'm afraid the livestock smell does tend to permeate everywhere.' He opened the door. 'This is our central observation room. The best place, I think, from which to give you a flavour of our activities.'

To Luke, the words *observation room* conjured up images of shining white tiles and a huge transparent panel overlooking a pristine science area where important science things were being done by important science people in nice white science coats.

This observation room was nothing like that.

Yes, it was a room and yes, it was painted a white more brilliant than the snow outside. And yes, there were three large, dark windows, evenly spaced out around the curved walls, with rows of comfortable seats for viewers. They sloped upwards in three tiers and the whole effect was that of a very tiny cinema.

'You will get a good view from up here,' said Mr Geoffrey, leading them to the front. 'And for your comfort and convenience, we provide refreshments for our guests.'

Jane looked across. Tiny triangular sandwiches, vol-au-vents, canapés, petits fours, flasks of coffee, jugs of fruit juice. It was all laid on. 'You knew we were coming?'

'Oh no,' said Mr Geoffrey, 'they're laid out every day. For any guests who . . .'

'Happen to be passing,' said Luke, spoiling his joke.

'Exactly. No alcohol, I'm afraid, but you can ring for fresh coffee at any time.'

'Never mind all that,' said Luke Parrish, playboy. 'I've got a table booked at Fiori this evening, so is it possible to speed things up a little, please?'

'Of course. Please be seated.'

Mr Geoffrey operated some kind of control and suddenly the room was filled with strange animal noises. It's a zoo, Jane thought. That's why it smells. I'm in a zoo. I'm in a prehistoric zoo.

'Oh my God,' said Luke, remembering his role as eager investor. 'Listen to that, Jane. They must have at least one mammoth in here. Or sabretooths. Or giant bears. I can't wait to see. Can you?'

Having built his moment and with a flourish, Mr Geoffrey activated the viewing screens. Jane and Luke both craned their necks for a better look.

There were no mammoths. Or sabretooths. Or giant bears. What there was defied belief. For what seemed like a very long time, Jane's shocked mind refused to take it all in. She stared and stared, looking without seeing, unmoving, unspeaking, while her brain scrambled to comprehend.

They were looking down into a vast space, most of which must surely be underground. The floor was of a thick, black material, possibly rubber. For easy hosing down, she realised later. Transparent cages were arranged around two walls, all in neat tiers. Two rows of five on each wall. A mini forklift stood nearby with a bored operator picking his teeth.

The third wall was taken up with illuminated tanks. For one mad moment, Jane thought they were aquaria. Just normal, pretty aquaria with normal, pretty tropical fish flitting in and out of the coral.

She was completely wrong. These tanks were not filled with fish. These tanks were filled with . . . things. And parts of things. Heads, organs, limbs, bits of limbs, all floated gently in a pretty iridescent blue fluid. A head, eyes staring blindly, rotated slowly in a jar. Some trick of the fluid seemed to give movement to its features. For one horrifying moment, Jane thought it might be still alive.

She wrenched her eyes away, back to the cages and their inmates. Twenty cages but not all were occupied. Two of them held nursing mothers with their young. Two more held heavily pregnant females, shifting restlessly to find a comfortable position in a too-small cage. Two bigger cages on the top row held the big males.

Except under very special dispensation, animal experimentation was mostly banned. How could this be possible? She stared at the occupants in disbelief. They were all showing signs of considerable distress, crying and wailing. One repeatedly banged her head against the transparent side, leaving a smear of blood every time. Another slumped, blank-eyed in her cage, listlessly awaiting her fate. One lay ominously silent on the grid floor of their cage.

'Our social enrichment units,' said Mr Geoffrey, gesturing proudly.

'They're cages,' said Jane, flatly refusing to buy into this social enrichment crap.

'We don't use that term here. We prefer to call them social enrichment units.'

'I prefer the term rich and beautiful,' said Jane, 'but that still doesn't make me anything other than poor and plain. They can't even stand up in those pokey little . . . cages.'

'Oh, they don't live in these,' said Mr Geoffrey, quite shocked she could think such a thing. 'Their habitat is in quite another part of the facility. These are just today's subjects. Brought in on a daily basis as required. Now, as you can see, the modules are interchangeable and interlocking, allowing optimum viewing and access. Very light to transport. Very convenient.'

For whom? thought Jane.

'Robust polycarbonate construction,' continued Mr Geoffrey, mistaking her silent outrage for interest. 'Rear flush for easy cleaning.' He sighed. 'We do what we can but they still stink.

380

And sometimes we need access for discipline. As you can see, there's been some resistance.' They could clearly see old blood and faecal smears across the transparent sides of the units.

Seemingly oblivious to the lack of enthusiasm from his audience, he continued. 'Food and water are delivered automatically, although we do have problems in that area. They starve themselves, you know. And they're surprisingly resistant to force-feeding. Often, it's a race to finish the treatment before they croak and we have to write that one off and start again. Still, it does mean the feed bill is negligible, so swings and roundabouts . . . you know.' He waved an airy hand.

The centre of the room was a large laboratory, divided into individual working areas by transparent partitions. Which meant that what was being done to those spread-eagled face-up on the tables was visible to all. Including those waiting their turn in their social enrichment units.

Masked people in sterile scrubs bustled around with clipboards, or stood silently around a table, watching with intense concentration some sort of surgical procedure taking place. So thickly were they clustered around that Jane was unable to make out the patient.

Mr Geoffrey was complacently regarding the activity below. 'What do you think?'

Luke turned to face him and Jane realised suddenly she'd never before seen Luke angry. Contemptuous, yes. Insolent, yes. Impatient, dismissive – all of those – but never so utterly, totally, fundamentally, dangerously furious as he was at this moment. His mouth was set in a hard line. She wondered if he knew how much like his father he looked. His eyes glittered. He was silent and she knew he was, for the moment, beyond words.

381

Because the occupants of the cages weren't animals. They weren't even primates. They were people. Real people. Jane and Luke stared, silent and unbelieving. Jane took in the low foreheads. The prominent brow ridges. The receding chins. The wide nostrils. These were the local indigenous people. These were Neanders and Site X was a people-experimentation unit.

31

Time Police training is arduous and thorough. There are procedures for everything. Jane stepped back from Geoffrey, closed her eyes and counted. According to her instructors, the brain prioritises counting to the exclusion of everything else. Anyone who tells you to calm down and count to ten is giving good advice. Jane counted to ten, took a breath, braced herself for what she would see and made herself look.

Neanders appeared to vary in size and shape as much as modern humans. Their skin colour was darker – almost a terracotta colour – but their hair colour ranged from black to what might have been fair if it wasn't so caked and matted. No white or grey hair. She wondered whether, in Mr Geoffrey's world, old people were worthless for his purposes or whether Neanders simply didn't live that long.

In addition to being caged, the two males were manacled. Jane could see bald patches where their hair had been ripped out. Could these injuries be self-inflicted? She knew parrots frequently plucked themselves bald. Her grandmother had owned a naked pink thing that crouched malevolently on its perch, taking great chunks out of anything approaching too closely – including itself. Even from up here she could see all the Neanders bore the marks of electrical burns where they'd been zapped too often.

The one making the most noise was keening in a corner. The sounds of her grief drifted through the intercom.

One of the masked figures – Jane refused to think of them as scientists – turned his head, demanding irritably, 'Why is she still making that fuss?' His voice sounded tinny over the intercom.

A technician answered. 'It's her kid on your table and I can't get her to shut up.'

'Well, do something. How can anyone work in this racket?'

Laying down his clipboard, the technician picked up a metal bowl and banged on the front of the social enrichment unit. 'Shut up. Shut up. Shut up.'

It had no effect. Her eyes glittered hatred as she rocked back and forth and the wails of her loss rose even higher. And now they were all off. Shouting, roaring, hooting, pounding their fists and throwing themselves against their cage walls. Such was their force that one or two of the cages jerked and shifted. And the noise was overwhelming.

'For God's sake, Jenkins, now look what you've done. Someone activate the . . .'

Someone already had. Water sprayed into the cages, drenching the inhabitants. The screaming set Jane's teeth on edge.

'The water's icy,' said Mr Geoffrey complacently. 'They really don't like that.'

The screaming reached ear-damaging levels.

Beneath them, out of sight, doors opened and half a dozen overalled figures wearing rubber aprons entered, each armed with what looked like some kind of long cattle prod.

'And,' said Mr Geoffrey, 'they like these even less.'

Men strode around the cages. The air was thick with the smell of burning hair.

It took a while, but eventually things settled down. Except for the female in the corner, shrieking and frantic, glaring with hate-filled eyes at her tormenters. She was repeatedly jolted until she was unconscious. Eventually, finally, silence fell.

'Thank God for that,' said someone.

'Yes, thank you. She was really beginning to get on my nerves.'

'She's no good,' said someone else. 'We're going to have to euthanise. Someone see to it.'

The figures bent over the operating table again.

'What's happening down there?' enquired Luke, not because he particularly wanted to know, but because it was all adding to Mr Geoffrey's charge sheet.

'Oh, yes. We're very proud of this one. Sterilisation for infants. Completely reversible later on, of course, but it does do away with the need for contraception entirely. And, although it's not politically correct to say so, of course, it opens up all sorts of possibilities for population control. No more unwanted pregnancies from certain social groups and so on, and the best bit is that they'll never know what's been done. Bit of a delicate procedure on a baby, as you can imagine, but we think we've nearly cracked it.'

Jane was unable to speak.

'What exactly is the problem?' said Luke, far too casually.

'Oh, the procedure is fine – mostly – it's the anaesthetic we have so much difficulty with. Their body mass is very dense, you know, and they're much more resistant to anaesthetic than we humans are. Especially the bigger ones. Keeping *them* under is a real problem, so usually we don't bother. We just strap them down hard and have at it. Fortunately, they don't feel pain like we do and I have to say, it does help to keep the costs down.'

Jane stepped back from the window. Even now, her mind refused to take it all in. This was impossible. This could not be happening.

She nodded at the female on the end, still unconscious. 'Do you have to euthanise her?'

'Speaking as a potential shareholder,' said Luke, 'surely that's a shocking waste of resources, don't you think? And I don't suppose any of them volunteered to be here, so I'm assuming you have to go out there and find replacements. And since they're indigenous and you're not, I should imagine that takes time and effort on your part.'

Mr Geoffrey shook his head. 'Well, a couple of high-beam, wide-angled sonics generally do the trick, but again the dose that quells is frequently the dose that kills. The wastage rate is enormous. I mean, yes, people think we get the research material for free, but that's not so. We have to employ people to capture them – they don't come willingly, believe me – then we have to feed and house them, and that's not easy. We tried all sorts of cages and they didn't respond well to any of them so now we go with what's best for us. As I said, the buggers try to starve themselves, and having them die halfway through an expensive trial is so infuriating. We have to restrict their rations anyway – we don't want them strong enough to break out. Which they probably could do if they ever realised it. So we keep them perpetually NQD.'

'Which means?' said Jane, certain she knew the answer.

'Not Quite Dead. The perfect state. And much better for them. They're more easily handled and much less likely to injure *us*. We're quite safety-conscious here, you know. It's taken some time, but I think we've got it pretty much cracked now. Although it hasn't been easy.'

He paused so they could appreciate how difficult his life was.

Jane's fingers itched for a tyre iron. Luke's thoughts were far more dangerous.

'Of course,' continued Mr Geoffrey, people-reading possibly not being one of his major talents, 'this isn't our only enterprise here. The wildlife provide excellent hunting opportunities. You won't believe how much we can charge for the opportunity to shoot mammoth. There are people out there who will pay literally anything.'

'But is it safe?' demanded Luke. 'Mammoths are dangerous, surely?'

'Very much so,' said Mr Geoffrey. 'I myself won't go anywhere near the buggers.'

'I meant, to the – our – customers.'

Mr Geoffrey shook his head. 'If you're thinking of giving it a go, Luke – and I do encourage you to – I can assure you that high-powered weapons mean you don't have to get any closer than a quarter-mile away. And you'd be escorted by two experienced gamekeepers, as well. There is absolutely no personal risk, take it from me.'

'Phew,' said Luke.

'But,' continued the oblivious Mr Geoffrey, happily surfing his wave of pride and insensitivity, 'the most popular prey is . . .' He gestured at the cages.

'Really?' said Luke, tightly. 'How does that work, then? Do

they lie down in the snow too sick to move and people empty their guns into them? That sort of thing?'

'Oh no, no,' said Mr Geoffrey, distressed at this misunderstanding. 'Our customers demand better than that. The big males – the really big ones – we fit them with a tracker and let them go. Our customers are offered the full stalking experience. And then there's the traditional après-hunt activities afterwards as well, which I have to say we do rather well. Sauna, beers, bragging, you know the sort of thing.'

Jane was torn between throwing up and throwing a punch.

Mr Geoffrey poured himself a cup of coffee. 'Well, what do you think?'

Jane didn't stop to think at all. Her reaction was entirely instinctive. Her arm shot out of its own volition, seizing Luke's wrist. His arm was as rigid as an iron bar. He almost certainly wasn't aware of her. And he was about to do something highly commendable and extremely stupid. She dug her fingernails into his wrist. Hard. Then harder still.

It worked. She felt him relax slightly. And now she had to get them out of here. And, sadly, save Mr Geoffrey's life.

She allowed herself to sag. 'Oh. I'm sorry . . . I feel . . . It's so hot in here.'

Luke seized one arm, Mr Geoffrey the other. Regrettably, at the one time in her life when it would have been socially acceptable to have vomited all over someone – she had nothing. They dragged her out into the mercifully cooler corridor.

Luke fussed around, using physical actions to dissipate his overwhelming rage.

'Jane, Jane. Just take it easy. Breathe deeply. Should you put your head between your knees?' There was a brief pause and then he enquired, hopefully and nearly normally, 'Would you like to put your head between my knees?'

She reached out and thumped his arm. He took her hand and held it between his own warm ones.

'I'll get some water,' said Mr Geoffrey, as uneasy as most men are around fainting women. He disappeared down the corridor. Jane straightened up and took two or three deep breaths.

Luke looked down at her, saying softly, 'All right?'

'Yes. You?'

'I am now.' He squeezed her hand once more and then altered his position slightly so he was taking her pulse when Mr Geoffrey returned and handed her a glass of water.

'How are you feeling, Miss ... um ... Can I fetch anyone? I believe Captain Smallhope is still in the building.'

Jane shook her head and sipped her water. 'No. I'm all right now. I'm so sorry. I don't think I should drink alcohol during the day.'

Luke abruptly turned on Mr Geoffrey, pushing him hard against the wall. Anger and indignation would be a perfectly normal reaction, and while he was grateful to Jane for bringing him back, the missed opportunity to rip Mr Geoffrey's glutinous head from his oleaginous shoulders would always be regretted.

'What do you think you're doing? For God's sake – those are people down there.'

Mr Geoffrey pulled himself free and smoothed his suit. 'No, they're not, Luke. Your concern does you credit but is entirely unnecessary. This is a common misunderstanding frequently experienced by those making their first visit to this facility. Let me put your mind at rest – they're not human.'

'How the hell do you come to that conclusion?'

'Well, for a start, they're not like us. They're inferior. Their brains are inferior. They don't feel pain like we do. They don't think like us. They can't speak properly. They don't build. They don't have art or music. They barely have family groups. They grunt, eat and fu— mate. Basically, they're just animals. Which is why our standing instructions insist we always refer to them as livestock. Makes things easier for everyone.'

'Easier for whom?'

'Luke, it's natural selection at work. If they were of any use – if they deserved to live – then they would have survived. But they didn't. They died out. They're one of nature's dead ends. Nothing we do here makes any difference to the outcome of their race, but at least this way, they are serving a useful purpose.'

Jane stiffened. She'd had to listen to diatribes of this sort from her grandmother. The exact subject varied but the theme was always the same. Everyone who isn't like me is bad. Everyone who doesn't think like me is bad. And all of them are worthless.

There was a long silence. Luke stared at the floor. Jane sipped her water. Mr Geoffrey waited. Luke stared thoughtfully at the door to the observation room.

'You are telling me,' he said, sounding every inch the privileged arsehole, 'that they actually *deserve* what is happening to them?'

'Well . . . yes . . . more or less,' Mr Geoffrey said, beaming, and digging his own ditch every time he opened his mouth.

Jane found her voice. 'But the things you're doing to them . . .'

It was obvious Mr Geoffrey was accustomed to working

through this type of reaction, but their inability to see the reasonable point of view was beginning to irritate him. 'We're not doing *anything* to them. This is legitimate medical research. Testing new drugs. Developing new vaccines. Trying out chemicals to make sure they're safe for public use. Experimental surgery – such as the infant sterilisation you saw earlier. And don't even get me started on organ transplant research. You can strip these things down like an engine. All for the benefit of mankind.'

'It's barbaric.'

'It's necessary.'

Luke frowned. 'How did you ever get permission to do this?'

Mr Geoffrey was eager to explain. Words tumbled from his rubbery lips. 'That's the beauty of it, Luke. We don't need permission. They're not human so they have no rights. They're not animal either, so we don't have all the do-gooders to worry about. Not that we would bother with permits anyway. After all, we can hardly approach the authorities and say we're illegal time travellers and we're using non-humans to test our drugs and procedures, could we?'

'But it's illegal,' cried Jane.

'It's *not* illegal. Yes, all right, the time-travelling bit is illegal, I'll grant you that, but there are no laws anywhere prohibiting the work we do here.'

'It's wrong. Morally wrong.'

'But hugely lucrative. Trust me, Big Pharma pays very, very handsomely for the use of our facilities. Do you know how much research costs them? Licences, development costs, welfare inspections, legal fees, disbursements and inducements, compensation, bribes . . . To say nothing of *time* wasted pursuing dead ends or unprofitable research. Here,' he gestured grandly, 'we can take as long as we like, test to destruction, and get the results back to them only a few days later. In their time.'

Jane was on the verge of tears. 'But you're experimenting on *people*.'

'*Again – they're livestock.*'

Luke judged it time to intervene. 'Jane, you're not listening. He said they're not human.'

She spun around as if she could hardly believe what he'd just said. '*That's not the point.*'

Scenting an ally, Mr Geoffrey made haste to strengthen the argument. 'Actually, Luke's right. It's exactly the point. And we had no choice. The world demands safe drugs. There's an insatiable need for pills for this, that and the other. The animal rights bigots pushed through their stupid legislation so no one's allowed to test their products on animals any longer. And we can't test them on criminals – we tried. Or the elderly – big uproar over that one. Or the mentally confused – whom I'm convinced never knew anything about it anyway, so what was the problem? The bastard human rights people saw to all that, so we really didn't have a choice. Don't look at me like that. Blame the stupid liberals, burdening society with their morals and having no concerns for anyone else.'

Jane said it again, but quietly, as if the fight was going out of her. 'But they're people.'

'*No, they're not.* They're not real people. Not like us. And they're tough little buggers – they can handle it. Their endurance and capacity for pain is enormous, and we've had more than a flicker of interest from the military over that. And there are certain areas of the sporting world beginning to pay attention as well. I'll say it again – we're not doing anything wrong, because these things don't have any legal rights. They're just livestock.'

Without warning, Luke punched Mr Geoffrey on his deeply unpleasant nose. Hard.

Geoffrey fell back with a cry of pain and shock, dragged out a spotless handkerchief, uttered another cry at the sight of his own blood and tottered off down the corridor.

Luke turned to her with a rueful grin. 'Sorry, Jane. You were doing a great job and I've screwed everything up, but I can't tell you how good that felt.'

'Never mind – I don't think anyone will weep for Mr Geoffrey.'

'They'll be weeping for us if we can't get out of here.'

'We could try and get back to the pod,' said Jane, looking back the way they'd come. 'If we can get it to jump, then they're all stranded here. Easy for our people to pick up. We should go while we can.'

'Except Smallhope and Pennyroyal might be there. They'll want to know what's happened to bollock-brain Geoffrey. I think we should take this opportunity to have a look around. I have a feeling we'll be ushered off the premises asap so I think we should seize the moment, so to speak.'

Jane shifted uneasily. For some reason, Ellis's remark about the perfect moment to withdraw came to mind, but Luke was hurrying on.

'Don't worry. We don't have to go back into the observation room again. Let's try this way, shall we?'

'Circular layout,' observed Jane as they followed the corridor round its gentle curve. Everything here was white and spotless.

There were notices everywhere exhorting people to keep the doors closed and conserve heat. More notices informed all personnel that decontamination between floors was imperative. Fire notices posted every few yards gave full instructions on the actions to be taken in the event of fire. There were extinguishers everywhere. Jane could imagine the fear of fire. Burn to death in here or freeze to death out there.

Unhelpfully, not only were none of the doors they encountered labelled, but they were locked as well. They seemed to be trapped in an endless curving corridor of anonymous doors.

'This never happens to James Bond,' said Luke, gloomily, as they tried the sixth or seventh door. 'The villain always explains his plans for world domination, brings up the building schematics to show them what's where and then helpfully points to the big red button and says, "As long as no one presses that, then nothing can stop me from taking over the world."'

'We don't have that sort of luck,' said Jane.

As it turned out, they didn't have any sort of luck at all.

'Remember,' said Luke, trying another door. 'We've been abandoned – which is true – and we're just trying to find our way out. Which is also true. For all we know, any one of these doors could take us back to Kansas.'

'Kansas is a real place?'

'I believe so, yes.'

The corridor remained empty. 'Where is everyone?' said Jane.

'I'm wondering if this area might all be residential. Which would make sense, if all the work is on the lower floors.'

Jane nodded. 'That does make sense. And I bet there's some kind of barrier or wall between the staff and . . .'

'And their livestock,' said Luke, grimly. 'Sensible. In case any of the Neanders escape. Imagine waking up after a hard day in the lab to find a couple of them sitting at the bottom of your bed.'

Jane shivered.

Finally, the corridor widened out into what seemed to be some kind of common relaxing area. Other corridors fed into it – like the spokes of a wheel. There were no windows, but everything was painted in relaxing shades of soft grey and blue. Tables and chairs were scattered around in informal groups. Comfortable-looking armchairs faced an entertainment wall fitted with all the latest gear. Shelves held a good supply of books, magazines and other electronic devices. The room was actually very well equipped. It would have to be, reflected Luke. Given the hostile conditions outside, coupled with the horrors of what was happening downstairs, the facilities would need to be first-rate.

A pleasant smell of coffee wafted towards them from a modern kitchen area in the corner. They could hear male voices and the sound of a blender. An open door gave into a smart-looking dining area. The overwhelming impression was of warmth and comfort. He closed his mind to the contrast between this and what was probably happening downstairs in the laboratories at this very moment.

'They don't stint themselves, do they?' whispered Jane.

'Well, it's not as if they can pop down the pub or send for a takeout, is it?'

As if to confirm this, a large notice on the wall warned that all alcohol was forbidden, spot checks would be carried out and possession was punishable. Rather ominously, it didn't say with what.

The rest area was occupied. Five or six people were scattered around, reading or writing. Two men were engaged in some sort of multi-level chess game. Another man had pulled up a chair and was observing. Everything was peaceful and quiet.

They looked up as Luke and Jane entered. Obviously, visitors were not unknown, but unaccompanied visitors were. Everyone looked at everyone else.

'Hello,' said Luke, brightly. 'Not sure we're in the right place. Mr Geoffrey was showing us the way out and then he had a bit of a nosebleed.'

For one wild moment, Jane thought this was going to work.

'Down there, mate,' said a very young man, turning from the coffee machine with a steaming mug. 'Back the way you came, past the observation room. Second door on your left. Don't forget to pick up your cold weather gear on the way out. Weather's taking a turn for the worse out there.'

'We certainly won't,' said Luke. 'I expect he's waiting for us there.'

'I do hope he's all right,' said Jane, making an enjoyable detour into the world of hypocrisy. 'He was rather gushing.'

'He always is,' said someone, drily, and someone else sniggered. No one expressed any sort of concern for their unfortunate colleague.

'We'll go and look for him,' said Luke. 'Thanks for your help.'

'No worries, mate. Have a good one.'

They so nearly made it.

As they turned to go, as if summoned by the mention of his own name, a door was pushed fully open and Mr Geoffrey appeared. He looked rather pale and there were blood spots all down the front of his paper suit.

'Shall we be getting back?' said Luke, as if nothing had happened. They hadn't explored all the complex but their priorities had changed. Now he and Jane needed to get back with what they knew. Details of this place. Shoreditch. The King's Arsenal. More than enough for the Time Police to be getting on with. Others could take it from here. For himself, he wanted a stiff drink and a hot bath. And another stiff drink while in the hot bath. And then another stiff drink. Somehow to erase the memories of this place forever, although he knew that would never happen.

How Mr Geoffrey would have responded to this face-saving way out was never known. Before he could say a word, he jumped a little, as if someone standing behind him had poked him in the back.

Which, as it turned out, was exactly what had happened.

Frowning, he looked over his shoulder, smiled slightly in recognition and stepped aside with an apology.

'Thank you, Geoffrey,' said a familiar voice and Imogen Farnborough swept into the room.

32

For once in his life Luke could think of nothing to say. Disbelief paralysed his thoughts. Those fire-trucking dickheads had let her go. One of the few people in the world who could identify them as Time Police and here she was. Right in front of them. And he still couldn't think of a single thing to say.

'Immy – how are you?' hardly seemed to cut it.

A cheery 'Out of prison, then?' – ditto.

A remark on her altered appearance? – the same. In Luke's experience, anyone spending quality time with his colleagues tended not to look so good at the end of it.

Imogen Farnborough was changed forever. Gone was the sparkling girl he'd known. In her place stood a woman. The slight lines of discontent had evolved into deep nose-to-mouth lines. She was managing at the same time to look both skinny and flabby. And she had the complexion of one who hasn't seen proper daylight for some considerable time. Unusually, her hair was several shades darker than before. She's going grey, he thought, and she's coloured her hair to cover it. Imogen might have served only eight years, but he was willing to bet she wouldn't have managed her imprisonment well. Eight years in a Time Police institution, thought Luke, dismally. For which she blames me. Hell – I blame me. And now she's out and she's here and Jane and I are in deep shit.

Pinning on a smile, he said, 'Imogen – fancy seeing you here.' He pointed to her paper suit. 'Are you investing, too?'

The old Immy would have gone for his eyes – via his testicles, probably. This one stood looking. Her eyes flicked from Luke to Jane and back again. Jane could think of nothing to say that wouldn't make this situation considerably worse. Casually, she moved behind Luke. To watch his back, ready for the moment they would have to fight their way out.

Mr Geoffrey halted in surprise. 'You two know each other?'

Luke's brain finally ground into gear. 'Oh yes,' he said, easily. 'Immy and I are old friends. How's your mother?' He glanced back at Jane. 'Actually, I'd love to catch up, but given Jane's fainting fit in the corridor, I rather think we should be off, don't you?'

He began to edge backwards. Jane put her hand in the small of his back – part comfort and part encouragement.

Imogen turned to Mr Geoffrey. 'What's he doing here?'

'Never mind that,' said Luke, shutting down that enquiry before it could get off the ground. 'What are *you* doing here?'

Mr Geoffrey had stopped smiling. 'Miss Farnborough is here in the same capacity as yourself.'

'Oh?' said Imogen, unpleasantly. 'So I'm a Time Police spy as well, am I?'

Mr Geoffrey's jaw dropped nearly to his knees. '*What?*' and for one gratifying moment, Luke realised he'd genuinely had no idea who they really were.

We were doing so well, thought Jane. A quick jump back. Into a water taxi and off to TPHQ to tell them everything, a nice cup of cocoa, followed by an early night and possibly even a medal at the end of the day.

Luke followed Mr Geoffrey's example because imitation is the sincerest form of flattery. His jaw dropped too. 'What?' Imogen snarled. 'You heard me, Geoffrey.'

Luke took Mr Geoffrey's arm and edged him away. 'Look,' he said confidentially, man to man. 'I don't know what's happening here but . . .' he glanced at Imogen. 'I don't think Miss Farnborough is very well. There have been rumours . . . you know.'

'Well, I . . .' began Mr Geoffrey.

'Apparently, her last spell in the clinic was not as successful as one could have hoped. Word on the street is that she's . . . well . . . you know . . . women's problems. And, you do know she doesn't have a bean, don't you? It's all Mummy's money and I doubt *she'll* be sympathetic to your cause.'

It was plain Imogen's financial status was of far more importance to Mr Geoffrey than her mental state. He stared thoughtfully.

'Don't listen to him,' shouted Imogen. 'That's Luke Parrish and she's Jane Lockland.'

'Yes,' said Mr Geoffrey. 'We know.'

Jane sighed. Now he remembered her name.

'Immy,' said Luke, gently. 'Are you certain you want to continue this conversation? Here? Now? In front of all these people?' He turned to Mr Geoffrey. 'I'm so glad Immy's taking advantage of the opportunity to invest here.' He turned to her, smiling. 'After all – in a roundabout way, she's the reason we're here, aren't you, Immy?'

He's threatening her, thought Jane. She's the one who grassed them up. They won't like that. Will she understand she could be in as much danger as we are?

Mr Geoffrey frowned. 'Our understanding was that Miss Farnborough had been availing herself of the facilities of an establishment very similar to your own. And there's no doubt of her financial status. She's been sponsored by Mr Portman himself.'

'No,' exclaimed Luke, blinking at her. 'You're still with him? If you'll take a spot of advice, Immy, I'd get him to pay for a little work if I were you. You're looking very . . . tired.'

Luke and Imogen were watching each other like a pair of cats. Jane held her breath. Luke had offered Imogen a way out. If she could recognise it. But Imogen was too far gone to listen to his words. Resentment – eight years' worth of it – not unreasonably boiled over in the froth and frenzy of revenge.

'They're Time Police officers, you morons!' Spittle flew from her mouth with the vigour of her shouting. 'They're spies. There should be another one around somewhere. A little runt with funny eyes.'

'Immy,' said Luke, gently. 'Don't you think you might benefit from a bit of a lie-down?'

'No,' she shouted. She turned to the room, desperate to make them understand. 'Why are you all just standing there? The Time Police are on to you.'

No one moved.

They don't believe her, thought Jane. Or, given who they think Luke is, they don't want to believe her. Mr Geoffrey won't easily let someone like Luke escape his clutches.

Immy clenched her fists in frustration. 'Don't you understand? They're the Time Police, I tell you. *Time Police.*'

And finally, it penetrated. Slowly, people began to get to their feet.

'Time Police bastards,' said someone.

Luke shook his head. 'You are mistaken.'

Imogen punched him hard in the stomach and he doubled up, retching and coughing.

'Liar,' she spat. She looked around. 'For God's sake, there might be any number of them on their way here *right now.*'

'Unlikely,' said Mr Geoffrey, a touch uncertainly. 'As far as we know, the Time Police are still unaware their original officers are dead – our contact certainly hasn't heard anything – so why would they send two more?'

He stared at Luke and Jane – the unspoken implication being why would they send these two?

'Look,' said Imogen to Geoffrey and anyone else whose eye she could catch. 'You know what happened to me when I . . . became separated from Eric on our jump – for which he paid you an enormous sum of money, Geoffrey – and I got lost. Mummy went to the Time Police to get me back and they sent these two bastards. And another one. Where is he?'

'Where's who?' said Jane, tearful, frightened, bewildered, and entirely playing to her strengths.

Imogen ignored her. 'And they dragged me off and arrested me and –' It seemed to occur to Imogen for the first time that this was an area of her story that should be glossed over as quickly as possible – 'and Mummy did a deal with them – if I got myself sorted out, then they'd let me go. And that bastard . . .' she pointed at Luke, 'got me sent to prison just because I dumped him for someone else.'

'I'm sorry,' said Luke, wearily, straightening up again and

402

wincing. 'I'm not sure where Miss Farnborough's getting all this from, and I don't want to be unkind, but I strongly suspect her last spell in the Happy Home didn't go so well, but that's not my problem. And now, if you don't mind, I'd like to go home now. On reflection, Mr Geoffrey, I think Jane and I will *not* be investing . . . in your organisation. And – I never thought I'd live to say these words – but when my father finds out about this, there will be an enormous amount of ordure impacting the air-circulation system.' He paused meaningfully. 'And now, I'll leave you with the delightful, if slightly unbalanced, Miss Farnborough and her paranoia. And the best of luck to all of you.' As he finished speaking, he became aware of an electronic whine in their vicinity.

'No,' said someone, running their electronic tag reader over first Jane, then Luke. 'No tags or tracking devices of any kind. Nothing electronic at all.'

'Not sure what that means,' said Luke, 'but it sounds good. The exit door, please.'

'I'm telling the truth,' shouted Imogen.

'Of course you are,' said Luke, patting her on the shoulder.

'He shouldn't have done that,' thought Jane. Imogen's face had turned white with rage.

During their training, one of their instructors had warned them to watch for this. 'Angry people come in two categories,' he'd said. 'Red-faced and white-faced. Red-faced – duck. White-faced – run away. They're dangerous.'

Imogen had mastered herself. She'd stopped shouting. Now she was dangerous. Turning to Geoffrey, she spoke quietly. 'These two people are Time Police officers. Forget his invest-ment. Parrish doesn't have a penny to his name. His dad kicked him out six months ago. The Time Police were the only people who would have him. If you fail to deal with this issue now – right now – I *will* speak to Eric. I will tell him this organisation is no longer secure. That under *your* auspices, Geoffrey, the Time Police have infiltrated the entire establishment – top to bottom. I promise you, Eric will have his money out of this venture before you even have time to regret not believing me. And once that happens, how long do you think you'll be allowed to wander around, Geoffrey, knowing what you know?'

Mr Geoffrey blinked. 'He's Luke Parrish. Son of Raymond Parrish and . . .'

'The name on my arrest docs said he was Trainee Parrish of the Time Police. You're a fool, Geoffrey. But this situation is not beyond saving. We get rid of these two right now and no one will ever know what became of them. Problem solved.'

Luke was never sure whether Geoffrey truly believed what Imogen was saying or not, but the face he turned to them was ugly. And afraid. He wouldn't take the risk of losing a giant investor like Eric Portman. And Luke was very much afraid he and Jane were another risk Geoffrey wouldn't run.

Jane pulled on the back of Luke's paper suit. Above their heads an electronic alarm shrieked and blue and red lights flashed. Heavy doors clunked shut and locked themselves, blocking their path. There was no way out. They were unarmed, and trapped.

'Don't fight,' said Luke, backing them both against a wall. 'Stand quietly. Cooperate. Let's try and stay alive for as long as possible.'

Those were the last words he was able to say for quite some time.

They were seized by the men around them. Not gently. Luke was thrown to the floor and disappeared from view. Jane struggled in the grip of two others. That they weren't security professionals was apparent by the way in which they handled her. *Get your opponent on the ground and then do everything to stop them getting up again* was always Rule 1. Jane was pinned to the wall which was all well and good but left her legs free. She kicked out. At what, she had no idea, but the sharp pain in her toes and ankle told her she'd connected with something. A man's voice shouted out. She was all set to follow through when, suddenly, Mr Geoffrey was in her face. He slapped her hard enough to knock her off-balance. One of her captors lost his grip on her arm and she pivoted and punched Mr Geoffrey in the stomach. Not hard – Grint would have laughed at her – but Mr Geoffrey was soft and flabby. He doubled over. More arms seized her, pushing her back against the wall. Before she could kick out again, Mr Geoffrey straightened up and hit her for a second time, putting a surprising amount of force behind the blow. Her vision blurred. Pain burned all down one side of her face. Even through the pain she thought how typical this was of him. Hitting a woman held back by other men was just about his level. He didn't even have the balls to be one of the many putting the boot into Luke.

Jane shouted to them to leave him alone and struggled hard. She had nothing to lose. No one was listening to her. They pushed her hard back against the wall and she banged her head. Someone held his forearm across her throat. All around she could hear the sounds of grunting and punching. She wondered if it would be her turn next.

Imogen stood watching. There was no compassion in her gaze.

The vivacious girl was gone forever. A small smile curved her lips. With a slight shock, Jane realised Imogen was enjoying this.

After what seemed a very long time the men drew back. Everyone looked at everyone else. Jane wrenched an arm free and pushed her hair out of her eyes. The original group of civilians had been augmented by a team of security guards. Escape, never very likely, was now impossible.

'Get him up,' said Mr Geoffrey, flushed and dishevelled. Slapping Jane had obviously taken it out of him.

They hauled Luke to his feet. He looked dreadful. One eye was closing fast and blood ran from a deep cut above his right eyebrow. He tried to pull himself free from their grasp.

'Christ almighty, are you out of your minds? I'm Luke Parrish, for God's sake. Do I look like a Time Police officer? Does Jane? I mean – look at her.'

Everyone looked at Jane, who did her best to look as unlike a Time Police officer as possible. For her, not difficult.

She tried to take advantage of their uncertainty. 'Wait, wait. If I'm understanding this correctly, Miss . . . Farnley . . . ?'

'Farnborough,' spat Imogen.

'Sorry. Miss Farnborough is a regular customer of yours. Together with her friend . . . Eric. She's claiming the Time Police somehow arrested her but let her go? Why would they do that? I've heard the Time Police will kill you just for looking at them wrong.' A thought apparently occurred to her and she turned to Imogen. 'Did you perhaps do some sort of deal with them?'

'That's a very good point, Jane,' said Luke, swiftly. 'No one gets off scot-free from the Time Police. Not unless they've got something those bastards want.'

'Scot-free?' shrieked Imogen, enraged beyond discretion. 'I did eight years thanks to you two. Eight fire-trucking years.'

'Eight what?' said someone in puzzlement.

'I think,' said Jane, 'she means . . .' She paused, closed her eyes, swallowed hard and said in a tiny voice, 'Fuck.'

'Oh my God,' said Luke in delight. 'You did it. Your first faltering steps on the primrose path, Jane. Well done you.'

'Shut up, Luke.' She looked at Imogen. 'You say I was one of the people who arrested you and you served eight years?'

Imogen, suddenly wary, said nothing.

'Well,' continued Jane, diffidently, 'when was this? Because eight years ago I was still at school.'

This was undeniably true. The grip on her arms slackened slightly. Heads turned towards Imogen.

'They're the Time Police, you idiots,' she shouted. 'They take you to another time – you serve your sentence – and then they bring you back and only a few months have passed.'

Jane was clearly puzzled. 'Why? Why would they do that?'

'Because they're bastards,' yelled Imogen. 'I mean – *you're* bastards.'

'Now I'm completely confused,' said Jane. 'Because everyone knows the punishment is usually either execution or a really, really long spell in prison. Why did you only get eight years?'

'Well,' said Imogen, off-balance. 'Because of Mummy, of course.'

'But I still don't understand,' continued Jane. 'They're utter bastards, but you only got eight years because your *mother* complained?' She turned to Mr Geoffrey. 'How likely is that, do you think?'

'Jane's right,' said Luke before Geoffrey could reply. 'They're the Time Police. They'd just laugh at her. Why *did* you get such a lenient sentence, Imogen?'

Imogen said nothing.

My God, thought Jane, conscious of a warm glow of hope rising in her aching body. We might just get out of this alive. She can't say anything without implicating herself. Turning to Mr Geoffrey, she said faintly, 'I'd like to go home, please.'

Luke had finally pulled himself free. 'Of course you do, Jane.' He turned to Mr Geoffrey. 'Now, if you don't mind.'

Mr Geoffrey hovered, indecision written all over him. Imogen made up his mind for him. Seizing a weapon from the man standing next to her, she levelled it at Luke. 'Admit it or I'll kill you.'

Luke sighed. 'Very well. I'm a Time Police officer. Happy now?'

'Allow me,' said Mr Geoffrey, relieving her of the weapon and examining it closely. 'Ah, one of our more potent stunners.' He handed it to the man next to him. 'Shoot Lockland.'

'It won't be fatal,' said the man, mystified.

'Not initially, but repeated blasts will be. Eventually. And every one of them will be exceedingly painful, of course.'

The man stared at him. 'What?'

Mr Geoffrey's patience snapped. 'Oh, for God's sake, just keep shocking her until Parrish tells us the truth. Or her head bursts. Whichever comes first.'

The man looked at Lockland, his reluctance plain. 'It'll have to be you,' said Luke to him. 'Our friend Geoffrey here just doesn't have the balls.'

408

'Oh, dear God,' cried Imogen, in exasperation. She snatched the weapon back. 'I'll do it.'

She will too, thought Jane. She's probably got more balls than any of them.

The same thought had obviously occurred to Luke. 'All right,' he said, quickly. He looked at Imogen. 'You just made a big mistake.'

'I'm the one with the gun, Parrish.'

'But I'm the one who can tell them what you told everyone at TPHQ.'

For one fatal moment, Imogen froze. The man next to her snatched back his gun and stepped away from her. Now they were all looking at Imogen.

'She gave you all up to save herself,' said Luke, quietly. 'She gave us the King's Arsenal. She gave us you, Geoffrey. By name. And then we just sat back and waited for you to invite us to meet you. From there we were led to Shoreditch. By you, Geoffrey. And then again, from Shoreditch to here. Nice little trail. Escorted every inch of the way. Again, by you, Geoffrey, because you're a stupid, greedy little oik.'

Mr Geoffrey's face was so twisted with rage as to be unrecognisable. Clenching his fist, he punched at Luke. Again, it was more of a slap than a punch, but it opened up Luke's lip.

Luke grinned the irritating Parrish grin. 'You even punch like a girl.'

'Hey,' said Jane, trembling but defiant.

Luke spat blood on to the pristine floor. 'Sorry, Jane.'

'You will both be sorry,' hissed Mr Geoffrey, seemingly unable to resist the temptation to behave like a Bond villain.

Imogen shifted her weight impatiently. 'You should kill him. Kill them both.'

She thrust her face into Luke's. 'You piece of shit, Parrish.' She stepped back. 'Shoot him. Shoot him now.'

'I give the orders here,' said Mr Geoffrey, now bespeckled with Luke's blood as well as his own.

'Actually,' said a voice behind Jane. 'I think you'll find it's Mr P who gives the orders here.'

'Really?' said Jane, trying to distract attention from a suddenly frozen Luke. 'Sorry, I hadn't realised. Isn't Miss Farnley the one actually in charge?' She turned her head to look at Geoffrey. 'Not you, anyway.'

Mr Geoffrey slapped her again. 'No, we won't shoot you. Too quick. Too easy.' He turned his head to address the man who had been watching the chess match earlier. 'Throw Mr Parrish and Miss Lockland outside. If the cold doesn't get them, then the local wildlife will. Or even, if they're really lucky, our friends outside might find them first. You won't enjoy that. They really don't love us at all.'

'Ha,' said Imogen in satisfaction.

Geoffrey turned on her. 'And you, Miss Farnborough, have problems of your own. Problems that I, alas, do not have the authority to deal with. For now.'

Luke and Jane were seized again. Fire truck, thought Jane. I'm going to die. I'm actually going to die.

'Wait a minute,' said Luke, and amazingly, they did. 'Imogen – how on earth did you get mixed up in this? Have you *seen* what happens here?'

'Eric *cared*, Parrish, which was more than you did. He took me back – Mummy wouldn't. He brought me in on everything here. I'm going to be rich.'

'Immy, for your own sake – persuade them to let us go. Mr Geoffrey knows what you did now. And even if he lets you live – unlikely – then trust me, the Time Police will hunt you down. They'll never rest until they find you and when they do . . .'

She laughed. 'Don't threaten me, Parrish.'

'Immy, we're not the only ones facing a nasty end here.'

Imogen was dragged away. Geoffrey stepped up. 'Throw them outside. Just as they are. Throw them out.'

Jane and Luke fought every inch of the way. They had nothing to lose. It took three or four men to manhandle Luke into the dressing room. Jane only rated two which, strangely, made her angrier than ever. She struggled and twisted and kicked them until a couple of heavy slaps made her ears ring.

'Steady on,' said Bolshy Jane. 'You don't want to be unconscious when they throw you outside. You won't last two minutes if you can't keep moving.'

'She's right,' said Wimpy Jane.

Great – now the two of you decide to work together.

'It's for your own good, Jane.'

The locker room was empty. Wherever Smallhope and Pennyroyal were, they weren't here now.

She heard someone open the outer door. Windblown snowflakes danced into the room and the temperature dropped sharply. Luke was shoved out of the door. He staggered out into the snow and fell heavily.

Mr Geoffrey nodded in satisfaction. 'Thirty minutes. If that.'

Luke rolled over and tried to sit up. His efforts were painful to watch. Dribbling blood on to the pristine snow, he squinted up at Geoffrey. 'Do you expect me to beg for mercy?'

Geoffrey laughed. 'No, Mr Parrish. I expect you to die.'

Someone grabbed Jane's ankles and she was swung out of the door to fall heavily on top of Luke. Someone else laughed. Jane rolled over and staggered to her feet, all ready to make a fight of it. Too late. The door was closed. They hadn't even hung around to gloat. Not that she blamed them. Not in these temperatures.

She pulled at Luke's arm. 'Get up. You must get up.'

He groaned but lifted his head. 'Jane . . . ?'

Her teeth were chattering and she could barely speak. After the warmth inside, the cold was so intense she could only take very shallow breaths. 'Luke, get up. We have to find some shelter.'

'Hurting me . . .'

'Good. Get up now. Because I won't leave you, so if you don't get up then we'll both die here.'

Groaning, he rolled on to his front and from there on to his hands and knees.

'That's good, Luke. That's really good. Now stand up.'

'Jane, you're a hard woman.'

But he did. Somehow, he pulled himself to his feet and stood swaying and shivering.

'Well . . . here I am. Now what?'

She pulled them both against the wall where they could shelter a little from the wind.

'Now we think of something.'

33

Matthew stared unseeingly at the lines of data flickering across his screen and thought furiously. Jane's daily report was late. She'd never been late before. Others might be a bit slapdash about this sort of thing, but not Jane. He bent over his console, ostensibly plotting and replotting old time-slips, and surreptitiously checked his scratchpad again.

Nothing. The screen remained obstinately blank.

They'd discussed what to do should this happen.

'I don't envy you,' Luke had said. 'If you've got to go and tell Hay we've disobeyed her orders, then I reckon you've got the most dangerous part of the assignment.'

Jane had nodded and they'd all grinned at each other because, of course, that wasn't something that would ever happen. Only now it had, and he had to go and confront Commander Hay.

Should he give it another hour? There might be any reason why Jane hadn't been able to make her report. No, there wasn't – this was Jane. Jane did things by the book.

He hesitated. This next bit was not going to be pleasant. It seemed unlikely that either Ellis or Hay would come at him with a cudgel and break his arm . . . or light a fire beneath him to make him climb the chimneys more quickly . . . but it still wouldn't be pleasant. But . . . this wasn't about him. This was about Jane and Luke. His quietly cherished friends.

Sighing, he flashed a request for an urgent meeting with Major Ellis. Who sent for him, listened to what he had to say, cursed mightily and lengthily, and requested an urgent meeting for them both with Commander Hay.

Who was bowel-twistingly furious.

'*I gave specific instructions to the contrary.*'

Matthew, standing on the other side of her desk, said nothing. It seemed the wisest thing to do.

'There was to be no contact. Of any kind. It was deemed – by me – to be the safest way to proceed.'

He remained silent.

She leaned over her desk. 'You say her latest report is late – how do you know it wasn't intercepted? How do you know any of her reports weren't intercepted? Thanks to you, they could both be dead. Why are you incapable of following even the simplest instruction? Do you think I forbade all contact simply because I like throwing my weight around? This was a carefully thought-out course of action designed to give two operatives the freedom to achieve their objective without imperilling their own safety. But you thought you knew better, didn't you? And now, thanks to you, all their efforts are in vain. I swear, Farrell, if you have jeopardised this operation, I will have your head. I don't care where you're from or who your parents are – I will *end* you. Now get out.'

A shaken Matthew made his wobbly-legged way to the door. A silent Captain Farenden watched him grope his way out into the corridor.

Taking a deep breath, Matthew leaned against a wall. In

general, those who were familiar with his early history – the abuse, the violence – as was Commander Hay – were careful to keep the shouting to an absolute minimum. His instructors had yelled at him, but in a general sort of way – nothing personal, he understood that. Yes, he was aware he was as scum beneath their boots, but so was everyone else. But this was Commander Hay. Someone whom he held in high regard, whose opinion mattered to him. And running underneath everything was the horrible certainty that she was right. His idea to stay in touch with his teammates had been too clever for Luke and Jane's own good.

He closed his eyes and waited hopefully for his heart to stop pounding. Vomiting in Time Police corridors was not a Time Police-approved procedure. Straightening up, he dragged his sleeve across his face and opened his eyes to find Officer North standing in front of him. This day was not getting any better.

She regarded him without sympathy. 'You should go on leave.'

He stared at her. 'What?'

She frowned. 'That's "What, ma'am".'

'Sorry. What, ma'am?'

'You should go on leave.'

He was bewildered. 'Why would I do that?' The thought of leaving TPHQ now with no news of Luke and Jane and not knowing what was happening . . .

Her expression never altered. 'You're supposed to be bright, Farrell.'

'I can't leave now. Not when no one knows . . .'

She sighed heavily. 'You're not wanted here, Farrell. You're not *needed* here.'

He stared at her, unable to believe what he was hearing. From Lt Grint – yes. From Officer North – no.

She rolled her eyes. 'We don't want you here. Go *home*, Trainee Farrell.'

He stopped breathing and stared at her. She stared back at him and the Elephant of Enlightenment landed squarely on his shoulders. He said hoarsely, 'You're right.'

She gave him the patented North *I'm always right* expression and then strode off down the corridor, leaving him to stare after her.

Finding a quiet corner, he carefully completed his leave application and flashed it to Major Ellis, who requested his presence again. North stood at his shoulder.

'Purpose of leave?' said Ellis. 'You've left it blank.'

'I wasn't sure what to put.'

'Why not?'

Matthew summoned his words and channelled Luke Parrish as hard as he could go. 'Well, no one but us knows my team-mates are missing, so writing *can't bear to stay around here any longer watching senior officers getting it so completely wrong* probably isn't an option. And the box isn't big enough anyway. Which is a bit of a design error when you think about it. After all, most officers need to write in large capitals. Or even crayon.'

Ellis stared in disbelief. 'Are you *asking* for trouble, Farrell?'

Matthew swallowed hard. 'No, I'm asking for leave. Before I do something our senior officers will have to officially regret. You should be grateful.'

'I'm considering showing my gratitude by having you banged up for forty-eight hours for insubordination.'

Behind Ellis, North twitched a frown.

Matthew took a deep breath and changed his tactics. 'My apologies, sir. Concern for my teammates and the apparent inaction of senior officers has caused my behaviour to become inappropriate. I recommend forty-eight hours' leave to alleviate the situation.'

Ellis twisted in his seat. 'North? Any comment?'

'I find it hard to believe TPHQ will benefit from Farrell's continued presence at this time, sir.'

Holding Matthew's eye, Ellis tapped his scratchpad. 'Take this to the Senior Mech. I don't want to see you until forty-eight hours has elapsed, Farrell. Understood?'

'Completely, sir.'

He took his scratchpad down to the Pod Bay where the Senior Mech grudgingly gave permission for him to use a pod. 'But not by yourself. You're not qualified yet.'

Matthew nodded.

'And we're not a bloody taxi service, right?'

Matthew shook his head.

'Take that one.' He pointed and Matthew set off.

A grumpy mech programmed in the coordinates.

'Can I do it?' asked Matthew.

'No.'

'Only I'm nearly qualified and . . .'

'No.'

'Everyone says I'm quite proficient and . . .'

'No.'

Both occupants scowled at each other.

'Commence jump procedures.'

The AI responded. 'Jump procedures commenced.'

*   *   *

The mech had the ramp up and the pod away again before Matthew barely had time to get out of range. His hair swirled wildly around his head which, he considered, was probably his own fault for not getting it cut when so instructed.

He trudged across the grass in the direction of Hawking Hangar where he was met by a sandwich-munching Mr Evans, second in charge of the Security Section.

'Halt. Who goes there? Friend or Foe?'

'Me,' said Matthew simply, wondering if anyone had ever actually answered 'Foe'.

Evans continued to munch. 'You armed?'

Matthew shook his head.

Evans took another big bite and enquired somewhat thickly whether Matthew had brought any contraband from the future.

Matthew shook his head.

'You up to no good?'

'Absolutely up to no good,' said Matthew.

Evans grinned. 'Then pass, Friend.'

St Mary's was, as it always was, completely unchanged. It was a bright, cold day and the building basked in the sunshine. A traditional representation of rural England. Serene. Peaceful. *Deceptive* . . . Matthew picked his way across the grass and entered via Hawking Hangar.

'Hey,' said Leon, emerging from Number Five. Inasmuch as it was possible for a piece of technology to look bedraggled, this pod did. Scorch marks decorated the side and the door looked as if a randy rhino had conducted a one-sided love affair. 'We weren't expecting to see you.' He peered closely at his son. 'Something wrong?'

Matthew nodded.

'Your mother's in her office. Go on up. I'll just finish off here and then I'll join you.'

Matthew made his way along the Long Corridor. The sun slanted through the windows, highlighting golden dust motes. He walked from shadow to sunlight and back again. A small brown and white rabbit lolloped alongside, keeping him company.

Emerging from the Long Corridor, he passed the kitchen, waving to Mrs Mack, who waved her ladle back again. The rabbit, wisely, veered off to pursue its own concerns.

The Great Hall was, as usual, littered with files, folders, whiteboards, sticky notes, mugs of tea and half-eaten sandwiches. There were also seven or eight rabbits hopping around the table legs, which was slightly less usual.

Exchanging greetings, he stepped carefully over a couple of furry *Leporidae* and climbed the stairs.

Max was in her office enjoying a vigorous discussion with her personal assistant. Time might pass but some things never change.

'Hey, Mum.'

'Matthew, hi.' She looked blank for a moment. 'Were we expecting you?'

'No. Can I have a minute?'

Rosie Lee grabbed her bag. 'I'll go and get the post. Nice to see you, Matthew.'

He nodded. 'How's Benjamin?' Benjamin was her son.

'Very well, thank you. He's off to college in the autumn to do electrical engineering. That's not the official name of the course, but apparently it's too difficult for non-electrical engineers to understand, so they call it electrical engineering.'

Matthew looked down. 'Mum, why are there rabbits everywhere?' Using his foot, he gently shunted a very pretty *Oryctolagus cuniculus* out of sight under his mother's desk.

Max smiled blindingly. 'Napoleon.'

'What?'

Max crossed to the window. 'Come and see. Ah, here he comes now.'

Professor Rapson appeared from an outside door, crossing the car park and swinging a bucket. Miss Lingos stood behind him, clipboard and stopwatch in one hand and the rather large handbell normally used for alerting all staff to the need for rapid evacuation in the other.

She paused a moment. 'Ready, professor?'

'What? Oh, yes, yes, ready when you are, Miss Lingoss. Activate the rabbit-alerting device.'

She swung the bell with a vigour that would lead to her being known as Quasimodo Lingoss for some considerable time afterwards.

For a second nothing happened. Other than the professor and Miss Lingoss, the car park was devoid of life and movement. And then, from nowhere, what looked like ten thousand rabbits emerged. As Mr Bashford attempted to explain afterwards – well, they were rabbits, weren't they; their numbers had probably increased three-fold since breakfast.

They came from everywhere. One moment the car park was a completely rabbit-free environment and the next . . . They emerged from behind the bins, from under cars, from bushes, from doorways, even from nowhere. White rabbits, brown rabbits, piebald rabbits, big rabbits, small rabbits . . . As Markham

420

said afterwards – it was like the Pied Piper. But with no rats. And no Pied Piper. But other than that, identical.

It was immediately obvious that whatever the professor had been expecting, it wasn't this. He stood for a moment, staring at the advancing tide of *Leporidae*, his hand raised, as if he could hold them back by force of will alone. As Mr Evans said afterwards – it was like Knut and the approaching waves. But without Knut. And no approaching waves. But other than that, identical.

The professor dropped his bucket and fled. A few rabbits stopped to feed but the majority were made of sterner stuff and kept going. As Miss Lingoss said afterwards, 'It was fascinating, Max. You could see the exact moment the entire species made the evolutionary leap from herbivore to carnivore. I feel privileged to have been there.'

Professor and pursuing rabbits thundered around the corner, heading for the traditional St Mary's escape route – the library windows.

As Dr Dowson said afterwards, 'Well, how was I to know it was an emergency? That I became aware of a strong draught just at that very moment was, believe me, merely an unfortunate coincidence. Well, yes, obviously, I shut all the windows. Well, yes, I thought I might possibly have heard some banging on the glass, but it was a very busy afternoon, you know how it is. Well, yes, I thought I might possibly have heard the odd scream for help but this is St Mary's, you know, and if we all downed tools every time we heard a scream for help, we'd get nothing done at all. Do I understand there was a problem?'

To return to the matter in hand, back in her office, Max closed the window. 'Apparently, the story of Napoleon being routed by hundreds of hungry rabbits is entirely credible. A good morning's work, I feel.'

'Well, I'm not going out there and picking them up,' said Rosie Lee.

Max pulled out her chair and sat down again. 'No one's asked you to.'

Miss Lee scowled. 'Yet.'

'Ever. Rabbits are charming, fluffy creatures of a nervous disposition. People like you should be kept away from them at all costs. Go away and turn someone into stone somewhere.'

'I heard that.'

'Well, that's astonishing. You didn't hear me when I asked for a mug of tea.'

She blinked. 'When was that?'

'Your first day here. Remember? I'm still waiting.'

'I'm taking the post down now.'

'There isn't anything to go. It's only ten thirty in the morning.'

'Then I'll go and bring it up. Bye, Matthew.'

The door slammed. Mother and son looked at each other. The door opened and Leon entered. 'So, what's the problem?'

Matthew blinked rapidly. 'Dad, I think I've been too clever and it's all gone horribly wrong.'

A mug of tea later – not made by Rosie Lee – Matthew had outlined the problem.

Max frowned. 'So why exactly are you here?'

'I want to borrow St Mary's.'

Leon frowned. 'Are you sure?'

'Absolutely. Luke and Jane were chosen because they weren't typical Time Police officers. I want to borrow St Mary's for the same reason. I thought a few of us could just drop in – casually – and see what we could find out.'

'And all you have for certain is this King's Arsenal place?'

'Yes.'

'And even that might be a bit iffy, given the source – this Farnborough girl?'

'Yes.'

'And no one's willing to go after Luke and Jane?'

'No. To be fair – everything might be fine. There could be any number of reasons Jane hasn't checked in, and Commander Hay's point that blundering in would jeopardise them and their mission – well, I do understand that.'

'Then we'd better not blunder,' said Max.

'Tricky,' said Leon. 'Blundering is the History Department's default state.'

She opened her com. 'Markham? Are you busy? . . . No, you're not . . . Nothing you do is important. You don't even know the meaning of the word. Can you spare me a moment?'

The door opened and Markham was among them.

Max blinked. 'Bloody hell, that was quick.'

'I set out as soon as Evans told me the young master was here.'

'Hi,' said Matthew.

'Good morning,' said Markham formally, maintaining standards, although whose standards was anyone's guess. 'How can the Security Section be of assistance today?'

'You're unusually cooperative.'

'Don't want to spend the day picking up rabbits. Their bite is poisonous, you know.'

423

Max nodded. 'Good point.' The door opened again. 'Oh God, what are you doing here?'

Peterson drew himself up. 'My office is temporarily unusable. Mrs Partridge is dealing with the . . . situation.'

'Aw . . . Did the nasty rabbits frighten you?'

'Bloody things chased me all the way from the car park.'

'What were you doing in the car park?'

'Trying to get back into the building. I had to hide in Mr Strong's potting shed in the end.'

Leon sighed. 'Can we get on?'

Max nodded. 'Lock the door and put the red light up.'

'It's not top secret,' said Matthew, startled.

'No, but it'll annoy the hell out of Rosie Lee.'

34

'So,' said Max, an hour later. 'To recap . . .'

'Good briefing, by the way,' said Markham to Matthew. 'Can tell you're not an historian.'

Max scowled. 'If I could continue . . .'

Markham amiably waved his permission.

'The only definite in all this is the King's Arsenal. That's the name supplied by this Farnborough girl. And we're sure she's reliable?'

Matthew nodded. 'She was desperate to reduce her sentence. She wouldn't have given up anything that could be so easily disproved. They – *we'd* have stuck a nought on the end of her sentence just to show the world what happens if you mess the Time Police about.'

'And Luke and Jane went to check this place out?'

'Not immediately. They had three or four high-living weeks – Luke wanted to make sure everyone knew he was back, full of money and high spirits and boredom – and they waited for an approach to be made.'

'Smart,' said Markham, nodding. 'I liked him.'

'And, presumably an approach was made.'

'Yes. One of Jane's sober counsellor reports mentioned a possible job offer.'

'The reports she wasn't supposed to make.'

'Yes.'

'Could it have been intercepted?'

'Perfectly possible – she didn't make any attempt to secure her account – but it wasn't anything a sober counsellor wouldn't say and it was addressed to a perfectly legitimate rehab centre.'

'But something has gone wrong?'

'I think so.'

'How overdue is Jane's last report?'

'Twenty-four hours.'

'Could that mean that she simply isn't here in this time? That she isn't here to make the report?'

'Yes.'

'She and Luke could in fact be off somewhere gathering vital info, and will return safe and sound tomorrow? Or the next day, or whatever?'

'Yes.'

'And precipitate action on anyone's part could not only screw up the entire assignment, but place Luke and Jane in severe jeopardy as well?'

'Yes.'

'Which is why Commander Hay won't take any action at this stage?'

'Yes.'

'How long will Commander Hay wait before she initiates a possible rescue?'

'Probably . . . quite a long time. Possibly until two more bodies are washed up.'

Markham sat back, deep in thought. Leon stared out of the window. Peterson was frowning, his chin sunk on his chest and his long legs stretched out in front of him. Max was apparently doodling squares on a piece of paper, joining them with lines until the whole thing looked like a badly designed spider's web.

'I think . . .' said Markham eventually. 'I think, for a number of very good reasons, this will need to be a very . . . informal assignment. Our priority is not to upset any arrangements that Jane and Luke might have in place.'

Max nodded. 'I concur.'

'And we don't want to upset the Time Police.'

'Don't we?' said Peterson.

'Matthew's in enough trouble.'

Matthew nodded. He was.

'So in the guise of happy trippers, we drop in on this King's Arsenal place.'

'You can't get in from the river unless you take a private water taxi,' said Matthew quickly. 'The public clipper doesn't stop there.'

'A land approach,' said Markham.

'An *informal* land approach,' said Peterson.

Markham looked at him. 'You're going?'

'It will do me good. I don't get out much. Besides, you'll need someone respectable with you or they'll never let you in. So – as I said – an informal approach.'

'Made by informal people.'

'Informally.'

'Absolutely. We need to put together a team that looks as unlike the Time Police as anything could.'

'Emphasising informality.'

'Exactly.'

Max was scribbling a list of personnel. Markham scanned it. 'Looks good. Add Evans, though. Just in case there's any trouble. Then I can sit down and watch him sort it out.'

He passed the list to Leon, who counted up the names. 'Ten people. I'll go and ready Tea Bag 2.' He left.

'What's the weather like?' asked Max.

'Moving into summer,' said Matthew. 'Hot and dry.'

'Oh good,' said Markham. 'I can wear my new summer outfit.'

Peterson twisted in his chair to look at him. 'I am concerned at the ease and rapidity with which you assume women's clothing.'

'Someone has to bring style and class to our assignments. Right. This all starts at the King's Arsenal – so do we. We'll get them talking – somehow – and see what transpires. Max, pull our people together. Briefing in ten minutes. Leon's working on pod availability. I'll sort out weapons. Matthew – what do we do for money?'

'Plastic,' said Matthew, pulling out a card.

'Then let's go. Downstairs in twenty, everyone.'

They lined up outside the big pod, Tea Bag 2.

Present were Dr Maxwell, Chief Technical Officer Farrell and Dr Peterson. Miss Lingoss represented those scamps from R&D. Mr Markham and Mr Evans brought brains and style to the assignment. Professor Rapson, fresh from rabbit trauma, and Dr Dowson, fresh from complaining about rabbit trauma, accompanied them, together with Amelia Meiklejohn, ex-teapot terror. And Trainee Farrell, of course.

A quality cast, as Peterson said.

Max pulled Markham to one side. 'You do realise if this goes wrong, none of us will ever be able to come home again.'

'Not a problem for me. I've been considering becoming a Time Pirate.'

She stared at him. 'That's a thing?'

'It will be when I do it. Har-har, me hearties. Shiver me timber.'

'We've had this conversation before,' said Peterson. 'There isn't a person on the planet who would touch your timber – far less shiver it.'

Max stood at the top of the ramp, checking everyone over as they entered. Everyone wore their idea of informal summer gear. As Markham said, even for St Mary's, this was certainly the most weirdly dressed team he'd ever seen.

Max wore a top and loose linen trousers. Lingoss set her own style in a short, flared dress in crimson silk, with a black corset over the top and Doc Martens. Today's hair was black tipped with crimson.

Mikey wore jeans and a white silk blouse with a leather jacket. Max had managed to dissuade her from actually wearing her trusty goggles, although they hung from her belt, all ready to be donned should an emergency arise. Her white-blonde hair stood out around her head like a dandelion clock. She and Matthew stood close to each other.

Professor Rapson and Dr Dowson wore light linen jackets. Dr Dowson had gone one step further, sporting a cream panama hat at a jaunty angle.

Peterson had made an obvious effort with a smart jacket – his only smart jacket, as Max had pointed out – and with his hair very nearly combed.

Leon brought respectability to the groupability in simple jacket and trousers. Evans pointed out he'd washed his face. Max congratulated him on his dedication to the assignment. Evans replied he grudged no effort and Markham pushed him into the pod.

Markham himself was wearing a blindingly bright Hawaiian shirt, on which giant pineapples, palm trees and unrealistic-looking flowers battled for technicolour supremacy.

Leon turned to Max. 'I don't know what effect this lot will have upon the enemy, but by God they frighten me.'

'Would you find it more reassuring to regard this as a kind of a works outing?'

'You're enjoying this, Max, aren't you?'

'Oh God, yes.'

They landed in a narrow lane at the bottom of a canyon. At least that was how it seemed. The pod was jammed between two sky-high modern concrete-and-glass buildings. The sky – a postage-stamp patch of blue – seemed a very long way above them. The trapped air was hot and still.

Max ran an experienced eye over what might loosely be described as her team. 'All right, everyone. We don't want to go in mob-handed. Divide yourselves into individual groups. Low-key, everyone.'

'We'll follow you,' said Markham to Matthew, and off they set, Leon and Matthew at the front. Markham and Max at the rear. The rest in groups of twos and threes.

Professor Rapson's joy and excitement at encountering his first energy-generating walkway was clearly audible. A complaining Mr Evans was tasked with separating him from this phenomenon and returning him to the job in hand.

'I'm always disappointed at the lack of flying cars,' said Peterson, looking around him. 'Every comic I read as a kid had flying cars in it.'

'And personal jetpacks.'

'You wouldn't get me in one of those,' said Evans.

Peterson looked him up and down. 'It would take more than one to get you off the ground.'

'That is true,' said Evans complacently.

Peterson appeared poised to comment further, but at that moment, they rounded a corner and there before them, glittering in the sunshine, lay the River Thames.

'Try not to fall in this time,' whispered Markham to Max, and went off to deploy his troops.

Leon and Max, together with Matthew and Mikey, sauntered down to the river to take in the sights, with Matthew pointing out various landmarks on the way. Peterson and Lingoss circled around the pub so as to approach it from a different direction. Evans announced he was too thirsty for subtlety and he and Markham walked straight in through the door.

The King's Arsenal was very quiet at this time of the afternoon. No customers were enjoying a peaceful drink in the garden.

'Are they even open?' enquired Peterson.

Markham and Evans emerged.

'Three bars,' reported Evans. 'One restaurant. A couple of miscellaneous function rooms. Two offices. One kitchen. Cellars and storerooms. The place is practically empty. Lunchtime trade over. Evening trade not yet in. Two barmen setting things up. Four kitchen staff prepping stuff. One gardener/caretaker. There'll never be a better opportunity.'

Markham nodded. 'Secure the front door. Never mind the back. No reason the kitchen staff should even know we're here.'

Evans nodded and pulled a carefully prepared sign from under his jacket which he began to fix to the door. That done, he ushered them all in, and closed and bolted the doors behind them. 'That should keep people out.'

'Good work,' said Peterson.

'All right,' said Max. 'Remember, everyone: a happy family and friends outing. Smile. Enjoy yourselves. Try not to kill anyone. Let's start in here, shall we?'

They found themselves in a small, comfy room. The bar was set in the back left-hand corner and the rest of the room contained small groups of tables and chairs. There was no thumping music or slot machines. The atmosphere was quiet and intimate.

'Cosy,' said Markham, looking around. 'We should be able to fill the room quite nicely.'

'And only the one door,' said Evans, parking himself nearby. 'Mine's a pint.'

They spread out to mark their territory.

It was busy, reflected the barman, polishing a glass. Normally this, the smallest and quietest bar, was only ever sparsely populated. People did not usually come to the King's Arsenal for a quiet drink. As the youngest and most recent member of staff he was always dumped in here. It was a constant source of resentment to him. Lack of customers meant lack of tips. His colleagues in the other bars and the restaurant frequently did better than he did. Tonight, however . . . and to have a full house this early in the evening. He didn't mind betting he had the only customers in the place. He finished his glass and picked up another.

And they were so quiet and well behaved. The first things he always looked for in a punter. Lots of money and no trouble. They'd shambled into the bar, gone back for a missing professor, and then the shock-headed kid had enquired whether his friend had arrived yet. Luke Parrish? Did he know him?

The barman had been more than happy to inform them that Mr Parrish wasn't in yet, because he thought it made him look as if he was acquainted with all the punters and that this poxy little bar was the centre of the universe. He'd even remembered to add that the evening was still young. Never mind, had said the shock-headed kid – he'd have a drink while he waited.

One couple sat in the corner, nursing their drinks and chatting. A margarita and a pint. An old married couple, he decided. Nothing much left for them at their age other than to chat. He wondered if he'd ever get like that.

Over by the wall, two elderly gentlemen played virtual chess. Two dry sherries. Both of them were far too old to be any trouble.

The shock-headed kid and his girl sat by the window. The low sun streaming through the window lit up her hair like a halo. He'd suspected there might be trouble from these two. Not old enough to drink had been his first impression, but they'd solved his problem for him by ordering two orange juices. They sat now, quietly enough, holding hands under the table. The barman thought they were rather sweet.

Not like the woman in the corner. Black hair tipped with red. Gave him the creeps. As if she'd dipped her hair in blood. Dark red dress, black corset over the top, and boots. Sitting next to

– would you believe? – a quiet bloke with a smart jacket and hair like a haystack. She'd ordered a port. Matched her dress. He was a single-malt man. A Goth and a banker. Who'd have thought? Still, it takes all sorts. He sighed and picked up another glass.

The Goth and the banker were joined by a short man wearing the world's most blinding Hawaiian shirt and jeans. A cider for Hawaiian shirt.

Sitting alone with his pint, the big bloke – nearly as big as Johnson, the bouncer – sat by the door, arms folded, legs stretched out, almost blocking the door should anyone wish to get in. Although with this lot in here, he already had nearly a full house. And they weren't giving any trouble. He wished it was always like this.

The last sun slipped from the window. This was the fag end of the day. Not late enough for the real punters. The ones who splashed the cash probably weren't even out of bed yet, and the afternoon trade had gone on elsewhere. He turned his back to the room and ran an eye over his shelves to see if anything needed restocking.

When he turned back, for some reason, the big bloke had pulled his chair and table right across the door. What a clown.

Squaring his skinny shoulders, the barman assumed all the squeaky authority of his nineteen years. 'I'm sorry, sir, you can't sit there. No one'll be able to get in or out.'

Suddenly, everyone was looking at him and equally suddenly, they didn't look so nice. He wondered if they were an outing, perhaps. From one of those homes where people over forty went to live. Although they didn't seem to have any carers with them. And surely, they wouldn't let old people out on their own.

434

'Now then,' he said, wishing his voice didn't sound so squeaky. He went to reach for the in-house telephone to summon assistance and found himself face to face with the little bloke. The one with the sunny smile and the blinding shirt.

He stepped back.

'No, no,' said the little bloke, smiling amiably. 'Out from behind the bar, please. We wouldn't want to do anything inadvertent, would we? You know – set off the panic alarm. That's always so embarrassing, isn't it? Shall we sit down? Oh, don't worry about the boss seeing you – no one can get in.' He paused meaningfully. 'Or out.'

Abruptly, he pushed the suddenly frightened barman into a seat. 'Now, we're going to ask you one or two questions, and you're going to tell us what we want to know, and then we'll go away and you can continue polishing those glasses – very nicely kept bar, by the way, well done – and we can all pretend this never happened.'

'I don't know what you want,' said the barman nervously. 'I just work here.'

'Which renders you just perfect,' said margarita woman, and the young barman unexpectedly remembered what his old gran had always said about redheads. 'When you're ready, please, professor.'

The barman tried to get out of his chair. 'What are you going to do to me?'

One of the elderly men – the one with hair like Einstein – bustled forwards. 'This won't take a minute. Could we hold him down, please?'

'What are you doing?' he said again, struggling to get to his feet.

'Hardly anything at all,' said the professor, reassuringly. 'Unfortunately, we don't have time to mess about – a half-hour window is about all we can hope for – so I need to get cracking.'

The young barman began to struggle in earnest. 'No, you can't do this.'

The redhead shook her head. The young man resolved to pay more attention to his granny in future and even take her a bunch of flowers on her birthday.

'Well, obviously we can. And are. You see, this isn't our time. We don't belong here. We'll be gone in thirty minutes. And no one will ever know it was us. And we don't care anyway. So the professor's come up with a little something to make you talk. I'm afraid, because time is short, we'll have to give you a whopping big dose. Normally it's best to increase the dose quite slowly, but as I say, we don't have time. If it does kill you, we'll be awfully sorry about it, but we'll just chuck your body in the river – because it's important to be tidy, don't you think? – and move on to someone else. Until someone talks. And someone will. Too late for the ones already floating down the Thames, of course, but that's not our problem. Off you go, professor.'

Wielding a hypodermic that could have felled a horse, the professor moved in. The young man proved instantly cooperative. Unfortunately, he had nothing interesting to tell them. But he did give up his supervisor, that bastard Dave.

'Mr Evans, if you would be so kind.'

Evans nodded and disappeared in search of that bastard Dave.

Who took one look at the sleeping barman and gave up *his* supervisor, Kevin.

Who took one look at that sleeping bastard Dave laid neatly next to the sleeping barman and gave up the boss, Mr Desai.

Who refused to talk. They could do whatever they liked, he said, jaw jutting pugnaciously. He wouldn't talk. From the many glances he cast towards the door, it was obvious he was expecting rescue at any moment. Even with his unconscious staff stretched out on the floor around him, it was obvious he was more frightened of his employers than he was of his hypodermic-wielding captors.

Markham and Max exchanged glances. They had nothing further with which to frighten him. Their truth-serum bluff had been called. Now what?

Dr Dowson bustled forwards. 'Stand aside, everyone. Andrew, did you bring . . . ?'

'I did, Occy.' He looked around. 'Everyone, step back out of range, please.'

Markham looked uneasy. 'Professor, what are you doing?'

'Making him talk.'

'How?'

'Oh, it's quite easy. Leon, dear boy, I wonder if you'd pop behind the bar for a moment, please. I need half a lime and two beermats if you'd be so good.'

Leon moved behind the bar. Everyone turned their heads to see what he was doing.

An ear-splitting shriek filled the room and was cut off in half a second as Dr Dowson clapped his hand over Mr Desai's mouth.

Evans eased the door open a fraction to check no one had heard.

Mr Desai's face was red. Tears and mucus ran down his face. His right leg juddered uncontrollably.

Of his audience, Max was the first to pull herself together. 'Have you changed your mind?'

He nodded. Frantically.

Markham pulled Professor Rapson to one side. '*Professor, what did you do?*'

'An old trick I learned during the Civil Uprisings.'

'How?'

'Mm?'

'How did you learn?'

'Well, it was done to me several times so I know it works.'

Markham stared at him then wisely decided not to pursue that any further. 'So what were the beermats and the lime for?'

'A distraction. Trust me, it's not a trick you want other people to know.' He nodded at Mr Desai. 'If you ask him now, I think he'll tell you everything you need to know.'

It took a while for Mr Desai to recover the power of speech, but once he did there was no holding him. He gabbled something about occasionally being required to pass messages on to a telephone number in Shoreditch. No, he had no idea of the location or who was at the other end of the phone. No, there was never a word spoken from the other end. And no, he hadn't written the number down, but he could remember it and for God's sake keep him away from me. He wrote down the number with a shaking hand.

Max passed it to Matthew who pulled out his scratchpad. Thirty seconds later he nodded. 'Got it.' He nodded to Mr Desai. 'The Time Police thank you for your cooperation.'

'Never mind the sodding Time Police – just keep that old bastard away from me.'

Matthew continued, because he was still under training and Major Ellis was a stickler, 'You will receive an official acknowledgement thanking you for your cooperation and assistance and making sure the entire world knows you sang like a cassowary.'

Professor Rapson approached with the hypodermic.

If he had been pale before, Mr Desai was now ashen. 'What? I told you everything. You bastards.'

Markham shook his head. 'Can't have you tipping them off. Whenever you're ready, professor.'

'No. Keep him away. Don't let him—'

There was the hiss of a hypodermic and Mr Desai went limp and smacked his face on the table. Several people winced. 'That's going to sting in the morning,' said Evans.

'Well,' said Max, as they carefully propped all the unconscious staff in the recovery position, 'they sang like . . .'

'Cassowaries,' said Matthew, again.

'What's a cassowary?'

'A small Australian bird,' said Matthew, after only a very short pause. 'Noted for its placid temperament and affectionate nature. If you ever meet one, they love to be stroked under the chin.'

'Oh, OK. Time to go, everyone. Mr Evans, please put that pint down.'

'What about the bouncer?' asked Peterson.

'Asleep in an outhouse,' said Evans. 'And there was a gardener, as well.'

'Tell me he's asleep, too.'

439

'Well, not really. He was a tiny little man – built like a leaf – I was scared I'd break him, so I just sat him down on a sack of something and left him there.'

'Didn't you threaten him at all?'

'Of course I did, but he folded his arms and said did I know he was a gardener and like gardeners everywhere, he'd inhaled so many substances over the years – recreational and professional, intended and unintended – that he reckoned he could withstand anything I could throw at him and to bring it on, buster. He seemed quite disappointed when I just left him sitting there.'

They secured the building behind them. Using Mr Desai's keys, Evans locked the front door and readjusted the already crooked notice for maximum impact.

There had been vigorous debate as to whether E. coli or salmonella was the more dangerous, and since a consensus could not be reached, St Mary's, ever flexible, had gone with both. The extremely official-looking notice informed anyone seeking access that the twin scourges of salmonella and E. coli were currently sweeping through the premises known as the King's Arsenal, which was now closed for the foreseeable future. Anyone who had visited the aforementioned premises over the last three days was advised to seek immediate medical advice. While they still could.

'The skull and crossbones are a particularly nice touch,' said Markham approvingly and Dr Dowson beamed.

'Off to TPHQ, I think,' said Max, setting off towards their pod.

Leon took her arm. 'We need to disappear, Max.'

'Why?'

440

'Because if Hay finds out Matthew's called in St Mary's, then the kid's finished.'

'But suppose our intervention saves the day?'

'I think that would make it even worse.'

'But he did the right thing, Leon.'

'I don't think that would help his case in even the smallest way. We need to step back and let him get on with it.'

'You think she'll throw him out?'

'He went behind her back. To St Mary's. Of course she'll throw him out. After he's done some time. Hard time, if she has anything to do with it.'

She shook her head. 'Just a moment.'

Matthew was talking to Mikey. Max gently touched his arm. 'Hey, got a minute?'

They moved a little way off and sat on a low wall overlooking the river.

'Matthew, how much trouble are you in over this?'

He shuffled his feet. 'I suspect quite a lot.'

'All right. Hear me out before you say anything.'

'I know what you're going to say, Mum.'

'I'm going to say it anyway. You don't have to go back to TPHQ. You can jump with us. St Mary's will protect you. Why deliberately return to a world full of trouble? You're valued at St Mary's. You don't have to pretend to be something you're not. You don't have to get your hair cut because some pillock thinks it's conducive to efficiency. Look at Grint. If his hair was any shorter, he'd be bald, and he's the thickest person in the Time Police. And trust me, there's a lot of competition for that slot. Look, if you want to work on the Time Map, then I'm sure you and Professor Rapson and Miss Lingoss can come up with something bigger and better than we've got at St Mary's. And it would be *your* project – not following in someone else's footsteps. And,' she paused significantly, 'Mikey's at St Mary's.'

She stopped speaking and stared fiercely out over the river, much in the way Knut might have tried to subdue the waves.

Matthew sat very still for a moment and then took her hand. 'Mum . . .'

'You told me yourself you can leave any time during your training. There wouldn't be any loss of face. You can say you tried it and it wasn't for you. No one will blame you.'

'Mum . . . I'd blame me.' He looked down at her hand. 'This isn't easy for me and I'll use the wrong words and I don't want to hurt you. Or Dad, but mostly you. I want to do this because it's something I can make my own. It's not something that St Mary's has handed me. And you can't stop me, Mum. You mustn't. You went out into the world and found somewhere you belonged. You carved yourself a place in it. You shaped your world to suit you. It wasn't easy but you always say if something's not difficult then it's not worth doing. You never accept help from anyone and I thought you would understand that I want to do the same. At St Mary's, I'm always your son. Your influence is everywhere. No, don't cry, please. I just want something of my own that I made for myself. And I have to *earn* Mikey. I'm not a little boy any more. I'm growing up and I want to have something to present to her. I want to say, "I'm Matthew Farrell and this is what I've done. This is what I've made. This is what I stand for."' He swallowed. 'I want to be awesome. Like my mum.'

Chief Farrell approached. 'Time to make ourselves scarce, I

think.' He looked at Max, who was still staring into the distance and then back at Matthew. 'You know what you're doing?'

'Not a clue, Dad.'

He sighed. 'You two are so alike.'

Max stood up, keeping her face averted. 'I'll get them all back to the pod, Leon.' She clapped Matthew on the arm. 'Good luck. Give Grint a good kicking from me if you get the chance.'

She walked quickly away.

Leon looked down at Matthew. 'Everything OK?'

He nodded. 'Absolutely fine, Dad.'

35

Reporting the results of his recent adventure at the King's Arsenal to Major Ellis, however unpleasant, was the easy bit. Being marched in to Commander Hay for a second time was much, much worse.

She said nothing for a very long time.

He waited. Captain Farenden waited. Major Ellis waited.

As the silence lengthened, it slowly dawned on Matthew that this was going to be even worse than he had anticipated. Slowly, his excitement and elation at what he'd discovered ebbed away, leaving a nasty cold sensation in the pit of his stomach.

Eventually, she picked up a file and, for no good reason that he could see, moved it to the other side of her desk and stared at it. Surprisingly quietly, she said, 'You went over my head.'

Matthew's insides slid south. He nodded.

'You called in St Mary's. You involved St Mary's in what is purely a Time Police matter.'

He managed to nod again.

He'd heard people say the Time Police were utter bastards. The three of them, Luke, Jane and he himself, had often made a joke of it. Now, he saw, very clearly, what utter bastards they truly were. The officers' faces were carved of stone. No one would help him. He'd committed another cardinal sin. Less than twenty-four hours after committing the first cardinal sin.

Commander Hay stood up. She was a slight, short woman, but to Matthew, it was as if a mountain was unfolding in front of him. He tried to stop his legs trembling.

'Mr Farrell . . .' Mr – not Trainee. The writing was on the wall. 'It would appear your first loyalties are not to the Time Police. As you wish. You have made your choice. From this moment you are suspended. Once this mission is completed – when I have time to deal with you properly – a hearing will be convened, the purpose of which will be to confirm your dishonourable discharge from the Time Police.'

The perceived injustice spurred him into speech. 'I got you Shoreditch. You didn't get that from Imogen Farnborough. I got you that.'

It was as if he hadn't spoken. 'You are confined to your quarters. Meals will be brought to you. You will speak to no one. You will surrender all communication devices. You are dismissed.' No one said a word. No one moved to help him. His eyes were blurred, but somehow he found the door, wobbled through Captain Farenden's office and out into the corridor.

He was vaguely aware people were waiting for him.

'I've got this one,' said North. His arm was taken in a firm grip and he was marched away. Only once did she speak. As he opened the door to his room, she said, without looking at him, 'You did the right thing,' and then walked away.

Back in her office, Commander Hay was engaged in damage limitation.

'Well,' she said, sinking back into her seat. 'Now we have no choice. We have to move. And quickly. Before their people at the King's Arsenal regain consciousness. Or someone investigates that stupid notice. Our hand has been forced. Let's just hope we can salvage something out of this.'

'He left them out cold, ma'am,' said Ellis. 'They'll be unconscious for at least a couple of hours.'

'Which means no senior staff will be answering the phone to deal with the rumours of E. coli flying around. And salmonella, for God's sake, because those witless morons from St Mary's never know when to stop. There'll be enquiries from the food authority. Enquiries from the council. Customers panicking in their droves. That won't set anyone's alarm bells ringing at all, will it?'

Ellis chose his words carefully. 'Our hand has been forced, ma'am, but that may not be such a bad thing.'

She picked up her paper knife and twisted it between her fingers. 'I will have them. One day, I swear, I will have St Mary's at my feet and I will *obliterate* them.'

She straightened up. 'In the meantime – Major, assemble a task force. Empty the building. Send three teams to the King's Arsenal. Arrest everyone there. Staff, customers. Everyone. No one slips through your fingers. Secure the building and hold everyone in isolation here until I return.

'Another six teams to Shoreditch. We don't know what we're dealing with there. They may be operating out of there or it may only be another link in the chain, but we have to move now, and thanks to St Mary's we'll be going in blind. You'll lead that mission. I'll be going along to observe. We go by pod. Too long by river. I want everyone prepped and ready to go in ten minutes. We hit the two sites simultaneously. I don't want them tipping each other off. We use whatever force is necessary. Just make sure there's someone left alive at the end of it for us to question. Now move.'

Sitting in his room, Matthew heard the alarms, the shouts, the running feet. TPHQ was being emptied. In the distance, he could hear the teams being called together. Hear people answering their names. Hear the rumble of heavy equipment. They would be loading the building-smashers in case they had to force their way in. He could feel the excitement pulsing through the building.

And what of Jane and Luke? If they were still alive, what would happen to them after he left? A team of three was just about acceptable. A team of two was not. And they'd almost certainly share in his disgrace. 'You see,' people would say to each other, 'I told you they weren't Time Police material.' And they weren't. Their first major task and they'd screwed up. Well, he'd screwed up. He'd screwed everything up.

Matthew Farrell never cried. He'd learned very early on – the hard way – that crying only made things worse. He clenched his jaw, stared at his feet and tried to think of something else. Anything else. He would not cry. He would not. He was Time Police and Time Police don't cry. He blinked furiously.

Five minutes later the alarms fell silent. The Time Police had departed.

Whatever their faults, the Time Police were a professional outfit. From muster to move-out – seven and a half minutes.

Major Ellis's teams landed at Shoreditch and exited their pods. Identifying their target, they lined up along the wall as someone from the mech section disabled the external cameras.

'Pretty colour,' said someone, admiring the pastel green.

'Not for long,' said someone else.

The Time Police hit the front and rear simultaneously. There was no namby-pamby girlie stuff about ringing and waiting. They just blew the doors off and poured straight in, dispersing their forces around the building, clearing rooms and roaring at everyone to put their hands where they could see them and get down on the ground.

Major Ellis's contingent stormed straight through the front waiting room and into the main body of the pod bay. Resistance was, in the words of that famous phrase, futile. And there was very little resistance. In fact, far from putting up any sort of opposition, most of the on-site staff tried to run away. One or two even burst into tears. The Time Police had had more exciting incursions in their time, but on the other hand, there hadn't been much on recently and it did you good to get out.

Most of the people there were mechs and completely taken by surprise. Even the security staff would have laid down their weapons immediately – if they hadn't already set them down to enjoy a nice game of cards in the staff room. It would seem that while Mr Geoffrey was away, the mice seized every opportunity to play.

Everyone was herded together in the big pod bay and pushed face down on the floor while officers went around zipping them.

Commander Hay made her entrance.

'Over here, ma'am,' called Major Ellis.

She stepped carefully across the floor. 'Are you able to guarantee no one could communicate with anyone outside the building?'

'Absolutely, ma'am. We hit them with an EMP burst before we blew the door. Captain Simon at the King's Arsenal confirms the same there. In fact, most of them were still groggy from whatever it was St Mary's did to them. There was no fight in them at all. They're all being shipped back to TPHQ as we speak. He wants to know if we need any assistance here.'

She opened her com. 'Thank you, Captain Simon, but I want King's Arsenal secured until we've had a chance to go over it. Make sure nothing happens to any of our guests on their way back to TPHQ. I wouldn't put it past their own people to try to take them out to protect themselves.'

'Yes, ma'am.'

'Be alert, Captain. No interaction with anyone who isn't known to you personally. And don't relax until they're safe with security. And probably don't relax even then. Who's on duty there?'

'Filbert and Varma, ma'am.'

'All right. Keep me informed and don't let *anything* happen to your prisoners.'

'Yes, ma'am.'

She closed her com and turned to Major Ellis. An officer approached. 'Ma'am, sir, Officer Dal found these.' He held out Jane and Luke's proximity bracelets.

Ellis and Hay regarded them in silence.

'They were here, then,' said Ellis. He turned to the officer. 'No sign of Lockland or Parrish?'

'None, sir. We've searched the whole building and they're definitely not here.'

'Right,' said Hay. 'Your team is to strip this building. Records, equipment, pods – everything. The transports are on their way. Be ready for them. I want everything loaded and taken back to HQ.'

'On it, ma'am.' He turned and trotted back down the hangar, shouting, 'Open the pod bay doors, Dal.'

'I don't think I can do that, sir.'

'*Open the pod bay doors.*'

The mech bent over his equipment, cursed mightily and fetched the recalcitrant doors a vicious kick. They opened smoothly. 'Doors open, sir.'

Ellis turned to Hay. 'Our prisoners, ma'am?'

'Call up the river launches and get them back to TPHQ. Same instructions as King's Arsenal.'

A mech approached. 'Ma'am, we've rebooted the mainframe console. If you can give us a few minutes . . .'

'Quick as you can, please.'

They waited while the mechs jacked themselves in and hunched over the equipment.

'Right,' said Hay, turning away. 'To recap. We've secured Shoreditch. We've secured the King's Arsenal. We'll see what the mechs can tell us and then hunt the rest of them down and find out what's going on.'

'You're trying to take down the whole organisation at one and the same time, ma'am?' said Ellis.

'Yes, and I'm furious, because this isn't how I planned it. Yes, we'll deal them a mighty blow but I'm pretty sure we're going to miss the big boys. The money. Whoever is behind all this.'

Ellis surveyed their prisoners being led away. 'I suspect they're all too scared to speak, ma'am. And that's supposing that at this level they know anything anyway. Which I doubt.'

450

They were joined by the Head of IT. 'Doesn't matter, ma'am. Their systems will tell us everything we need to know. And much more quickly, too. One thing I can tell you now – there's a pod missing.'

Ellis jumped. 'Highest priority. I want details of all jumps over the last twenty-four hours.'

'On it, sir.'

Another mech turned up. 'Ma'am, I think you might want to see this.'

He led them into a big pod and pointed. Giant images of Abu Simbel were flashing up on the screens.

Hay frowned and looked around. 'Is this actually a pod?' Her face flushed with anger. 'Don't tell me we've given ourselves away just to arrest a bunch of fraudsters?'

'Yes and no, ma'am. It is a working pod. It can jump. It didn't jump today. This holo runs for about ninety minutes.'

'For what purpose?'

He shrugged. 'Promotional material, perhaps?'

'Or the whole thing's a big con.'

'Possibly, but there *are* pods here and there's been actual pod activity so . . .'

A breathless mech appeared at the door. 'Got it, sir. And ma'am.'

'Where?'

'The missing pod is in the Pleistocene period, ma'am. Jumped about an hour and a half ago. And there are other jumps. Scores of them. They've been all over the place. There's a couple to the 17th century . . .'

Hay glanced at Ellis. One of those would have been Imogen Farnborough's jump.

'. . . A couple more to Tudor England. One to 10th-century England, as well, but mostly the Pleistocene. A *lot* of jumps to and from there. Regular intervals but always the same location.'

She turned to Ellis. 'I wonder what's the attraction? There's nothing there, surely?'

Ellis was listening to a voice in his ear. 'Lt Grint is reporting a large part of the pod bay appears to be stuffed full of supplies and equipment. Mostly medical, ma'am. It looks as if they're taking medical stuff in and out for some reason.'

'Get your men together, Major. Leave enough to escort the prisoners back to TPHQ, but otherwise I want everyone you can lay your hands on. We're going to the Pleistocene.'

36

It was the thunder of feet running past his room that woke Matthew. And the shouting. And then the alarms went off. All of them. Again. For a moment he blinked in confusion. Were people still turning out to invade King's Arsenal and Shoreditch? For how long had he been sleeping? And then he felt the building shake as the blast doors came down in the Pod Bay. And then shake again with another, different impact.

It seemed unbelievable but . . . were the Time Police under attack?

He swung his feet off his bed and wrenched open the door. Further along the corridor, those sleeping off night-duties or just taking the afternoon off ran towards him, shouting orders. He fell in behind as they raced along the corridors and up and down stairs, finally bursting into the wreckage of the atrium where officers crouched behind counters and tables, shouting demands for assistance into their coms. Smoke and dust swirled wildly. Those unfortunate civilians having the misfortune to be attending TPHQ today screamed and ran aimlessly. Outside, where the Time Police gardens lay, several smoking craters had appeared. People lay spread-eagled on the ground.

Out on the river, the two Time Police launches, now only

yards from returning to their moorings, were under attack. One boat was listing heavily, on fire at its stern. Matthew could see dancing orange flames. Dark smoke curled upwards. An anonymous black launch, slim and wicked, was closing fast, raking the shore with fire as it came. Officers returned shots as best they could as the gardens disintegrated around them. Fragments of trees, bushes and benches exploded into the air.

A voice rose above the mayhem, shouting for all officers to form up. Matthew recognised Captain Farenden, who must, at that moment, be the ranking officer.

'Lieutenant, take a team and secure the front doors. Then set up a defensive position to cover the retreat. You,' he pointed to another officer, crouching behind an overturned table, 'take another team and cover the boats. Protect the prisoners at all costs. Get them disembarked and into the building. We'll retrieve the wounded. All right, everyone. Move forwards. Double time. Everyone stay alive. Charge.'

They charged, kicking their way through the remains of the front doors and into a war zone. The air was sharp with the smell of burned paper. There had been blaster fire.

Matthew found illusory safety behind a planter containing a former flowering tree. He'd been stripped of all his equipment after his audience with Commander Hay. He didn't even have baton and string. He nudged the officer next to him. 'Got a spare weapon?'

'For God's sake . . .' The officer pulled out a small sonic and a can of liquid string. 'All I've got.'

Other than the truck-sized blaster slung over your shoulder, thought Matthew enviously.

Two yards away, a civilian woman lay face down. Part of his

mind registered she was in running gear. She'd certainly picked the wrong afternoon to get fit with a run along the river. She was bleeding from a head wound. As he watched, she woozily lifted her head and tried to get up.

'Stay down,' shouted Matthew. 'Stay down, ma'am.'

She ignored him, either because she couldn't hear because of the noise all around them or was still unaware of what was happening.

Leaping up, he caught her under her arms. She seemed very heavy. He could hear the impact of bullets around him. He had no idea whether they were aimed at him and he certainly wasn't going to stop to find out. It was a struggle to get her back behind his planter.

'Can you hear me?'

She nodded blearily.

'Stay here until someone tells you otherwise. Do you understand?'

She nodded again and closed her eyes.

He could hear the whine of charging blasters. New forces were entering the fray. Major Callen erupted through the front doors, leading another team through the hastily assembled barricades. They were firing as they came. Everyone seemed to know what they were doing. Everyone was part of a team. He could hear Farenden ordering people to fire at will. He could hear the clatter of a heavy-duty automatic gun somewhere and the bullets impacting the building behind him. Tiny – and not so tiny – fragments of brick and mortar fell around him. And sometimes on him. From where he was crouching, it was impossible to tell from which direction they were being attacked. There was the black launch on the river, but from which direction the rockets were coming, he had no idea and it was vital not to be pinned down.

The same thought had obviously occurred to everyone else. Five or six officers were moving forwards as those behind them laid down covering fire.

Someone shouted that he'd located the source of the rocket launcher.

'Return fire,' shouted Callen. 'Take them out.'

A team of two took up position. One hefted his rocket launcher on to his shoulder. The other rammed the shell home and slapped his partner's helmet to confirm all clear. The rocket launched with a roar and a belch of smoke.

Callen appeared in their midst. 'Everyone else – to the river. Cover those in the water. Farenden – take out that bloody boat.'

Matthew hauled himself to his feet and ran with everyone else, expecting at every moment to feel a hail of bullets between his shoulder blades or the heat of a blaster sear his skin. Like everyone else he was unarmoured. There hadn't been any time. They'd been caught completely unawares.

The burning Time Police launch was listing badly. Their second boat, ignoring fire from the black launch, nudged closer, officers leaning over the sides and heaving people on board. Tiny tongues of flame ran across the oily water. Matthew found himself a shelter behind another concrete planter where he was joined a second later by Farenden.

'Sir,' he said, pointing. Another black launch was racing towards the stricken craft, bouncing on the waves and firing as it came on. He experienced a second's disbelief. The incongruity. This was the centre of London – the capital city – a sunny afternoon – and there was a small war being fought here.

His sonic was useless against the boat – the range was too short – but Captain Farenden had acquired a blaster from somewhere. Shouting, 'Cover me,' he rose above the cover of the planter and fired. There was the traditional whine, then the familiar roar as a blast of hot gas erupted from the business end, igniting as it went.

The blast hit the water just to the left of the oncoming launch.

Farenden swore and raised the blaster again. A shot from nowhere caught him squarely and he spun around, dropping the blaster as he fell.

'No,' shouted Matthew.

The second black launch was between the stricken ship and the bank. They raked the shore with fire. Matthew crouched, wrapping his arms around his head as soil, pieces of shattered tree, lumps of concrete and God knows what fell around him. He wondered what had happened to the normal everyday shipping – the barges, the water taxis, the commercial craft – surely, they'd all fled. Together with those who'd mistakenly thought a stroll along the Thames might be a pleasant way to spend the afternoon. In the distance he could hear sirens. A small black dot hovered overhead. A helicopter. Whose helicopter remained to be seen.

Afterwards, the only impressions he retained were of chaos. The noise – men shouting incomprehensibly. The clatter of automatic fire. A row of holes appearing in the planter to his left. The smell of cordite, of burned paper, of burned people. People running directly into the line of fire as they tried to escape. Civilians caught up in the violence. Officers shouting instructions to clear them out of the way. People screaming. He shut down his mind to what was happening. Farenden first.

His own contribution to the battle would be negligible but he could do something here.

His mind flashed back to Team 236's first proper mission to Ancient Egypt when he'd stood in the desert, frightened and alone, with illegals pounding towards him, and he had only his string to bring them down. He'd stood his ground on that day; he could do the same today.

There were illegals running towards him now. He knew they weren't Time Police because they were fully armed and helmeted. And he and Captain Farenden were directly in their path.

Standing up, Matthew hefted the blaster and shouted, 'Halt!' hoping against hope they would stop because the time had come for him to fire upon someone for the first time in his life and he was wondering whether he could do it.

He was about to find out. No one even slowed down. Of their objective, he had no idea, but his duty was clear.

He lifted his blaster and fired a short, sharp blast, aiming from right to left. He'd never fired a blaster before – training came after qualification – and was unprepared for the massive kick that nearly sent him over backwards.

One man went down but the others came on. The two in front lifted their weapons. Matthew flung himself sideways. For all the good it would do. But it would seem he was not their target. They were heading towards the doors. Access to the building.

Regaining his balance, he fired again. A longer blast this time, playing the flame in a semicircle. The smell of burned paper and burned metal was nearly overwhelming. He was enveloped in smoke and could barely see. He wished he had a helmet. A heads-up display on his visor would be very useful just at the moment. And no one had ever told him how heavy these things were.

Some instinct made him look around.

Two men had somehow bypassed him and were heading towards the building. His blaster was too unwieldy. He shoved it to one side, snatched at his sonic and dropped to a crouch. Bullets sprayed above his head. Expecting to die at any moment, he fired his sonic. The two men wavered and wobbled but not for long enough.

There was more movement behind him. He was facing fire on two fronts. The thought flashed through his head: act now or he would die. And so would Captain Farenden. He yanked up the blaster, flipped the setting to high and sprayed a full circle of red fire around his position. The heat was immense. The tree in the planter burst into flames. Figures reared up all around him. He wondered if anyone else was even half as scared as he was. He became aware he was yelling at the top of his voice. No words. Just yelling. Spraying round and round. Round and round. Get them before they got him.

His weapon was burning his hands. He had no gloves. No protective gear of any kind. Sweat poured down his face and still he could see black figures beyond the flames. A tiny voice whispered that once his blaster was empty, he would have no defence at all.

He became aware someone was shouting at him. He could hear another voice over his own. Someone was shouting his name. A voice he knew. Someone caught hold of his ankle. He looked down. Farenden, lying in a pool of his own blood, was shouting his name. Shouting for him to ceasefire.

Somehow his stiff fingers obeyed the command from his

brain and relaxed. He stopped shouting. The flame disappeared. The blaster whined down to silence. Smoke poured from the nozzle and drifted out over the river. Suddenly everything was very, very quiet.

A black and bloody figure who looked very like Major Callen pulled himself to his feet. Armoured but no helmet. 'All right, lad?'

Matthew nodded. With a shuddering breath he looked about him. Captain Farenden lay at his feet. People were on the ground everywhere. Callen's voice said quietly, 'Now then, son, better let me take that,' and the blaster was lifted from his hands. The weight was gone. He became aware he was drenched in sweat. That the muscles in his forearms were killing him. With every movement, tiny pieces of broken glass and concrete fell around him. They were caught in the creases of his clothes, his hair, everywhere.

Something warm and wet was running down his face. He put up his hand and discovered that at some point he must have been hit by ricocheting concrete because he was bleeding from a deep nick over his right eye. His legs trembled with strain and reaction.

'Medic,' he shouted and his voice belonged to someone else. 'Medic over here. Officer down.'

Medtecs were running from the building, medkits in hand.

'Sit down, lad,' said someone. Not Callen. Matthew could see him supervising the transfer of surviving prisoners from the boats.

He didn't have to sit because his legs gave way all by themselves and he collapsed gracelessly to the ground.

'I need your help here,' said a medic. 'Put some pressure on this.'

460

He felt his hand guided to the wound on Farenden's blood-soaked chest.

He tried to ask if Farenden was still alive but his voice was just a croak.

'Yes,' said the medic, apparently understanding this. 'Just keep the pressure on while I sort out a dressing.'

In a dream, Matthew did as he was told. He could not have said for how long he knelt while the medtec worked on Farenden, until eventually, along with the other wounded, he was stretchered away.

'Let's have a look at you now,' said the medic, peering at his eye. 'That's deep. You're going to have a scar there. Badge of honour, mate. Let's just stick a quick dressing on it, shall we, and then off to MedCen for you. We'll need to check for damage to your eye.'

'Actually . . .'

'What's the problem?'

'I'm not sure I can get up,' whispered Matthew, embarrassed. 'And if I do, I'm not sure I can stay up.'

The medic snapped his case shut and stood up, extending his hand. 'Up you get. If you fall over, I'll tell everyone you have a leg wound.'

Matthew grinned and reached up. 'Did we win?'

'We always win,' said the medtec. 'Even when we don't.'

He gave Matthew a gentle shove in the right direction and went off to treat someone else.

Back at Shoreditch, Major Ellis and Commander Hay were conferring together when Major Callen's voice spoke in their ears.

'TPHQ has been attacked, Commander. An attempt has been

made either to eliminate or rescue our prisoners as they disembarked. A second force attempted to access the building.'

She turned and took a few paces away. 'Tell me they didn't succeed.'

He replied most emphatically, 'No, Commander, they did not. We were taken by surprise but managed to regain control of the situation. However, a substantial number of the prisoners did not survive. Either shot or drowned. A few are missing. Washed away, we assume.'

'Or escaped to warn their masters.'

'Possibly, Commander.'

'Damn and blast. Time Police casualties?'

'Substantial, ma'am. No one dead. But . . .' He stopped.

'Who?'

'Captain Farenden, Commander. He led the first wave. Held on long enough to give the rest of us time to get organised. I'm afraid it's not looking good.'

Her damaged face was never capable of much expression, but Ellis could see the stricken look in her eyes. 'Is the building secure?'

'A temporary barricade has been erected outside the front doors.'

'Well, I gather barricades are a tradition in that part of London.'

'Indeed, Commander. The blast doors are down. The Pod Bay and Security Section are locked down. The atrium took heavy fire but nothing's in flames, nothing has fallen down, and probably everything is repairable and it could have been worse. Except . . .' He stopped again.

She sighed. 'Give me the bad news, Major.'

462

'They destroyed the clock.'

Every organisation has its symbol, its totem, its logo. The Time Police had their clock. For them, the clock symbolised Time. Every year, on a certain date, at a certain time, they Stopped the Clock – the ceremony in which they honoured those lost in the Time Wars and afterwards. The ceremony was important to them. The clock was important to them. And now it was destroyed. Its giant tick silenced. Its mighty pendulum still.

Hay gritted her teeth. 'They'll pay for that, Major.'

'I am gratified to hear you say so, Commander.'

'What about civilian casualties?'

'Some. And front-of-house staff, too. The civilian police are calling it a terrorist attack.'

Ellis frowned. 'Why would they attack their own people, ma'am? There wasn't anyone of any value captured. They probably can't tell us anything we don't already know.'

'Perhaps,' she said slowly, looking around, 'they thought there *was* someone of value here and they couldn't take the risk.'

He looked around. 'So where is this valuable person? Or persons?'

'Not here, obviously. And there's a missing pod . . .'

'And two missing operatives.'

'That would be Nuñez and Klein?' said Callen in her ear. 'Are they accounted for?'

There was a long pause. Commander Hay swore silently. This was not how she would have chosen to break the news to Nuñez and Klein's commanding officer.

His voice sounded in her ear. 'Commander Hay . . . are you still there?'

'Major Callen, could you join me here at Shoreditch, please.'

'Now?'

'Yes, now, please.'

'The situation here is not . . .'

'Elect a replacement and join me immediately, please.'

'As you wish, Commander.'

The line went dead.

She turned back to Ellis. 'They're sending a message to anyone who might have thought of spilling even a few beans. *Nowhere is safe from us.* And a message to us too. *We have the resources. We can take you on.*'

Ellis nodded. 'And don't forget, ma'am: Imogen Farnborough said in her statement that there are moves afoot to change the legislation. Perhaps to allow time travel again. If so, these people would be well ahead of the game. All set up and ready to go. Someone could make an absolute packet.'

'Someone with pods, resources, people, equipment, customers, everything they need already in place.'

'Exactly, ma'am.'

'And, I'm sure this is no coincidence, at exactly the moment politicians are endeavouring to clip our wings.'

'Exactly, ma'am.'

'Assemble a strike force, Major. We'll wait for Major Callen. In the meantime, I want to know where Lockland and Parrish have got to. I want to know who was here they don't want us to speak to. I particularly want to know who "they" are, because at the moment we don't have a clue. And most importantly, I want to know where that missing pod went. And what it did when it got there.'

'Already on it, ma'am.'

464

37

Jane and Luke huddled together in the scant shelter of the Site X building. The wind was getting up and more snow swirled around them. Jane had propped a shivering Luke against the wall and was trying to think thoughts that didn't centre on how cold she was. What to do next. Where to go. How to survive. The landscape was monochromatic. The sky was grey and heavy with snow. In the mid-distance, cliffs reared up, dark against the sky. There might be caves, perhaps. Although it seemed safe to assume they would be occupied already. At the foot of the cliffs Jane could see trees, thick with more snow. In fact, white snow lay over everything. If the sun ever shone, the sight would be dazzling. For the two of them though, it would be deadly. They couldn't withstand these temperatures. Not without cold weather gear. And probably not with cold weather gear, either.

Luke leaned against the wall, feeling the cold surface through his clothes. He was shivering uncontrollably and his chest hurt badly. A couple of damaged ribs, he guessed. Even breathing hurt. His eyes had swelled to such an extent that he couldn't see that well either.

'Jane, I'm sorry,' he said through chattering teeth. 'In addition to being the brains of the team, I'm afraid you're going to have to be the eyes and the muscle as well while we work our way out of this particular predicamentette.'

'Well,' she said, trying to stamp her feet, 'our first priority should be . . .'

She fell over.

Luke blinked. 'Jane – where did you go?'

'Down here,' she said. 'I tripped over something. Oh.'

'What? Hurry up, I'm freezing here.'

'Not for long. Look.'

'Can't see very well.'

'Clothing, Luke. It's snowsuits. Cold weather gear.' She held up a grey and white jacket.

'You're kidding.'

'I am not.'

Luke began to wonder if he was light-headed. 'I don't believe it.'

'Neither do I,' she said, 'but I'm not going to argue.'

'How did it get here?'

'Who knows? Who cares? Let's get you dressed.'

He wrapped his arms around himself. 'Actually, Jane, no. It's going to take me ages. Do yourself first.'

'Luke, I . . .'

'No – it's sensible. Of the two of us, you have the greater chance of survival. If you're alive you can do your best to keep me alive. If anything happens to you then I'm finished too, so get your gear on.'

She dragged the clothing out of the snow and shook it hard. 'It's all here, Luke. Both suits. Even our overboots.'

'Dress first. Talk later. Shake the snow off your clothes

first because when you warm up it'll melt and you'll have wet clothes next to your skin and all the cold weather gear in the world won't save you when that freezes solid. Hurry, for God's sake.'

She did. Brushing herself down as best she could, Jane shook her gear hard and gave the jacket to Luke to hold while she scrambled into her trousers. The jacket followed. The zip gave her some trouble because her hands were shaking with cold but she got there eventually. She leaned against the wall and tugged on the overboots and finally pulled up her funnel hood. She felt no warmer afterwards – she'd already been cold when she donned the gear – but at least the wind chill was gone.

Dressing Luke took far longer than either of them anticipated. He was clumsy and every movement hurt him and his clothes were caked with more snow than Jane was happy with, but it was vital to get him covered up. She pulled up his hood, zipped him up and found his gloves in his pocket. When he was fully dressed, she finally pulled on her own.

'Well done,' he said, leaning against the wall, trying not to shiver, pant or cough. 'Thanks. Feel much better now.'

He was lying and they both knew it.

Luke looked around. 'Perhaps we could find the pod.'

'It might not let us in. You know, biometrics?'

'It's a shuttle, Jane. People are in and out all the time. There's a good chance it's open access.'

She scanned the landscape. The light was failing but the one thing she could say definitely was that there was no pod anywhere in sight.

'It must be here, somewhere,' said Luke, his voice muffled because she'd zipped him all the way up to his eyes.

'It might well be but they've probably operated the camouflage device.'

Luke refused to be daunted. 'We could . . . follow . . . the footprints.'

'Sweetie, they disappeared a long time ago.'

'Don't . . . call me sweetie,' said Luke. 'Revolting habit.'

'Don't kill him,' said Bolshy Jane. 'He doesn't know what he's saying.'

He never knows what he's saying, thought Jane. And what to do next? Where to go? Staying put was not an option. Keep talking. They had to stay conscious or they'd be frozen stiff in minutes.

'Do you think,' said Jane, 'that Imogen will be presenting Eric with two glittering ice statues as a wedding present? That would appeal to her. She could stand me in the entrance hall as a work of art and you in the loo to hang the toilet rolls off.'

'Actually,' said Luke, wrapping his arms around himself. 'I've just had a stonking idea.'

'Does it involve escaping to safety?'

'Not as such.'

'Not interested then.'

'No, I was thinking – about the statues, Jane. How about . . . them coming out tomorrow and finding . . . the two of us frozen together in a passionate embrace. A look of . . . sublime fulfilment etched forever upon your frozen features. How impressive would that be?'

Jane tried not to laugh. 'I don't believe you. We're dying here and you're thinking of sex?'

'To be fair, Jane . . . I think of sex even when I'm not dying. Don't you?'

'Not with you – no.'

'Who then? Come on, Jane, tell me.'

She heaved his arm over her shoulder.

'Ooh,' he said. 'I knew . . . my persuasive arguments would win . . . you over.'

'While you're wasting time, Parrish, I'm using my brains. We'll head for those trees over there. Shelter from the wind.' They set off through the snow with Jane staggering slightly under his weight.

'Good thought. And perhaps, once there . . . you know . . . in our final seconds . . . the unutterable joy of Luke Parrish?'

'Let him drop,' said Bolshy Jane. 'Just step over him and keep walking.'

'Or . . .' said Wimpy Jane. 'You could take him up on his offer.'

Both Actual Jane and Bolshy Jane regarded her in astonishment.

'Why have we stopped walking?' slurred Luke. He broke off for another fit of coughing. Red-hot pain lanced through his chest.

'Lean on me,' said Jane. They set off again.

It was hard going. In some places the snow barely covered their boots and in others it came up to their knees, slowing their speed to almost nothing.

Every step was painful for Luke, jarring his bones from top to toe. Breathing made him cough. Coughing made him cough even more. On one occasion, the force of his hacking drove him to his knees. The temptation to keel over and just lie there forever was overwhelming.

Jane tried to make her voice urgent. 'Luke, you must get up. It's not so far now. You must get up. *Get up.*'

469

Leaning heavily on her shoulder, he heaved himself to his feet.

'I think,' he said, teeth chattering, 'it's the bloody irony of it all that's pissing me off. Just think, Jane. If we'd disposed of Imogen Farnborough – just chucked her out of the pod in the 17th century – and don't say you weren't as tempted as me – then she would never have walked through that door back there and we wouldn't be here now.'

'And we'd never have had the intel about King's Arsenal.'

'And still we wouldn't be here. We'd be back at TPHQ. In the warm . . . Say what you like, Jane, no good deed ever goes unpunished.'

Their progress was slow. Looking back while Luke recovered from another fit of painful coughing, Jane was discouraged to see they'd barely covered a hundred yards. The good news was that between the snow and wind, their footsteps were slowly disappearing. Looking ahead, the trees seemed no closer. The whole world was white. She was up to her knees in white stuff. More white stuff fell from the sky. And it wasn't as if being under the trees was likely to be any better. The best they could hope for was to die slightly more slowly.

She sniffed. Even her snot was frozen. 'Luke, whatever are we going to do?'

'We survive,' said Luke with determination. 'For as long as possible. People do live here. So can we.'

'What's the point, though? If we're still alive in the morning, they'll just come out and shoot us. And if they don't kill us, then the Neanders will. They won't know the difference between us and the people at Site X. They'll slaughter us on sight. If a sabre-toothed tiger doesn't get us first. Or a sabre-toothed wolf. Or a sabre-toothed bear.'

'Could we . . . have a little less emphasis on the sabretooths, please?'

'I think you mean sabreteeth. Here.' She pulled his hood even closer around his face. 'There, that's better.'

It would have been if he hadn't been cold and wet to begin with. He could feel his wet clothing cold against his skin, lowering his core temperature. The moment he stopped moving it would freeze. He would be encased in a sheath of ice. As would Jane. They had to keep moving.

He had no thought they would be rescued. No one at TPHQ knew they were here. They had no back-up. No support. No hope.

But – that was what Team 236 had agreed to. Hay had laid it on the line. She hadn't held back. They would be completely alone. Nuñez and Klein had died – possibly because they'd maintained a link with the Time Police which had been discovered. Total immersion in their roles had been the best way to go, he was convinced of it. And it would have worked. No one could have foreseen that Imogen Farnborough would have chosen that particular moment to walk through that particular door. So fire-trucking frustrating. They'd so very nearly had it all. They could have returned to London, gone straight to TPHQ with what they'd discovered – names and locations – and then sat back with a well-deserved drink and let everyone else do the hard work. There would have been congratulations. A possible commendation even – and wouldn't that have stuck in the throats of those who thought they were so useless? They would have completed their

471

training. They would have had a future. They would have had a life. Instead of which . . .

The weather was getting worse. Snow swirled around them. The wind cut like a knife. Luke hurt all over. Anything more than shallow breathing was too painful even to think about. And the almost incessant coughing wasn't helping.

Beside him, Jane plodded on, taking as much of his weight as she could. They were nearly at the trees. There would be shelter from the weather although not the cold. Deep snow was unbelievably tiring to walk through. Luke was aware he was being more of a burden than a benefit.

No change there, he thought. We're not going to make it. We'll never get out of this. Even if we're sheltered, how long before we fall asleep? And never wake up.

He allowed himself the luxury of a few unkind thoughts about Imogen Farnborough and then turned his attention back to their current predicament. A good word, predicament, he decided, and one that in no way conveyed the catastrophe this assignment had turned into. One moment they'd had everything they needed – and more – and the next moment they were dying slowly in the snow. He'd laugh but he needed all his breath to keep going. If he fell, then Jane would as well and neither of them might ever get up again.

The ground sloped slightly downhill. A hollow, perhaps, protected from the snow, which was much shallower here.

Something moved beneath his feet. At the same time, Jane stumbled. 'Oh my God, what have I just trodden on?'

Something long and white protruded from the snow. A stick? Jane stirred it with her foot. It was a long bone.

'An animal,' said Luke. 'Something died here.'

'And there,' said Jane. 'And there. And over there. Luke, they're . . . they're everywhere.'

Luke's frozen brain struggled. Dirty bones lay all around them, half in and half out of the snow. And then something rolled under his foot and he nearly fell again.

'Oh my God,' said Jane. 'That's a skull. A human skull.'

They were standing in a bone pit. Barely more than a few inches of snow covered the iron-hard ground. All the better to see who they were standing on. Long bones, short bones, ribs, pelvises, eyeless skulls. Bones everywhere. Some of the bones hadn't been picked quite clean but they all had a scattered, higgledy-piggledy look about them. Giant paw prints tracked everywhere. Frozen rusty-red patches in the snow provided an unwelcome clue. This must be where Site X dumped its waste.

'Predators,' said Luke. 'They've dragged the bones about as they fed.'

He struggled in his mind for the word. The thoughts wouldn't come. Depredation? He cudgelled his frozen brain. No – predation. That was it.

He was too cold to feel the slow burn of fury. Too tired. 'I imagine,' he said, trying not to cough, 'that this is where they dump the Neanders. When they've finished with them. They can't bury them because the ground's too hard so they bring them out here. To be covered by the snow.'

'You mean after they're dead, they drag the bodies out here and just leave them?'

'Yes,' he said, just a little too quickly. 'After they're dead.'

'And then the animals . . . feed off them?'

'Yes, and we shouldn't hang around here.' Because predators solved Site X's problem of waste disposal. In fact, they probably hung around this area just waiting for the next meal to be served up. He and Jane should get away as soon as possible.

'We need to . . . go,' he said, trying to cough quietly. 'And we shouldn't make a lot of noise.'

'But . . .'

'Now, Jane.'

They struggled on, fighting their way over the frozen body parts scattered across their path. It was almost a relief to be back in the deep snow, and the trees were now only yards distant.

They were wasting their time, thought Luke. Any predator would easily be able to pick up their scent. And – and he tried not to think about this but the thought kept forcing its way into his brain – so could any Neanders still lingering in this area. Would they be out in this weather? He imagined angry eyes watching their struggle across the snow. At this very minute, he and Jane could be surrounded by those who had no cause to love his kind. Humans . . .

'Do you think,' said Jane, quietly, echoing his thoughts, 'that Neanders would come here? To gather up relics of a loved one to take away for a religious ceremony? To honour the dead? After all, they were people just like us.'

Luke coughed. 'I suspect they're considerably better than us.'

The trees did not seem to be getting any closer.

'Jane . . . Jane . . .'

'What? Am I hurting you?'

'No, I'm . . . fine. Don't . . . worry about me.'

'We're nearly there, Luke. Please hold on.'

'Good. Once we're under the trees, things will be better.'

'Yes,' she panted. 'It'll be warmer and we'll be out of the

wind. Once we're under the trees. We can make a nest or shelter or something and . . . think of . . . a plan.'

'Jane, I want to tell you . . .'

'Luke, save your breath. Wait until we're . . .'

'Under the trees,' he whispered. 'Yeah, I know.'

They staggered on. Luke was unable to catch his breath. Which made him cough. Which made excruciating pain shoot through his chest. Which made him unable to catch his breath. Which made him cough. Some days, he reflected, it's just not worth getting out of bed.

'What?'

He realised he must have said that aloud. Had he started to talk to himself? 'I said . . . some days . . . it's just not worth . . . getting out of bed.'

'I'm inclined to agree,' said Jane through gritted teeth, struggling up a slight incline. But there were trees over on their left. The wind was dropping.

It was, of course, very possible that any comparatively warm and sheltered spot would already be occupied by someone or something that would be very unwilling to give it up. Or even to share. But one problem at a time.

A little to their right a large conifer of some kind stretched its lower branches almost to the ground. Snow lay thickly upon it but there might possibly be some form of protection underneath. Less snow, certainly.

Carefully she lowered him to the ground. 'I'll go first. If anything tries to eat me . . .'

'I'll cough and shiver at them,' he promised. 'North is always telling us to play to our strengths.'

Being very careful not to dislodge any snow from the

branches, Jane crawled underneath. Whether anything already occupied the small space between the branches and the ground she was unable to say and her hood made it impossible to hear if anything close by was breathing. Tiny tracks, bird and mammal, she guessed, criss-crossed the snow but there was no rank animal smell. And none of the big paw prints they'd seen at the body dump. She pushed on, eventually banging her head on the tree trunk. A little snow fell on her head.

No time to wait for her eyes to adjust. She turned to pull Luke inside with her. He crawled in behind her on his hands and knees. She could see that every movement hurt him.

'That's it. Nearly there. Just a little further. Well done, Luke. We've made it.'

'Where are we?'

'Under a tree. Does it hurt less if you sit down or lie down?'

'Everything hurts all the time, Jane. I'll sit.' He awkwardly manoeuvred himself into position. 'I'll sit . . . against the . . . trunk. Like this. You . . . sit between . . . my legs.'

'Oh God, Parrish. This is just some complicated plot to get me between your legs, isn't it? Why can't you just do flowers and dinner like normal men?'

'I . . . am . . . Luke Parrish . . .' he said with dignity. 'I don't operate like normal men.'

'You got that right,' she muttered, easing herself carefully into position.

'That's right,' he said. 'Now lean back against me. No, it doesn't hurt. Then I can put my arms around you. Then I can keep you warm and you can keep me warm. Perfect.'

She leaned back very gently. He slid his arms around her.

'Can you pile the snow up around us a little? It's insulation against the wind.'

Using her gloved hands, she piled the snow up around their legs. 'How's that?'

'Perfect,' he said, again. 'We can last here for ages.'

She sighed and laid her head back against his shoulder and they sat in the strange half-light as the snow fell. The tree protected them from the worst of it. Only a few flakes filtered softly through the overhanging branches. The cold was biting, though. Half an hour, she thought. If that.

'All right, Jane?'

'Yes. I'm very warm, thank you.'

Even through all their layers he could feel her shivering, but shivering was good. When the shivering ceased – so would they.

'Jane, I have to say something.'

'I think you should conserve your strength.'

He took no notice. 'I really screwed this up, Jane. All this is my fault. I've got everything wrong. Story of my life, really. If I'd handled Imogen better – not just at TPHQ, but if I'd worked a little harder on our relationship . . . if we'd parted on better terms. She must really hate me.' His voice faltered for a moment. 'It's not a good feeling, Jane . . . to know someone hates you *that* much. And I don't think I'd feel so bad if it was just me. Anyone could make a good case for saying I deserved it . . . but not you, Jane. You're a good person. You deserve . . .'

'Luke . . .'

He would not be stopped. 'And then we had them. We had them at the King's Arsenal. We had them again at Shoreditch.

I got greedy. I wanted it all. I wanted to go back to TPHQ and fling it in their faces. Do *you* hate me?'

She smiled inside her hood. 'Sweetie, everyone hates you. You're the most irritating person on the planet.'

He coughed a laugh. 'I can live with that if you don't hate me.'

'I don't hate you. I am constantly battling the urge to slap you senseless, but no, I don't hate you.'

'No, you don't understand, Jane.' He stopped to catch his breath and then said quietly, 'Not only is everything my fault, but it's my dad's fault as well.'

Now they were out of the wind, she rather thought she might be feeling warmer. In fact, she was quite comfortable. It would be nice to just close her eyes and go to sleep. 'Mm? How's that, then?'

'You didn't see it, did you?'

She said drowsily, 'See what?'

He sharpened his voice. 'Jane, wake up. This is important. This is something you have to know.'

She jolted awake. 'Know what?'

'The locker room? At the facility back there?'

'Mm?'

The words were forced out of him. 'My dad built it.'

The words ran around inside her head while she struggled to take in what he was saying. 'What?'

'Didn't you see it? On the inside of the locker? And in the pod? The Parrish Industries logo?'

'I don't think I'd know it if I saw it.'

'A diamond with a P inside.'

'Oh . . . yes . . . saw that. Was that Parrish Industries?'

He felt suddenly very tired.

'Yeah. And once I saw it – it was everywhere. Lockers, equipment, the lot. Parrish Industries built it all. Everything. And to think I was just coming around to the idea my dad might not be such a bastard after all. You know . . . after what Birgitte said . . . about that night . . . but obviously not. The Parrish family showing their true colours, eh, Jane?'

She tried to cudgel her brain into action. Her lips felt almost too stiff and cold to function. 'No. Wait, Luke. They know who you are. They wouldn't kill the son of the man who . . .'

She tailed away and closed her eyes. Too much effort.

'Wouldn't they? We both saw what they're capable of. Think of the money they must be making . . . Always knew he was a bastard.'

Jane closed her eyes again, the better to consider this information. This idea of getting out of the wind had been a good one. Finally, warmth was beginning to creep through her bones. She was actually very comfortable.

'Jane, stay awake. Don't go to sleep.'

'I'm not,' she said drowsily. 'I'm fine.'

And she was. Heat was flowing through her body. She could feel her toes and fingers again. Everything was soft and comfortable. All she had to do was lie back and recover. Everything would be fine.

She was jolted awake by Luke trying to scoop more snow around them. At least that was what she assumed he was doing, although his movements were so jerky and uncoordinated it was hard to be sure.

She blinked. Even her eyelashes were frozen. 'Luke, where's your glove?'

'Eh? Oh. Dunno. Must have come off sometime. Doesn't matter. Feeling fine.'

'No, no. We must find it.' She tried to sit up but it seemed so stupid to move and let all that cold air in when they'd just managed to get themselves so warm. Must conserve body heat.

She could still hear his voice. Fainter now. He was saying words.

'If it wasn't . . . for the fact that I've dragged you down with me, I'd be inclined to say this was . . . the . . . ideal outcome for me. You wouldn't believe the amount of damage I've done in this world. The sooner . . . I'm out of it the . . . better. Sorry, Jane. So sorry.'

She made a half-hearted scrabble in the snow. 'I can't find . . . glove. Dark. Can't see.'

'Jane, must tell you . . . about my dad . . . saw his logo . . . Site X . . .'

She became aware she was digging in the snow. Whatever for? Why would she do that? 'Sorry . . . what? Say . . . again.'

'What?'

'About the thing . . . you were going . . . to tell me.'

'My dad. Site X. Must . . . tell you.'

'Mm.'

'When I wake up . . .'

He leaned his head back against the tree trunk and closed his eyes. Jane slept in his arms.

38

The Time Police have always had a reputation for hitting a place hard, blowing up everything in sight, shooting everything that moves until it doesn't, and then enjoying a well-earned coffee and chat around the smoking crater. Commander Hay had been at considerable pains to change this attitude but now, suddenly, she found she had no problems with it at all.

She stood inside Site X, in the observation lounge, noting the comfortable chairs, the food, the drink . . . as if all this was some kind of spectator sport. And then there was the view . . .

They'd hit this place hard and they'd hit it fast. The outer door had been blasted into non-existence. Two clean-up crews went in first, pouring down the corridors, driving people ahead of them and sonicking the reluctant until either they complied or were incapable of non-compliance. Or, indeed, anything at all.

The main force drove forwards, sweeping everything ahead of them until their targets had nowhere to go and were invited to surrender or die. It was made very clear that the Time Police weren't bothered either way.

The secondary force swept up behind, picking up those who thought they'd escaped the attention of the main force.

The third force – mechs, medtecs, the infants from IT, and so forth – followed on at the rear. Their job was to investigate, download, upload and generally remove everything that could be removed. People, equipment, records – everything. Once they had what they needed – and it wouldn't take long – the Time Police would hit the facility with simultaneous EMPs so ferocious as to ensure anything left would never function again.

Resistance was not only futile but almost non-existent. The Time Police had the advantage of surprise, superior numbers, superior weapons and their famous *couldn't give a rat's arse* attitude. A winning combination in any situation.

More and more Site X staff were marched into the central rest area and pushed on to their knees. The less conscious – those who had been zapped – now found themselves enjoying the other half of the equation and were unceremoniously dropped to the ground and zipped. Zapped and zipped – the traditional Time Police way.

Major Ellis found his commander still in the observation room.

'All secure, ma'am.' He pushed up his visor. His face was rather pale. 'You wouldn't believe this place, Commander. Some of the things going on . . .'

She was still looking down into the science area below. 'Oh, I think I have an idea.' She roused herself. 'Any signs of Parrish and Lockland?'

'None.'

'Pick someone and hit them until they tell us where they are.'

'That might not be necessary. Imogen Farnborough is here.'

'Really? The rat returned to the sinking ship?'

'So it would appear.'

'I gave instructions she wasn't to be released until my say-so.'

'We were the victims of our own secrecy, ma'am. Not knowing anything of this mission, Captain Filbert saw no reason why her release shouldn't proceed as normal.'

She said thoughtfully, 'It would give me enormous pleasure to slap that little bitch unconscious.'

'Not necessary, ma'am. She can't talk fast enough.'

She nodded. 'Even her mother won't be able to get her out of this one.'

'No, indeed. And a second offence. It's not looking good for her. There's also an oily little snake called Geoffrey who I think can be induced to rat out his colleagues in return for his life.'

He joined her at the window. 'What do we do with *them*, ma'am?'

They gazed down at the Neanders below, thoroughly agitated by the events of the day, which they couldn't possibly understand. Some were screaming. Others cowered. Several were hurling themselves at the walls of their cages.

'And there are others, ma'am. Some sort of habitat in the basement – but anyone venturing close enough to release the cages runs a very real risk of being torn apart.'

She nodded. 'Leave them where they are for the time being. I don't want any of our people having to shoot them in self-defence. They've suffered enough. When we leave, we'll fry this place with the usual EMP. That'll unlock the cages; they can free themselves and find their own way out.'

'Very well, ma'am.'

'Where is Major Callen?'

'Supervising the illegals, ma'am.' He hesitated. 'I think it would be fair to say he's feeling a little aggrieved at the moment.'

She nodded. 'I don't blame him. I'm going to have to mend some bridges there. However, first things first.'

She opened her com. 'Major Callen, I want every scrap of data we can retrieve. Quick as you can, please.'

'Yes, Commander.'

She closed the link. 'Let's go and meet the delightful specimens responsible for all this, shall we? You might want to put the word around, Major – I am not in the best mood today and anyone even so much as looking at me wrong will regret it bitterly for the very short period of time I allow them to live.'

'It will be my pleasure, ma'am.'

'How many illegals have we got altogether?'

'Twenty-five, ma'am.'

'Alive?'

'Mostly, yes. Three dead. Three wounded but not seriously.' He consulted his scratchpad. 'Plus, three security types, six suspiciously silent so-called doctors and/or scientists, six people assuring us they're lab assistants and only following orders, a couple of all-purpose cooks and bottle-washers who say none of it was anything to do with them, one known illegal – Farnborough, Imogen – and the aforementioned piece of grease who must be senior management and calls himself Geoffrey.' He stored his scratchpad and said thoughtfully, 'I wonder, ma'am, if he might be the person they were so anxious we wouldn't get to meet?'

'Let's go and have a look, shall we?'

*   *   *

Nineteen people knelt with their hands secured behind them. Imogen Farnborough was crying. So, on closer inspection, was Mr Geoffrey.

'He did it,' she burst out. 'He made us do it. It's all his fault. I tried to save them.'

'You lying bitch,' he shouted. 'It was you.' He turned to Callen. 'I swear it was her. It was all her.'

An officer lightly sonicked the pair of them and they crumpled to the floor.

Commander Hay stared at them for a long while. Everyone here was silent. The only sounds were those of the Time Police, still tearing through the place and boxing up anything they could find. Pulling everything apart. Generally wrecking the place. And downloading everything.

Major Ellis, who had, on several occasions, seen his commander in full frontal fury was suddenly aware he would much rather face that Commander Hay than this one.

'I can give you names,' slurred Mr Geoffrey, struggling to rise with his hands zipped behind him. 'I can tell you everything.'

An officer with an IT flash on his shoulder emerged from a shattered doorway. 'Lt Fanboten sent me, ma'am. Some of it's a bit fried because they tried a mass delete when they saw us coming and their system couldn't cope, but we've got most of it. He says another ten minutes and he'll have everything worth having.'

'My compliments to Lt Fanboten and his team. Carry on.'

'Yes, ma'am.' He trotted away.

'Major Callen.'

He turned, his face expressionless. 'Ma'am.'

She indicated Mr Geoffrey. 'Ask him once – where are my

people? If he doesn't reply, shoot him dead and move on to Farnborough. If she doesn't cooperate, shoot her dead and move on to the next one. Make it very clear that if they cannot produce Parrish and Lockland – alive – I will feed everyone here to their friends downstairs.'

'My pleasure, ma'am.'

The threat was unnecessary. Mr Geoffrey and Miss Farnborough couldn't gabble their stories fast enough.

Imogen Farnborough, nearly hysterical, had, apparently, done her best to save her friend Luke, even to the extent of hurling herself at Mr Geoffrey, no matter how unpleasant she found him, and pleading for Luke's life.

Mr Geoffrey's version fully described his horror and disbelief at Miss Farnborough's revelations concerning Luke and Jane's day job.

'I just thought they were a nice couple,' he wailed, piteously. 'Here for a nice afternoon out.' He appeared to remember the activities of the science area downstairs and wisely veered away from the niceness of the activities at this facility. 'I didn't believe a word she was saying. She obviously had it in for Luke Parrish. Spiteful little cow, she is.'

Even more tears ran down his cheeks than Imogen's.

'So where are they?' roared Grint, shaking him by the scruff of his neck.

Having no hands free, Mr Geoffrey intimated with his head. 'There.'

Grint dropped Mr Geoffrey, who thudded painfully to the hard floor, and looked around. 'Where?'

'There. Out there.'

'They're outside?'

486

Geoffrey nodded vigorously.

'And you've waited until now to tell us?'

Mr Geoffrey almost physically disappeared behind a welter of apologies, self-justification, pleas for mercy, Farnborough-based accusations, and snot-snivelling self-pity.

Grint turned to Commander Hay. 'With your permission, ma'am.'

'Granted, Lieutenant, and with all speed. *Find them.*'

Grint set off for the door, calling for two teams to follow and to bring tag readers, proximity alerts, the lot.

Ellis turned to his commander and said quietly, 'I hate to say it, but it's most unlikely anyone could survive out there for more than about thirty to forty minutes and we've been on site for over half an hour. Their bodies could already be buried in the snow.' He stopped and took a deep breath. 'Ma'am, I'd like to join in the search.'

'I understand, Major – you are their team leader – but I want you and Callen supervising events here. If they are already dead, we owe it to them to make sure we miss nothing. I think we can safely leave the search to Lt Grint. He has ground to make up.'

Reluctantly, Ellis nodded.

'We will find them. I promise you, Major, we won't leave without them.'

Outside Site X, Grint was dividing his teams into pairs.

'Fan out. Stay within visual range of each other at all times. We know who we're looking for. Lockland and Parrish will almost certainly be unconscious by now so you need to *look* for them. Check everywhere. Under trees, behind rocks, inside caves. Look for disturbed snow. Footprints. Blood, even. You won't be surprised to hear that someone's given Parrish a good seeing-to, because we all know what a gobby bastard he is, but he's *our* gobby bastard, so find them. Go.'

They fanned out, trudging through the snow in pairs – one officer to check visually for signs that anyone could have passed this way, and the other to consult his equipment.

Grint and Rossi both set out for the stand of trees at the foot of a black cliff in the distance. The light was going and Grint could feel the temperature dropping. It was hard to see how either of them could still be alive. Especially if Parrish was injured. The scent of blood would carry in this clean, cold air and there would be plenty of predators about looking for a quick and easy meal.

Grint pulled out his torch and shone it around. The snow glittered in the bright light. Over to his right, Hansen and Kohl trudged through the snow, heads down, checking every inch.

The cold was intense. The wind moaned rather than howled. A miserable, lonely place inhabited by people he hadn't liked the look of when they were safely behind bars. The thought of encountering them out here in this bitter twilight . . . He couldn't wait to get out of here. History – you could keep it.

Knee-deep in snow, they ploughed on.

Beside him, Rossi stopped, shining his torch on the ground. 'Are these footprints? I know the wind's covered them over but . . .'

At the same time, their proximity meters bleeped. 'Over there,' said Rossi. They struggled up the slope. 'Can't see anyone,' he said, panting. 'Trees too thick.'

They flashed their torches about. There was no one here but the meter was still bleeping.

The same thought occurred to both of them. 'They're under the trees. Here.'

Grint and Rossi moved from tree to tree, carefully lifting the snow-laden lower branches. And there they were. Luke and Jane huddled together, their faces the same colour as the snow. Deeply unconscious. Probably dead.

About to investigate, Rossi found himself knocked sideways. He sprawled in the snow as Grint literally clambered over the top of him.

'Jane. Jane. Can you hear me?' He opened his com. 'Major, we've got them. Rossi, alert the medics. Tell them to get heat sheets ready.'

'They're still alive?'

'Unknown and no time to investigate. Get a couple of others over here to give us a hand.'

Hansen and Kohl appeared, running clumsily through the snow.

'Right, let's get them out. You three take Parrish. I'll see to Jane. Be aware – handle them gently. Don't rub or chafe their skin. You know the drill. OK, let's get them off the cold ground.'

'Their clothes are wet, sir.'

'We can't undress them here. Let's get them back to a pod asap. Keep them as flat as possible. Gently now.'

Grint scooped up Jane and set off, leaving his grumbling team to manhandle Luke Parrish.

'Wouldn't it have made more sense for *him* to take Parrish?' enquired Kohl, stumbling under the combination of an

489

unwieldy Parrish and knee-high snow. 'Lockland probably weighs less than an After Eight mint.'

'Yeah,' grinned Hansen.

'What are you grinning at?'

'Nothing.'

Slipping and stumbling through the snow, they made their way back down the slope. Grint carrying Jane, Kohl and Hansen carrying Luke. Rossi was on his com, alerting the medtecs. Who had a pod door open, ready for them.

'OK – set them down here. Are they alive?'

Hansen shook his head. 'Don't know.'

'Right, let's get this wet clothing off them. Quick as you can. Out, you lot.'

Grint and his team were chivvied from the pod.

'Heat pads to groins and armpits,' instructed the medic. 'Lowest setting. We want to warm them, not cook them.'

Grint's voice sounded in his ear. 'Is she alive?' There was a pause. 'Asking for Commander Hay.'

'Yes, they are. Barely. We aim to keep them that way. Now let us get on with it.'

Back inside the facility, Callen was reporting to Hay. 'They've found Lockland and Parrish, Commander.'

'Alive?'

'Unable to say at this moment. If they are, then it's only just and they might not be for long.'

She nodded. 'Keep me posted. Whichever way it goes, I want to know.'

He looked at her. 'Did we know they were here?'

'I did, yes.'

He regarded her for a long moment and then said, 'Do you want me to make arrangements for a detention pod to transport the illegals?'

'No.'

'Are we – will we dispose of them . . . here?'

A ripple ran through the illegals' ranks. Imogen Farnborough, who had just hauled herself to her knees, began to cry again.

'No.'

'Then . . . what, ma'am?'

She pitched her voice so it could be heard by all. 'We leave them here.'

There were shouts of protest. Imogen Farnborough began to cry properly. 'You can't do that. My mother will . . .'

'Will never know. To the rest of the world you were released from prison and disappeared from sight. Just another missing delinquent. No one will weep. Not even your mother.'

'But I'll tell you everything.'

'I already know everything.'

Imogen suddenly looked sly. 'No, you don't.'

'Oh, I think I do.'

Callen lowered his voice. 'Commander, do you mean . . . ?'

'Yes, I do, Major. Having seen this sample of their work, I think the sooner these specimens are removed from the gene pool, the better for humanity, don't you? We leave them here. Unless you have any better ideas?'

He surveyed the prisoners still herded into a corner. For a moment, his eyes lingered on Farnborough and Geoffrey. 'No, I don't think I do, Commander.'

Ellis felt compelled to speak. 'Ma'am, we blew out the

door. The electrics will be fried. They won't be able to shut themselves in and once the indigenous people find out . . .'

'Yes,' she said, not bothering to lower her voice. 'Suddenly they'll be at the mercy of their victims. They can try and barricade themselves in here but I don't know how successful their efforts will be. We won't be leaving them any weapons or ammunition, so not for too long, I suspect. Then their supplies will run out. There'll be no power. I suspect they have very few survival skills between them. My best guess is the oily bastard in the grey suit will go first. It's very obvious he has no value at all. Farnborough might persuade some man to take her under his wing but if it comes to a choice between eating her and fu— Well, I think we can guess. I suspect they will either die quickly at the hands of their former prey or slowly starve to death in the cold. I must confess I really don't care.'

'A warning to others,' said Callen.

'Exactly, Major. Does anyone have any strong moral objections?'

Apparently, no one did. Only the now hysterical illegals themselves and no one took any notice of them.

A breathless officer appeared. 'Ma'am, the medtecs want to get Lockland and Parrish back to TPHQ asap. Can you manage with one pod less?'

'Yes. Go. Tell the doctor if they die, I'm coming for him.'

She turned to Ellis. 'Reigns of terror are quite enjoyable. I'm beginning to see the benefits.'

'I'm very happy for you, ma'am. All team leaders report they have what they need in the way of equipment and records. With our lost lambs recovered, all search parties are now on their way back to the pods.'

'Then our work here is done.'

Ellis watched Geoffrey's shoulders sag. Had he been holding on for a rescue? Given what had just happened at TPHQ – were those the standing orders? Say nothing and wait for us to get you out? If so, he was out of luck today.

'Let's get back to the pods, Major.'

There were screams of protest. 'You can't go. You can't just leave us here. We're still zipped. What about what's out there? You blew the outer door. What about us?'

'What about you?'

'You can't leave us. We can't even secure the building any longer. It's not safe.'

'Not safe for whom?'

Silence as the implications sank in.

Major Ellis considered a timely reminder. 'What of the indigenous people, ma'am? We left them in their cages as you suggested, but we can't leave them there to starve.'

'No, indeed. Make sure we're all well clear and then hit them with the EMP. That should knock out the locks on the cages and they can free themselves.'

Major Ellis, recognising the glint in her eye, knew his duty. 'And what then, ma'am?'

'Oh, well,' she said carelessly, 'I suspect most of them won't be inclined to hang around . . .' She smiled at her prisoners. 'You hope. On the other hand, of course, it's very possible that revenge will be uppermost in their thoughts. An interesting situation, Major.'

'Indeed, ma'am. I wonder if, perhaps, you might care for a small wager.'

'To make things interesting, you mean?'

'Exactly.'

'Excellent idea, Major. Open it up to everyone. Excluding our friends here, of course.' She smiled wolfishly. 'Well, can't hang around here all day. Places to go, people to see, winnings to collect. Lead on, Major.'

There were screams of protest. 'We can tell you everything you need to know.'

She turned. 'I already know everything I need to know. We have files, downloads, uploads, records, photos – the lot. And what's missing here will be provided by your colleagues from the King's Arsenal and the pretty green building in Shoreditch. I don't *need* any of you. You are of no use to me at all. Or the world in general. On the other hand, I'm certain you'll be an excellent source of protein to your former . . . guests. Lovely to have met you.'

They left with Imogen Farnborough's screams ringing in their ears.

Once outside and out of earshot, she said to Ellis, 'Give them twenty-four hours to experience real cold and real fear and think seriously about in which order they'll eat each other and then go and pick them up. They'll sing like cassowaries.'

Halfway back to the pods, and flanked on either side by Majors Ellis and Callen, she halted suddenly. 'The missing pod.'

Ellis stopped too. 'Ma'am?'

'How did they get here? Where's their pod?'

Major Callen shook his head. 'It's not here, Commander. I checked all pod signatures myself and records show their pod left again shortly after landing. Not sure of its ultimate destination at this moment but we can get people on that.' He paused. 'I know you'll find this interesting – the pilots' names were Smallhope and Pennyroyal.'

She nodded. 'Yes. We should have guessed, I suppose.'

'They make me nervous.'

'They make everyone nervous.'

'Including anyone stupid enough to employ them, I suspect. Well, that changes things slightly, Major. Leave a small team here to keep an eye on things – just in case anyone turns up. As soon as we get back home, send a rescue team for our friends back there. We can't risk them falling back into the hands of their employers.'

'Yes, Commander.'

She and Ellis set off towards the nearest pod. Major Callen stood for a moment, staring at a patch of empty snow some one hundred yards from Site X. His face showed no expression. Then he hitched his blaster over his shoulder and followed his commander.

39

A safe distance away, two people, very carefully camouflaged in the snow and with only their eyes showing, watched the Time Police emerge with box after box, crate after crate. Lines of officers passed them to each other for careful storage in the three black pods lined up to the north of the facility.

'Well, this didn't end quite as expected, Pennyroyal.'

'No, my lady.'

'Not quite sure what our employer's going to say about this.'

'No, my lady.'

'And we haven't been bloody well paid, yet.'

Pennyroyal sighed. 'They're stripping the place, my lady.'

His companion nodded sadly. 'Bastards. Did they find the other two? Those young people?'

'I believe so, my lady.'

'Our good deed for the day, Pennyroyal.'

'Indeed, my lady.'

They resumed their careful scrutiny.

Some twenty minutes later the Time Police had all gone and the landscape was as empty as before.

Until . . .

Slowly, a dark head emerged from the broken doorway. Then

another. Then a whole group. Still very carefully concealed, Smallhope and Pennyroyal watched the Neanders depart. Single file. Hastening through the snow towards the cliffs. The last one, a female clutching a tiny infant, could barely walk. Two of the bigger males helped her through the snow. No one was hanging around. They all moved as fast as they could go.

'Oh good, Pennyroyal, they've let them go. Compassionate Time Police officers. Who'd have thought?'

'Indeed, my lady.'

'Not that that helps us, of course . . .'

Her companion maintained a gloomy silence.

Stillness and silence descended again as they watched the Neanders disappear into the deepening dusk. When complete stillness had returned to the landscape, they emerged, brushed off the snow and regarded the destruction around them.

The facility had a battered look about it. The outer door lay some yards away in the snow. A plume of black smoke drifted out into the ice-cold air. Discarded boxes, crates and equipment lay in the trampled snow. There was a desolate and deserted air about it.

'Sodding arseholes, Pennyroyal. Those bastard Time Police have just walked off with the equivalent of a year's income for us.'

'Indeed, my lady.'

'In fact, Pennyroyal, sodding *bloody* arseholes.'

'Eloquently put, my lady.'

'We've been working on this for bloody months.'

'We have indeed, my lady.'

'We've had to put up with that great greasy, pus-sucking troglodyte Geoffrey . . .'

497

'As you say, my lady.'

'And now a bloody fortune has just slipped through our fingers.'

'As you say, my lady, but in this case, perhaps . . .'

'Oh yes. Can't begrudge those poor buggers their freedom, I suppose. It's just that we'd have got a tidy sum for this lot and I had my eye on a rather nice little property in Tuscany. How about you?'

'A very promising two-year-old, my lady. Rather appropriately named Daughter of Time.'

'Oh, what a shame. Never mind. And those poor sods deserve their freedom. Don't mind betting they'll all be a long way from here by morning.' She looked around at the smoke pouring from the broken door and the trampled and bloody snow. 'Mind you, I can't help feeling that the shit's really going to hit the fan chez Parrish.'

Pennyroyal shrugged. 'What else is shit for, my lady?'

'Very true, Pennyroyal, and very profound, but the trick is always to ensure the fan it hits is not one's own.'

'A little late, my lady.' He surveyed the empty landscape, turning slowly. 'It would appear that at this moment we're right royally buggered.'

'I'd be inclined to agree, Pennyroyal, if I didn't know you better.'

Glove in his teeth, Pennyroyal was rummaging in an outside pocket, pulling out a small hand-held device. He turned slowly and then his snowy face cracked into a grin.

'*Nil desperandum*, my lady. If you would care to glance over your right shoulder . . .'

She did so and their pod materialised. Untouched. Unscathed.

498

'Oh, I say, Pennyroyal. Camouflage device. Jolly well done.'

'I can take no credit, my lady.'

'No, no. Beg to differ. You take as much credit as you like.'

'Not sure how the Time Police managed to miss it, my lady.'

'No – you'd have thought they'd have picked up the signature. And that major at the back looked straight at it, didn't he? Still – I do think we should bugger off while the buggering's good.'

They set off, crunching through the snow, their breath steaming. The snow had stopped but the night skies were now clear and bitterly cold. The stars were coming out. The moon had risen over the horizon. Somewhere a wolf howled.

'A trifle on the nippy side tonight, my lady.'

'I commend your restraint, Pennyroyal. I'd describe it as brass monkeys, myself.'

'Never mind, my lady. A nice cup of tea once we get inside. And I have some Battenberg put away for a special occasion.'

'Bugger the Battenberg, Pennyroyal. I intend to give the nearest cocktail cabinet a bashing it won't forget in a hurry.'

'Very good, my lady.'

40

MedCen was packed. Busy medtecs trotted from one bed to another, snarling at the security guards to get out of their way. The guards ignored them. With so many illegals receiving treatment, the number of security staff actually exceeded medical teams.

And there were civilians, too. The more serious had been air-evacked to civilian facilities, but a handful remained and were being regarded with deep suspicion by everyone.

The wards were bustling. The only quiet space was that around Captain Farenden's bed. He lay flat, staring up at the ceiling. Which was never a good sign. His face was white and drawn with shiny purple shadows under his eyes. Commander Hay paused on the threshold, took a deep breath, straightened her shoulders and crossed to his bed. Pulling up a chair, she fixed him with a fierce stare.

'You're not allowed to die, Charlie. I refuse to have bad news brought to me by anyone other than you.'

His voice was still very weak but he made a heroic attempt. 'In that case, ma'am, I shall make every effort to do the not-dying thing.'

'Thank you, Captain.' She sat back in her seat and looked

around. 'Well, this brings back memories, doesn't it? You malingering away and me at your bedside trying to work out what I'll do without you.'

He smiled. 'Oh yes . . . the helicopter crash. What a long time ago that seems now. It's a bit more than . . . just my leg this time, ma'am.'

She patted the small part of him that wasn't bandaged. 'A piece of sticking plaster and two aspirin and you'll be fine in the morning.' Her gaze roved around the crowded MedCen. 'Everyone turned out to fight, didn't they?'

'They did, ma'am . . . even the civilian staff.'

They watched a long-suffering medtec endure a female civilian admin clerk instructing him on how to bandage a wound *properly*.

At the end of the ward, next to a curtained-off corner, Matthew Farrell sat on an uncomfortable visitor's chair, his bandaged head in his bandaged hands.

Hay raised her eyebrows.

'It's the closest . . . the doctor will let him get, ma'am.'

'How are they?'

He shook his head slightly.

She sighed.

'Farrell fought well, ma'am. Saved . . . a civilian woman. He certainly saved me. Stood his ground and roared like a lion.'

She sighed. 'He is very like his mother, isn't he?'

'With the bad comes . . . the good. You know that.'

'Get better soon, Charlie. The front of the building looks like a bomb site and most of our garden has fallen into the river. The press are all over us and the Corporation is out for blood. I need you on it.'

'With that incentive, ma'am . . . how could I fail to make a spectacular recovery?'

'The doctor tells me you'll be sitting up tomorrow and taking nourishment.'

'Ah. Something . . . to look forward to.'

'I shall come and watch.'

The words *something else to look forward to* were not spoken.

She smiled. 'Get well, Charlie. That's a command.'

An hour later, back in her office, Major Callen was presenting his report.

'My sitrep, Commander.'

'Thank you, Major. Your main recommendations?'

'That we admit the gardens were a bad idea, concrete over the front area, sow a few anti-personnel devices, and install two miles of razor wire and a couple of gun turrets.'

'Ah, still favouring the warm and fluffy approach, I see.'

'Someone has to, Commander. We made things too easy for them. Plenty of cover for the enemy and none for us. It's a miracle there wasn't more of a bloodbath.'

'No one died, Major. At least, not on our side.'

'We won't always be so fortunate, ma'am. If you read my report, you will see I've recommended . . .'

She let his report fall on to her desk and sighed. 'I don't have to read it, Major. I know without looking that there will be three pages of I told you so, another three pages of how badly everything has been handled and ten pages of how much better you would manage things given even the slightest opportunity.'

There was a red-hot silence.

She leaned over her desk. 'I know what you want, Major.'

He appeared to come to a decision. Subtly moving to a fighting stance, he said very quietly, 'No, you don't.'

'I think I do.'

'Actually, I don't think you've got a clue what I want.'

'Well, let's find out, shall we? Let's drag it out into the open. Tell me what it is I think you want.'

He was very white. 'I can assure you, whatever you are thinking, you are completely wrong, Commander.'

'Am I? I think not.'

On the other side of the wall, the very young lieutenant currently standing in for Captain Farenden listened to the rising voices and redoubled his prayers for Captain Farenden's complete – but above all, immediate – recovery.

'Very well, since you insist, Commander. You initiated an entire operation without any reference to me. You knew two of my people – *my* people, Commander, from *my* division – had been murdered and you said nothing to me. You left me in complete ignorance of current events. You could not more clearly have demonstrated your complete lack of confidence in me. I am your second in command and officer i/c the Hunter Division. I have *never* failed in my loyalty to the Time Police, Commander, but now . . .'

'And I *command* the Time Police. What about your loyalty to *me*?'

The silence lay like a chasm between them and then he said very quietly, 'You're a fool, Marietta. A blind fool.'

Kicking a chair aside, he strode from the room.

Commander Hay sat down. Very slowly. After a while she reached for the file, opened it, stared blindly and then closed it again. She picked up her scratchpad and then put it down again. Then she turned her chair to stare out of the window. For a long time.

Back again in MedCen, Jane was struggling to open her eyes. They felt gummy and disinclined to cooperate. The first thing she saw was Matthew, illegally easing himself through the curtains.

'Hey, Jane. Can you hear me?'

Her mouth felt gummy as well. Everything was a tremendous effort. 'Yeees.'

'How do you feel?'

'Worn . . . out.'

'Yes, you will for a bit.'

'Did . . . we get . . . them?'

'Yep. Every last one.'

'Luke?'

He nodded. 'There.'

She summoned all her strength and turned her head. Luke lay in the next bed, white, silent and hooked up to any number of machines.

'They're still rewarming him. Don't worry. He's doing well.'

'What's the matter with his hand?'

'He lost some fingers.'

Jane closed her eyes. 'I couldn't find his glove.'

'Not your fault, Jane. He'd be the first to say that.'

'Will they chuck him out, do you think?'

'They won't chuck *him* out, no.'

Something in his voice made her ask, 'What . . . do you mean?'

He didn't reply.

She seemed to focus more clearly. 'Why are you in civvy clothes?'

'Suspended.'

'Oh my God, what did you do?'

He looked around but they were alone. 'I went to St Mary's for help. They tracked you to Shoreditch and I took the information to Hay.'

'You saved us?'

'I think the emphasis is more on – *so you went over my head to those morons at St Mary's.*'

'And she did her nut?'

'I deserved it. I did go over her head. Is there a worse crime?'

Jane thought of some of the things that had gone on at Site X. 'Yeah. Trust me. There are worse things out there.'

He remained silent.

'What's going to happen now?'

'Dunno. Some kind of hearing. If I'm lucky, they'll just boot me out. If not, I could be doing some time.'

'Surely not.'

'She's really not happy with me, Jane.'

'Well,' said Jane, weak and wobbly, but decisive. 'If you go, then so do I.'

'You don't mean that.'

'I do. I won't stay without you and I suspect Luke won't, either.'

He shook his head. 'The end of Team Weird. We didn't get far, did we?'

'Well, you can't say we didn't have an impact. Just not the right one.'

Luke stirred.

Matthew pressed the call button.

The dark-haired doctor turned up and regarded his patients gloomily. 'Out, young Farrell.'

Reluctantly, Matthew wandered away.

Luke croaked something Jane didn't catch.

The doctor sighed. 'Your hand was a mess. You lost your glove, didn't you?'

'I never noticed,' said Luke in a tiny thread of a voice. 'And then we couldn't find it.'

'Well, we've salvaged what we can. We've debrided to remove dead tissue. We're waiting for new tissue to regenerate – which it will, but – I'm sorry, lad – you've lost two fingers. There was nothing we could do.'

There was a long silence. Luke stared stupidly at his bandaged hand. 'So – I've lost two fingers?'

'I'm afraid so.'

'Off my left hand.'

'Yes. Your records show you're right-handed.'

'Does that make it all right?'

'No.'

'Couldn't you just . . . sew them back on?'

'No. We took them off to save your life.'

'Well, I'm sorry I'm not more grateful.'

'That's all right. We're none of us in this job for the gratitude.'

There was another long silence.

'Parrish, there are people here with prosthetics.'

'And they're functioning?'

'Of course.'

506

'Within officially recognised Time Police parameters?'

He's being sarcastic, thought Jane. He's going to get himself into even more trouble.

The doctor, however, was very patient. 'Of course. We wouldn't keep them on otherwise. This is the Time Police – not a sodding garden party.'

'Well, good for fire-trucking us.'

'Parrish, this is difficult for you, I know. You've had no time to prepare yourself for this. For some people, amputation can be like a bereavement. The same shock and grief experienced when someone close to them dies. I think this is what you're experiencing at the moment.'

'Nah – not really,' said Luke carelessly. 'I'm fine. Although I'd be finer if you hadn't managed to lose my fingers.'

The doctor was silent for a moment and then said, 'Would it help if you could see your fingers? If you could see how bad the damage actually was?'

'You've got them on you?'

'Well, they're not in my pocket, but, yes. Sometimes it helps if people can see there really was no way of saving them. Gives you a chance to ditch the resentment and anger and concentrate on self-pity and damaged body image.'

'All right,' said Luke. 'Bring them on. I warn you now if I'm not convinced, you *will* be sewing them back on again.'

'Deal,' said the doctor.

She heard the clatter of a metal bowl.

There was a very, very long silence.

Finally, Luke said, 'You do know that nothing pisses people off more than a doctor who's always right, don't you?'

'Yeah,' said the doctor, covering the bowl again. 'There's a lot of pissed-off people in this world. Happy to think you're one of them.'

He stood up, put a hand on Luke's shoulder for a moment and then departed.

Jane looked across at Luke. 'Do you want to be alone?'

'What are you going to do, Jane? Get up and go for a walk? You don't look much better than me.'

'It's my fault, Luke. I couldn't find your glove. And then I forgot what I was looking for. You lost your fingers because of me.' She was crying now.

He shifted in his bed, looking anxiously at the door. 'Jane, stop crying – you'll rust your machines. And they'll all turn up to find out why you're sobbing your heart out and everyone will automatically blame me.'

'But your fingers, Luke.'

'I shall wear a glove. A sinister black glove. I shall be known as Seven-Fingered Luke.'

'Eight,' said Jane, unable to help herself. 'Or six, if you exclude thumbs.'

'I shall stalk the corridors exuding sinister menace,' he said, not listening. 'I might even get a Persian cat.'

She frowned. 'We're not allowed pets.'

He still wasn't listening. 'I shall hire a gorgeous blonde to cut up my meat for me.'

'There's no earthly reason why you can't cut up your own meat.'

'And perform other, more intimate tasks.'

'I don't understand.'

'And to type my reports for me.'

'You can dictate your reports. Even death couldn't stop you talking.'

He sighed. 'You suck all the joy out of life, Jane. Have you ever considered a career in Health and Safety?'

'I doubt they'd have me. I didn't keep you very safe and you're definitely not looking that healthy, so I'm probably not eligible. And did you know Matthew's been suspended? We could all be out of a job.'

'Oh, for God's sake. I take my eye off the ball for one minute and this team falls to pieces. Literally.'

Jane steeled herself. 'I said that if Matthew left, then I would too.'

'Bloody hell, Jane. Impressive. Did you say that to Hay?'

'Um, no – I said it to Matthew.'

'Well, not quite so impressive, but a good start. But it won't come to that.'

'How do you know?'

'Team Two-Three-Six is currently flavour of the month. That'll change, of course. Probably by this time tomorrow.' He closed his eyes, suddenly looking very tired. 'They'll offset our achievements against Matthew's transgressions and everything will carry on as normal.' His voice died away. 'Trust me, Jane . . .'

41

Major Ellis had requested an interview with Commander Hay. 'I'm worried they'll leave us, ma'am.'

'So am I. I'm seeing them on Friday afternoon. I'd like you to be here, obviously, Major.'

'And the purpose of the interview, ma'am?'

'To ensure everyone gets what they want without loss of face.'

Luke had taken one look at the Time Police-provided sling for his arm and rejected it with rude words.

'What's the matter with it?' had said a medtec, loyal to his equipment.

'It's salmon pink.'

'It's flesh-coloured.'

'What the hell colour is your flesh?'

'We have five other colours – this was closest to the Parrish complexion.'

'No,' said Luke firmly. 'Forget it – I'll get my own.' By which he meant he'd scrounge a silk scarf from Jane's newly extended wardrobe, recently recovered from his flat. He was now appearing around the building sporting a dashing and very non-regulation black-and-white spotted sling.

They filed into Commander Hay's office. She regarded the three of them in silence, eventually saying, 'I still haven't received your D12s.'

'We've been busy,' said Luke.

'Nevertheless, you are, apparently without effort, again managing to interfere with the smooth running of the Time Police.'

'Are we really?' said Luke, enjoying that deceptive sense of immunity frequently engendered by a recent near-death experience. 'Yay, us.'

Ellis stirred. 'Parrish, shut up.'

'And so,' she continued, 'because time is now short, I felt it would be easier for you to register your preferences verbally. Parrish – you go first.'

Parrish was silent.

She sighed. 'While we wait for Trainee Parrish to assemble his words, shall we pass on to Lockland.'

Jane went scarlet. 'Um . . .'

'Oh, for God's sake,' said Bolshy Jane. 'We're not back to this, are we?'

Jane closed her eyes and spoke. 'We've been discussing this, ma'am, and we'd like to stay together.'

Commander Hay blinked. 'Why? If you think this is because no one else will have you, then I can assure you this is very much not the case. I've had several expressions of interest.'

'We'd like to stay together,' said Jane again.

'I'm not sure you've quite grasped how this works, Lockland.'

'We want to stay as a team,' said Luke, cutting to the heart of the matter. He added pointedly, 'The three of us.'

She sat back in her chair. Captain Farenden, not yet fit

511

enough to return to duty, had sent a message on ahead and Major Ellis had prudently placed her paper knife out of reach.

'Do I need to point out that Farrell is on suspension?'

'Well, when he comes off suspension, obviously.'

'*If* he comes off suspension. That is by no means certain.'

'Then, with regret, Commander, Trainee Lockland and I must tender our resignations.'

'Indeed?'

He assumed a woebegone expression. 'Ma'am, I've only been here eight months and I'm two fingers down already. Extrapolating forwards, there is a very good chance there won't be anything left of me after two years.'

'Well, speaking for Major Ellis and myself, let's hope your attitude is the first thing to go.'

'I highly doubt that, ma'am. I rather think that will be the last thing to disappear. Like the Cheshire Cat.'

'I beg your pardon?'

'His grin, ma'am. He would slowly fade away until only his grin was left.'

'Shut up, Parrish,' said Ellis.

Baulked of her paper knife, Hay slapped her desk. 'Resigning from the Time Police is no longer an option for you. You've long passed the training period.'

'True, ma'am, but we haven't yet graduated. Officially we're still trainees and can leave at any time.'

'You and Lockland are up for a commendation.'

Even Parrish dared not utter the words *We can pick it up along with our discharge papers* but they hung in the air nevertheless.

'So, you think you can force my hand, do you?'

Silence.

Matthew stepped forwards. 'Ma'am. The fault here is mine and I apologise.'

The Gates of Wrath swung open again.

'*You went over my head.*'

'Yes, ma'am.'

'*To those morons at St Mary's.*'

Luke's instructions had been for Matthew to agree to everything. 'She knows they'd never have got near Site X if you hadn't forced the issue. Not in time to pull us out, anyway. They owe us and they know it.'

'But don't mention that,' had said Jane. 'Just agree to everything and say as little as possible.'

'Not a problem for you,' said Luke.

Obeying his instructions to the letter, Matthew said again, 'Yes, ma'am.'

'They – St Mary's – could easily – very easily – have ruined everything. In fact, I'm astonished they didn't.'

'Yes, ma'am.'

'You could have placed your colleagues in the gravest danger.'

'Yes, ma'am.'

'Do you have nothing to say to defend yourself?'

'No, ma'am.'

Major Ellis stared at his feet.

She swung back to Luke and Jane. 'And Farrell's reinstatement is the price I must pay to keep you two?'

Silence. No one moved a muscle.

She flipped open a file.

'Lockland, there have been three requests for you to join various sections.'

Three? Jane glowed. For the right reasons this time.

'Parrish, I have received an astonishing two requests from section heads wishing to avail themselves of your talents.'

Luke frowned. 'Only two? What is the matter with this place?'

'Farrell, I've had the Map Master in here three times this week already.'

Everyone nodded gravely. Enough said.

'Having given due consideration to your various . . . requests, I have come to the following decision. Your collective failure to submit your D12s constitutes failure to comply with an order from a senior officer. I cannot allow that to stand. However, this is offset – to some extent – by your recent meritorious behaviour, and I have therefore decided it is necessary for this team to undergo a period of further training. Major Ellis has agreed to supervise you for another month, at the end of which, the situation will be reviewed.

'Farrell, you are docked one week's pay and if you ever, ever do anything like this again then I'll dock you your head. Now get out, all of you.'

The correct procedure was a smart about-turn and march to the door. Team 236 shuffled disjointedly from the room. They heard Parrish say, 'Well, that went quite . . .' and then the door closed behind them.

She sighed. 'I'm not sure I didn't prefer them when they were three disconnected individuals with more personality issues than you could shake a stick at.'

Ellis drew breath. 'Nevertheless, ma'am, nicely played.'

'Yes. Everyone got what they wanted and no one died.' She

eyed him. 'This is usually the part where Captain Farenden and I high five.'

Major Ellis was a battle-hardened veteran. He started nervously and eyed his commander. 'Er . . .'

'What are you waiting for, Major?'

'For the courage to inform you I am a decorated officer with the Time Police, ma'am, and my superior skills lead me to believe you're making fun of me.'

'Quite right, Major. Now give me back my damned paper knife.'

Two weeks later a ceremony took place.

Team 236 were the first trainees ever to receive a decoration. Less impressively – although as Luke said, only *slightly* less impressively – Matthew was the first trainee ever to be suspended. As Ellis said to Officer North, 'You never knew whether to kiss them or kill them, did you?'

Officer North stared at him, managing to convey the message that, in relation to this particular team, she personally was suffering no such indecision.

'What about you, Celia? Are you happy to spend another few weeks with Team Weird? Or have you decided your future?'

'My future is still under review, sir, but yes, I'm happy to put in another few weeks. They gave me a Team Two-Three-Six mug and I feel I'm under an obligation. Plus, I'm beginning to regard Parrish as a personal challenge.'

'Yes. A pity to waste all that potential, don't you think?'

The ceremony was to take place in the patched-up atrium. Unwilling to display their broken clock, the Time Police had draped their flag across the wreckage. Strategically placed smaller flags concealed the worst of the damage to the walls and windows. As Luke said, the effect was overwhelmingly . . . Time Policey.

'Never does any harm to send a message,' said Major Callen. 'Too many people out there willing to take a pop at us.'

Major Ellis was concerned at possible poor attendance. 'None of them have any relations, ma'am – none that would be interested, anyway – and I'm afraid there won't be many people present. They'll be lost in that great space. Would you prefer to hold the ceremony in your office?'

She considered. 'No, I don't think so. Our ceremonies always take place in the atrium – in full view of the public. I'm particularly anxious this team shouldn't be treated any differently.'

'As you wish, ma'am.'

As it turned out, their concerns were groundless. A surprising number of officers were lining up under the clock. Their reasons for doing so were unclear. Luke was convinced that despite Ellis's reassurances, a good number of them were almost certainly expecting Team 236 to be publicly disbanded. If not publicly shot.

Grint, Rossi, Hansen and Kohl stood at the front, lined up with military precision. The Map Master led a small contingent of her own people, all of them blinking in the unaccustomed daylight and whose attempts to achieve two neat lines had led to some amusement. Captain Farenden was there, healing fast and expecting to return to duty any day now. There was even a contingent from security – because, as Luke said, most of them were on first-name terms with that reprobate Lockland and probably wanted to see who she'd kill next. Ellis and North stood at each end of Team 236 – to foil any chance of escape, as Luke said in a loud whisper. And quite a large number of people – who presumably couldn't quite believe what was about to happen – were present as well. All in all – quite a respectable turnout. There were even groups of civilians who had collected on the walkway above.

The ceremony began at eleven on the dot. Major Callen called the room to order. Commander Hay entered and took her place by the podium. One by one they were called forwards.

'Trainee Farrell.'

Matthew stepped up.

Her voice carried around the atrium. 'For conspicuous bravery displayed during the recent attack on Time Police Headquarters.' She handed him a certificate. 'Congratulations, Trainee Farrell.'

'Thank you, ma'am.'

She smiled brightly and said more quietly, 'I've never before handed out a commendation with one hand and a formal warning with the other.'

He swallowed. 'No, ma'am.'

'Let us be clear, Trainee Farrell. If you ever go over my head again, I will reopen every investigation into every St Mary's-related offence on and off the books, and – trust me on this, Trainee Farrell – I will not rest until I discover exactly how your mother lied and cheated her way out of the Troy investigation – and once I have her, I have them all. Do we understand each other, Trainee Farrell?'

He nodded dumbly and stepped back.

Next up was Jane. Scarlet-faced and vibrating at an even higher rate than usual at the thought of being the centre of so much attention.

Commander Hay affixed the medal. 'For commendable service. Congratulations, Trainee Lockland.'

Luke was able to reassure Jane afterwards that she did, in fact, remember to say thank you.

'Trainee Parrish.'

Luke stepped forwards and grinned down at his commander. No words were exchanged but he was given to understand, very clearly, that if medals were still pinned instead of fastened, then his would almost certainly have been skewered to his still-beating heart.

'Congratulations, Trainee Parrish.'

'Thank you, ma'am.' He squinted down at his chest. 'Who'd have thought?'

'Who indeed? Love the glove.'

'I'd like to be known as Cool Hand Luke in future, ma'am.'

'Get back in line, Parrish.'

Up on the walkway the applauding crowd shifted to reveal a solitary man standing slightly apart. His face expressionless, Raymond Parrish watched his son receive his medal. His hands gripped the railing tightly, turning his knuckles white. As Luke stepped back into line, his father cast one last look down into the atrium and then turned away. The crowd closed behind him and he vanished from view.

NEARLY THE END

Epilogue

Sometime later, an almost completely healed Captain Farenden gathered his briefing notes together and entered Commander Hay's office for their morning meeting. The signs were not good. She was sitting back in her chair, arms folded and scowling at her paper knife. Obviously, the failure to identify, far less arrest, those in charge of Site X still rankled. Mentally discarding most of the morning's business, he carefully pulled out a file, waited a moment or two and then coughed.

'Good God, Charlie, don't *do* that.'

'Sorry, ma'am.'

'Had you been there long?'

'Quite a long time, ma'am.'

'Why the hell didn't you cough or something?'

'I believe I did.'

She eyed him for a moment and then said with enormous patience, 'Are you here for a reason or just to frighten the shit out of your commanding officer?'

He passed over the file.

'What's this?'

'Mrs Chubb.'

'Who?'

'Mrs Chubb. To be precise, Mrs Cherry Chubb.'

She stared at him. 'What?'

'Mrs Cherry Chubb of Acacia Road, Chorley, Cheltenham, has reported a Time Vortex in her fridge.'

'In her *fridge*?'

'Yes, ma'am.'

'And this has manifested itself – how?'

'Every time Mrs Chubb opens the door, the interior of the fridge is filled with a cacophonous wailing and the tentacles of dread Cthulhu try to drag her into the clutches of the deadly Time Vortex.'

'How old is Mrs Chubb?'

'Quite old, ma'am.'

'And presumably up to date on her medication.'

'I have no information on that score, ma'am.'

'And Mr Chubb?'

'Sadly, Mr Chubb is no longer in this world.'

'Ha! Fell a victim to dread Cthulhu, did he?'

'Number fourteen bus, ma'am.'

'He was run over?'

'He fell down the stairs. After a possibly too convivial night celebrating his team's success in some sporting event.'

'Hm. Returning to Mrs Chubb.'

'Yes, ma'am.'

'And her Time Vortex.'

'Yes, ma'am.'

'Did we take any action?'

'We did indeed, ma'am. Lt Grint and one other were despatched to investigate.'

'And?'

520

'Events proceeded, ma'am.'

He paused.

After a while, she said, 'Am I to know in which direction they proceeded?'

'Not quite in the direction expected. However, all's well that ends well. Sleeping dogs and all that. Now, if I could bring the senior officer rota to your attention . . .'

'Stuff the senior officer rota.'

'Ma'am.'

'Are you hiding something from me?'

'I wouldn't dream of it, ma'am.'

'Don't make me come over there, Charlie.'

'Heaven forbid, ma'am. Well, perhaps if I tell you the A.N. Other officer despatched along with Lt Grint was Trainee Lockland, you will begin to perceive just the faintest glimmer . . .'

She put her head in her hands. 'Oh God.'

'No, no, ma'am.'

'Just tell me, Charlie.'

'Well, Lt Grint and Trainee Lockland were despatched to investigate this really not very likely claim.'

'Before we go any further, and to avoid wear and tear on your commanding officer – *was* there a Time Vortex in this lady's fridge?'

'No.'

'No?' She poked the file on her desk. 'So why am I looking at what appears to be a sixty-page report on Mrs Chubb's apparently perfectly normal fridge?'

'It was the aftermath, ma'am.'

'Oh God. If ever a word was a harbinger of doom, it's aftermath.'

'There's another one, ma'am.'

'Another what?'

'Word, ma'am.'

'What?'

'Harbinger.'

'You have two seconds, Charlie, before I reach for my paper knife.'

'Moving swiftly along, ma'am. Our officers arrived at Thirty-Four Acacia Avenue, Chorley, Cheltenham at 0900 hours.'

'That's Mrs Cherry Chubb of Chorley, Cheltenham, Charlie?'

'Exactly, ma'am. Obtaining access to the premises, they entered the lady's kitchen to investigate the contents of her fridge.'

He stopped.

'And . . . ?'

'There weren't any.'

'There weren't any tentacles belonging to dread Cthulhu?'

'Any contents, ma'am. At all.'

She sat up. 'Oh.'

'Exactly, ma'am. Officer Lockland's opinion was that Mrs Chubb appeared to be having difficulty separating fact from fiction due to the empty nature of the fridge. No eggs, no butter, no cheese . . .'

'No tentacles.'

'If there had been, ma'am, they weren't there now.'

She put her hand over her eyes. 'I hardly dare ask.'

He started to get up. 'Then I shan't worry you with any further details, ma'am.'

'Living dangerously this morning, Charlie.'

'I am your adjutant, ma'am. It's in my job description.'

'I am assuming, given the size of this report, that Lt Grint and Trainee Lockland did not, having ascertained the Time Vortexless nature of the fridge, return to TPHQ to resume their allotted tasks for the day.'

'Well, I think that would have been Lt Grint's first choice, ma'am, but it would appear the mission did not work out quite as planned.'

She sighed. 'I'm actually considering making that our new motto. *Did not work out quite as planned.* How would that look in Latin, Charlie?'

'Er . . .' He closed his eyes. 'Um . . . *Quod non satis elaborare sicut cogitavit* is the best I can come up with off the top of my head, ma'am.'

'It's a bloody sight more accurate than *Protecting the Past to Ensure Your Future.* Have it printed on all our stationery in future.'

'I shall do so as soon as I receive written confirmation of that instruction, ma'am.'

'Please tell me we've reached the point where Lt Grint and Trainee Lockland returned quietly to TPHQ.'

'Not quite, ma'am. Trainee Lockland had other ideas.'

'This is still *our* Trainee Lockland? Tiny, underweight, shy, low self-esteem?'

'The very one, ma'am.'

'Only, you know, I wondered if, perhaps, somehow, we'd acquired another.'

'I can check the staff roll, ma'am, but I believe not.'

'Oh. Proceed.'

'According to Lt Grint, Trainee Lockland was considerably incensed at the emptiness of Mrs Chubb's fridge. As was Lt

Grint himself but, it turned out, their incensedness had two separate causes.'

'I feel sure I should, at this point, question your use of the word incensedness, but I have been seized by a dreadful foreboding.'

'There's another word, ma'am.'

'What?'

'Foreboding.'

Commander Hay's hand strayed towards her paper knife. 'I am assuming Lockland was incensed at the lack of food and Grint at the lack of tentacles?'

'Exactly. Well, it would seem a flurry of instructions were issued and Trainee Lockland set off for the local shops while Lt Grint was despatched to the social offices.'

'Do I gather the driving force behind these instructions was not the officer nominally in charge of this particular investigation?'

'No, ma'am. Apparently, it was felt – by Trainee Lockland – that a six-foot-four, sixteen-stone Time Police officer with the social skills of a T-rex with barbed-wire-encased haemorrhoids, and in possession of enough weaponry to level a street, would . . . induce . . . the officials to regard Mrs Chubb's predicament in a kindly and timely manner.'

She closed her eyes. 'Tell me Lt Grint has not razed these civilian premises to the ground.'

'Not . . . quite, ma'am.'

'Oh God.'

'It would appear that being handed a number and invited to wait stretched Lt Grint's already limited . . . social proficiency . . . to the limit. Announcing his disinclination to comply

524

with their request, he discharged his weapon . . .' he consulted the file, 'in a timely and effective manner as required by Regulation Twenty-Two open bracket small letter b close bracket sub-sections eye, eye-eye, and eye-vee – and quite a large section of the ceiling fell in.'

'What happened to eye-eye-eye?'

'No idea, ma'am. Would you like me to . . . ?'

'No.'

'After that, Lt Grint had only to read out the list of demands drawn up in advance by Trainee Lockland, for emergency procedures to be immediately initiated. Mrs Chubb now enjoys the benefits of meals on wheels, a twice-weekly home help and a weekly visit to the social centre. And her request for additional benefits has been expedited. Trainee Lockland herself has packed the interior of the fridge to such an extent that dread Cthulhu couldn't get a tentaclehold in there even if he wanted to. Furthermore . . .' He paused.

'There's *more*?'

'Possibly to compensate for his loudly stated disappointment at missing the opportunity to grapple with dread Cthulhu – that morning, at least – Lt Grint was encouraged to visit Mrs Chubb's landlord, who was tracked down to a local establishment where he had been, until that moment, enjoying a lunchtime pint and a game of snooker. It appears, thanks to the combined efforts of the aforementioned landlord, together with a man designated as his brother-in-law, that Mrs Chubb now has hot water and a working downspout. Not forgetting, with hardly any prompting at all from Lt Grint, a new lock on her back door. Trainee Lockland reports that improved nutrition will almost certainly ensure the non-appearance of dread Cthulhu in the future.'

He sat back and waited for his commanding officer's response.

'I'm sorry, I'm still struggling with the idea of Lockland issuing a stream of instructions to what, I am certain, would have been an extremely reluctant Lt Grint.'

'She was responsible for the entire episode, as she makes clear in her report. Lt Grint, she says firmly, was not to blame in any way.'

'He could have refused – he has seniority and he's three times bigger than she is.'

'I don't think it entered his head, ma'am. Trainee Lockland was, apparently, quite forceful.'

She gestured at the file. 'And what am I expected to do about all this?'

'Well, that's entirely up to you, ma'am.'

She sighed. 'Lose the file, Charlie.'

'And if we should receive a complaint?'

'From whom?'

'Well, the property owner, possibly, or the social office staff . . .'

She sighed. 'We who know and love Lt Grint are fully aware of his many endearing qualities, but I suppose it is possible he and his blaster could come as quite a shock to strangers – as, indeed, he is supposed to.' She drummed her fingers on her desk. 'Should the situation arise, tell everyone – *everyone* – we've lost the file and are therefore unable to confirm or deny their complaint.'

'As you wish, ma'am.'

Silence fell. She eyed him. 'There's more, isn't there?'

'Well, not regarding that particular issue, ma'am, but certainly Team Two-Three-Six-related.'

'Oh God, what have they done now?'

'They haven't done anything. It's other people.'

'Has there been fighting in the corridors again? I'm prepared to turn a blind eye occasionally, Charlie, but it's becoming a war zone out there.'

'No, no. I have here . . .' he pulled out several pieces of paper, 'three applications to join Team Two-Three-Six.'

He placed them gently on the desk before her.

She gazed at them in stunned disbelief. 'From whom?'

'From serving officers, ma'am.'

'To join Team Two-Three-Six?'

'Yes.'

'To be clear – Team Weird.'

'Yes.'

She stared. 'You cannot be serious.'

'Indeed I am, ma'am.'

She was silent as the implications sunk in. 'But this means . . .'

'It does, indeed. People – not everyone, but some – are beginning to appreciate the way Team Two-Three-Six works. They like the . . . unconventionality . . . of their methods.' He looked at her. 'Congratulations, ma'am. The mould is cracking. There are officers out there who are openly discussing different ways of doing things. Your way of doing things.'

She got up to stare out of the window.

'It's not an avalanche, ma'am, which is probably just as well. I agree with you that a gradual change is what's called for here, but these are, perhaps, the first few small pebbles.' He smiled. 'Even Lt Grint is seeing the funny side of this morning. Yes, a few officers did venture to offer their own opinions on how the situation *should* have been handled – torch the kitchen just to be on the safe side and arrest Mrs Chubb for time-wasting – but I believe that was all settled after a small – and surprisingly bloodless – scuffle in the corridor.'

'A scuffle in the corridor?'

'A *very small* scuffle in the corridor, ma'am. Hardly even worth mentioning.'

'A scufflette, in fact.'

'Another excellent word, ma'am, but you may rest assured most people are now fully on board with what is generally reckoned to be Lt Grint's imaginative and sensitive handling of the situation.'

He paused for them both to get their heads around the words Grint, imaginative and sensitive together in the same sentence.

She closed the file. 'A busy morning for everyone.'

'Indeed, ma'am,' he said, beginning to shuffle his papers together.

'Deny their requests,' she said suddenly.

'Ma'am?'

'I don't want Two-Three-Six diluted. If teams want to reproduce their working methods then they should be encouraged to do so, but no – Team Two-Three-Six remains unchanged. Ellis, North, Parrish, Lockland and Farrell.'

He nodded and closed the file. 'As you wish, ma'am.'

NOW IT'S THE END

Acknowledgements

Thanks, as always, to everyone at Headline. My editor, Frankie, and Bea, Jenni and everyone else who had a hand in making my scribblings fit for human consumption.

Thanks to my agent – the prosecco-draped, diamond-drinking Hazel, righting the world armed only with her knitting sticks.

Thanks to Phil Dawson, whose knowledge of weapons, tactics and violence in general is alternately useful and disconcerting.

Thanks to everyone who's had to put up with me while I wrote this. You are unsung but not unappreciated.

The Time Police will return in

SAVING
TIME

To discover more about

JODI TAYLOR

visit

www.joditaylor.online

You can also find her on

Facebook
www.facebook.com/JodiTaylorBooks

Twitter
@joditaylorbooks

Instagram
@joditaylorbooks